Under the Red Moon

A CHINESE FAMILY IN DIASPORA

AMY S. KWEI

Second Edition 2018

ISBN: 0981549969
ISBN 13: 9780981549965

US Copyright registration TXu1-091-237

Interior layout by www.gopublished.com

By the same author

Intrigue in the House of Wong
A Concubine for the Family

Acknowledgement

Thanks to my uncle, the "old Tom cat," who connected me to my dispersed relatives, and renewed my interest in telling the stories of so many Chinese who survived the non-stop traumatic upheavals in their lives during the 20th century.

Again, my gratitude goes to my husband and family for their loving support that gave me the emotional strength to continue writing. So many friends have also offered sustained encouragement, helpful criticism, and editing that shaped this book. Josephine Fang always asked about my writing and made sure to tell me how she enjoyed my stories. My college era friends, Doreen Grayson and Josette Davison, never gave up on me. Dalia Geffen, Jenna Johnson, Nancy Stiening, Ali Oliva, Evie Bromiley, Xiaofan and Suwei Zhou, Chris King, Jean and Ron Young and the Aspen Tuesday evening writers all helped me. Some sections of the book were written many years ago and I thank the Taconic Writers, the Tuesday Morning Writers in New York. As always, I particularly appreciate the support of the Aspen Writers' Foundation.

Aside from the many famous history books, I learned a great deal from Henry Kissinger's *On China*, James Bradley's *The Imperial Cruise and The China Mirage: The hidden History of American Disaster in Asia*, Barbara W. Tuchman's *Stillwell and the American Experience in China, 1911–45,* John S. Service's *Lost Chance in China: The World War II Dispatches of John S. Service, ed.,* Iris Chang's bestseller: *The Rape of Nanking,* Joseph W. Esherick, and Regina M. Abrami, William Kirby & F. Warren McFarlen's *Can China Lead? Reaching the Limits of Power and Growth,* and Kirby, William C., Gong Li and Robert Ross, eds.'s *The Normalization of U.S.— China relations: An International History,* Orville Schell and John Delury's, *Wealth & Power: China's Long March to the Twenty-First Century.* I also enjoyed reading Li KunWu and Philippe Otie's *A Chinese Life,* which is an autobiography in graphic novel form. I learned a great deal about modern China through Evan Osnos's *Age of Ambition: Chasing Fortune, Truth and Faith in the New China,* Peter Hessler's books: *River Town, Oracle Bones and Country Driving.* I appreciate the local Chinese Newspaper "Kan Zhong Guo" which published explications of the *Three Character Book,* that is central to a Chinese' child's education in the old days.

"Men build too many walls and not enough bridges."
Isaac Newton (25 Dec. 1642 — 1727)

MAJOR CHARACTERS IN THE NOVEL

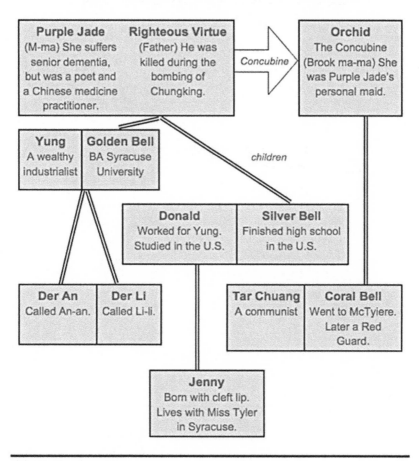

Other major characters:

Miss Tyler - A missionary who tutored Golden Bell in Hangzhou.

White Lily - Corel Bell's friend from childhood.

Golden Bell

Syracuse University, May 1945

AUGUST OF wind whooshed into my room, rustling the book on my chest. It settled into a steady breeze, shaping the lacy curtains into two filaments of light fluttering in the eerie dusk. Suddenly I sat up in bed. Was someone here? I was bathed in a warm stream of unnatural brightness. I turned my face away.

"Who is it?" I asked out loud.

Silence. The stillness was so intense, I sensed the hollow sound of floating dust particles roving in the blazing light, as if I was in a dream or some projected image from an old silent movie. My eyes began to tear. I shaded them and squinted into the glare. A shadow shifted across the bookcase, dresser, and desk. My room seemed cavernous in the glowing whiteness.

A figure in a Chinese robe solidified; the face was a patch of darkness, but the hands, gently knotted at the back, the slow pacing with an abrupt turn — these were distinctive traits . . .

"Father!" I whispered, and fell to my knees.

He came closer, but remained a blur. He appeared to be refraction.

"Father," I cried out louder.

He did not look at me, but resumed his pacing. Unlike the old days, his back was bent. As he turned, his face became visible.

1

My voice came out shrill and sharp. "Father, you've come to me!" I stretched out my hand, but he stepped back.

He frowned and lowered his head. His mouth quivered, as if he wished to speak. Though his shoulders were no longer thrown straight back, and his gait was hesitant, there remained an air of solemn grandeur about him.

"Speak to me!" I started to weep, and couldn't ask the questions needling me.

I stood up to pace after him, feeling heavy-headed, breathing in long gasps. I knew I was not dreaming. I just wanted to be close to him.

"Where are you?" I asked.

The glare dimmed to soft amber, centering on my father. He moved toward me and motioned for me to sit. His gesture was so gentle; I felt he had stroked my soul. I sat on the edge of my bed, contentment settling over me as if I had changed into my old silk garments. Father sat before me, in his favorite chair from the study of our Hangzhou house. The amber glow expanded to show his shiny rosewood desk and his calligraphy on the wall. A forlorn smile stole to his lips.

I noticed drops of blood splattered on his robe. "Are you hurt? What happened to you?" I moved forward to touch him, but he raised an arm, pushing his open palm toward me.

He grimaced, and then folded his arms in front of his chest, partially covering the stain. His kind eyes filled with regret; in a choking voice he said: "You must be strong now, my precious Golden Bell. I am here to say g . . . good-bye."

I stepped toward him. Again, he raised his arm and stopped me.

"Take care of your mother," he implored. He rose and turned to walk away, his hands again knotted at his back, his head lowered as if unspeakable burdens weighed on his shoulders.

"Father, Father!" I raced after him, more bewildered than alarmed. But he was gone. His figure dissipated in the amber light, trailing away into darkness. As my curtains flapped in the window, I was overcome with a chilly dread.

I was certain my father was dead.

Was it a dream? I pinched myself and felt the pain. My heart thumped against my chest and I heard myself call out, "Father, Father, come back!"

Only the swishing sound of curtains in the wind answered.

I stared into emptiness and decided to turn on the radio.

The announcer was talking about local casualties. "Lawrence Grant, son of Kathy and Robert Grant of Maple Street, is listed missing in action . . ."

I wondered if this Lawrence was Elisa's brother. If so, people would gather around her tomorrow, hug her, and cry along with her. Many would eye me with suspicion. Some would point; others would turn away. They couldn't tell one Asian from the next. They would probably assume I was Japanese. Even for the few people who asked me about myself, my description of the war in my homeland and of my scattered family often led to cold curiosity rather than sympathy. Most people were ignorant of Chinese history. Last July, the Guam invasion had given me hope that America would help liberate China. Then came the big triumph — Iwo Jima in February of this year. I would have given anything to join the WACS, but of course I could not. Not being a citizen, I felt excluded from the camaraderie and high-minded goals of my classmates.

Father's letters from Chungking had been my only tonic. His exciting reports on the war and his little four-page weekly, the *Chungking Critic,* filled me with pride but also invited guilt to nibble on my conscience. *I should be doing more for my country and my family. But what? How?*

The last four weeks had brought no letters from Chungking. Was Father busy? Was Chungking under attack again? Mother had not written since she'd returned to Shanghai from Hong Kong in 1941. This was right after Pearl Harbor when the Japanese attacked the British colony and Father escaped to Chungking while Miss Tyler, my teacher, brought my sister Silver Bell to me in Syracuse. Thank God Brook ma-ma, once Mother's personal maid, Orchid, still served her with unwavering devotion. Since Brook ma-ma had become my father's concubine, she had taken on more and more of Mother's responsibilities, including her correspondence. She imitated Mother's elegant style — as well she should, since Mother had taught her how to read and write. In her last letter, she said Mother "is the ideal woman — like supple silk; she weaves patterns of peace and harmony into glorious designs." What was she talking about? Between Mother, Brook ma-ma, and her daughter, Coral Bell, my half sister, there couldn't be any disharmony. I suspected that Mother had become placid and removed from reality. Brook ma-ma's description of Shanghai sounded as if everything had remained the same under Japanese occupation, except she never mentioned Mother's practice in acupuncture and midwifery. She sounded desperate when she asked for news of Father. Had Mother become passive and distracted? She was never quite the same after the Japanese burned down our mansion in Hangzhou. Her mental state had further deteriorated when Brook ma-ma's first daughter, Jade Bell, was killed during the Japanese invasion of Hong Kong and the family dispersed. Lately, I had heard nothing from Shanghai. The mail was slow because in these times of war, it was delivered from Shanghai to Hong Kong to Macau and then to the United States through friends and distant relatives.

In Hangzhou, light and darkness, right and wrong seemed self-evident. I was sure Mother was hopelessly old-fashioned, and the bold new world of the United States was mine to explore. When Miss Tyler suggested I attend Syracuse University, from which she had graduated, my father and mother supported the idea. After moving from Hangzhou to Shanghai to Hong Kong to escape the war, they wanted me to pursue an education in peace. I was happy to comply.

The girls here treated me like a jade vase — a delicate, decorative, and strange creature. They oohed and aahed over me and urged me to wear my cheongsam. They kept their distance and whispered behind my back. They expected me to need help in English and philosophy. As it turned out, they were envious because, in spite of my accent, I earned top grades. I felt so lonely! After Silver Bell arrived in December 1941, she attended a public high school in Liverpool, outside Syracuse, and lived with two retired missionary spinsters who were Miss Tyler's friends. She was only thirteen. Whenever she came to visit, my cottage mates were full of sympathy for her tales of bombs and destruction during the Japanese invasion of Hong Kong. In contrast, my earlier arrival in July and insularity in Syracuse made me appear unseemly lucky and unscathed by the war. Miss Tyler traveled often, giving lectures. She had been on a fund-raising tour since the previous fall. Even when she was here, it was uncomfortable for me to confide my difficulties to her because she had taken me out of danger, and I might appear ungrateful. I kept them to myself.

When I was young, I was afraid to go near the ancestors' room. Trestle tables hemmed the far end of the wall, where all the tablets, with names of our ancestors, were lined up like a pyramid. The rows of red wooden blocks, filled with black characters, looked innocent enough, but Mother said the spirits of our ancestors lived in their names, and whenever we were in their presence, we must either bow or kowtow.

I was the firstborn. My parents had no son, and whenever I didn't learn my lesson, Mother would send me to kneel in front of the tablets. I dreaded this punishment not because it was uncomfortable, but because I was afraid of being left alone there with all the spirits hovering over me. I would kneel down, place my book on the ground before me, kowtow three times by knocking my head on the ground, then read and reread the text until I had memorized everything. I never dared to look up for fear that my ancestors might be looking down at me. I was sure they would be very angry with me for being a dumb egg and losing face for the family.

Once I told Father about my fears of the ancestors and their tablets. He said, "Nonsense, Golden Bell. Our ancestors' spirits will only protect us and help us uphold the integrity of the clan."

"What if some of our ancestors were wicked?"

"Their names would have been erased from the family roster, and their spirits would not remain here."

In time, I became accustomed to the idea of the ancestors as benign spirits living among us. On festival days, all the relatives came to honor them. It seemed only natural that those who had watched over our welfare should be included in our family celebrations.

Mother had presented her personal maid, Orchid, to Father as a gift, a concubine for his fiftieth birthday. Everyone praised Mother for her wise and noble act; our family needed an heir. But I was most uncomfortable. My studies with my American tutor, Miss Tyler, had made me aware of Westerners' disdain for concubines. Perhaps I was not convinced that Mother had done the right thing. Maybe I had hoped the spirits of our ancestors would show some sign of approbation.

On their wedding day, when we followed Father to pay obeisance to the ancestral tablets, my heart popped like a chestnut on hot coals. First, members of the older generations bowed. I perspired and waited. Then Orchid kowtowed. I was next. Silver Bell, my younger sister by five years, followed in turn. My sister rose from her kowtow, tripped on the hem of her long silk skirt, and fell forward. She stretched out her hands and grabbed a leg of the table for balance. The tablets listed toward us. Mother blanched; I rushed up to set them right. I was so quick that people barely had time to wince at my sister's clumsiness. Nevertheless, I trembled with fear. I was certain the ancestors had sent us an ill omen. No one mentioned the incident again. But sure enough, later that year the family had to move to Shanghai to escape the encroachment of the Japanese. Then when the Japanese occupied Shanghai, Father fled to Hong Kong because he was shipping materiel to the Nationalists. The family followed after the birth of Brook ma-ma's first daughter, Jade Bell. After Coral Bell was born in Hong Kong and I was preparing to leave for America in July 1941, Mother came into my room to help me pack. Holding my gray silk scarf, which was woven from the silkworms bred in Hangzhou, with the yellow iris she had embroidered, she said: "Remember, Golden Bell, you held up the ancestors' tablets during Father's birthday celebration. The Huang family still has no son. Our ancestors have clearly intended for you to hold up their names and act as our son."

Perhaps my long engagements with the ancestors had prepared me for Father's visit. Though I might have questioned the benevolence of my other ancestral spirits, Father's presence had always filled me with warmth. I moved to the window and hoped he might appear again.

Our garden in the French Concession of Shanghai had been largely free of the sights and sounds of nature. In Hangzhou, birdsongs had led to thoughts of romantic love and freedom. In Syracuse, the seemingly infinite expanse of fields and wildlife made me long for the protective walls and cultivated gardens of our homes. The houses for the male students and cottages for the women cast somber shadows on the lawn of the university. In the fading light, I saw fireflies rise from the bushes and remembered the times when Silver Bell and I would go to the lotus pond to catch them. We held them in glass jars covered by pieces of gauze. The fireflies glowed and flickered all night, like snatches of our secrets and confidences shared in the dark.

Now the fireflies, faint and inadequate in the vast wilderness outside my window, reminded me of folk tales about hungry ghosts who wandered the land and haunted people because no one kowtowed to them or brought them food and drink.

"Oh, Father, please, please visit me again!" I wailed. I don't know how long I cried. I resolved to do whatever was necessary to honor Father's name.

I grabbed my gray silk scarf — the threads that had connected me to my family — and left my room to buy the necessary offerings. It must have been dinnertime. There was hardly anyone around. The Gothic spires of Crouse College looked like obsidian spikes, piercing the darkening skies. Passing the rise overlooking the city, a flock of starlings swooped down to the meadows. The screeching, fluttering black cloud sent me running toward town.

Back in my room, I locked the door. Calligraphy always calmed me down. Even after years of arguing with Mother about my Western inclinations, painting or practicing calligraphy on a vertical easel in front of me seemed impossibly difficult. I liked to sit or stand in front of a table, in the Chinese way, with the paper lying flat. "The Westerner," as Mother used to call me, was now desperately trying to preserve her Chinese heritage.

Fingering my sable-haired brushes and turning on the lamp, I took out my ink stone and a cup of water and wet a large character brush; then I dripped some water on the stone and ground the ink stick on it. Round and round I ground, the motion restoring me to peace. The familiar smell of the dark ink brought childhood memories of Father's study and Mother's writing corner in her bedroom.

When the ink was at the right consistency, I brushed Father's name on red construction paper. Then I attached it to cardboard and set it against the wall, between candles on my desk, making it look just like a tablet from the ancestral hall. I poured out a cup of wine and placed it, with fruit, in front of Father's tablet on my desk. I kowtowed to it. Exhausted, I lay down to sleep.

A flash of lightning woke me. Loud claps of thunder and sheets of pouring rain soon followed. My head throbbed with pain. I stumbled out of bed and gulped down some aspirin with the cup of wine on my desk. At home, we always feasted on the offerings to our ancestors, so it was proper to drink the wine. I refilled the cup, and kowtowed repeatedly to Father's name. When my head still ached, I took some sleeping pills and drank more wine. My head was pounding again, or was it thundering outside? I pulled my blanket over my head and slept on.

Someone was shaking me violently. "Wake up, wake up, Vicky." Katie's words broke through my sleep.

"How long has she been like this?" Josie asked.

"I missed her at dinner last night," Katie said, her voice filled with concern.

"Oh, my God. Isn't that an altar?" Josie cried.

I sat up in a stupor to see Josie pointing to the red tablet with Father's name and the wine and fruit lined up in a dutiful offering.

"What is this?" Katie asked.

I tried to explain: "My father came to visit me last night. I think he is dead."

The girls gasped. They looked at each other.

"You're ill, Vicky," Josie said finally. "You should go to the infirmary."

"Wait," said Katie. "This telegram came for her this morning, and I slipped it under her door." She handed it to me. I could barely read it.

The message was from Chungking, dated May 3, 1945. My father's cousin had sent it. My father was killed in an air raid two days before. My mother had already been informed. Without a word, I handed the telegram back to Katie, stumbled out of bed, and fell in front of my desk.

"Father, Father," I cried, and kowtowed over and over again to the name tablet.

Four arms pulled me away from the desk. They straightened my knees, holding me upright.

A stream of amber light and a warm hand led me forward. I was sure it was Father's.

Adjustments

THE INFIRMARY WAS a bright but dank place. While there, Brook ma-ma's letter arrived.

She wrote that M-ma did not become delirious when told of Father's death, but she was often in tears. She focused on her Tang poems and rocked herself, reciting Tu Fu's dream of his friend Li Po:

> *Boundless sorrow filled our parting.*
> *Death brings mourning, never-ending.*
> *No word from your lonely exile —*
> *That forlorn place, south of the river.*
> *You appeared to me in a dream,*
> *As you were always on my mind.*
> *Perhaps it was only a shadow —*
> *Too far to send an image.*
> *When you appeared, the trees turned green.*
> *When you left, the mountains turned dark.*
> *Were you detained down under?*
> *Did you try for freedom?*
> *Did you leave your spirit,*
> *While moonlight shone upon the rafters?*
> *Giant waves churn the murky waters.*
> *Beware of the water-dragons.*

Why had Brook ma-ma sent me this poem? Was it her way of telling me that Father had also visited Mother? For many days, I sat in bed drenched in tears, swayed, and recited the poem in solidarity with my mother.

After a few days under sedation, I was allowed to walk in the garden and receive visitors. Silver Bell came after school one day. "You look better, Golden Bell." She greeted me in Chinese, smiling. She was wearing a pink linen skirt and a matching pink blouse with eyelet collars and cuffs. Despite the cheerful color, her outfit had a gray sheen of weariness.

"Another outfit from the charity bin?" I bit my lip, knowing that since the family's dispersion, we had to economize.

Silver Bell grimaced. "No, but yes. Doris gave me this outfit. I thought it was rather springy."

"Let's go outside." We walked into the garden, heading toward the edge of the campus. The fresh air felt invigorating.

"Doris gave me lots of old clothes too," I said. We passed students standing about or walking to class. "One day at breakfast, she asked me in front of everyone: 'Vicky, you're wearing my favorite wool skirt. Why aren't you wearing the jacket that's supposed to go with it?'" I felt I could say all this because we were speaking in Chinese.

Silver Bell lowered her head.

"I know our savings are depleting, but you don't have to go around and advertise it." My voice rose to a shout. "Anyway, we're in mourning. Why aren't you in black? Oh, no, no, in white. That's the Chinese way."

"I don't have any black clothes, and white is for the summer," Silver Bell cried. "Oh, Golden Bell, what are we going to do?" She hugged me and choked on her sobs.

I couldn't stand to see Silver Bell cry. She could be such an exhibitionist, and so gullible. Whenever people told her what a pleasure it was to hear her sing, she believed them. I pushed her away.

"You must set up a name tablet for Father," I told her. "And offer fruit and wine."

"People will say we're practicing idolatry. I've said prayers for him." Silver Bell averted her eyes.

"We're Chinese!" My shrill voice seemed to spring from my constricted stomach. "How's Father going to benefit from useless prayers?" I didn't wait for an answer. "He's already a disconsolate ghost roaming the world! I've prayed almost nonstop for our family's reunion. See what that brought us?"

"My prayers have not been answered either." Silver Bell nodded. "But Christian charity will always sustain us."

"Does that mean we have to abandon our own culture and become charity cases?" I almost screamed.

"Shhh, shhh . . . not so loud, please, Golden Bell," Silver Bell implored. "People will think you're crazy!"

"I'm crazy, am I?" I shouted in a rush of anger. "Did your new Western learning make you lose all sense of filial piety? You should be ashamed of yourself, dressed in pink under these circumstances!"

We arrived at a ravine. The sides were steep but grassy. I reached out for Silver Bell's hand and stepped sideways down the bank. Silver Bell slipped on the damp grass and we tumbled together to the bottom, where puddles of water had muddied the grass. Silver Bell jumped to her feet. I landed on my face.

"I'm not hurt." I spat energetically, allowing Silver Bell to pull me up. Then I took a deep breath and looked my sister in the eye. "Father appeared to me. He wants me to take care of the family."

Silver Bell tried to brush the mud from her blouse, sputtering, "Miss Tyler said the Holy Spirit moves in mysterious ways. I . . . I am so confused." She finally gave up, buried her face in her hands, and sobbed.

13

"All right, all right. You're totally useless!" I spat some more and shook my muddy shoes. Water had seeped through the leather. Dirty water streaked down our clothes.

"From now on, wear white — that's the proper color of mourning." I punched out the words, as befit the head of the family.

"I'll do that," Silver Bell said, nodding. She was almost too eager. We scaled up the bank, falling forward and sliding back. Our clumsy attempts gave us beads of sweat, and cascades of hair ran down our foreheads and cheeks. A cold wind refreshed us as we finally crawled to the top, puffing and disheveled. My throat felt raw from shouting, but we faced each other, bursting into fits of wailing, laughter, and tears. We held on to one another as if we had just reached a mountaintop.

Silver Bell mumbled something I could not make out. When I pressed her, she shook her head. "This would have been so much fun in Hangzhou."

The sober remark calmed my hysteria. I took in the endless expanse of green meadow, shimmering in the setting sun. My mind searched for the clumps of bamboo, the graceful willows, the flowing river, and the flight of rooflines on our Hangzhou house. The linear simplicity before me ended at the edge of the woods, where brambles, rough bark, and gray branches formed a wall of impenetrable darkness. "Yes." I nodded. "This is not home. Let's go back to the infirmary to change. You can wear one of my outfits."

"I'll be confirmed next week," Silver Bell said as she trudged beside me. Then she stopped, twisting a corner of her blouse in her hands. "You were already confirmed in Hong Kong, but they say you're acting strange."

"Remember you wanted to be baptized when you were nine because you wanted to wear a lacy white dress and hoped they might allow you to sing at your baptism? Did you ever believe Jesus would save you from harm?"

"I don't know. So you don't believe in Jesus?"

"I believe in the charity he preaches, but I'm not sure he is God." I shook my hands in frustration. "He doesn't seem to want to deal with the chaos in China."

Silver Bell nodded. "I wish Miss Tyler were here to explain!"

"Oh, yes, Miss Tyler can always explain," I said. Wet hair slashed my face as I blurted out the thoughts I had never dared tell anyone. "No matter how well I do in English literature and American history, I'm always a surprise to them. I'm an astonishing creature, incapable of sharing their culture! It is only when I put on a Chinese dress and stand beside Miss Tyler, like an antique decoration, while she explains her missionary work, that they think they understand me."

"Oh, Golden Bell, Miss Tyler will be so upset."

"I'm sure she will be. Don't you have any pride? You're giving up your identity — adopting something that can never be yours! Where is your gray silk scarf?"

"I . . . I stored it safely in my trunk."

"Wear it as often as you can," I shouted. "Mother embroidered a peony on yours and an iris on mine. They are the names of our personal maids. They're family too!"

"Oh, I miss Peony so much." Silver Bell began to cry.

I fixed my gaze on the somber buildings looming in front. "Miss Tyler is never around," I whimpered, and hugging myself tightly, I ran to my room in the infirmary. Silver Bell followed, and wrapping our arms around each other, we wept.

A day later, Josie and Katie also came to visit, bringing me flowers and chocolate cookies. I thanked them.

"You're looking well," Josie said.

"Yes, I hope to be back in our cottage tomorrow."

Josie eyed Katie, shifted from one foot to the other, and came over to hug me. "Oh Vicky, we're so sorry for your loss!"

I sobbed and buried my head on her shoulder. Katie joined us in a three-way hug, but I couldn't stop crying.

After a while, Josie took my hand. "We never realized how lonely you must have been, conjuring up your father's visit."

"But he did come!" I exclaimed.

"Yes," Katie grabbed my other hand. "We've heard of cases where the dead reached out to their beloved, but no one can prove it wasn't caused by the intensity of their longing."

I almost nodded. I knew that intensity well.

Josie quickly continued, "At any rate, we should have paid closer attention to your situation. You did so well in school and spoke with that crisp British accent. We thought you wanted your privacy."

"You must have felt awful when so many of us thought you were Japanese! We were ignorant of Chinese history and culture," Katie added.

I gaped. I had often emphasized my British accent to disguise my Chinese inflections, which often slipped out. I never dreamed that it would seem off-putting to Americans. I never thought that people would avoid me for reasons other than physical differences.

"I'm sorry we never seriously considered how the Japanese and Chinese are enemies. We've since done some research." Katie said.

"Some of us knew you were Chinese, but we thought China was just as aggressive a nation as Japan, because China must have grabbed a lot of land to become such a large country." Josie scrunched up her eyebrows.

I nodded and whispered, "Most people don't seem to know that Genghis Kahn conquered China on his way to India and his grandson adopted our Confucian culture to form the Yuan Dynasty, adding Tibet to our country. The Yuan ruled for over one hundred years."

"Oh yes," Katie said. "I read that the Mongols were so eager to copy Chinese customs that their princesses demanded to be supported by a servant under each arm even though they did not have tiny 'lotus' feet, like the Chinese princesses."

"Silly, isn't it? What people are willing to do to follow what they think is fashionable." Josie chuckled.

"It is cruel to bind women's feet," I mumbled, remembering my arguments with Mother in Hangzhou about liberal Western customs.

"Oh, God, it is beastly!" Josie made a face. "I hope that is no longer allowed!"

"No," I replied immediately. "It was abolished in 1911 when China became a republic." I did not tell them about my mother's bound feet. The grotesque image of Brook ma-ma washing mother's little stumps floated to my mind and I winced. Perhaps someday I would tell them how the last two toes of a two-year-old girl's feet were crushed under her soles, and later the heels were pushed to meet the toes. I used to rail against Mother's acceptance of her fate and her insistence on the supremacy of everything Chinese. But I've come to understand her suffering, her staunch devotion to her family, and her need to maintain her identity.

"Yes, the Chinese were conquered many times," I said, eager to switch the talk to politics. "According to family legend, my great-great-grandfather lost his head because he refused to wear the pigtail that the Manchu forced on all Chinese after they breached our Great Wall." I patted the back of my head.

"So the Chinese did not wear pigtails originally?" Josie asked.

"No," I replied. "The Chinese were forced to conform to Manchu customs, but the Manchu adopted all aspects of Confucian culture and added all the northeastern provinces to form our Chin Dynasty. They all became Chinese instead." I smiled. "It is too bad that this three-hundred-year-old dynasty was decaying just when Western imperialism came. The depredation of our civilization started with the Opium War in 1839."

"Yes, we read about that — Britain wanted the free export of Indian opium into China. They won the war and Hong Kong became a British colony." Josie patted my hand. It was obvious they were proud of their research and had already discussed this.

"Japan westernized early, learning imperialism from the West," Katie added. "They also grew opium in the provinces near Manchuria and flooded China with cheap opium."

"Yes, people smoked opium instead of taking aspirin because it was cheaper." I nodded.

"You know, we're thinking of presenting this information to our 'world interest' forums in the sorority." Josie nodded to Katie and me.

"Oh, that'll be wonderful." I squeezed their hands. "I'd like to attend some of your world interest forums."

"Oh, great! We were preparing to talk about Susan B. Anthony, but with the women helping out in the war effort, women's rights are no longer an issue. First, we'll have to sponsor you for Kappa Kappa Gamma."

"I don't know if I can contribute anything to the sorority, but I'll try." I was so happy to find camaraderie and diversion from the troubles at home. Perhaps it was Father's hand guiding me, or was it Jesus' hand?

"You must come and talk to us about Chinese history."

I remembered my inadequate and unsatisfactory British/Chinese pronunciations. "I've never given talks before. Perhaps I can help you with the research."

"We'll do the presentation together," Josie exclaimed. Katie and I will first write up a rough draft and then you can rearrange and add things. Will you answer questions?"

I nodded.

"This will be the most authentic presentation of world events in our sorority!"

The next day, while Silver Bell was visiting, Josie brought me some literature about Susan B. Anthony. I read it with interest and passed it on to my sister. I said, "A woman's movement could not happen anytime soon in China." Silver Bell agreed, adding, "We had never even heard of any women organizing to ask for anything. We might have been too young to know, but all the protests in China seemed to have only male participants."

"The women's issues seem so remote when the Japanese are controlling our country," I told Josie.

After Josie left, Silver Bell asked, "Do they know about our family problems?"

"No." I answered. "I prefer to keep them private. We'll speak in Chinese anytime we talk about home."

I took out Brook ma-ma's last letter and said, "They have sold our old burned-down homestead and other properties in Hangzhou to fund life in Shanghai."

"No doubt Mother was paid far less than the fair value, because the buyers were dealing with a distracted woman and her former personal maid," Silver Bell grumbled.

Oh, I miss Uncle Dragon! He would have protected them."

"I am proud of him." Silver Bell almost shouted. "To die on the battlefield in Changsha and singlehandedly to take down three tanks made him a true hero!"

"I'm proud of him too. But I often wonder how the relatives are surviving now. They studied the classics, but depended on their tenant farmers and Uncle Dragon's business acumen for their livelihood. Knowing Mother, she's probably sharing whatever she has with these leeches."

"Mother is so old fashioned." Silver Bell stamped her feet. All our old studies about honoring our parents, showing respect to authority, cultivating propriety, and harmony are useless!"

"Don't talk about Mother like that!" I glared at my sister.

"Mother is thought to be the quintessential Confucian noblewoman. She does her duty; is completely trustworthy, and practices mutual support with all members of her family. A strong family is the foundation of being Chinese."

"With all the wars, who is Chinese anymore?" Silver Bell sneered.

"You are becoming what is called a banana — yellow on the outside and white inside." I snickered. "Whether you like it or not, you'll always be seen as Chinese."

Silver Bell lowered her head, and I continued, "If and when the war ends, you and I will have to return to Shanghai to support Mother and, according to tradition, help all the relatives as well."

"I'm not going to help those degenerates. Some of them must still be addicted to opium." Silver Bell answered, punching the sofa.

"You're going to lose face for the family! But we may have bigger trouble before then: Brook ma-ma's last letter suggested that they wanted to sell the Shanghai house and move to a small apartment."

"So Mother really has no money to share with the relatives. Besides, that's the male heir's problem. We will not be expected to help those relatives." Silver Bell shrugged. "I have to run. I have choir practice."

Golden Bell's Journal

A T ALMOST SEVENTEEN, Silver Bell Seems better adjusted to American life than I. She is confident of her place in spite of our situation. She is practical and confronts life as an individual. She does what interests her rather than worry about the subtle ways of exclusion that dominate my consciousness. Both parents told me, in death and in life, that I am to be the male heir of my family. I have no edifying example to follow. I do not know another respected Chinese woman who works to support her family. In China, women can help their families only on the sly, assuming they marry well. Miss Tyler is now taking care of Silver Bell and me. She makes me believe in Christian charity, but how have I become so thoroughly Chinese? My earlier experiences must have influenced me.

Back in July 1941, a steady gale blew me from Hong Kong to the United States on an ocean liner. Certain of Miss Tyler's connections and my family's support, I felt no fear, but I was not prepared for the dislocation. I was wide-eyed with wonder — the open spaces felt daunting and overwhelming. Even in populated neighborhoods, there were so many open lawns, with no walls separating them. Often, it was difficult to tell where the property of one house ended and the neighbor's began. The flower beds were scattered in small patches so all passers-by could enjoy them — unlike the rambling gardens, with lily-pad ponds, flowering bushes, bamboo groves and pavilions — that wound from court to court behind high walls at home.

After attending the all girls' McTyeire School and the French Convent School, I had difficulty grappling with the new social norms and mores. Men and women talked openly in public, often kissing or hugging each other in greeting. Students walked hand in hand on campus, and no adults admonished them. No one even paid attention. I was curious about everything, but I remained a mute observer. Soon I was swept into a bewildering forest of Western art, music, American literature, and history. Math and science courses carried no cultural baggage, and I studied them like old friends. The English I had learned in the French convent school in Hong Kong was more than sufficient for me to handle class work, but I was not used to speaking up in class. At first, people were solicitous, but when I did not respond quickly enough, some would raise their voices as if I were old and hard of hearing or had trouble with the language.

In Hong Kong, I had loved sitting with *Jane Eyre, David Copperfield, Great Expectations,* and *Wuthering Heights,* turning the pages that thrust me into the protagonists' tumultuous lives. I even had dreams of romantic love. To me, Nathaniel Hawthorne and Washington Irving's stories seemed eccentric. The Transcendentalists were idiosyncratic, but they reminded me of the Taoist philosophy — "Wu Wei." Little did I suspect then how these spiritual messages of individualism and independence is somehow helping me navigate my chaotic life.

I loved Robert Frost, but couldn't understand the strength he drew from a nature that was wild and uncultivated. Often feeling homesick, I found it hard to love literature that glorified the untamed, open spaces and the solitude, though I thought Mother would love Emily Dickinson.

Adding to my struggles with the overwhelming dissonance I felt, I had to deal with male attention. Syracuse was proud to be the first co-ed university in the country. Soon after I arrived, Steve Russell took an interest in me. He was a redheaded history major, flat-footed and therefore exempt from the draft. He wanted to learn Chinese. He spoke softly. We had a riotous time laughing over transliterations of Chinese names. I said, "Do you know that 'Steve' could be translated as 'Silk Buddha,' 'Time Flourishing,' or 'Death Flourishing'?"

"No contest," he replied. "Call me Silk Buddha!"

So "Hi, Silk Buddha!" was how I greeted him every day. He urged me to talk about my home, and I was glad to reminisce about the many courts and meandering garden in our Hangzhou mansion.

He invited me for Thanksgiving. Initially, I was shy and could not find my voice when I was introduced to his family. Soon his father addressed me. "I hope you like-kee turkey?"

I froze.

"She speaks perfect English — with a British accent, Dad!" Steve interjected.

Steve's father did not apologize, but scrutinized me as if I were a creature from outer space.

"Where's your family, dear?" Steve's mother asked sweetly.

"My family is in Hong Kong," I mumbled.

Everyone nodded. Then the usual series of questions followed about my father's occupation and how long I had been in the country. I answered everything as simply as I could, mentioning how we had fled the encroaching Japanese invasion, leaving our home in Hangzhou for the safety of the foreign concessions in Shanghai and again, due to my father's patriotic activities, to the British colony. No one asked what "foreign concessions" meant and didn't seem to know what to say about our family odyssey. Instead, the parents stared and praised my "remarkable" British accent and other attributes. "You are unusually tall for a Chinese, aren't you?" "You are more fair than most Chinese." "Your eyes are wider than most Chinese." I thanked them and told them that the Chinese have many minority tribes because we were conquered many times. Steve mentioned that the Manchu, not the majority Han people, were the last imperial Chinese government until the Westerners came to trade, wage war, and take territories in all the major Chinese cities. I added that our family lived in the French Concession, on Petain Road.

"Named after the French general?" Steve's father asked. I nodded.

As we sat down to dinner, Steve's mother announced sweetly: "We have extra side dishes — just in case Vicky misses Chinese food!" She proudly produced a plate of gooey rice and fried meat they had ordered from a local restaurant.

Afterward, Steve told me his parents liked me. I knew they meant to be kind, but I couldn't help but feel disappointed that they were so unlike Miss Tyler's circle of mostly missionary friends, who were much more knowledgeable about Chinese culture.

After the meal, friends of Steve's blond, blue-eyed sister dropped by. They lined up, pressed their palms together in front of their chests, and bowed. Steve's parents smiled and said, "Such interesting Chinese manners!" I did not know how to respond. That was certainly not how we greeted each other at home. We simply bowed our heads, and curtsied slightly when greeting the older generation.

Everyone asked me questions about China as if I were an expert on the entire country. If I happened to declare my ignorance, it seemed that I was denouncing my heritage. I didn't dare mention the traumatic events of the early twentieth century, when China was almost carved up and dismembered by Japan and the Western powers. Whenever I remembered these Chinese humiliations, my heart felt like I had just run a marathon.

No one bothered to tell me their backgrounds, but the girls didn't hesitate to ask the most intimate questions about mine. I said as little as I could. Somehow Steve brought up Brook ma-ma. In a moment of intimate discussion, I had explained to him that my mother had given my father a concubine because the family needed an heir and that Brook ma-ma had given birth to two more daughters. After Japan occupied Shanghai, we moved to Hong Kong. There, Mother served the boat dwellers as a midwife and acupuncturist. She had always been a caregiver in our Hangzhou household, and in Shanghai she had practiced Chinese medicine with a Chinese doctor as well as helped an American female doctor deliver babies, using her skills in acupuncture. Steve was impressed by my mother's unusual occupation. He mentioned that Susan B. Anthony was from Syracuse, and that he admired the courage and solidarity of women, especially during traumatic times. He never asked how I felt about having a concubine in the family.

During the meal, I had neglected to mention Brook ma-ma to his parents, so I was surprised when Steve now brought up the subject in front of his sister's friends. I blushed, but Steve tried to explain the necessity of the situation because my mother had bound feet and could not handle household chores. The girls giggled and rolled their eyes. When Steve asked me to explain, I didn't know how to respond. I was devastated and felt that he had betrayed my confidence, though I had never specifically told him to keep this a secret. I could feel my face burning and tears filling my eyes. I used to think Steve's sparkling blue eyes showed a fiery interest in me. Now he seemed merely inquisitive, cold, and impersonal. I wanted to scream, "I don't belong here!"

The girls looked at me pityingly. One of them mumbled, "Vicky, it is not your fault." Another said, "The Chinese are so cruel." She gave me a sideways glance, and then corrected herself. "I mean the old Chinese."

I started to say that I liked Brook ma-ma and was forever grateful to her for her devotion to my mother. But shock and incomprehension shone through the girls' eyes. I didn't know how to clear up the misunderstanding. Tears brimmed in mine, and I blinked to hold them back, but some coursed down my face. I wished I had been able to keep my composure and explain the tradition of having the male heir making seasonal offerings in the village temple and in front of the ancestor tablets. The necessity of maintaining the prestige and continuity of the family would be something they could have understood; hadn't they read *Pride and Prejudice*? Of course, this being America, they probably didn't have much interest in the British classics. I wiped my face and held my handkerchief to my mouth, trying to stifle a flood of expletives that wanted to rush out. Steve took me back to my cottage, but it was obvious that there were too many misconceptions between our cultures.

For many nights I sat up in bed drenched in tears, rocking and hugging my legs to my chest, bemoaning my past and pondering my future. I blamed myself for being embarrassed. After this one "attachment," I concentrated on my studies and rebuffed all male attention, especially when they wanted to invite me somewhere private to study.

Mother had always opened her fan with a swish of her wrist — sometimes to hide a giggle or a hearty laugh. She had a way of staring into my eyes when she had something important to tell me. Father paced when he was worried or wanted to concentrate. Silver Bell loved to blow her silly whistle and always had a song ready. Seeing Steve's American family life had led me to draw sustenance from my home culture, but it also aroused my longing and stripped me of all protective layers, revealing my barren cultural pride. I finally decided that Ms. Tyler's total devotion to teaching would be the most acceptable course for me too. I would also major in mathematics because it was grounded in certainty. The logical thinking it required would be a diversion that would leave all my cultural baggage behind.

All that changed when Japan invaded Hong Kong right after Pearl Harbor. Pearl Harbor had been the storm that shook Americans from their complacency. But the occupation of Hong Kong was the knife that stabbed my being to the core. This upheaval gave me a keener awareness of the sea of strange faces, sounds, and smells around me. I was chronically anxious about the safety of my family, and I did not learn of their fate until Miss Tyler came to Syracuse with Silver Bell. My sister's presence did nothing to ease the pain of knowing my family had dispersed and little Jade Bell, my first half sister, had died in the Japanese bombing. Mother, Brook ma-ma, and Coral Bell had returned to Shanghai for safety and protection; Father had escaped to Chunking. It became difficult to write to my parents. I fell into a fog of desolation in spite of Miss Tyler's solicitude. Finally, when a circuitous route of communication was established, I calmed down.

Silver Bell had experienced firsthand the Japanese invasion of Hong Kong and witnessed the death of little Jade. She seemed grateful to be here with me and away from the anguish of war. The ladies she lived with treated her like a daughter, and she had even started favoring American food. She clung to Miss Tyler and me whenever we met but appeared composed and happy with her school and her special singing lessons. Sometimes I felt she was better adjusted than I am. Although Miss Tyler encouraged me to pray, I was determined to cultivate inner strength, like the Transcendentalists. But I would also brace myself against the headwinds of each day by practicing Wu Wei.

There were no other Chinese female students at the university. Except for Silver Bell, I had no one of my own kind to cling to. One male undergraduate spoke the Fukien dialect, which I didn't understand. He had so much trouble with English, I could find nothing in common with him. I hardly saw the few Chinese graduate students. Miss Tyler said that most were married, with wives and children in China. The American students were all caught up in the country's entry into the war and seemed totally unaware of the struggles in China. They remained forward-looking and energetic. Until Josie and Katie's visit during my stay in the infirmary, only Silver Bell's presence had given me hours of escape from the worries of war and my jittery concerns for my family.

During the early years of my stay in the United States, I felt a cynical detachment from our family's fortunes. Since Silver Bell's and my expenses were depleting the bank account Uncle Dragon and Father had set up for us, Miss Tyler had helped us become work-study students. I worked in the kitchen, and Silver Bell helped to take care of all the indoor plants at her high school. Now that Father had died, I was plagued with many sleepless nights and constant worries and concerns about what to do. The distractions of everyday life could not erase my burdens. I paced, twisted my gray silk scarf, and chewed my nails. Josie and Katie looked forward to graduation so they could join the workforce and take jobs vacated by the men at war. I knew I had to go home and take care of my family, but that only intensified my anxiety.

Silver Bell is still too young, but what can I do, after the war? I know the allies are winning. I hope my major in mathematics will be a marketable skill. With no business experience and no powerful male sponsor, who will give me a position that will help provide for my family and not lead me to unsavory compromises? My only option will be to teach in the McTyeire School, which Silver Bell and I had attended during our short sojourn in Shanghai. I am sure Miss Tyler can arrange it, though the thought of becoming an overworked spinster makes me ill. Still, my obligations leave me no other choice.

A New Man

IN HOPES OF lifting my mood after my stay in the infirmary, Miss Tyler had brought me to the Sino-American Amity dance in New York City. Under the high-domed ornate ceiling of a small hall near Columbia University, echoing voices confused my hearing but added to my excitement. Tiny tables surrounded a dance floor. I sat with Miss Tyler, Dr. Charlie Chu, a physics professor from NYU, and his wife, Sophie. I had not seen so many Chinese together since I had left home.

We helped ourselves to cups of soup, dumplings, stir-fried meats and vegetables, and tea from a buffet supplied by a Chinese restaurant. People arrived in various groups. The men who came with women were obviously older and probably married. They were mostly professors, research assistants, or graduate students. Many young men sauntered in and congregated in circles. Most tried to edge close to circles that had a young woman among them. I was sure everyone noticed me because I was one of only a few single young women there. This was no surprise. Traditionally, Chinese families spared no expense in educating their sons but kept their daughters at home. I had never met so many young Chinese men in one place. They soon swarmed all around me. Throughout the evening, one young man after another came to ask me to dance or cut in while I was dancing. I danced with everyone, and hardly had time to sit down for a bite to eat and talk to the Chus. All my dance partners introduced themselves by their Chinese names, the university they were attending, and their majors. They might not have met a Chinese girl in months or years, but they all seemed to have been schooled in the Chinese mode of sobriety and modesty. A few bold ones referred to their proudest achievement: full scholarships. Soon I was mixing up their names and faces. Tossed into this sea of young men, I felt so lost — as if I were wobbling on a boat, unstable on my feet. I gazed at the pictures on a distant wall to steady myself and kept quiet. Some young men must have felt the same. Many were so shy and looked so uncomfortable that they just mumbled their names and the college they were attending. Almost all of them seemed to be majoring in engineering. They were from various provinces in China and spoke different dialects. We mostly resorted to speaking English, but some had such thick Chinese accents that I could hardly understand them.

I was introduced as Vicky, the English name my father had given me when we lived in Hong Kong. No one mentioned anything significant to distinguish himself, except for a very tall young man with gold-rimmed glasses. I could hardly look into his eyes because of the glare. "Miss Tyler told me you're from Shanghai." He smiled, and the cleft on his chin deepened.

I nodded, wondering how he knew Miss Tyler.

"I'm from Shanghai too," he continued. "Just call me by my family name, Yung."

Suddenly I became alert. "Why?" I ventured to ask.

"The Americans have trouble calling me Hsien-kung, and I don't fancy myself as a Tom, Dick, or Harry." He smiled smugly. His English had almost no Shanghai accent, and when he detected a touch of British inflection in my speech, I had to explain how our family fled to Hong Kong because of my father's patriotic activities and how the missionary school in Hong Kong insisted upon the proper King's English. He laughed and said that in spite of British

32

snobbishness, it was America's entry into the war that was saving the British Empire. I agreed and mumbled something about preferring the missionaries of Western imperialism to the brutish Japanese. He complimented me on my observation.

I had heard of a famous Yung family in Shanghai, which dominated the textile industry. I was sure he was from that family when he said he was majoring in textile engineering. I felt intimidated. He did not look like the hero of my romantic dreams, but could he be the blind Mr. Rochester? I so shocked myself with this bold speculation that I didn't utter another word. We couldn't continue talking because another young man had elbowed his way in and wanted to dance with me.

The next day Miss Tyler drove me through New York City. The numerous steel-and-concrete buildings made me think that the Shanghai Bund had proliferated here. Miss Tyler told me the names of the architects and pointed out the fine details of friezes, scones, gargoyles, and Greek columns and capitals. I had not noticed the embellishments on buildings in Shanghai, nor did I know that all these details had names. I was impressed and said so. Miss Tyler smiled and patted my hand. Then she took me to Central Park, where the spring flowers were in bloom.

The day turned out to be sunny, but gusts of cold wind sent debris swirling down the avenues and rattled the tree branches, clothed in a tender light green. The cracking and snapping sounds did not brighten my mood. Miss Tyler showed me the Obelisk and Turtle Pond. The wind buffeted us enough that we almost jogged around the reservoir, all the while ignoring the budding fruit trees and the swaying tulips and daffodils along the paths. There were few people in the park. We finally headed toward the Belvedere Castle, which was more sheltered. As we leaned against the castle wall, tears streamed down my cheeks.

"What happened?" Miss Tyler hugged me.

"Some dust must have gotten into my eyes." I lied. I was remembering the walk with Miss Tyler in our Hangzhou garden through the lily pond, the moongates, the bamboo groves, and the Taihu rocks. She had taken a picture of the moon-viewing pavilion and told me that she had come to China to capture such scenes. Miss Tyler must have been thinking of the same. She was quiet for a long time. Soon she said, "I was told that you helped to plant the little skywell in your Shanghai house."

"Yes," I replied. "My science teacher helped me select the flowers suitable for our Shanghai garden. Our rickshaw puller was a farmer in Hangzhou. He did all the work. It was not really a garden. It was tiny." I was glad to talk of the old days. "I never went to the park in Shanghai, because Mother said it was meant for foreigners only. Is it true that there was a sign that read 'Chinese and dogs are not allowed'?" I asked. The idea sounded outlandish here in New York.

"I'm not sure." Miss Tyler hesitated. After a pause, she said, "I know the gardeners were Chinese, and Chinese nannies always brought their foreign charges to play there."

I almost asked Miss Tyler if the Japanese now permitted the Chinese to enter the park. I didn't, because Japan had so successfully imitated the Western powers in empire building that they were unlikely to favor the occupied Chinese. I wondered how we were so lucky to have connected with Miss Tyler, who identified with the Chinese while most foreigners only wanted to grab as much as they could from our country. I rubbed my eyes, made complimentary comments about Central Park, but inside I felt as if I had bitten into a red, luscious peach and tasted only a bitter fruit.

Miss Tyler had invited several Chinese couples and singles to come to the mission house for a potluck brunch in two days.

The next morning, Mrs. Chu and a Mrs. Wong arrived to help us make dumplings. They brought most of the ingredients and had the party all planned out. In my family, cooks did all the work, and I had never gone near the kitchen, but I loved eating Chinese dumplings. I was glad to learn some cooking and see how the Chinese Americans lived. Mrs. Chu had brought lean ground pork, carrots, celery, Napa cabbage, and garlic chives from Chinatown.

"Sophie, do you think you can use these seaweed sheets someone left in the cupboard?" Miss Tyler asked.

Mrs. Chu looked at the package, and one corner of her mouth curled up in a sneer. "Huh, Japanese. We Chinese have many kinds of seaweed; we don't need what they stole from us!"

"Sorry." Miss Tyler blanched. "I didn't know these were Japanese."

"No need to apologize." Sophie snickered. "Americans usually think everything is Japanese — bonsai trees, painting on silk, origami, the Koto, drumming, calligraphy, etcetera." She swallowed. "Vicky, have you studied Chinese history in school?"

"Yes. My parents taught me, and Miss Tyler talks about it whenever she can," I answered. "She knows more about Chinese culture than I do."

"Vicky knows her Chinese history," Miss Tyler told everyone. The remark reminded me of feeling outraged at how the Western nations and Japan competed to grab Chinese territories and forced the opium trade upon us. When the Chinese refused to trade, seven Western nations invaded us. They burned the emperor's favorite garden. The prime real estate in port cities became the famous foreign concessions. By 1900, the boxers — Kung Fu zealots — attacked and killed the missionaries, so eight nations joined in another invasion, looting the Forbidden City, the surrounding towns, and the countryside. China had to pay huge indemnities and could not collect its own import and export taxes. I felt peevish just remembering the sight of so many desperate beggars in Shanghai. I turned to look into the refrigerator to distract myself.

"Sorry, Miss Tyler," Sophie said. "I know the wonderful work you've done. I certainly do not hold you responsible for the suffering in China." She mixed the meat with salt, soy sauce, and sesame oil, and asked me to help wash the vegetables. "Young people are the logical keepers of our heritage. They must know how the foreigners bullied us. Vicky, do you know that China allied with the winners during WWI, but the Paris Peace Conference awarded the German Concession in our Northeast to Japan?"

"Which allowed them to appropriate Chinese resources and use Chinese slave labor to start World War II!" Miss Tyler spat out her words in anger. "Otherwise, as a small country, they would never have dared to challenge the world!"

Bathed in this peevish mood, I wanted to add that my father had been a member of the T'ung Ming Hui and had established his patriotic credentials by participating in the May 4 movement of 1919 — when students agitated against this arbitrary disposal of Chinese territories. But I kept quiet.

"Let's not talk about the arrogance of white people." Miss Tyler sighed. "Now the allies are dying under the Japanese. We've been rewarded by the mad dog we fed!"

"Let's give credit where it is due." Mrs. Wong dried the vegetables. "We Chinese were always too proud and smug, taking solace in our fine, gentle culture. We were disdainful of Western technologies and refused to trade with them. The Japanese opened their country to Western ideas and became strong."

"Yes, Jane, we invented gunpowder and became masters in fireworks displays, but they developed guns and warships. By the way, Vicky, even though you're from a younger generation, just call us Sophie and Jane; just be casual like Americans." Sophie took the seaweed sheets from Miss Tyler and mixed them with the vegetables. "Miss Tyler will always be Miss Tyler to us because she is older and must be honored for her good work."

"You can call me Nancy," Miss Tyler said.

"No, no, no." Jane and Sophie answered almost at the same time. "You are the best friend any Chinese can ever have; you deserve our every respect."

"I'll never be able to call you Nancy." I nodded.

Sophie showed me how to chop everything together by banging two cleavers like drumsticks. I chopped with a vigor that belied my deep uncertainty. When I was done, Sophie stirred in the meat and added more seasoning. The aroma was heavenly and my mouth watered.

Miss Tyler brought out a half package of whole-wheat flour. "Can we use this up and mix it in our dough? Someone in the mission thinks this flour is better."

"Aiyaa," Sophie exclaimed. "The country folks at home eat brown rice and use whole wheat, but the wealthy households want everything white, soft, and sweet."

"Americans are the same." Miss Tyler laughed. "But someone in the mission likes to find new things to improve our lives. Many have come to believe whole grains are more nutritious."

Jane poured the two kinds of flour into a large bowl and made a well in the middle.

I had seen the tomato juice in the refrigerator. I fetched it.

"Auntie Sophie and Auntie Jane, let's make the dumplings red. That's a lucky color," I said, surprised at my audacity.

"In China, you would call us Auntie Sophie and Auntie Jane. Here, we're just Sophie and Jane!" Jane said.

Sophie opened her mouth and stared at the bottle.

"We'll make something different in America," Jane said. "These are going to be colorful, healthy Chinese American dumplings."

I shifted my weight, knowing I was inaugurating something unorthodox.

"You'll be the model for our new China." Jane poured the

tomato juice into the flour bowl. "Creative." She smiled broadly. "Now, you can help."

She mixed the white and whole-wheat dough and sprinkled more white flour on the table; she taught me how to knead. She rolled the dough into long, thick ropes, and then cut the ropes into small balls. With a small rolling pin, she rolled each ball into a circle. My hands grew tired, and soon after, I rolled a large glob of dough into a huge flat piece and started using a cup to cut circles.

Everyone watched me. "You are so innovative, we're entering a new era!" Sophie laughed.

Miss Tyler was smiling and nodding at me. I felt happy, but also strange that everyone had accepted my improvised ways so quickly.

We took turns rolling out large sheets of pasta until the dough was only one-eighth of an inch thick. My mind twisted and turned, wondering how I could get them to tell me about living in the States. "So how do you like living in America?" I finally asked directly.

"American ways are so different. No one has servants here," Mrs. Chu answered. "Life can be difficult: cooking, cleaning, shopping in Chinatown, and trying to fit into the white community." She pursed her lips and sighed stoically.

"So do you have many friends in Chinatown?" I asked.

"No, most of them speak a different dialect," Jane said.

"The Chinatown people have lived here a long, long time. They were early traders and railroad workers who suffered under the Chinese Exclusion Act," Sophie joined in. "They were not allowed to bring their families. For decades, they lived in a bachelor society. They never went to American schools and could only speak Pidgin English. Most of the people in our small community uptown who are connected with the colleges and universities find it hard to communicate with them."

"Still, the Chinese immigrants here never suffered like people in China." Jane added. "Yes, Vicky, your studies in Chinese history must have told you that China went through a hundred years of *luan*—chaos."

"Let's not talk about the Chinese trauma anymore," Sophie said. "Tell us about your family. How did you meet Miss Tyler?"

I obliged. "Miss Tyler was my private tutor in Hangzhou — mainly in English and science. My parents taught me Chinese history and the classics," I whispered.

"Then you must have come from a book-fragrant family," Sophie said.

I nodded, but mumbled that our homestead was burned—and with it all our books. My eyes welled up.

"Sorry I brought up the unpleasant." Jane patted my hand. "You are not alone! Every Chinese here has a family at home who has suffered disastrous losses."

"We're all in the same boat." Sophie came to stand beside me while she helped with the rolling. She eyed Miss Tyler. "Meaning no disrespect to the good work done by the missionaries, all the guns and warships of Western empires helped turn us into a desperately poor country. It was as if the sun had turned pale and the moon spat fire!"

Her statements came like thunderbolts out of a clear blue sky, but I recognized Sophie and Jane's anguish. What might their families have endured under the Japanese? I did not have the courage to question them. The trauma of our family's dispersal flooded my mind, and I trembled. I remembered Father's visit, and knew Mother's mind had retreated to her beloved old home because Brook ma-ma made oblique references to it. I wanted to run somewhere to cry, but I swallowed and turned away to cough.

"In early 1937, just before Japan declared war, my family bought a house in Shanghai's French Concession," I continued. "We felt it would be safer to leave our family compound in Hangzhou and go to the French territory. Of course, we thought it would only be temporary." I slammed down a plastic cup and twisted to cut circles from the sheet of thin dough. Anger energized my movements, and the dumpling skins piled up quickly. A few slipped to the floor. I apologized, picked up the pieces, and threw them away. "When the Japanese came into Shanghai in the fall of 1937, we fled to Hong Kong."

"So how did you come to the States?" Sophie asked.

My past came to me in a torrent. "Miss Tyler arranged to have me come here in July 1941." I took a deep breath and almost choked. "When Japan invaded Hong Kong, my father fled to Chunking; he was killed there during the bombing." I held one hand in front of my mouth; afraid I might tell everyone how my father had appeared to me in Syracuse. Instead I said, "My mother, Brook ma-ma, the concubine, and her daughter Coral Bell returned to Shanghai, and Miss Tyler brought my sister Silver Bell to high school here." I turned to wash my hands and collect myself. "We owe so much to Miss Tyler."

"If the Western world truly practiced Christian charity, the world would be at peace," Jane mumbled.

The ladies did not question me about the concubine. It was a common practice in China. It was so much easier talking to them about my family than to Steve's parents. Miss Tyler huddled close and handed me tissues. I could not help mentioning my worries about my mother: "After all the dislocations, poetry became my mother's only refuge." I banged and twisted the plastic cup on the sticky dough, regretting my lack of control in blurting out my family history. My heart raced as if the horror stories were coursing through my veins. The dough circles came out all wrong.

"Vicky's father was a founding member of the Kuomintang." Miss Tyler proudly filled in the details of my history. "He never stopped writing articles and sending aid to the Nationalists. That's why the family had to flee when Japan occupied the east coast of China."

Warmth enveloped me. I was proud that my father had not collaborated with the Japanese and that Miss Tyler told these ladies about it.

"Let's not talk about this anymore. China has suffered under this fiery red moon since the turn of the century." Sophie's voice wobbled. "We've all heard about the Nanking Massacre, and most of us come from dispersed families. We are lucky to live in peace here, but it is hard to ignore the suffering at home."

"We're all praying for peace," Miss Tyler said.

"I hope to return home and help rebuild our country," I added.

Miss Tyler wrung her hands and exclaimed, "How are we to stop the world from going mad?" After a pause, her quiet authority returned. "Sophie and Jane, will you please show us how to fold the dumplings, now?"

"China will rise again with young people like Vicky," Sophie said. She placed a spoonful of filling in each dough circle. Folding the circle into a half-moon shape, she pinched a scalloped ridge at the top and put it on a baking sheet where she had spread white flour. The dumplings lined up like the fancy friezes on New York buildings.

Finally, I fell into the rhythm of dumpling making — brushing a drop of water around the circumference of dough before pinching the ridge over the filling.

Sophie stepped back and laughed at our creations. "These reddish brown dumplings will be the laughingstock of our refined Chinese friends. But we are in America." She looked at me as though she was seeing a stranger. She returned to her work.

"Ah, some people are blessed with good fate." Jane laughed, changing the subject. "That young man, Yung Hsien-kung, never suffered a day! His family sent him out of Shanghai before the Japanese came, and even though he is separated from his family, he has some relatives here."

My heart fluttered when I remembered the tall young man.

When we were almost finished, Sophie steamed some dumplings for us to sample, and then helped Jane place sheets of dumplings into the freezer for the next day's party.

The following day dawned sunny but cool, brightening the mood in the mission house.

"Oh, thanks!" I said, accepting a heaping bowl of stir-fried seafood noodles from a Mr. Yan; I rushed it into the kitchen's warming oven. Mrs. Yan followed with pork-fried rice.

Then everyone headed into the kitchen. Lucy Zhou placed her spicy green bean salad in the refrigerator.

"You have sprouted good fortune, Peter," Miss Tyler said by way of greeting.

"Yes, I'm getting fat, Miss Tyler." Peter Zhou laughed. "It is all Lucy's fault. She is such a good cook!" He nudged his wife and handed Miss Tyler a plate of five-spiced beef. "This is also from Lucy."

Several other young men came bringing Peking duck and other delicacies from Chinatown. With the many visitors crowding the kitchen, I almost bumped into Yung. He smiled, and again the cleft on his chin became more prominent. He gave me a box of Swiss chocolates. "I am Yung. Remember? Thanks for including me."

I almost answered that Miss Tyler had invited everyone and I had not planned anything.

The jolly atmosphere had changed my mood. I felt as if I was back in the crowded bustle of a family gathering. "Nice to meet you again," I said. Instead of shaking hands, I spun around and waved the chocolates at him. A strange light-headedness made me behave like a flirt. I avoided eye contact and reached up to put the chocolates on a shelf. "We'll serve these for dessert," I told everyone.

42

As people drifted into the living room, Lucy drew me aside and whispered, "Yung is an only son. His father is a textile tycoon in Shanghai."

I might have said "Oh," but wondered if Miss Tyler had used her connections to invite the eligible young man. For some reason, I didn't bother to greet the other two young men.

"I've learned some cooking," I heard Yung say to Miss Tyler as they went near the stove. "What can I do to help?"

"All the food is ready," Miss Tyler said. "Why don't you help Golden Bell set the table?"

"So that is your Chinese name, Vicky?" Yung asked in Shanghainese.

Blushing and feeling hot, I nodded. *He knew I spoke Shanghainese!*

I handed him the dinner plates and chopsticks and went into the dining room. I tried not to stare at his slightly hunched broad shoulders. He was almost a head taller than I was. No one would have considered him handsome. He had a bulbous nose, and at certain angles, his glasses looked opaque, giving the impression of a blind man. In any case, his glasses were so thick I could hardly see his eyes. Somehow this gave him a clownish look, but I thought it bespoke intelligence as well. I reminded myself that intelligence could be very seductive. Engulfed as I was by worries about my family and accustomed to repressing my youthful desires, I might have avoided him. Yet he seemed anxious to please in spite of all the talk of his family wealth. His guileless smile was the most attractive feature about him.

As I walked around the dining table, putting down placemats, he followed me and juggled three plates in the air, then caught and landed each one neatly on its mat. Obviously his eyesight was no impediment. I could not help but watch his every move, walking backward to do so. I tried not to focus on his cleft chin.

"Now catch!" he called out to me and made a throwing motion with a chopstick. I snapped to attention. But he swung his body around in a fancy turn and caught the flying chopstick himself. A rush of energy sent me to the other side of the table, laughing and calling to him: "OK, we'll start from here."

"Ready?" Yung shouted.

"Yes," I shouted back, opening my hands to show my "catch" position.

The sticks came flying, first slowly, then faster as I managed to place them on the mats and move around the table. I missed some sticks, but caught most. People laughed and urged me to go right, go left, and try harder. I was giggling so hard, I had to wipe tears from my eyes.

Afraid that Yung would break the rice bowls, teacups, and drinking glasses, I handed them to him one at a time. He threw each glass or cup into the air and did a backhand catch. All eyes were on him. Sometimes he threw them really high so he had time to straighten the chopsticks on the mats before catching the cups and glasses. There were curious moments of suspension until each cup and glass was in its proper place. We cheered and clapped.

"Miss Tyler," Yung called out. "See how fast Golden Bell and I have finished our work?"

"Neatly done too," Miss Tyler answered, laughing. "Now, go and call everyone to come and eat."

Chinese etiquette dictated that people first serve their neighbor, before eating. Since I'd had my meals in the cafeteria during the last years, I'd forgotten this custom. By the time I remembered, everyone's plate was already full. As usual, the married ladies played host, piling food onto others' plates. Everyone had a glint of merriment in their eyes as we chattered on and off in English and Chinese while Miss Tyler exclaimed how happy she was to be able to speak Chinese among her "own chosen" people.

"Ah, these dumplings are unusual!" Yung said. His soft voice was arresting. Everyone seemed to come to attention.

"Vicky suggested we make these colorful dumplings because we're in America and we can do things differently," Mrs. Chu said.

I blushed and lowered my head. *Are my reddish dumplings to become the laughingstock of these real Chinese?*

"Um . . ." Mr. Yan plowed into the seafood noodles, and Peter Zhou took two more helpings of beef, but Yung asked for more dumplings. Saying "Yum, yummy," he gobbled up three more while Miss Tyler said, "These are my favorite too."

The food disappeared so fast that I felt it was the best meal I had ever had in America.

Yung had brought beer, and most men and a few women began to toast and thank Miss Tyler.

"I think Schlitz is a German beer," Miss Tyler said, reading the label. "Do you think people know that?"

"I think it is American made — just like our beer from Sing Tao, which was in the German Concession," Yung answered. "Some day the Chinese will make German beer from Sing Tao."

"Yes, but the Japanese are making it now and drinking it!" Mrs. Wong said grumpily.

"Kang bai, Kang bai." Mr. Yan drained his beer and held his cup upside down. Other guests followed suit.

After brunch, the men went outside to play basketball on the driveway while the women and I wiped the table, soaked the chopsticks and silverware, and washed the dishes, pots, and platters.

"That young man, Yung, is really a wonderful boy," Lucy said, eyeing me.

"I heard his family is really rich," Mrs. Yan added.

Lucy nodded. "The family factories seem to still prosper under Japanese occupation."

I felt a bit guilty listening to gossip, and uneasy about Yung's family thriving under the Japanese.

"Poor Yung." Lucy sighed. "He always sounds apologetic. He feels he is spending dirty money, since his fortune now comes from collaborating with the Japanese."

I kept busy wiping the counters, the stove, and the table. *We both live in peace. Why isn't he as tormented as I am? Does he feel as conflicted? Is that why he wants to please? Are his antics a façade?*

In spite of my doubts, hearing about Yung's family background filled me with an unfamiliar lightness, relieving me of my obsession with my own family and the war.

"Oh, you're working too hard, Golden Bell," Sophie exclaimed. "Go join the young people outside."

I shook my head and murmured, "I like to help."

"It is so good of Miss Tyler to invite us here," Mrs. Yan said. "Mrs. Chu told us Miss Tyler had tutored you since you were a child. Where are you from?"

"Yes," I replied. "When Mrs. Chu and Mrs. Wong came to help us make dumplings yesterday, I somehow blurted out how my family had dispersed during the war and my father died in Chunking." My voice wobbled. I really didn't want to go into my family history again.

Lucy turned pale. "My family was decimated in Nanking," she whispered. She was on the verge of tears.

I immediately regretted being so insensitive. What had possessed me? Every family had suffered dislocation in these years. It was more traumatic for those who had witnessed torture or death. My father had died, but Lucy might have known worse. My mention of death and dispersion must have fallen like icy raindrops on her bare head. "I'm sorry," I whispered.

"You're still young." Lucy took a deep breath and put a hand on my shoulder. "Time will heal us."

I said nothing, but frowned. With these older married ladies, it felt like being among my older relatives. I needed to be more circumspect.

"The next time we get together, it'll be in my house," Lucy said loudly to change the subject. "It'll be a dumpling party, and Golden Bell will teach us how to make these healthy dumplings!"

"I am returning to Syracuse tomorrow."

"Then we will wait for your next visit!" Lucy turned to put away another pot.

"The school year is almost ending, and we hope the war will end too!" Jane said. "Let's hope many of us will be able to return home."

While everyone was saying goodbye in the front hall, Yung whispered, "May I call on you?"

Asking for my permission seemed very old-fashioned, but asking me and not my father was such a modern gesture that it startled me. "But I don't live here," I said.

"That's OK," he said. "My finals are coming up, and then I must write my graduate thesis. I can take the train as soon as all my classes are done. I can work on my paper while I visit you. Miss Tyler said she can arrange lodging for me."

I smiled, happy that Miss Tyler approved and seemed to have maneuvered this young man into my life. I became tongue-tied, as I was prone to be when faced with something embarrassing. I could not open my mouth to say "I look forward to seeing you." Instead, I nodded and murmured "good-bye."

"In the meantime, write to me?"

I could feel my heart thumping against my chest and didn't answer. But I nodded again.

When we shook hands to say farewell, Yung's thumb stole under my palm and stroked it.

His glasses lit up his childlike smile, deepening the cleft on his chin. He looked very pleased.

47

A New Romance

BACK IN SYRACUSE, a subdued joy permeated my whole being. The five days in New York City had been an uplifting interlude. They had relieved me of my obsessive thoughts about our future, Father's visit, and Mother's sanity. Plus, my acceptance into Kappa Kappa Gamma fortified my sense of a newfound connection. Calm at last in my bleak, isolated life, I found the warm spring days pleasant and agreeable. The happy, jostling people at the New York party had changed my perceptions. In my room I took down the altar that had offended everyone. A shaft of brightness kept my thoughts lingering on Yung. I reran images of his large hand and long fingers tossing and catching the cups and glasses and juggling the plates. The way he clutched every cup to his chest and caressed each glass with both hands before placing them gently on the mats was alluring. There was also a delicacy and tenderness about the way he tossed the chopsticks horizontally, like tiny logs, rather than shooting them at me like spears. The light glinting from his glasses had lit up his face, and his voice was strangely calm and soothing when he told me to "watch it," or "look, here comes another one!" I sat for hours every day, mesmerized by the details of my memories of him.

Is he arrogant? Does he hog all the attention? His good humor and playfulness can be deceptive. And yet . . . and yet, I sense no trace of arrogance at all. He is eager to please — almost childishly so. He is perceptive and seems such an unusual character. Perhaps that is because he has never been scarred by war. And he shared the stage with me. Catching the chopsticks was the first time that people focused their attention on me and cheered me on! Since most people know of his family's wealth, why hasn't any young woman snatched him up?

When Silver Bell asked me about the long weekend, I blushed as if just talking about Yung would invite illicit thoughts. To play down the attention I was giving this new man in my life, I told her that I was afraid Father might not find him acceptable because his family was collaborating with the Japanese. Deep inside, I still longed for the return of the amber light and the warm hand that had led me forward. I was sure it had been Father's hand.

"His family maybe, but you don't know that he collaborated!" Silver Bell retorted. "Perhaps Father sent him here to help us!"

I was surprised by my little sister's observation. I stared at her for a long time. *Surely, if Father can visit, he can find ways to help me support my family.* I promised Silver Bell I would tell her everything after Yung's visit.

In the meantime, Yung and I corresponded every day. At first we talked about the weather, our school work, and, later, our loneliness. I was luckier than Yung because Silver bell was nearby.

Soon, Yung arranged to have a telephone installed in my room. We'd had no telephone in Hangzhou, and I had seldom talked on the phone in Shanghai and Hong Kong. When he first called, my heart was in my mouth and I could hardly speak; I let the static fill my head with his image and his voice. I replied in disjointed words and phrases. Gradually we began talking about our classes and school life. "I'm a member of the Kappa Kappa Gamma sorority. My friends Josie and Katie sponsored me. In fact, many women from my cottage are members."

"It must be so quaint to live in a cottage."

"Oh no, it is just a house, but people call the men's dorms houses and the women's cottages."

I still preferred writing to him, when I had time to think about what to write. I sat beside the phone when I wrote and couldn't wait to hear his voice once a week. We told each other about our families. He confirmed all that I already knew about his charmed life: his coming here for high school and graduating from Columbia University, and now he was almost done with his doctorate. It was no wonder his English hardly had a Chinese accent.

"I feel more like an American sometimes," he said. "But being Chinese, I can never be free from the strong family ties dominating my existence. Before Pearl Harbor, my mother visited me frequently. She made sure that the family's wide connections and an aunt kept track of me. I only have an older sister, so everyone impressed upon me my responsibility as the heir."

I told him my family history as if I were writing a story. It was cathartic and distracted me from my constant worries about my mother. I wrote to him what Mother had told us about witnessing the burning of our home in Hangzhou:

"The gates burst open. Japanese soldiers charge into the silent house. Blood, sweat, and soot cover their uniforms. Torches light up their coarse, drunken faces as their ominous shadows swarm the halls. Brandishing bayonets, bellowing for women, gold, and wine, they smash earthenware in the kitchen, porcelain and ink stones in the family quarters. Two East Ocean Devils chase down Silver Bell's whimpering puppy, Ah Joy. Shouting, they spear him again and again. A trail of blood follows the carcass to the bonfire. A rifle flashes, discharging a round into the antique Ming desk. Trunks and cupboards are ransacked. I am hiding in a hollow behind the cupboard, where the family treasures are stored.

A thin wail drifts through the darkness — it is Peony pleading for mercy — her eerie call answered by an onrush of stomping feet and smoking torches . . ."

Yung called me right away when he read that letter. This was the first time I'd told anyone of Mother's trauma. I couldn't control myself and started sobbing, clinging tightly to the telephone, as if his voice were an amber glow and I was clutching his warm hand. I felt his kind nature even on the phone.

When I finally calmed down, he said, "I feel guilty that I have not shared the suffering of the other Chinese."

"I feel guilty too. I never witnessed any bombing, fighting, or people being killed," I joined in. "Silver Bell witnessed the Japanese invasion of Hong Kong, but I already came here. I was young when we moved from Hangzhou to Shanghai to Hong Kong. They all felt like adventures. I'm sure Mother and the rest of the family felt differently."

"I truly appreciate our parents' burdens. I don't like my father's collaboration with the Japanese, but so many lives are dependent on the company's success that I see how it is necessary."

"I understand," I said. "My jeo-jeo, Glorious Dragon, worked with the Japanese and prospered — supporting the whole family. He probably helped to pay for my sister's and my schooling in America. So in a way we also benefited from collaborating." After much talking, I mentioned my suspicion that my mother's mind was drifting, as she no longer wrote to me. I was sure she would be a completely lost vessel without Brook ma-ma's constant care. Even before I left Hong Kong, Mother's eyes would sometimes glaze over and she would recite her favorite Tu Fu poems.

Instead of expressing more sympathy, Yung asked me to recite a poem. The one that popped into my mind was Tu Fu's quatrain Mother had shared with the whole family when we took a leisurely walk around the path on Victoria Peak.

Birds flash white against the blue water,
Flowers flame brighter against the green mountain.

52

Spring speeds past before my eyes.
What year will I return?

My voice trembled when I explained Brook ma-ma's status. I told them that when Orchid was five years old, Mother saw her gnawing on a tree trunk and bought her in to serve as a personal maid. Mother taught her how to read, write, sew, embroider, and all the fine manners of a lady. Our household had no son, so my mother presented her as a concubine to my father. "We all call her Brook ma-ma now," I said.

Yung told me not to feel embarrassed. "Anyone who expressed shock just forgot human history," he said. "Miss Tyler's missionary friends must all know that Abraham in the Old Testament had a concubine. Then there was Henry the Eighth, although he never had a concubine because he just executed his wives one after the other!"

I laughed.

"By the way, I know my father had mistresses and would have taken many concubines, but since I was born, my mother has not allowed another woman into the house." He stated flatly, "I think my mother was wise because concubines usually bring chaos into the family." He added, "Sure, some were oppressed; others schemed against each other and created tension and constant squabbles in the house."

"My mother had bound feet," I mumbled. "She could never have survived without Brook ma-ma."

"My mother would say your mother was very wise." I imagined Yung nodding here. "If a strange woman were brought into the house instead and bore a son, your mother would have to swallow bitterness for the rest of her life."

"Although Brook ma-ma felt it was the greatest honor of her life to be selected, from all the maidservants in the house, to become a concubine for my father, I could not understand how my father, a very progressive man by all measures, would take one."

"Well, in the old days, with the country in turmoil, Chinese traditions gave us order. When a man died, his male heir had to place his head on the pillow in the coffin. No one would perform such a task without first being named an heir. So, did your Brook ma-ma produce a son?"

"No," I answered. "She bore Jade Bell and Coral Bell. Jade Bell was killed when Japan invaded Hong Kong."

"Oh, Golden Bell, how horrible!" Yung exclaimed.

"I was already studying in the States, but the rest of the family endured all that." My words slurred after one another. A leaden weight seemed to have latched on to my thoughts. I swallowed and tried not to choke.

"I know exactly how you feel," Yung whispered. "I have been spared the trauma too."

"Mother would say it is fate, and no one couldn't give me a simple Christian explanation. Miss Tyler mentioned something about Christ dying on the cross and something about redemption of sin."

"Christ chose his path, but the Chinese didn't ask to be invaded."

"So, I suppose you're not a Christian?"

"No, I was never baptized, though the high school I attended is Christian. The minister befriended me, and most of my friends are Christians. Are you?"

"Yes. Miss Tyler's generosity and kindness moved me. Silver Bell and I owe our safety to her and her mission."

"I suppose I owe her for bringing you to me."

I reddened and changed the subject. "I don't think Miss Tyler could understand why Brook Ma-ma felt she had been ungrateful for her failure to produce a son. That's why she swore she would devote the rest of her life to serving her kind mistress — my mother."

"Do you understand why?"

"She is a noble woman." But my confusion rushed out of my mouth: "It is not her fault! Modern science says it is the man's sperm that determines a child's gender!" My heart twitched at the idiocy of the whole affair. "Besides, why would my mother, or any woman, give her husband another wife?"

Yung paused and coughed, perhaps unaccustomed to such a forthright outburst from me. "This is a new scientific theory. People in our parents' generation didn't know about it. My mother is forever grateful that I was born so our family fortune would not land in the hands of my uncle."

The custom was irrefutable, but acid churned my stomach. "At any rate, Brook ma-ma is now Mother's alter ego. Without her, Silver Bell and I would not be able to connect to our mother," I said. "Brook ma-ma used to call Mother the silk of our family. Now she is the silk, because she, alone, provides warmth and supple strength during our Diaspora."

"Your mother did a very noble thing when she chose the concubine. She had the welfare of the family in mind all along."

I could not help remembering how differently Steve's family's reaction had been to my family's concubine. Yes, it was so much easier talking to Yung. We had been cut from the same cloth. I decided to write to him about my "American boyfriend" adventure. He wrote back about the clash of cultures right away, because he had a similar experience with a brilliant young woman in college.

Anna Maria's father was an Italian bricklayer. Since Yung loved Italian food, Anna thought he would fit right in with her large, warm family with two older sisters, their truck-driving husbands, their broods and innumerable cousins. She had heard that the Chinese were family oriented and valued family solidarity. But a single visit to her jostling, beer-drinking, wine tossing, backslapping family was enough for Yung to realize the enormous gulf that separated the two cultures. As soon as they were introduced, Anna's father and mother both said they understood how lonely he must be in a strange country. They gave him a bear hug, which he didn't know how to handle. Hugging a stranger was simply not something a sane Chinese would contemplate.

I saw Silver Bell only on the weekends when we were not otherwise engaged, and I'd missed the deep attachment of a family. I'd yearned for the daily conversations, consultations, and revelations that I used to share with my mother. Now writing and talking to Yung every day, I was no longer awkward and reticent but felt a new intimacy. When he called, I imagined his cleft chin touching the speaker. I rubbed my chin against my speaker as well. It felt like a kiss almost.

"My parents did everything to protect the integrity of the family." I sighed. Anguish gnawed my insides. I finally told him about my father's visit.

"Oh, what a strange experience," Yung cried. "But I've heard of the dead reaching their beloved in desperate situations! Your father's spirit is surely watching over you."

"I hope so," I said. "I wish he would visit again!"

"I'm sure you miss your family, but you must move forward in the land of the living. By the way, my exams will be over next Thursday. I'll be in Syracuse Friday. I can write my thesis there." Yung spoke with confidence. "Hold tight there, little one, and everything will be all right."

A wave of soothing warmth washed over me; an amber light seemed to be glowing, and I smiled into the phone.

Blessings of Love

"WHERE DID YOU go?" Yung asked as soon as he saw me taking off my wet shoes in the vestibule of my cottage. I had been so nervous all day awaiting his arrival that I couldn't sit still.

"I went for a walk in the woods and almost forgot the time. I ran back." I puffed. "Sorry I didn't have time to change."

"I am so happy to see you again." He surveyed my flushed face. He pointed to the bulletin board. "This sign says they'll be doing maintenance work today and the water is shut off from noon to six. Do you want to come to my house to shower and change?"

I blushed and shook my legs to cover my anxiety.

"Miss Tyler has arranged for me to housesit for a professor on sabbatical," he continued. "I went there first to drop my luggage. It's a lovely house. They must have just renovated the bathroom. It is all green and sparkling." He took my hand as if to shake it, but he just held on. "It's on the next block."

Since my experience with Steve, I had considered several American college men my friends. Most of them dumped me because I refused to become intimate and go to secluded places. I knew I needed some distraction from my obsessive worries about my family, but I had an old habit of not wanting to put on a "dog and pony" show for any man. I slipped easily into my fortress

57

mentality. "I'm used to just cleaning up in my dorm," I said. "But I had forgotten about this notice."

"I'm an old-fashioned Chinese." Yung looked down at his shoes. "I don't mean to sound as if I have ulterior motives."

Yung's soothing voice on the phone had become very precious, and his existence had settled in a special place in my mind. He was someone I could talk to and perhaps the only one who understood me. Silver Bell was too young and too eager to fit into the American landscape. She said confidently that Miss Tyler would never let us starve and that I was worrying enough for both of us. She sounded so logical; I had no words to refute her.

Now Yung's tangible presence threw me off balance. I blushed furiously and couldn't find a word to say.

"Well, it is almost five. I have to get something to eat. I didn't have lunch on the train."

I hadn't even thought about lunch. "I skipped lunch too," I whispered. In fact, I hadn't eaten breakfast either, but I didn't say it out loud. I had rushed into the woods to stave off my agitation.

There is no water in the dorm, and Yung will feel very uncomfortable waiting for me in the common room where the girls congregate to giggle and gossip when I try to tidy up and change. "Oh, sorry I messed up my schedule. I'm so confused." I kept stepping in place so that my red face and my huffing and puffing would mask my bewilderment.

"Miss Tyler has invited us for dinner tomorrow. She told me about this Chinese restaurant not too far from the campus. We'll have dinner there." Yung smiled. "I am so hungry." His clasp on my hand tightened. "We'll walk to my house, make tea, and have a snack. You'll be so much more comfortable after a shower." His firm grip and gentle tone conveyed authority and security. He was dressed formally, looking like a man in control. Intoxicated by his white shirt, blue tie, and dark suit, I felt the stability I had longed for from my parents. I gleamed with the certainty that my father's protective arm had reached me. I ran upstairs and quickly packed a change of clothing. As soon as I came down, I took his outstretched hand and proceeded across the campus toward his house. I would soon turn twenty-one. For some time now I had been aware of my maturing body — the strange stirrings in my groin and around my breasts. I told myself innumerable times that my attraction to Yung might be just an infatuation or simply a way to satisfy my physical yearnings and my need to find safe harbor. Now with Yung standing before me, I seemed to have suspended all caution, and smiled up into his eyes.

It had rained the night before, but the sun had already dried the walkways. Lingering moisture dressed the trees, grasses, and roofs in a bright sheen. We meandered, admiring the budding tulips and daffodils. Hyacinths perfumed our path, and I felt rejuvenated by the clean, fresh beauty of this little walk. "Look," I said. "Everything happens later here than in New York City. These flowers are just opening."

Yung squeezed my hand. "The sign of an auspicious beginning! Notice the tender light green of the trees? This rain has cleansed our old world."

Several robins flew in to peck at the still damp ground. Their twitter cheered me up. If my schoolmates saw me walking hand in hand with a young Chinese man, they might tease me. But I didn't care. I felt the certainty of our two minds discovering camaraderie amid the tumult of war and isolation.

Two college kids ran by us, laughing and shouting, as they passed a football back and forth between them.

"American kids enjoy such freedom," Yung said. "They are an active, optimistic people."

"The American students amaze me," I replied politely. I was glad to talk about anything that showed our shared understanding. "The Chinese are more subdued. At home, I was taught to honor my instructors as second only to my parents. Here, teachers want to please the students. I'm confused when some of them try to make their material interesting by adding jokes and letting their voices rise and fall. Lately, instead of feeling entertained, I can't wait for the classes to end so I can rush to my room and let the strange longings for my Chinese world take over."

"I'm afraid the old Chinese world is disappearing. Perhaps that's liberating? Old-fashioned Chinese parents like ours worry about their children's future. They push us to excel in school, but they can become really intrusive — set goals for us and manage our lives," Yung muttered. "If America weren't at war with Japan, my parents would have sent me a wife by now. Some parents don't bother to bring their sons home but simply ship a young woman overseas after a wedding celebration in China. They've been scouting among their friends and relatives for a suitable match for a long, long time —since I was a child. In fact, I dread visiting my relatives here, because they're always matchmaking. I can't tell you how many times they've urged me to take a wife. If I hadn't resisted, they would have had me married a long time ago."

I remained silent. I missed my parents so much, I would have loved to have them interfere with my life. *Did my father send Yung here? Would I want such intervention if times were different?*

"When you came to the party in the mission house, how did you find out that I spoke Shanghainese?"

Yung shifted his glasses and pulled me closer. "When I first saw your melon-seed face and dimpled smile during the Sino-American dance, it was as if the sky had opened up and a ray of sunshine pierced my heart. You were so busy dancing and talking with everyone, I could hardly get near you. So I asked Miss Tyler about you. The potluck brunch in the mission house was my suggestion!"

I was dumbfounded. No one had ever singled me out for such attention. I took a deep breath to steady my racing heart.

Yung's little Cape house looked neat and compact.

"I agreed to a reasonable rent, and the owners pay the college service to maintain the grounds and clean the house," Yung said. After a brief tour, he led me to the bathroom and handed me towels.

A giddy recklessness came over me. I forgot to thank him and tiptoed to give him a peck on the cheek.

Yung raised his eyebrows. "As soon as I saw you, I tried hard to control my urge to kiss you!"

I ran into the bathroom and locked the door before he could grab me. Lingering in the shower, I let the steamy water blast into my every pore. As my muscles relaxed and the giddiness dissipated, I realized I had been impulsive and presumptuous. What if his parents disapproved of me? What if he was toying with me? What if my father had nothing to do with sending him?

In my mind, I rationalized my presence in his house as a necessity, because I wanted him to know me. It was so easy to write and talk to him about my responsibilities. He seemed to have already accepted my absent family and my sense of responsibility toward my mother, Brook ma-ma, Silver Bell, and Coral Bell. He had told me that he admired the courage and equal endeavors of American women in the war effort. Now, the freedom to unload my concerns on Yung was exhilarating.

It felt like I spent hours in the bathroom drying my hair, getting dressed, and cleaning up after myself. A fog shrouded the mirror. I gave it a quick swipe. The rosy, animated face that stared back at me looked like it had been immersed in an amber glow. I was smiling as if waiting to have my picture taken. Showering in a man's house was definitely something no one, not even Miss Tyler, would approve of. I winked at myself for being so bold. I shaded the hollows of my cheeks with a little rouge to emphasize my high cheekbones and wondered why I had thought to include a tiny comb and my small makeup pack. I splashed rosewater on my face. Its fragrance and chill startled me. The amber glow disappeared. "What do you think you are doing?" I shouted mutely to myself. I could imagine my parents scowling at me. "Your father is dead and your mother has lost her mind. You need someone to take care of you, but where is the honor in luring this young man for your needs?"

I washed off all my makeup and blotted the scent with the towel. Yung was reading the newspaper in the living room. He had already changed into casual gray pants and a blue cardigan. I wandered into the kitchen and noticed cookies and boxes of teabags on the table and a steaming kettle on the hot plate. I made tea for both of us.

Yung entered. He had taken off his glasses, and his deep-set eyes surveyed my body. It was unnerving. Then, without a word, he pulled me toward him. He nuzzled under my ear as if sniffing me. "I'm so glad to have found you," he whispered, but his nose and mouth were in wholehearted pursuit of the scent around my head as he pressed his body against mine.

I smelled the freshness of my clean hair mingled with his hot breath, and my hands rose to rest on his back. He cradled my head in his hands and tenderly kissed my forehead, my eyebrows, my eyes, my nose, and finally my mouth. He held me so close that we almost dissolved into each other. My head seemed to be floating, and my body went limp. I was drifting in the evening sunlight reflected off the white walls, setting the room on fire. The gold and fuchsia of the room matched my mood perfectly. When he kissed me again, I automatically whispered no. But then I responded so fiercely to his mouth that I could feel my heart burning, obliterating my cold, passionless past. Yung led me into the living room. On the sofa, he kissed me again, softly. I raised my hand to my mouth — an instinctive gesture meant to ward off further advances.

Yet I was warm and relaxed, and somehow my hand fell to his neck and I felt like lying down and yielding to him.

Suddenly I noticed the lingering scent of rose water. I straightened and moved away a little while still holding him. "I . . . I . . ." I stuttered. I let my hands fall to my sides. "You are hungry. Let's go to dinner."

"I had some tea and cookies." Yung shook himself. "Yes, we must not be too hasty."

I braced myself and moved back more, muttering, "We . . . must keep calm."

Yung nodded, and I stood up. Yung's face was flushed as he also rose slowly. "Where are my glasses?" he mumbled.

We found his glasses, put on our jackets, and walked out the front door while he gave me intermittent pecks on my cheek. I had to turn away my face when he sought my lips.

We held hands but remained silent during our walk. My mind kept returning to our brief love scene, and I tried hard to suppress my rising excitement by recalling my playful mood when his ebullience had filled the dining room in New York.

"I have never been kissed by a man before," I blurted out.

"Steve didn't kiss you?"

"He tried," I mumbled. "I let him kiss me on the cheeks, but never on the mouth."

I did not ask him about his experiences with Anna Marie. I had already thanked my father innumerable times for sending me this wonderful, sensitive, and loving man, and I didn't want to know anything that might make me feel different.

"Oh, I can just eat you up!" Yung brought my hand to his mouth and softly nibbled all over it. It was twilight, and I was afraid he would grab me and kiss me again.

I controlled my mounting excitement with an effort. "Come to think of it, neither of my parents ever kissed me. My father would pat my head when he was pleased with me. Mother would call me 'my heart-and-liver' and nudge me close."

"That's what my mother used to call me too." Yung smiled into my face. "Our book-fragrant families always inhibited spontaneity. I'm glad we met here."

My whole being tingled with joy. I wanted to shout to the world that I'd found the love of my life and that I would take care of the rest of my family as well!

As soon as we entered the restaurant, the Chinese husband and wife owners greeted us, telling us that they knew everyone in the Chinese community and how excited they were to see new faces. They served as cooks, waiters, and cashiers. They spoke Cantonese and were thrilled to know that I had lived in Hong Kong and could communicate well with them. Once they found out that we were from Shanghai, they offered to prepare special Shanghainese dishes for us. They recommended the stewed pork lion's head meatballs with Chinese cabbage, steamed fish with scallions, ginger, and garlic, and plain stir-fried tiny crystal shrimp.

"I'm so hungry, I could even eat the gooey Chinese American food," Yung said. I smiled, but noted in my head that this was going to be the first genuine, fancy Chinese meal I would have in Syracuse.

When the owners disappeared into the kitchen, Yung held my hands across the table and nibbled them again. It was past seven thirty, and no other customers were there. "I was so glad that I controlled myself." He lowered his head. "When I first kissed Anna Marie, our passion took over. She was so quick to take off our clothes that we rushed into lovemaking without proper preparation. I felt guilty afterward."

I lifted my eyebrow slightly and tried to smile. I was surprised by the confession, but also glad. I wondered if he had meant to marry her.

He must have read my mind. "I was not ready for marriage. There wasn't a single Chinese girl that I was attracted to. The one Chinatown girl I met spoke a different language and the Chinatown culture is really quite alien to my upbringing; the few women connected to the graduate school were either married or too old; the one or two college women I met happened to look like dogs. Most American young women I approached were not interested in me. I was considered too strange and different. You can't imagine how many young women rebuffed me." He looked at me to gauge my reaction. I was surprised to hear him say that, but if China were at peace and I had gone to college there, I probably would have rebuffed any foreign man who tried to become intimate too. I nodded. "I was so starved for female friendship," he continued, "that when Anna Marie showed an interest, I dove head-long into it. Anna Marie must have told her parents of my loneliness, because they went all out to embrace me in their folksy ways. I bought them lavish gifts. They were kind and I felt fortunate. But then I realized the enormous cultural gulf between us, and I grew scared. My parents also were alarmed and threatened to send a proper Chinese girl. I felt trapped and did everything to escape." He lifted his head, stealing a guilty look toward me. "Anna Marie always had to assure me she was a liberated woman, and she'd had sexual experiences before. She knew how to take precautions, but I was always careful not to leave anything inside her." He stared into my eyes. "It took me almost a year to break off our relationship."

I blushed furiously, but I was also excited. It was definitely not a Chinese custom to be so open about sex.

"I know you probably have never been with a man. I will teach you, and I want to marry you."

I was totally overcome by new sensations. My heart throbbed, and my tongue was glued to my palate. I remained mute while he continued to kiss my hands, kneading them in his. "My heart is exploding with love for you. I've spent so many sleepless nights longing for you. Will you marry me?"

I stared into his eyes for a long time and finally managed to smile. He smiled back. "I don't have a ring with me. My mother probably has many fancy rings waiting, but we'll go and get a simple one tomorrow."

Every beat of my heart was yelling, "Yes, yes, yes," but I only lowered my head and felt the blood rushing to my face. Finally I murmured: "Perhaps I should ask Mother first."

The food came. The owner pulled a chair near our booth. He assumed we were college students and asked about our families. We politely avoided most of his questions; Yung told him that the food looked great and we would come at least three times a week. I blushed when Yung groped for my hand. The owner understood and left us alone.

"Say yes. Say you will marry me. You said your mother is not herself. We are in America and we can decide for ourselves." Eyeing the closed kitchen door and seeing that the restaurant was empty, Yung slipped into my bench and drew my hand to his chest. "I hereby swear that I will love and cherish you, take care of you and all of your family for the rest of my life!"

I was stunned by this quick resolution of all my worries. A morsel of food must have slipped down my throat, as I started coughing. Yung hugged me, softly thumped my back, and kissed my head. After drinking some tea, I felt better. He kept repeating: "Say yes. Say yes." My heart going pitter-patter, my chest and hands shaking, I nodded. He slammed his mouth on to mine and kissed me with so much passion that I could hardly breathe. I moved away a little.

"Yippee," he whispered. "I wish I could shout like the cowboys. Oh, oh . . ." He kissed me again and again, pressing me into his chest. I felt a liberating surge, and responded by allowing his tongue into my mouth.

Finally, I wiggled loose and pointed to the kitchen and his bench. He slipped back across the table still holding my hand.

Thank goodness we were in a restaurant. We had to control ourselves.

"Ever since I met you, I wrote to my parents everything I learned about you. They said they were happy I had found someone from a book-fragrant family and that you must be a very special girl to be such a filial daughter. I think they're really glad I did not fall for an American girl. I always thought I wouldn't need their approval in my choice of a mate, but I was relieved that they accepted you. I think they had also heard about your father, the famous patriot. In fact, one of our factories supplied your father with cloth for the uniforms he shipped to Chungking after the Japanese occupied Shanghai!"

I was delighted to hear Father had known his family! Now I was more convinced than ever that Father's spirit had sent him. His candid words dispelled my jumble of doubts and legitimized my sweet tingling feelings. He had already talked about me to his parents as his intended wife!

Except for Silver Bell, I had not told anyone in my family about him. I took a tiny bite of shrimp and said: "I wish my parents could meet you." I wasn't sure of my mother's mental abilities. Would she understand my situation? I was certain she would consider Yung a good match. *There are questions I must ask. Since the party in New York, Miss Tyler has hinted I must find out more about his future plans, his dreams, and his intentions. Young men from wealthy families often become dilettantes, with no particular skill to make a living. I am sure Yung will have a job waiting for him in Shanghai if we ever get back, but will he be able to handle it? He speaks English almost without an accent. Will that help his career? He's been in America so long, is he really more American? Would he prefer to stay in America?*

We ate quietly for a while. Eventually I mumbled, "I . . . I'm twenty. How old are you?"

"I am twenty-eight." Yung grabbed my hand and kissed it again, rubbing his lips against it with a strange, delicate gentleness. "I would have been married a long time ago if I had been in China. I knew how old you are; I asked Ms. Tyler. I knew you would be the most precious person in my life when I first noticed you at the dance."

I wanted to say, "I felt the same," but refrained. My hand drifted lower to rub the dimple on his chin and felt the stubble around his mouth. "There are so few single Chinese girls here," I said instead.

"You are very tall for a Chinese girl."

"I am not quite five-five."

"That is tall for a Chinese girl," he repeated. "I'm not quite six feet, but everyone thinks I'm really tall."

I nodded and almost told him that I had observed how women preferred tall man.

"I think my parents fed me milk, cheese, eggs, and bacon every morning. That might have helped," he said. "The Chinese breakfast of soupy rice, pickles, and a few peanuts is not nourishing enough."

"I used to share Miss Tyler's Western breakfast during all those years she tutored me."

"See?" Yung exclaimed. "We even have that in common!"

I blushed.

"At any rate, it was my lucky day when I went to the dance. Your sparkling eyes and your dimpled smile so captivated me that I vowed to get to know you better. It was love at first sight!" Yung leaned forward. "Every time we talked on the phone or I received your letter, I felt the breath of spring touching my soul." His long hands pulled up my face, and he leaned over to rub his nose playfully with mine. "I've been here for so long that my behavior may not be typically Chinese." His forthrightness was certainly more American. "Still, I know what most Chinese families want in a daughter-in-law — bai (white), fu (wealthy), mei (beautiful). I told my parents you've never worked in the fields, so you are very fair and beautiful. Since they knew your father, they know you are no longer wealthy, but that is the fate of most Chinese these days."

I kept sipping more tea to disguise my unease with all the frank discussions of our courtship.

He added simply: "It looks as if the war will be ending soon. I plan to go back to Shanghai. I trust you also want to go and see your mother."

"Yes, I do." I swallowed. "I have been planning to find work. I'll have to help support my family now that Father is dead. I told Miss Tyler that after . . . after all the years of my American education, I would teach at McTyeire," I said unsteadily.

"You can do that if you want. You are a modern, liberated woman. But our factories will have to be reorganized when we return. We'll need to expand our overseas sales." Yung swallowed while helping me smooth down my tousled hair. "With your mathematics degree and your excellent command of Chinese and English, you can find a job anywhere, but you'll be a great asset for me in the Yung industries. Your English will be invaluable. You'll be my partner and a true helpmate."

The logic and elegance of the solution felt so spectacular. I was sure my father's spirit had a hand in this. Everything had happened so fast. I had known Yung for only a few months, but our letters and phone conversations made me feel he was my soul mate already. The fluorescent light seemed to burst red, yellow, and amber around me. I smiled and nodded. "Yes."

After a quick look at the closed kitchen door, Yung slipped back to my bench. He placed his glasses on the table. With our breaths heaving in the tiny space between our mouths, we paused for a long moment of aching suspense. We gazed into each other's eyes; the gray expanse of the restaurant disappeared, and we indulged in one probing kiss after another.

When Yung picked up his glasses to wipe them, I saw his dancing eyes.

"Aren't you proud we chose each other without busybody
matchmakers and our parents' meddling?" he asked.

I made some unintelligible noises about wishing my father
could meet him.

"I want my parents to meet you as soon as possible. They'll be
thrilled!" Yung exclaimed. "My, what a lucky man I'll be, having a
modern, educated wife!" He smiled into my eyes.

"Oh, I hope you are right." I rubbed my forehead on his cheeks.
"Miss Tyler told me I could always teach in the missionary school."

"It'll be a great help to have someone completely trustworthy to
check the books!" Yung squeezed my hands. "My father is getting
old. I hope he has been served well during all these years of war."
He put on his glasses again.

"The cohesion of the family brings success," I mumbled, trying
to calm myself. Marooned in a foreign culture, I had avoided
intimacy and entanglements that preoccupied most normal young
people. I sensed our soul's yearning for ecstasy, and our bodies
were parched deserts waiting to soak up all the love in the other's
heart.

"I think so too." He kissed me again. "If we were Americans, we
would marry right away, but we'll have to wait till we get back to
China and marry with the families present."

We restrained ourselves with great effort. "You are too precious
for me to take you immediately as I want," Yung said. "Thank God
we're in a restaurant."

I shook my head, trying to clear the warm, fuzzy sensation in-
undating me. "I . . . I . . ." I could not verbalize the yearning that
was flooding my senses.

"Yes, we must properly prepare ourselves for your first experience."

I shuddered, but could not make myself ask him what his first experience was like and who his partner had been. How many other women had he courted, seduced, and loved besides Anna Marie? Given his family's wealth and the Chinese tradition of allowing multiple wives, I was not surprised that he was not a virgin. The thought quenched my ardor. I could not ask him the questions that were at the tip of my tongue. *It'll be all right because Father must have sent him,* I told myself. I stood, pulled him up, and pointed him to his bench on the other side of the table.

We ate in a deliberate and unhurried silence. Finally, I asked if I might share our news with Miss Tyler, my mother, Brook ma-ma, and Silver Bell.

"Share with whomever you feel comfortable. Chinese families like to interfere with young people's plans. Some never know how to stay away from their children's lives!" Yung put down his chopsticks. "We are famous for building strong families, but I wonder how the American-educated Chinese will react to their intrusive ways. I mean to be my own boss as soon as I get home."

I wanted to say I still longed for my parents' advice, but I held my tongue.

"May I share the news with my sorority sisters?" I asked.

"Oh, yes!" He answered. "I'll really be part of your community then!"

It took us over two hours to finish the meal. It was completely dark outside, and a crescent moon shone bright over us. Yung wrapped his arm around my shoulder, pulling me close. This would become our mode of walking in the dark.

"Silver Bell will be coming to visit tomorrow," I said. "I hope you'll like her."

"I will, if she is not meddlesome." He stopped and gave me a lingering kiss. It was a slow walk because we were kissing every few steps. He was so much taller that I felt completely sheltered when he nestled me into him. We finally reached my residence. In the reflected light from the windows of the house, we embraced and reluctantly said good night.

Pinnacle of Love

AS SOON AS I introduced Silver Bell, Yung suggested we go to the jewelry store to buy me a ring. Silver Bell stared and didn't say a word. Then she laughed, giggled, and skipped around us. She was acting like a little girl, except she was not singing or chatting quite as nonstop as she used to. She finally grabbed me and whispered in my ear, "He is definitely gao (tall), fu (wealthy), shuai (handsome!). I told you Father sent him!"

I gave her a reproachful look, thinking some people might not find him handsome at all because of his bulbous nose and thick glasses. Maybe that was why no woman had snatched him despite his family wealth. Still, I also believed Father had sent him, because I felt such warmth and comfort when he was around.

We chose a simple golden band because Yung said his mother would want to shower me with her baubles. When I showed my ring to my friends, they exclaimed: "That's a wedding ring! Are you already married?"

I didn't bother answering. I was so happy I didn't care what people thought. In the evening, Miss Tyler was flushed with excitement. She knew my mother's mental state and thought it only right that a modern Chinese woman should decide her own fate. She prepared her signature roast chicken with salad and apologized that she'd be unable to celebrate our engagement properly because the next day she was going on another tour of the country. She brought out some wine, and we were toasted. She wished us good fortune and gave her blessing. Throughout the evening, we talked about Miss Tyler's Chinese experiences. Yung asked her about the topic of her talks and she replied that they were about the history and culture of China because most Americans knew nothing about China except that it was a desperately poor country. She felt the need to give frequent lectures because she was always surprised when people feared China, even though they pitied the Chinese. They thought China was like Japan — an aggressive, cruel nation bent on grabbing riches. She thought it important that people understand that the Chinese culture promoted harmonious living. During the Han Dynasty (206BC-220AD) China went to the NW and subdued several powerful nomadic peoples to establish the Silk Road. Since then, China had not occupied another country or exhibited warlike tendencies. We all agreed this was an important subject.

Yung dropped Silver Bell and me off at my cottage. He shook Silver Bell's hand and said: "Consider me your brother-in-law. Your sister and I are already married in our hearts!" He turned to me quickly, yanked me toward him, and gave me a big hug and kiss. I was so embarrassed that I ran into the cottage.

Once we were alone, Silver Bell couldn't stop talking about Yung. She was giggling and babbling about how happy she was that I'd found this ideal man for our family. She didn't bother to ask how I felt about it. I'd confided in her during my long-distance contacts with Yung, but I felt uneasy about Silver Bell's assumption that I had chosen Yung only because I wanted someone to take care of my family. I couldn't explain my tingling urges to Silver Bell, but under my bedcovers, I played with my breasts and poked and squeezed my legs. My heart and blood raced in a chaotic rhythm while I imagined the physical joys of a union with Yung. Was that love? I felt it must be. Silver Bell asked me how it felt to be in love. I couldn't tell her much. I said only that it felt good.

The following day, after church, with Yung holding my hand, we showed the ring to everyone.

Katie thought we should just get married in Syracuse right away. Yung explained the importance of the family in China, and I blushed and nodded the whole time, pulling my gray silk scarf from my bag and wrapping it around my neck.

Josie drew me aside and whispered, "Both Katie and I have boyfriends. Want to have lunch together in the cafeteria one day?"

I nodded, whispering, "Yes, yes." I realized most students probably couldn't afford to eat out like Yung.

I turned to let more people see my ring and congratulate us. Finally, we went to lunch with Silver Bell in the same Chinese restaurant.

The restaurant was almost empty. After we were seated, Yung asked Silver Bell about her schooling. Silver Bell said, "It was hard at first, but I've adjusted and now enjoy choral singing and American literature the most!"

"So, will you want to stay and go to college here after the war?"

"Oh, no," Silver Bell answered. "I can't wait to see M-ma, Brook ma-ma, and Coral Bell. Besides, kids here will never accept me as one of their own." She lowered her head.

I was surprised that Silver Bell felt this way. I had always assumed she was becoming more and more American since her singing made her many friends and she always sounded cheerful. Sometimes I had chided her for not worrying about Mother. "What do you mean?" I scrunched up my face as if I had just put something sour in my mouth. "I thought you were treasured in the choral society; they often give you solo parts."

"There is always so much competition," my sister whispered. "Some murmured that I had been chosen because of the novelty value — I'm the only Oriental." Her eyes reddened. "In English class last week, the teacher was asking about our reaction to Jo, in *Little Women*. Jo chose to take an independent path of working in the city, which was very unusual at the time. In fact, it is probably unusual even nowadays. Many girls put up their hands and voiced their admiration for Jo. When the teacher asked me about my thoughts, I became tongue-tied, wondering how to express myself in a different way, when the boy sitting next to me eyed me sideways and said, 'She is holding on to her ideas because she is planning a sneak attack and will then bombard us with her brilliant insights.' I felt as if I was hit by a rock. Was that supposed to be a compliment?" She stared at us for confirmation. Yung and I looked at each other. "At any rate, I was sure he thought I was Japanese. Many of my classmates assumed that the Japanese and the Chinese were the same unethical people who would take advantage of America's goodness." She put down her chopsticks, her face flaming with anger.

I reached over and rubbed her back. "You never mentioned these incidents before. People are just ignorant, that's all . . . don't take it personally."

"I know exactly how you feel, Silver Bell," Yung said. "Even before Pearl Harbor, they couldn't tell the Japanese and the Chinese apart, and they ascribed all our successes and failures to our race. Have you felt that, Golden Bell?"

I nodded.

"When I did a good job in my class," Yung said, "even some of my professors mentioned that they were impressed by the Oriental ethic of hard work and persistence — as if my individual aptitude had nothing to do with it." He huffed. "Then when I couldn't understand something, they assumed it was my deficiency in English that was hampering me. I guess I still have a trace of a Shanghainese accent, or maybe I just look different."

"Well, we'll soon be going home, I hope," I said.

"Yes, I can't wait!" My sister smiled. "I'll be graduating this summer."

"Me too," I said. "Still, it'll be hard to face how little remains of the family."

Yung reached over to hold my hand. "We'll all help to build a new China." He put food on Silver Bell's plate and commanded: "Eat! It looks like we're winning the war!"

The next day meant school for Silver Bell and me.

"I imagine you'll be working in the library tomorrow," I said to Yung. "I'll come find you after my morning classes."

"I'll be on the top floor, near a window where I can see you coming." He gave me a quick kiss on the forehead.

I had no trouble finding him. He had seen me coming and had closed his books. As no one was around, he drew me to him and started kissing me passionately. Basking in the warmth of his embrace and cushioned by his hot hands on my back, I clasped my arms tightly around his neck and giggled. "I'm glad this is not happening in your house."

Yung chuckled. I smiled, tucked my head into his chest, and burrowed into it. After rocking back and forth like a swaying column, we agreed to go to lunch.

Josie, Katie, Marcia, a bright-eyed freshman, and I spent many hours in the library preparing our talk to the sorority. Yung joined us. When we talked about the Opium War and how the Western nations raided, looted, and exacted one unequal treaty after another, Yung suggested we ask the librarians to provide pictures of life in the foreign concessions as well pictures of the country's war devastation.

Remembering the gruesome images of Chinese desperate poverty, versus the Western extravagances in the concessions, I began to dread the presentation. The research stirred my dormant feelings of loss and desolation. I refused to be a presenter. When the day came, Josie and Katie invited Yung and their young men — John and Sherman — to join us. Many Asian studies students also came and we had a full house. Marcia was eager to be the speaker. She gave an extensive talk about the Opium War and the treaties that ceded Chinese port cities to foreigners who extracted huge indemnities. Her voice rose when she mentioned the Paris Peace Conference, which arbitrarily awarded the German Concessions in Manchuria to Japan. She emphasized how China had been an ally through both world wars and was now suffering from further Japanese depredation.

Then she started talking about the Nanking Massacre. "In November 1937, after three months of fierce fighting, Shanghai fell to the Japanese. When the Japanese armies marched toward Nanking, reports of their savagery preceded them. They had raped and plundered all the towns and villages in their path. Many people took refuge in the ancient landmarks in Suzhou, which Marco Polo had called the Venice of China. They assumed that since the finest Japanese culture had come from the Chinese, the Japanese would protect these traditional treasures. But the Japanese destroyed the landmarks. Thousands of women were enslaved to 'service' the Japanese military." Tears rolled down Marcia's face and her voice shook.

"At first, people in Nanking thought their capital would be safe because General Tang Sheng-chih had vowed he would defend it to the death. There were almost 300,000 Nationalist troops left to fight only 50,000 Japanese soldiers, and a large swath of the countryside around Nanking had been burned and rendered useless to deter the Japanese advance. What most people did not understand was that the Chinese soldiers were untrained conscripts and spoke different dialects. Plus, the entire national air force had fled with the generalissimo.

"Days later, the Japanese bombarded the streets with propaganda leaflets about their benevolent intentions: All soldiers should abandon their arms; everyone would be given food, medicine, and work. Later, Emperor Hirohito chose his uncle, Prince Asaka Yasuhiko, as the commander-in-chief of the army around Nanking. However, the Japanese had neither the means nor the intention of feeding prisoners of war, and so the prince gave the order to kill all captives.

"The Japanese entered on December 13, 1937. Nanking fell in four days, and the Chinese soldiers, some of them twelve- and thirteen-year-old boys, tore off their uniforms and surrendered in droves. They were separated into groups of hundreds. The Japanese ruthlessly gunned them down; beheaded them; buried them alive; burned, mutilated, or strangled them; fed them alive to dogs; drove them into the frozen rivers and ponds; and even used them in target practice and staged killing competitions promoted as sporting events." With one hand stabbing the air, Marcia shouted out each gruesome killing method so forcefully, she started to cough. Katie brought her water.

"Then the Japanese soldiers went from street to street, looting the stores, burning what they could not use, and killing everyone in sight. The streets and rivers ran red with blood.

"The women suffered terribly. They were either herded into sex slavery or, if they were young and pretty, given to the officers. Many soldiers believed that raping virgins would make them invincible in battle and that wearing amulets made from the pubic hair of their victims would endow them with magical powers. After raping and torturing them, they killed their victims to erase all traces of their crime."

Pictures were passed around. There were many teary eyes in the audience and widespread expressions of outrage. One young man asked Yung and me why we were not organizing other young people to resist the Japanese. I was shame-faced and couldn't answer. Yung told them that the Chinese youth had always been in the forefront of protests and that my father had been involved in the May 4 movement after World War I, which later led to the formation of the nationalist party. But the Japanese had invaded our territories for many years and our people had never had the modern weapons or training to resist them. Yung held my hand throughout the talk. I was grateful for his presence. Without his support, I might have broken down into hysterical sobs. As it was, I had sucked in so much air, gulping down my emotions, that I was hiccupping by the end. Katie brought me water.

I thanked Marcia for her presentation and soon after, Josie, Katie, John, and Sherman joined us for lunch in the cafeteria. The two men were engineering students sent by the Department of Defense to prepare for the war effort. They both mentioned their total ignorance of China's history even though they knew they were at war with Japan. We all fervently hoped for peace. Sherman and Katie held hands throughout the meal and didn't say much.

John spoke with a heavy accent, and I had trouble understanding him at first. "I'm from South Carolina," he said.

"My family is in the textile business in Shanghai," Yung told everyone. "I've heard that South Carolina has many cotton mills and textile factories."

"What a coincidence!" John exclaimed. "My family owns cotton mills and textile factories too! In fact, there is a saying in South Carolina that we're very much like the Chinese — we eat rice and worship our ancestors!"

Everyone smiled broadly, and John and Yung went into deep discussions about cotton, new milling machines, and the need for chemical engineers to help with future products. John took down Yung's contact information in China, and Yung asked if he could visit John's family factories in South Carolina.

Josie and I smiled at Katie and Sherman's total immersion in each other and were thrilled that John and Yung had connected.

My final exams were approaching; I joined Yung in the library whenever I could. We usually sat across the table from each other so as not fall into each other's arms every other minute. I did not understand a thing about his thesis on textile engineering, but he helped me with my quadratic equations and algorithms. I moved to his side of the table, and as we pored over the figures, huddling close, he exclaimed: "I can't wait to be home and go through our company books with you. Why did you choose to major in mathematics?"

I explained the cultural neutrality of math and confessed my preference for history and literature. "Somehow, most women gravitate toward that," I added. "There was too much competition in my survey classes. Besides, I've never taken American history and literature, so I felt awkward. Now they've become my extra-curricular readings!"

"So you like to read?"

"Yes. I read a lot of American history and literature so I can understand my friends."

"Good for you!" Yung winked at me.

"I want to know what made Americans who they are."

"America grew strong because hardworking immigrants brought innovative ideas. Still, many Westerners are uncomfortable to know there is that strange, huge country in the East," Yung said. "Before Pearl Harbor, they consistently supported Japan, giving them Chinese territories and encouraging their territorial ambitions. I hope they've learned their lesson."

Yung looked at me with great intensity and continued, "Perhaps after America defeats Japan, you and I will help return the country to our Confucian roots. We have enjoyed centuries of peace and

81

stability by teaching the supremacy of education, proper behavior, and living in harmony," he said wistfully.

"That would have been my father's dream." I nodded. "Both my parents were devoted to the central Chinese tenet of propagating art, music, literature, and correct behavior."

"My family admired clever business maneuvers, but their most aggressive instincts were to push for the success of our family." He sighed.

Our smiling eyes locked, and we entwined arms under the table.

More than ever, I was convinced that I loved Yung, not only for the protection he gave me, but also for his mind, his sensitivity, and his heart.

Every evening, when the weather permitted, we took walks. When darkness fell, he walked me to my dorm. Kissing him repeatedly and unwilling to part, I would then walk with him to his house. Back and forth we went until we forced ourselves to say good night.

Yung stayed for almost six weeks. On the last day of his stay, he persuaded me to help him pack. As soon as I entered his room, he took off his glasses. He hugged me close, patting me like a child, and said, "My parents want me home as soon as my orals are over. Since they haven't seen me during the war, I understand their concerns. He held me at arm's length and scrutinized my face. I'll probably find some way to fly home as soon as I'm able — after a visit to John's family's cotton mills. I probably won't see you until you're in Shanghai. I'll be waiting on the dock when your ship arrives."

We had talked about all that before, and now the panic of losing him overwhelmed me. We fell into each other's arms and kissed passionately, murmuring how much we would miss each other. Before we knew it we were rolling in his bed, trying to get close.

For the first time since I'd met him, he sought my breasts. I did not resist. To me, he felt like a safe harbor where I could lie in the sun. He unbuttoned my blouse, and as he pushed away my bra, I froze. His mouth sought every crevice of my torso. When he sucked on my nipples, I played with his hair, feeling a warm, tingling dampness in my groin. I didn't want him to stop. I put my hand inside his shirt and rubbed his back. Suddenly, I understood how Anna Marie must have felt. With an effort, I eased myself from under him. I sat up but still allowed him to kiss my breasts. We lingered for a long time until I finally extricated myself, pulled on my bra, and buttoned my blouse. Yung lay down on my lap, nibbled on my stomach, and apologized. "I almost lost it!"

I nodded. We giggled.

"You know, Americans call it necking?" he whispered.

"It's really more than just the neck, isn't it?" I gave him a naughty grin, pushing his head away to stand up.

"Oh, but I almost forgot we're already married!" He shouted and grabbed me for another passionate kiss. "I am so starved for intimacy. I was still an undergrad when I had the affair with Anna Marie." We leaned back into the bed again.

Since puberty, I had hidden my passions inside an igloo. Sometimes I had intense feelings, but until now there had been nothing safe for me to hang on to. These last few weeks had been the happiest of my life. I felt my insides melting. His hands stole under my blouse, and this time he touched me ever so tenderly and helped me out of my blouse and bra. He rubbed his face against my chest as if inhaling my every cell. Strange warmth crept up from my abdomen to my head. I could feel my nipples stiffen and wanted to squeeze my legs. My usual inhibitions seemed to have departed. When his hand went inside my pants, I could not move. My heart was racing and I was embarrassed, but I did nothing. I felt breathless with desire. He poked me inside so gently, I felt I would burst with delight. Waves of a new excitement and tingling sensations flooded me. I groaned with pleasure and wanted to shout and cry. I dug my fingers into his back to steady myself.

When Yung slipped off to remove his pants, I stiffened. I had never seen a grown man's penis before, and his pulsating rod frightened me. He bent down, gently encouraged me to hold his member in my hand, and fell on top of me sucking gently on one breast. In a loud huff, he collapsed on my chest, wetting me all over. I withdrew my hand immediately. Still panting, he whispered, "don't worry. You won't get pregnant. You really haven't done it yet!"

I disentangled myself from him and ran into the bathroom. I took off my pants and tried to clean myself. A ball of fire seemed to have engulfed my heart, racing all over my body. I pressed a cool towel to my chest and repeatedly rinsed my legs with a damp cloth. Soon Yung was knocking on the door, shouting: "My fluids are not dirty! You're just not used to it!"

Is this what he meant by preparing me for my first time? I had never questioned him or consulted anyone because it was not a ladylike thing to talk about. My head was still reeling with the sensations he had stirred up, and every pore of my body longed for his touch. I let him into the bathroom.

He was still naked. As soon as he saw me, he hugged me, swaying gently, and helped me out of my clothes, saying, "You're used to handling menstrual blood. Mine is just less colorful!"

We kissed. Like two birds preening each other's feathers, we touched and rubbed our noses on each other's torso. "You may find it easier in the water," he mumbled. He ran the bath, and we both got in. We soaped each other, gliding our hands gently over all corners. I no longer feared his stiff rod. While kissing me, he guided himself into me, murmuring, "I want to be one with you . . . I want to be one with you. You're the only woman I'll ever want!"

I hugged him tighter. I felt anchored.

"Yes, you are ready, you are ready!" he shouted. He thrust deeper. Streaks of blood wiggled in the bathwater — proof of my virginity. "Did I hurt you? Did I hurt you?" he asked softly, soothing me.

I whispered no. My body was exploding with an excitement I had never experienced. All my mother's lectures on chastity and propriety flew from my mind. We both moaned our satisfaction and pledged our love anew.

We carefully toweled each other dry, seeking out every nook and cranny, and he kissed each one with such tenderness that we were aroused again. We ran to his bed. This time, his fingers gently traced every inch of my body, interrupted by slow kissing until I found myself cooing and bursting with desire. He came into me again and took his time moving inside so we would climax together. Exhausted after a whole afternoon of lovemaking, we dozed off. When we awoke, he brought me water. He guided my hand to explore his body the way he had done with mine. My finger traced the ridge of his nose, around his eyes, across his forehead, down his cheek, outlining his mouth and lingering in the cleft of his chin. I wanted to remember every inch of his face so I would have my finger memories to dwell on when he left.

We were famished. We raided the refrigerator and made a meal of everything we could find. We fell asleep. Waking up in the middle of the night, we made love again, until my vagina felt sore. Finally, after a shower, I said, "We'd better clean up the place, and I'll help you pack."

I put on one of his old shirts and shorts, and covered myself as best I could with one of his sweatshirts. He teased me about how I looked, and I was so exhilarated by the taste of my new freedom that I didn't even blush.

Yung dumped everything from his drawers into his suitcase while trying to peck me on my face. Afraid that he might want to make love again, I held up each of his shirts and trousers between us, then folded and rearranged them in the suitcase.

"What if you got pregnant?" Yung whispered.

"You'll have to marry me!" I eyed him naughtily.

"Oh, I consider myself already a happily married man!" He fell on his knee and kissed the ring.

"I can't wait to find out how it feels to carry your child!" I said.

"Our child!" Yung exclaimed, hugging and kissing me.

I ran out of the room and told him to change into his travel suit.

While I was cleaning up the kitchen and washing our dishes, Yung came in wearing his dark pants and white shirt." He led me to a chair and showed me two notepads and pens. "The minister who wanted to baptize me always reminded me to be grateful for all the good people and things that I've been blessed with. He also told me to never give up hope and wish for peace. Forgive me for being the engineer," he said. "I make lists and draw diagrams for projects."

"What do you plan to do?"

"Our future together is the biggest project in my life. Let's each make two lists. One is a Gratitude List. The other, a Wish List of what you want and what is important to you. We don't have to show anyone our lists."

I stared at him for a long time, tapping my pen on the pad. "Good idea!" I said finally. "This will be my project for the rest of the day.

Dawn was breaking. I peeked outside his house but saw no one. I ran to my dorm and stole into my room.

As soon as I changed into my clothes, I wondered if I should put Yung on my Gratitude List. Thoughts of my sexual awakening and our joy filled all the space in my head. I couldn't write anything. Several days after his departure, I calmed down and realized I could not change history or events, but he had released me from my emotional prison, from my fears and depression over my father's death. I put him on my Gratitude List, together with my parents, Miss Tyler, Brook ma-ma, my sister, and the many blessings I had taken for granted — my good health, relative financial security, finishing college in America, and so on. The list covered a whole page.

The Wish List included all the people on my Gratitude List. I wished them to remain in my life and prayed that God would grant joy to each. On top of it all, I added: "Immense gratitude and wish to have Yung in my life forever."

The New Girl

Shanghai, 1946

"MAY I SMOKE in here?" With a deft twirl, Silver Bell flipped a cigarette between three fingers.

"Don't see why not," Le-An answered from her desk across the room as she typed a letter. "Mr. Ching smokes in his office all the time." She tilted her chin toward the boss's room.

Silver Bell rested her feet on an open drawer and leaned back in her chair. The white patent leather bows on her new high-heeled shoes glistened. She lit her cigarette. The sparks from the match reminded her of the times she had stolen out at night with Golden Bell to watch the fireflies on the lotus pond in their Hangzhou mansion. They rose from the bushes, glowing and flickering, as if they were spies sending messages to their parents, reporting on what they were doing. Silver Bell shook her head to clear the memories.

She inhaled deeply and blew out jets of smoke, aiming them at the low ceiling fan. As the smoke rose in a steady plume, she felt a sense of accomplishment in sustaining it for a while. She smiled as she watched it disperse — the slow, rotating fan whipping it into thin air.

"You act like a carefree young man," Le-An said with a reproachful frown.

"It must be all that time I spent in the United States; women have more rights there than in China."

Le-An's eyes widened, and she stopped typing. "So you were in America?"

"Yes." Silver Bell smiled. "I was a high school student in New York."

"You're lucky to have learned the language when you were young. No wonder you can rewrite Mr. Ching's letter." Le-An said the word "lucky" in English.

Silver Bell wondered how many other English words Le-An knew and whether she understood what she was typing. In New York, she had dreamed she might work in the Empire State Building someday. Now she was in Shanghai, China's own New York City. But instead of working in one of the riverside colonial towers in the fashionable Bund area, she was stuck in the office of a textile factory compound. The walls and doors were made of plywood, and most drawers jammed. The only touch of luxury was in Mr. Ching's office, where a carved rosewood desk and other Chinese furniture reminded her of her father's study in Hangzhou.

"Here, I've finished typing it. Do you want to take another look?" Le-An stood, straightened the creases on her silk cheongsam, and put the English letter on Silver Bell's desk.

Silver Bell picked up the letter. It felt important to have her work going out into the business world.

"Did you buy your clothes in New York?" asked Le-An.

Silver Bell nodded. She was wearing her favorite beige linen suit, a hand-me-down from her sister. Not wanting to explain how the war had depleted her family's fortune, she crushed her cigarette and started proofreading.

Although Silver Bell was only seventeen, she had been given the job because Golden Bell would soon marry Yung, heir to the East

UNDER THE RED MOON

Pacific Textile factories. The families had agreed to keep her status a secret for as long as possible, so she could be Yung's "eyes and ears" in the office. Her assignment was to translate the English correspondence and proofread her boss's English letters. She was pleased that her ability to answer the phone in both Chinese and English was a marketable skill.

"When did you come back to Shanghai?"

"My sister and I came back late this summer. My sister finished college with a mathematics degree, but I did not learn anything practical, like typing, in high school."

"Oh, you're so lucky! I wish I could visit New York. You know, the Statue of Liberty!" Le-An raised an arm, holding an imaginary torch aloft.

Silver Bell did not know how to describe her life in Liverpool and Syracuse. In New York, she seldom wore makeup or high-heeled shoes. Le-An might have seen pictures of the city, but would she even know there was a New York State outside the city?

"I'll never go anywhere." Le-An lowered her head. "My husband was killed in thirty-nine when the Japanese came."

"I'm sorry." Silver Bell felt like running over to hug Le-An, but she dared not. Experience taught her that most Chinese did not understand the American way of showing emotional solidarity. They might interpret the gesture as a lack of self-restraint. She lit another cigarette and puffed away, creating a smokescreen.

"You're so lucky."

Silver Bell grimaced. Le-An's repeated use of the word "lucky" was getting on her nerves.

Le-An retrieved the letter from Silver Bell and placed it on Mr. Ching's desk, ready for his signature.

Silver Bell propped up her legs again and lit another cigarette. She had been working only for a few days. She met her boss when Yung brought her into his office the prior week; Yung had

91

told Mr. Ching that Silver Bell was young but spoke English. She could help with their increasing volume of foreign business dealings.

"Good morning, girls!" Mr. Ching marched in, wearing a navy pinstriped suit.

Silver Bell put her feet on the floor and kicked the drawer shut. The loud bang jerked her ramrod straight in her chair. Le-An was hardly a "girl" anymore, she thought.

Mr. Ching glowered at her. "When you're done smoking, bring me some tea."

Silver Bell asked Le-An's help to find the tea and china service. Le-An handed her a thermos and pointed toward the kitchen downstairs.

Rough-looking office cleaners had congregated in the hot, greasy kitchen to rest and gossip. Everyone stopped talking when Silver Bell appeared at the door. A few stood and bowed. Without a word, she stuck out her thermos. A young woman quickly grabbed it, bowing again. "Young mistress, I'll fill it for you," she said.

In Hangzhou, her personal maid, Peony, always fetched her tea. Peony, only five years older, was more like a sister or a playmate. All the other servants seemed like extended family members. A dull ache rose in her chest as she recalled how Peony anticipated her every need, made excuses for her when she misbehaved, and instructed her on the politics of handling the many other servants and relatives. Peony was never deferential.

Silver Bell knocked on Mr. Ching's door and brought in the tea tray.

"Ah, new girl." Mr. Ching looked up from his desk, fingering his mustache. The mustache made him look Japanese, she thought. Without thinking, she bowed like the kitchen servants.

Mr. Ching had taken off his jacket. "Put the tea over there and sit." He pointed to the coffee table and the sofa.

Silver Bell obeyed. She crossed her legs and smoothed down her Western-style skirt.

"I see you have entirely rewritten my letter." He came over to the sofa and sat uncomfortably close to her.

Silver Bell wriggled away a little. Her father was formal and had never sat so close.

"I've rephrased your thoughts to sound more the way English-speaking people might express themselves," she muttered.

"Your family is from Hangzhou, is it not? I heard your home burned, and you had to move from Hangzhou to Shanghai to Hong Kong and back to Shanghai during the war. You must have gone through some hard times." He turned to stare into her eyes.

For a moment, she gaped in silence. She had not expected her family affairs to be discussed. Since their return, Golden Bell had admonished her repeatedly not to be a fool for memories, to face life going forward and not to look back. Still, tears brimmed in her eyes.

She remembered going boating on the West Lake with her mother and Brook ma-ma, then called Orchid. Her own favorite game was playing hide-and-seek with Peony in their walled-in garden. There were so many places to hide. The garden paths were interspersed with lily ponds, marble bridges, Taihu rocks, cherry trees, azalea bushes, and moon-viewing pavilions.

Her stomach turned sour. She coughed to clear away the memories.

"I'm sorry to learn that your father also perished." Mr. Ching sounded sympathetic.

"My father died during the bombing of Chungking." She cleared her throat. She almost blurted out: *my mother now calls me Golden Bell, my sister's name.* How could she have come so close to telling Mr. Ching that since the war, her mother's mind was fixated

93

on the past, and that she was no longer in touch with reality? Was she not like her mother, also haunted by memories?

"So your father left the family and went to Chungking?" he asked with an ironic grin.

"He refused to collaborate with the Japanese." Silver Bell almost choked on her words. "We were refugees in Hong Kong when the Japanese invaded."

She fished out her handkerchief to cover her cough and wipe her eyes. She didn't want to continue this conversation.

With a valiant effort, she took a deep breath and said, "Have some tea, Mr. Ching." She stood, motioned to the tea service, and walked away.

"Pour me a cup and sit. I'd like to know you better." He pointed to the space beside him.

Silver Bell poured the tea, held out the cup to him, and re-mained standing.

Mr. Ching ignored the cup and gently but firmly grasped Silver Bell's wrist. "The ravages of war ruined so many lives. Want to tell me how you escaped it and learned such good English?"

His viselike grip shocked her. With her free hand, Silver Bell set the hot cup on the table and twisted free.

"Have a cigarette." He took out his golden case.

Silver Bell hesitated. Her heart was thumping against her chest, but she decided to take one. She needed a smoke to steady her nerves.

Mr. Ching popped a cigarette into his mouth and waited for her to light it. He signaled to her with a tilt of his head.

With her own unlit cigarette dangling from her lips, she struck a match and held it out to her boss. Her hands shook. Mr. Ching inhaled deeply. In one breath, he exhaled a stream of smoke and extinguished the match. Leaving the cigarette in his mouth, he grabbed Silver Bell's arm and yanked her onto his lap.

"Ah, h . . . help . . ." she gasped in surprise.

"Now, is this what you had to do to service the foreigners and learn their language?" With one hand he fondled her breast and with the other reached under her skirt.

Kicking, writhing, and fighting off his hands, Silver Bell screamed, "Help . . . help! Don't! Don't!"

"Lie down, Silver Bell, lie down!"

"I'm going to tell . . . tell Yung . . . he's going to be my brother-in-law!"

Mr. Ching froze and then released her. "What? He never told me!"

Silver Bell stumbled to her feet and made a dash for the door.

Mr. Ching jumped up to bar the way. He straightened his tie and opened his palms toward her. "No harm done, my pet! Just a bit of fun."

"Please . . . please let me go!" Crying and hugging herself to still her trembling, she again made for the door.

Mr. Ching blocked the way again. "Here," he sneered, giving her his lit cigarette.

Silver Bell took it in spite of herself. She turned and sucked on it heavily. It was no use. Her knees felt weak, and she had to sit down.

"Where did you learn to smoke?" he asked with a smirk. "No young girl in Shanghai smokes like that!" He put on his jacket and was instantly transformed into a boss again.

"Like what?"

"Like a whore!" He leaped to guard the door.

"I went . . . to school . . . in New York. Lots of women smoke there." The cigarette was having an effect; her trembling subsided. "I never had to do anything bad!"

"Yung told me you came from Hangzhou and grew up in the countryside, didn't you?" Mr. Ching made it sound like an accusation. "How did you get to America?"

"In Hangzhou I had a tutor, an American missionary, who got Japanese permission to leave China; she took me to my sister in the States."

"And your sister was already there?"

"Yes, she went first."

"How did Mr. Yung meet your sister?"

"They met at a Sino-Amity dance in New York City." Silver Bell sobbed as she choked on the smoke. She charged toward the door again.

He grabbed her arm. "So you went to dances?"

Silver Bell threw her cigarette at Mr. Ching and pulled away. She steeled her voice. "Miss Tyler, my teacher, said I was too young to go to the city . . . Get out of my way!" She made another dash for the door.

Mr. Ching stomped on the cigarette and ran after her. "Look, I'm really sorry." He reached for Silver Bell's arm, but she slapped him away.

She still quivered, but her anger had kindled her senses.

His eyes shifted. He saw her as dangerous.

He knelt down before her, crying. "Please don't tell Yung! I . . . I did everything, everything —entertaining, collaborating with the Japanese throughout the war—all for the Yung factories!" He tried to hold on to Silver Bell's wrist. She tore away. "My English is so poor. All the Japanese I learned is useless now!"

Silver Bell stepped away from him.

He stood up to collect himself and paced in front of the door. "The young Mr. Yung has been gallivanting around town with that Ting fellow, who just returned from America. That's where everyone is buying the new spinning machines. They talk of new manufacturing techniques I've never heard of."

He raked his hair and loosened his tie, mopping his face with a handkerchief. "They talk in English and have such laughs . . . I don't understand a word they're saying!"

Silver Bell shuddered.

"That new manager told me to have a go at you. He said you would be easy game. I swear, he put me up to it!"

"I don't know what you're talking about!"

Mr. Ching opened his arms and pounded his chest. "Please, please forgive me! In the old days, young girls who are so free . . ." He blushed, lowered his head, and peered at Silver Bell. "Who smoke like you . . ."

Silver Bell shoved him aside, threw open the door, and ran straight to her desk. She snatched her purse.

Le-An stood beside her. "It's not easy for a woman to find a good job," she said. She pursed her lips and was on the verge of tears.

Silver Bell stared for a moment and grabbed a cigarette from her purse. Flipping the unlit cigarette between three fingers, she charged out of the office, shouting, "bastard! Like hell I'm not going to tell!"

A Fraud?

Shanghai, 1946

WHEN GOLDEN BELL told her mother she would marry
Yung, the owner and chairman of the East Pacific Textile
Company, Purple Jade smiled and congratulated her. "Your mother
must be pleased you made such a good match."

"But you are my mother!" Golden Bell cried. "Don't you recognize me? I'm Golden Bell. You always said I stole your face and
these dimples."

Purple Jade looked devastated. She knew something was wrong,
yet was unable to say what it was. The woman in front of her with
wavy hair and a dress of a strange Western cut did not look like her
daughter. She searched each face until she settled on Brook ma-ma.
"Orchid, you know I never arranged any marriage for Golden Bell."

Brook ma-ma nudged Golden Bell out of the room. As usual, she
would soothe her mistress and clarify everything as best she could.

Twisting a handkerchief in her hand, Purple Jade mumbled,
"There will be a marriage, a marriage . . ."

Brook ma-ma smiled. "Great joy and good fortune await our
family."

Purple Jade did not seem to hear her. "Is Golden Bell marrying
a total stranger?"

"No." Brook ma-ma hesitated. "We've heard of the family, but we do not know them."

No, that woman could not possibly be my daughter. Purple Jade twisted her handkerchief tighter. "Where is the matchmaker? I must ask her to check on the lineage of the young man."

"Times have changed, Tai-tai. Golden Bell chose her own husband; there was no matchmaker."

"Then how are we to know if there are any idiots in his family? Hidden illnesses? Debts? And are they book-fragrant?"

Brook ma-ma had no answers.

"This woman is not my daughter!"

Brook ma-ma grimaced. It was not her habit to contradict her mistress. She had gotten used to deflecting Purple Jade's strange utterances by remaining silent.

"What is the name of the young man?"

"Yung Hien-Kung," Brook ma-ma replied. "We all call him by his family name, Yung, because when Golden Bell first met him in America, the foreigners found it difficult to call him Hien-Kung."

"She must call him Hien-Kung ko!" Purple Jade paused. "Golden Bell has been properly schooled. It is impolite not to address this man Hien-Kung as older brother. I'm sure this woman is not Golden Bell."

Brook ma-ma looked away.

"What sort of bride-price is offered? Who is providing the dowry?" Purple Jade asked urgently, her eyes bulging.

"The bride-price will be a new apartment for our family in the International Concession," Brook ma-ma answered. "And we will write a check of ten thousand American dollars as the dowry. However, since we don't have that kind of money anymore, it is agreed that her husband will tear up the check the following day so the Huangs can save face."

"A fraud? No, this woman cannot be my daughter."

Purple Jade paused for reflection. Gravely, she put forth more questions. "Did the matchmaker consult a medium? Or did they consult the I Ching? Did anyone compare the couple's birth signs?"

"Yes, the Yung family did all the checking."

"Who chose the wedding date? Tell Golden Bell it is important that all proper arrangements be made in order to bring the young couple many sons, prosperity, and good fortune."

"All the appropriate arrangements have been made. The Yung family is extremely wealthy. They certainly do not need our money, so you must not worry about Golden Bell's marriage."

Still fussing with her handkerchief, Purple Jade asked, "Who will plan the fireworks? The red beaded wedding gown, the mile-long procession of embroidered silk quilts, furniture, bridal bed, fancy silk gowns, and the chamber pots filled with red eggs to ensure many sons?"

"None of that will be necessary. Golden Bell and her future husband have chosen a Western-style wedding in a Christian church. A traditional Chinese banquet will follow, and a dance in the Yung mansion after that."

Purple Jade shook her head. "No, the real Golden Bell would not do that."

Brook ma-ma finally gave up trying to explain.

Days later, Purple Jade looked for the gray silk scarf with the yellow iris she had embroidered especially for Golden Bell so many years ago in Hangzhou. Brook ma-ma reminded her that Golden was taking good care of it. "Please tell Golden Bell," she said, "never to forget who she is!"

Golden Bell's wedding in the fall of 1946 was Shanghai's social event of the year. The bride wore a silk and lace white gown with an eight-foot train. Her young half sister, Coral Bell, was the flower girl, and Silver Bell served as one of three bridesmaids, dressed in flesh-toned pink. Purple Jade appeared briefly to sign the marriage certificate but became so disoriented by the Christian ceremony that she recited another Tu Fu poem, "The Lone Goose":

> *"Refusing to peck and drink, the lone goose flies,*
> *Recalling his flock, he cries.*
> *Who pities this sliver of shadow*
> *Searching in a layered cloud meadow?*
> *He sees them in his remembered formation.*
> *He hears them in his ululation.*
> *The callous crows keep squawking and cawing,*
> *Happy in their strident clamor and brawling."*

Brook ma-ma took her home immediately.

During the reception dance in the Yung mansion, Silver Bell noticed a tall, trim young man with an athletic physique. A nimbus of dark hair adorned his tanned face. She could not take her eyes off his smiling face: his piercing eyes, broad jaw line, and straight long nose. A group of young women already crowded around him, giggling and trying to flirt with him. He broke free and approached her. Introducing himself as Donald Ting, he shook her hand and said, "Congratulations! The weather is perfect! All the flowers make this mansion more magnificent than ever!"

Silver Bell wanted to disclaim any responsibility for the preparations but could not find her voice. His deep baritone and his handsome bearing created such an aura of self-confidence, Silver Bell felt as if he had just sucked all the oxygen from around her. She thought his name sounded familiar but couldn't remember where she had heard it or in what context.

They danced almost exclusively with one another that night. Donald's arms led with a gentle assurance, and they glided over the floor with such grace that during the Blue Danube Waltz people formed a circle around them to watch.

"So Golden Bell is your sister?"

"Yes." Silver Bell nodded, breathless with excitement and the dancing. She could feel his warm hand against her rigid spine.

"You look like a fresh budding flower. How old are you?"

"I'm seventeen."

"Ah, you are still very young. You float like a swan in my arms. Where did you learn to dance like this?"

It would have been the polite thing to say that it was easy to dance well when led so masterfully. Instead, with a racing heart, she stammered, "Our high school used to hold dances every three months."

"You must have been in the United States with your sister. No high school in Shanghai would have held a dance during the Japanese occupation." His booming baritone had modulated into flawless English. "I'm already twenty-five and only just finished my second engineering degree."

Silver Bell nodded. Though she had danced with American boys in America, she had never dated anyone. Whenever the girls whispered and giggled about their boyfriends, she felt left out. In the beginning, while she was still trying to fit in the new high school, the foreign boys had seemed even more intimidating than the girls. In their letters, her parents reminded her that she represented her family, her country, her race, and that she must not allow herself to become entangled in "boy-hunting."

"I just finished high school near Syracuse where my sister was in college. In a small town called Liverpool."

"So are you still in touch with your classmates?"

"No," Silver Bell answered. "Many girls went on to college, and some started to fill the veterans' still-vacant jobs. We really don't have anything in common anymore." She blushed, feeling overwhelmed by this handsome young man paying her so much attention. She had found it hard to describe her overseas experiences to those who had remained in Shanghai during the war. Now this modern man could speak her new, fashionable tongue. Wanting to sound worldly, she thought of asking him where he had learned English, but a tingling sensation muddled her head. Paralyzing warmth made its way up to her throat. Her face turned peachy-red and her eyes sparkled.

"Are you warm?" Donald smiled. He led her away from the dance floor. Placing her hand on his arm, he took her to the open bar. "You look lovely when you blush; your mouth looks like a ripe strawberry." He lowered his head and stared straight into her eyes.

Silver Bell's heart pounded so hard she forgot to say thank you when she accepted the champagne.

"Here's to our glorious return to our homeland!" Donald clinked his glass against hers.

Silver Bell wanted to ask "Did you study overseas also?" but her throat constricted. The moisture in the air seemed to have evaporated. She took long breaths to still her fluttering nerves.

Donald drained his glass. He lit a cigarette but did not offer her one. He blew his smoke sideways, so as not to cloud his view of the blushing girl. "You're lucky to have come from such a well-connected family. I'm an orphan. I studied in Japan and America, all on scholarships." His voice was both sad and intense, but his manner was so unassuming, he did not seem to be bragging.

She finally found her voice. "Where were you in America?"

"The Washington, D.C., area."

"So that's where you learned your English."

"Yes. Unfortunately, my story is only too common these days. During the war, our only chance for a future was to accept missionary charity. They offered us an education, and we tried our luck in the Diaspora, like the Jews."

They were now conversing exclusively in English. Silver Bell felt she had finally met a kindred spirit.

"I'm almost an orphan myself," she whispered. "My father died during the bombing of Chungking, and my mother is no longer herself." She sipped her champagne to choke back the lump rising in her throat. "My sister and I also were helped by a missionary—our tutor, Miss Tyler. She came from Syracuse, New York, and told us that she was one of the early coeds."

"So how did Miss Tyler help you get there?"

"Oh, I don't know how to begin." Silver Bell eyed his cigarette.

"Begin from the beginning. We have all night, don't we?" He took away her champagne glass, draped his arm around her shoulder, and led her out to the patio. A wide expanse of lawn planted with flowerbeds spread out in front of them. Everything sparkled with the early dew under a full moon.

Silver Bell drew a deep breath. "Most Chinese think it unseemly for a woman to smoke, but I need a cigarette."

"Oh, I'm sorry." He quickly put the cigarette in his mouth and extricated his cigarette case, bowing and offering her one. He struck a match and smiled. "I think it is chic for a woman to smoke."

Silver Bell felt her heart burst into flame. She inhaled deeply to still her trembling hand.

"I want to know everything about you. Tell me how you went from Hangzhou to America," Donald said.

Walking arm in arm and puffing with Donald in a warm, cozy haze, she began: "My father was a member of the legislative council in Hangzhou. He had always been a patriot, and when the Japanese were advancing, we moved to Shanghai, thinking it would be safer for us in the French Concession." She shivered.

"Are you cold?" Donald snuffed out his cigarette. He took off his jacket and draped it over her shoulders. Keeping his arm around her, he hugged her close and led her onto the garden path.

Silver Bell snuggled against the bulk of his shoulders and chattered rapidly. "My mother found it difficult to be away from home. She went back and was caught in the invasion. She hid behind a cupboard in our Hangzhou mansion while the front courtyards burned." Silver Bell sucked deeply on her cigarette to calm herself. "She was never quite the same after that. Don't be surprised when you hear her call me Golden Bell."

"She thinks you are Golden Bell?"

"Yes. My sister was around my age when she left for America."

He took the cigarette stub from her hand, dropped it on the path, and stepped on it. He held on to her hand, his fingers gently massaging her own. "I did notice she couldn't use the fountain pen to sign her name on the wedding certificate. When they gave her the ink stone and brush, her hand shook. I thought she looked distracted."

"Yes, usually she stares into the void, but then she will say something as if she were still living in our old home."

Entering a corner of the garden, he turned her around to face him. "It must have been hard for her to watch her home burn." Seeing no one around in the gathering dusk, he tucked her head under his chin and pulled her tightly to his torso.

Silver Bell wanted to stay there forever, but the heat of his body and talk of her family tragedy set her aquiver. She placed her arms in front of her chest and maintained a little space. "Oh, yes, all the Chinese hate the Japanese — even those who are opium addicts."

"Yes, the Japanese tried to poison us!" Donald frowned, and his voice wobbled.

Silver Bell stepped back to stare at Donald, surprised that he shared her outrage. "My mother always ranted about how they grabbed territories in the north and grew opium on all the arable land. Maybe that's why my father's younger brother, my snobbish Soo-soo, would smoke only the British opium cultivated in India."

"So, did your father also smoke opium?"

"No one smoked in my immediate family, even though my mother was given opium when she was only three years old — to help her endure the pain of foot binding." Silver Bell shuddered. "Luckily, my grandfather took pity on her and loosened her binding after her last two toes were turned under her sole but before her heels were pushed forward to meet the toes. That was really barbaric!" Tears welled into her eyes.

"Of course, of course . . ." Donald wrapped his arms tightly around her again. "But she is not totally deformed and her feet are still functional. The destruction of her home must have been more devastating."

"Hangzhou was not ravaged like Nanking, but there were atrocities." She trembled.

He pressed her head into his chest again, cooing and stroking her hair. Silver Bell felt him tremble along with her.

Nestled in Donald's strong arms, she felt the comfort of home and the urge to talk. "When the Japanese occupied Shanghai, we had to flee to Hong Kong because my father was shipping uniforms and war materials to Chungking." Warmth surged through her body. "Oh, I forgot to say that my mother's brother, my uncle Glorious Dragon —" She broke loose, hopped up and down a few steps, and smiled. Dewy-eyed and staring, she surveyed his face. Her heart pounding, the words rushed out of her mouth. "Oh, oh, oh. Now I know why you seem familiar! You really remind me of him!"

Donald folded her hands into his palms and stroked them gently with his thumb. "I hope he was an honorable man!"

Silver Bell knew she was babbling a fragmented version of her family's history. Still breathless, and with a strange sense of urgency, she blurted, "Oh, yes, yes! He saved our family in so many ways. He started a uniform factory in Shanghai with my father so that we could buy a house in the French Concession."

"Was he some kind of a hustler?" He bent to reach her at eye level and leaned into Silver Bell. Still holding her hands, he brought them up to his face, and gently ran her fingertips on his bristly cheeks.

Donald's face felt like sandpaper, but Silver Bell was overwhelmed by this masculine touch. She let her hands rest in his.

"Oh, no! Well . . ." She tried to collect herself. "He was resourceful." She could not concentrate. She shook her head, knowing she was confusing her listener. "He had an important Japanese friend and was able to arrange our family's flight to Hong Kong." She couldn't stop talking, even as her mind and her emotions raced in opposite directions.

"So your uncle collaborated with the Japanese?" Donald wrapped her hands around his face and peered into her shimmering eyes.

"No, not really. Well, he had this Japanese-American friend, who worked for the Kempetai and he saved our lives — helped us move to Hong Kong." She could not clarify what she was saying. Her hands felt the wonderful bone structure of his face.

"Tell me what happened. I would really like to know all about you." He grinned and slid her hands to his mouth and nibbled on her fingers.

Silver Bell closed her eyes and poured out everything in one breath. "We didn't stay long in Hong Kong. Golden Bell left to study in America the year before the Japanese came, but I was caught in the bombing."

Donald turned his face to the brightly lit house. "I know about being bombed. Most of us experienced that 'treat'." He snorted in sarcasm then sucked in his breath and drew her hands to his heart.

"As you know, the Japanese invaded Hong Kong the day after bombing Pearl Harbor. Miss Tyler, my tutor from Hangzhou, had to leave China as soon as she learned about the bombing. Still, my uncle's Japanese friend was able to route Miss Tyler through Hong Kong and bring me to my sister in Syracuse."

"So what happened to the rest of the family?" he asked. He was now kissing her hands.

Silver Bell could not see his expression but felt paralyzed by his ardor. She tried to fix her mind on his question and pulled her hands away. She was talking too much, yet she couldn't stop. She wanted to sound nonchalant, but her voice quivered. "At any rate, the Japanese friend also helped my father escape to Chungking, and my mother return to Shanghai with Brook ma-ma and the newborn Coral Bell."

"I'm glad you were safe." Donald stroked her back.

"But, my father was . . . was killed," she stuttered uncontrollably. She couldn't tell whether it was the retelling of the family's traumatic history or this young man's intoxicating attention that had thrown her nerves awry.

"Hush, hush." Donald drew her close. "War has given us such unspeakable pain . . . I've known much worse."

Suddenly his head lurched forward. His lips slammed into hers and he kissed her so passionately that Silver Bell responded with equal fervor. She had never been kissed like that before. She didn't know such violent desires existed. She only felt as if the earth had dropped from under her and the moon and stars swooned in the sky.

When they were calmer, Silver Bell groped for words to steady her turbulent heart. She whispered, "Tell me about your family. How were you orphaned?"

"It's not important." He kissed her again and again. She wanted to melt into him.

Yung's voice rang out from the patio, "Silver Bell, Silver Bell! Are you out there? It is time for you to sing to us." Donald and Silver Bell stood very still in the shadows. Yung returned indoors to continue his search in the dance hall.

Silver Bell ducked behind Donald, giggling and blushing. She wiped her mouth, allowing him to smooth down her dress.

"Your hair is a little tousled, but all everyone will notice are your heart-shaped lips. Now, let me help you repair your face." He took out his handkerchief, lifted her chin, and removed the lipstick smears around her mouth, punctuating each wipe with a peck on her forehead and cheeks. She stood meekly before him, clenching and unclenching her fists. "I didn't know you were scheduled to sing!"

"I had lessons in high school." She took the handkerchief and hurriedly wiped the lipstick from his mouth. "Are you sure I look all right?"

"You look radiant!" He took her hand, brought it up to kiss it on the knuckles, and then placed it on his arm. Slowly, he escorted her back into the ballroom.

Silver Bell had never felt such swelling sweetness in her heart. She sang the newly released popular tune "Some Enchanted Evening" with all the ebullience of her newfound passion.

Silver Bell married Donald Ting six months after Golden Bell's wedding. Brook ma-ma thought Silver Bell was too young, but Silver Bell was obviously in love, and with the whole family now dependent on Yung, Golden Bell and Yung's blessings sealed the deal.

Shortly after, Donald was appointed chief manager of all the Yung family factories, reporting directly to the chairman, his new brother-in-law, H. K. Yung.

Some months later, Silver Bell learned that Mr. Ching had resigned and became manager of a small steel mill in Wuhan, in the interior of China. Le-An now worked for Donald. It was then that Silver Bell recalled hearing Mr. Ching mention that an American-educated man had urged him to "have a go at her." Was that man Donald? Was his effusive affection a fraud? No other young manager from the Yung factory had been a returning student from America. In the excitement of her new love, she had ignored the possibility that her handsome, clever husband had manipulated Mr. Ching out of his position and courted her so he could join the Yung family.

Bitter Sweets

Shanghai, 1947

"MADAME CHIANG KAI-SHEK will be coming to our Phi Lambda Fraternity Day at the Shanghai Sporting Club," Yung announced during a family dinner in his mansion.

Donald said, "I hear she will be presenting trophies and prizes to all the young winners — not only in tennis and badminton, but also the three-legged race, the hurdle race, and pin-the-tail-on-the-donkey."

"They're going to have a huge chestnut cake, endless fancy sweets and treats for the children," Yung added.

"Too bad we don't have any children." Golden Bell sighed.

"Let's take Coral Bell!" Silver Bell's long eyes lit up, and her false lashes fluttered like wings. "It's no fun being left out of a family-day party. Besides, Coral is so smart. With her fine ear for languages and her improved English, she should see something of society."

"How are you going to introduce a concubine's daughter?" Donald glared at his bride of several months. "Phi Lambda is a fraternity for Chinese who have studied abroad. We're all westernized. Besides, Madame Chiang is Christian."

"We'll say she is our niece." Silver Bell plumped her lower lip, trying to squeeze her mouth into a pouting heart shape.

AMY S. KWEI

"There is no honor in lying. Tai-tai would not approve," Brook
ma-ma said. She sat down with the family but hardly ate anything.
Her attention was centered on her mistress, who smiled each time
Brook ma-ma turned to wipe her mouth to make sure she wasn't
drooling. To prevent her mistress from dropping food from her
chopsticks, she piled pieces of shrimp, vegetable, and meat into
Purple Jade's rice bowl so that she could just shuffle them into her
mouth with her rice.

"Oh, Brook ma-ma, please, please let me go!" Coral Bell
begged. "I can run ever so fast, and I shall win so many races!" She
popped her thumb into her mouth.

"Yes, yes, Silver Bell, you shall go." Purple Jade nodded and smiled
at Coral Bell. "Your uncle Dragon will take you." She turned to
Donald. "Dragon-dee, you must let Silver Bell go."

"I'm Sh . . . Shoral Bell," Coral Bell mumbled through her
thumb.

"Yes, yes, M-ma," Silver Bell answered for her half sister. Her
mother's disorientation confused her. She lowered her head and
laid down her chopsticks.

Brook ma-ma reached over to dislodge Coral's thumb and
whispered, "Now, who would want a thumb sucker in polite
company?"

The composed faces around the table turned into scowls and
frowns. Yung and Golden Bell shook their heads. Everyone was
through eating, and Yung stood up to leave. Golden Bell took a
deep breath and followed. She had hoped the family gathering
would help bring her mother closer to reality, but it had only led to
another display of her problem.

Everyone knew that Brook ma-ma would be pleased to see her
daughter among the children of the Western-educated business
class in Shanghai society. They agreed to the Phi Lambda party
and introduce their half sister as "their niece, Coral."

Golden Bell couldn't help thinking how her dream in Syracuse of returning to the bosom of her home had been so different from reality. Her mother had become an embarrassment. In spite of Brook ma-ma's best efforts, she and Coral Bell were additional burdens. Their poor relatives sometimes came to ask for help. They were sent away with small sums of money or old jewelry they no longer wore. Sometimes they were turned away empty-handed to discourage them. Even though she remained Yung's Western-educated trophy wife, their lovemaking was no longer as passionate. Maybe it was familiarity, or the many women who were eager to flirt with and throw themselves on a wealthy man. Golden Bell was afraid to learn the reason, so she never probed. It was the memories of her romance in New York and her contacts with Josie and Katie that made her happy. The two friends had written to her about the changing campus. It was now so full of returning veterans that the university had to install trailers and build temporary structures to house the older students. *Things change,* Golden Bell told herself. *We all have to adapt.* Soon both friends married. Katie moved back to Ohio and Josie went to South Carolina. They sent Golden Bell subscriptions to *Life* and *Look* magazines as wedding presents. Golden Bell was thrilled to remain in touch with America, where meeting Yung had been the highpoint of her life.

The crimson awnings of the Shanghai Sporting Club greeted the Yung party. Like most mansions, the club compound was walled in, bordered by sharp-edged fences and walls. Two dark-skinned men in maroon turbans and khaki uniforms opened the guests' car doors. The party followed the red carpet up a few steps, where Chinese boys, wearing blue uniforms and round blue caps with gold chinstraps, pushed the shiny brass handles and swung open the doors.

The guests passed through halls decorated with huge crystal chandeliers, potted palms, and gleaming marble columns. They spoke a Chinese smattered with foreign words or conversed only in English. They had come from many different provinces and spoke in different dialects; most members found it easier to talk in English. The men were often addressed by the initials of their Chinese names.

"H.K., want to play a game of tennis?" someone asked Yung.

"Sure, perhaps we'll play doubles with C.Y. and Donald."

Golden Bell, whom everyone addressed as Vicky, joined several other ladies in the back room to play mahjong. Silver Bell led Coral Bell onto the patio where children's games were about to start.

"Ah, Sarah!" a matronly woman called out to Silver Bell, addressing her by her English name. "You brought your niece as promised!" They winked at each other.

Silver Bell turned to her half sister. "Coral, this is Auntie May and her daughter, White Lily."

Coral Bell bowed and whispered "Auntie May." She stared at the petite girl of about seven — roughly her own age. But White Lily chewed on her lips and hid behind her mother.

The children addressed the grown-ups as "Auntie" and "Uncle" — whether they were related or not.

"White Lily will be going to the same school with you in the fall," Silver Bell informed Coral. "She and Auntie May just returned from Chungking."

"Why don't you both sign up for the three-legged race?" Auntie May suggested. "You're about the same height."

"Sure!" Coral Bell grabbed White Lily's arm and tugged. "Let's go!"

Having a companion emboldened Coral Bell. She had been concentrating intensely on keeping her thumb away from her mouth, and now her thumb throbbed and her mouth felt dry.

Thirty or more children milled around in groups — talking, giggling, and drinking sodas. A few played tag on the lawn. It seemed to Coral Bell that she and her new friend were the only ones there who didn't know anybody. White Lily tagged along but, unlike Silver Bell, did not sign up for the hurdle race and the twenty-yard dash.

When the races began, White Lily cheered and shouted on the sidelines. Coral Bell was sure her new friend's loud encouragements helped her win the dash, although a much taller boy won the hurdle race.

When Coral Bell and White Lily were preparing for the three-legged race, the tall boy sidled over to them. "You're joining a Communist race," he snickered.

"What's that?" Coral Bell glanced up, her face flushed from bending over to tie her leg to White Lily's.

"The Communists want everyone to share everything. When they come, you'll have to share three shoes between the two of you!"

Coral Bell stared blankly at the boy, but White Lily giggled. "I've seen lots of people in Chungking with no shoes!"

A teenage boy wearing a waiter's white jacket came by with a tray of sodas and juices. "Young master and mistresses, would you like to share four drinks between the three of you?"

Coral Bell laughed as she took a soda. "Why don't you join the race with this boy? You're both the same height."

"Sorry, but that wouldn't do." The waiter quickly bowed and left.

The boy introduced himself. "I'm Eddie. I'm twelve. Our family just came back from Calcutta."

"Oh." The girls looked at each other and shrugged. He might as well have said he had returned from the moon.

"That's in India, where people have dark skin. My servant always crawled behind me, picking up everything I dropped." He smirked. "Such stupid girls," he muttered to himself in English.

"Too bad you don't have a friend to run this race with you," Coral Bell replied in English, handing him her unfinished drink. "White Lily, let's go!" She tugged on her friend, and they hopped off to join the lineup while she translated her exchange with the boy.

"Where are your parents? Is your mother a foreigner?" White Lily asked.

"What makes you think my mother is a foreigner?"

"You have such fair skin and big eyes, and you speak English."

Coral Bell didn't know how to answer. She had heard people comment on her mother's "cow eyes." And everyone said she had inherited them. She slipped her thumb into her mouth. "My father died when the Japanese bombed Chungking. I was only a baby," she said instead.

"I'm sorry about your father," White Lily whispered. "There was so much bombing in Chungking!" Her hands covered her ears as she hunched up her shoulders and tried to stop shivering.

Coral Bell pulled her thumb out of her mouth, resuming her vigilance. She put one arm around her friend's shoulder, patting it as her mother had always done. They hugged each other close on the lineup for the three-legged race.

"Where's your father?" Coral Bell asked.

"He's not a member of Phi Lambda. Auntie Sarah invited my mother and me here. She and my mother were high school classmates in Hong Kong. So many of their friends died when the bombs fell on Chungking, just like your father."

As Coral Bell shuddered, a whistle blew, signaling the start of the race. Distracted by all the secrets they had just shared, the new friends had trouble coordinating their paces and lost.

Eddie came over. "Sorry you didn't win. No sweets for you," he said in English. "Come on, let me show you a poker game."

"We don't know how to play, but we'd love to watch." Coral Bell answered for both of them, translating for White Lily. They followed Eddie to a grove of pine trees where several older boys and girls were seated in a circle. Eight people were playing. Others stood around and watched. Eddie selected a good vantage point and whispered his explanation of the game.

Coral Bell sucked in a quick breath when a boy did not receive the requisite card.

"Shhh —" Eddie gave her a gentle nudge. He whispered again in English, "The whole game is won on a bluff. Look: He is adding his bet, pretending he received a good card. He keeps a straight face so no one knows what he's holding."

When the game was called, another boy with a full house won the game.

"I was so close!" shouted the boy who bluffed.

"He has a true poker face!" Eddie said, smiling and nodding. "A great poker player."

Coral Bell and White Lily looked at each other, noting the new phrase. Later they talked about how sophisticated Eddie was and how much they had learned from him.

Toward evening, Madame Chiang was introduced to present prizes. Coral Bell thought she had never seen anyone more elegant. The grand lady wore a loose-fitting royal blue sheath with a matte silk sheen. Her hair was neatly bound in a chignon at the nape of her neck. Except for red lipstick, she didn't seem to be wearing any makeup on her velvet skin. Eddie stood at her side, handing out prizes. When Coral Bell's turn came, Eddie announced in English, "Auntie, this girl speaks English."

Madame Chiang flashed a warm smile and asked Coral Bell her name and where she went to school. Coral Bell mumbled her name. But when she answered "McTyeire," Madame Chiang exclaimed gleefully, "That was my school! Good, good." She patted Coral Bell's head, and the next prizewinner was announced.

At the picnic supper on the lawn, White Lily confided to Coral Bell, "You're so lucky to have a mother who taught you English."

"Not my mother. My tutor and my sis — I mean my aunt — taught me." Coral Bell looked away, slipping her thumb into her mouth.

"Oh, do you have an English name too?" White Lily asked.

"No, I told you — my father died when I was a baby! He gave everyone else their English names, but the Japanese invaded Hong Kong shortly after I was born and everyone just called me Coral Bell."

"Where is your mother? Maybe your aunt will ask her and my mother to give both of us English names."

At the mention of her mother, Coral Bell removed her thumb and decided to explain to her new friend the complicated relationships in her family.

"My father named my sisters Victoria and Sarah," she finally let on. "I'm a concubine's daughter. I was never given an English name. That's why I call my mother Brook ma-ma and my sister's mother M-ma." Although only seven, both children understood that a concubine's daughter with a deceased father might never be fully accepted into high society.

"I'll keep your secret if you'll keep mine," White Lily whispered. "My father has another woman who gave him a son. Even though my mother is the number one wife, she only had me, a daughter. My father kept us in Chungking for as long as he could. That's why we've just arrived in Shanghai. I don't know anyone here."

Coral Bell nodded, smiling. Her heart understood the status of the outcast. Without the presence of supportive fathers or the generosity of Golden and Silver Bell, they might never attend these parties and meet children like Eddie again.

Silver Bell and Auntie May joined them as the two girls sat eating in the fading summer light. They watched the men on the grass tennis courts still swatting the ball back and forth while a waiter held a tray of drinks at courtside.

Donald, decked out in tennis whites, a soft knit shirt, and creased trousers, looked tall, athletic, and confident — unruffled by his exertions. Auntie May and Silver Bell whispered and giggled, gazing over at him.

"Such easy grace, so suave and tan!" they heard Auntie May say.

On the way home, Coral Bell, exhilarated after a day in the sun, fell asleep in the car, hugging her prize of fancy chocolates. At the door of their apartment building, she sleepily extended one arm and allowed herself to be helped down to the pavement.

No sooner had her feet touched the ground than a beggar boy charged toward her. He punched her in the chest, grabbed the box of chocolates, and ran down the street like a dust devil. He turned the corner and disappeared. The chauffeur started after him, but Silver Bell shouted, "Don't bother, the poor child must be hungry!"

Coral Bell burst out crying and Silver Bell hugged her, murmuring, "Now, now, you're not hurt?"

Donald remained in the car. "Silver Bell, come back in!" he hollered. "I have to get home. We'll get her more chocolates tomorrow!"

Coral Bell ran up to M-ma and Brook ma-ma. She howled like a wounded animal, "The beggar . . . boy took my sweets . . ."

"Life is so different outside the Sporting Club." Silver Bell sighed, leaning back into her seat. "Brook ma-ma said there were fewer beggars in the streets during the Japanese occupation."

"The Japanese probably just terminated them." Donald snarled, grinding his teeth.

"Where do all these people come from, I wonder?"

"There're millions of displaced people in the country. They flock to Shanghai because they hear of our lavish parties and wealth." Donald looked at his wife. "Your Christian brethrens have all learned to make money. Most Chinese remain desperately poor."

Silver Bell turned her face away, wiping her tears. "I have experienced Christian charity, but whatever I have, I owe it to my sister."

Donald did not respond. Silver Bell was surprised when he reached over and held her hand.

Slips of Memory

SILVER BELL'S HEART blazed with desire and excitement throughout her six months of courtship and two weeks of honeymoon. Strangely, Donald was never an urgent lover. He did his duty quickly and efficiently. He never asked how she felt and whether she was happy. Since Silver Bell was young and inexperienced, she didn't know what to expect. If she had even a glimmer of doubt, she dismissed it. Sex was certainly not something any respectable woman would discuss with anyone — not even with her sister. One day she tucked her head into Donald's chest and asked: "Tell me about your family."

Donald stopped breathing for a moment, and she could hear his heart pounding. Finally he stroked her hair and murmured, "I have been so busy, my memories have become shadows."

"How can your ancestors and family become shadows?" She broke loose to face him. "Do you mean ghosts? Are they all dead?"

He grimaced.

"Where were you born?"

"I was born in Nanking."

"Let's take a vacation in Nanking. Do you still have relatives there?" He pressed his lips tight and didn't answer.

She rambled on: "We'll find your relatives. You can show me your old school, and maybe some of the old missionaries will remember you and tell me how they helped you go to Japan and America."

"Oh, let's not talk about the past!" He tickled her and started kissing her all over. She giggled and moaned with pleasure as they made love and all further queries were deflected.

Sweet happiness enveloped Silver Bell. As always, her head was clouded by smoke — literally and figuratively. What really bound them, what truly made her feel his equal in worldliness and self-possession, was that they were an elegant team of tobacco lovers. Often, accompanied by the music of Glen Miller playing "The Little Brown Jug" or Tommy Dorsey playing "Indian Love Call," they sat side-by-side in bed after their lovemaking, or across from one another at dinner, and sucked furiously on their cigarettes, wordlessly squinting into the blue smoke. In a moment of rapture, she said, "This is the image of our hearts on fire, and the smoke, a symbolic emanation of our love."

"That's a beautiful vision," he replied. But sometimes he would laugh and wave the thought away and say, "Such romantic non-sense."

Amid the touring, feasting, and dancing during their honey-moon in Beijing, Donald often lapsed into silence. He would clutch her hand and frown. She thought it was because they were dazed, basking in the heat of a thrilling affection.

"It's really rewarding to know I am indispensable at work," Donald said one day. "Yung told me he trusts me more than his other brother-in-law." He chuckled. Another time, he muttered in the shadows, "I am only a working stiff. I don't own any part of my labor!" These remarks were as close as he ever came to sharing his inner self.

Finally, Silver Bell asked Golden Bell, "Do you know if Donald has a Chinese name?"

"I don't think so. He was an orphan, so maybe the missionaries gave him his English name."

"Then how did he get his family name?"

"I don't know."

"Do you know anything about Donald's family, the Tings, and how he went to Japan and America?"

"No, how did he?"

"I thought he might have told Yung," Silver Bell said, a bit crestfallen.

"No, I've never heard Yung talk about it. Why don't you ask him yourself?"

"He said he was from Nanking."

"So you do know something. Ask him more."

"I shall." Silver Bell blushed, not wishing to reveal the lack of communication in her newlywed state. "You know, Donald's been so busy lately."

"We have all heard about the rape of Nanking during the war. You'll just have to be patient, and maybe one day Donald will tell you." Golden Bell eyed her sister with sympathy.

There were so many stories about the unspeakable violence the Japanese had committed in Nanking that Silver Bell suspected Donald's family was also killed. Surely he would have a Chinese name, she thought. But why would he hide it from everyone? So many had suffered during the war that she wondered if he too had been traumatized and couldn't share his experiences. Her passion, inexperience, and fear of unspeakable truths left her bewildered and reluctant to broach the subject again. She would concentrate on their future instead.

After she and her sister had returned to Shanghai, Silver Bell had often complained about their reduced circumstances compared with their lives in Hangzhou. Since meeting Donald, though, she was no longer a "fool for memories," as Golden Bell used to call her.

One night after supper, they lit up as usual. A cloud of smoke was closing in on them, and she felt cradled and dreamy. "I've always wanted to have a house in the country, with a white picket fence and an apple tree. You know, something like what's in that movie: Jeanette MacDonald singing about springtime in May, and a cloud of apple blossoms showering down on her. Oh, it is splendid!"

Donald's gruff voice cut through the fog. "You've seen too many American movies. Where are you going to find a house like that in Shanghai?"

Silver Bell couldn't read his expression. She imagined him smirking. He leaned against the window — an Adonis in a smoky silhouette. "Perhaps we could buy some land near Shanghai and build one, say, in Hongkew?" She thought she sounded mature.

"Dreams, that's all." He turned to look at her, his lips curled down in a scowl. "I am a salary man, not a scion of a textile empire like your brother-in-law. We have a three-bedroom apartment with servant's quarters. That's enough room for us and all we can afford to rent. Why don't you go back to work?"

Silver Bell was taken aback. She had not thought of work for many months.

"Your sister goes to the office every day. Sometimes I think I'm taking orders from her rather than from Yung."

"Being the eldest, my sister is used to taking charge," she mumbled. She didn't know how to tell him about her experiences with Mr. Ching.

"I know you only worked one week, and Ching treated you badly. But now that I'm the chief manager, no one will touch you."

"I . . . I . . ." She stuttered, surprised that he knew but relieved that the incident had cleared up without any apparent aftershocks. Suddenly a bell rang in her head. She remembered how she'd first heard the name Ting — in Mr. Ching's office, the day Mr. Ching tried to molest her. She shuddered.

Maybe her mind had conjured up the wrong name. *No, Mr. Ching did say Mr. Ting, a name I had never heard before. If it was*

Donald, did he use me to cause Mr. Ching's downfall? Was that how he became chief manager? Her heart tightened in her chest, and she felt a headache coming. *Where did he learn to scheme like that?*

A barrage of questions swirled in her head. *Does Donald come from a book-fragrant family? Has he been taught the basic Confucian precepts of honor and righteousness? How old was he when he was orphaned? What happened to his parents? Regardless of what happened, how can he have encouraged Mr. Ching to play any part in that nasty drama?*

Then her loyalty to her husband took over. No, she must have remembered wrong. Donald couldn't possibly have done anything like that. Her face felt flushed and swollen, but she didn't cry. *Should I ask my sister? No, Golden Bell probably wouldn't know, because if she did, she would have told me long ago. If I accuse him falsely, our relationship will never be the same again. And even if my fears are on the mark, what can I or anyone else do about it?*

"It's decided then," he said, the cloud of smoke obscuring his profile entirely. "You can help Mr. Wang with his English correspondence."

She was speechless.

The very next day, Silver Bell called her sister and sought her advice on work. Golden Bell was practical. "Go back to work, and use your salary to take some accounting courses. Everyone needs to feel useful!"

The following week, Donald arranged for her to work in a Yung factory office five miles outside of town. The chauffeur drove her there; she had flexible hours. She worked only when English correspondence or translation was required. Donald was so busy that sometimes she didn't see him for days. To stave off loneliness, she often stayed over at her mother's apartment, sharing Coral Bell's bed. Gradually she came to enjoy both her accounting classes and her office work.

Whenever Donald returned home, she served his favorite dish, beggar's chicken, and longed for the magic moment when they would nestle in bed, forgetting their fears, suspicions, and dreams. After their lovemaking, they always lit up — two solitary figures cemented in a purple-gray haze of smoke.

"Hire Ah Woo as your chief housekeeper. That is what your mother would have done," Brook ma-ma advised. "There is no question of her loyalty."

Ah Woo was Old Woo's cousin. Old Woo had been the accountant at her father's estate in Hangzhou when the Huangs were prospering. These relationships in her parents' household went back for generations.

Since Silver Bell was only seventeen, just married, and knew nothing about managing a household, she hired Ah Woo as her chief housekeeper. Ah Woo kept a keen eye on all the servants in the house and reported every detail to Brook ma-ma.

Every day, Ah Woo brought Silver Bell ginseng tea brewed with gingko nuts and herbs. Brook ma-ma prescribed the drink based on her mistress's bygone medical studies. She thought Silver Bell was too young to work, and since she married well, she shouldn't worry about studying. Her task would be to prepare for children and become a full woman. Brook ma-ma wanted to build up her strength. The young couple laughed at her over-protectiveness, but Silver Bell drank her tea anyway because it made her feel more energetic.

One day, Brook ma-ma insisted that Silver Bell lend her the cook.

"I can't do that," Silver Bell said, glaring at her. "I know the cook is only in her twenties, but she is an expert on beggar's chicken. You know that is Donald's favorite dish."

"That is also your mother's favorite," she answered, fixing her gaze on her shoes. "Tai-tai has been feeling poorly and needs to build up her appetite."

"Really, Brook ma-ma!" Silver Bell rolled her eyes. "What's gotten into you? Take Mother to see a doctor. A cook trained to do banquets is not going to be happy working for you, Mother, and little Coral Bell."

"Tai-tai is not sick," Brook ma-ma whispered, looking past her toward the window. "Lend us the cook for a week, and your mother's spirits may revive."

Her gentle tone, sad brooding eyes, and quiet insistence left Silver Bell no room for retreat. "All right. Just one week." Her voice sounded strident and grating to her ears.

When Donald learned that Silver Bell had lent their cook to her mother, he pounced on her. "You did what?" He slammed down his hand so hard on the dinner table that the chopsticks jumped onto the dishes. He would not take a single bite, even though she had spent hours preparing the salad and hamburgers herself. *Why should Donald be so annoyed?*

Silver Bell tried to sound optimistic. "Mother needs cheering up. And I thought you might like to try some American food." She almost choked on the bit of bread in her mouth, feeling guilty and confused. She had never gone near the kitchen in China. Only in New York had she occasionally helped to make salad and hamburgers.

"Are you becoming senile like your mother?" Donald took a sip of wine. "That concubine is just using your mother to get a good meal," he bellowed. "Get that cook back, or I'm never going to eat at home again!" He stormed out of the house.

Silver Bell ran into her room and wept herself to sleep.

The next day, when Donald came home after work, the first words out of his mouth were to ask whether the cook had returned. Silver Bell answered no, and was about to explain how she had tried to reason with Brook ma-ma, when Donald threw her a disgusted look and bolted out the door.

A day later, Brook ma-ma sent Silver Bell a man named Loh Fan, who had been apprenticed to a famous chef. The new cook took over the kitchen with remarkable efficiency. His dishes were so delicious and beautifully presented that Donald could hardly protest, and all should have been forgiven. Still, Donald seldom came home for dinner.

Soon the former cook asked to leave her mother's service. She came to Silver Bell's house to pack her belongings and said that she was now serving a private patron who favored her beggar's chicken. Her face was flushed. Her buxom chest heaved while her guilty glances confirmed Silver Bell's suspicions.

She telephoned Golden Bell in the factory office to seek comfort. "Does Donald have to work so much that he can't come home for days on end?"

"Donald and Yung both work late — often traveling to factories in other cities and sometimes entertaining customers. I don't want to know anything else." Golden Bell used her business voice.

"Don't you worry that they might be dallying with other women?"

"I have my suspicions, but I don't worry." She chuckled. "Anyway, what can I do? There'll always be pretty young women who find successful men attractive."

"But . . . how can you stand it?" Her pride was broken, and she began to cry.

"Grow up, Silver Bell." Golden Bell sounded almost impatient. "Generations of rich men have had concubines in this country. We grew up with one in our family, did we not?"

"Yes, but Brook ma-ma is different."

"You're right. Brook ma-ma used to say Mother was silk — giving warmth and comfort to everyone she touched. Now Brook ma-ma has assumed her spirit. She is the silk of our family!"

"I don't think I could ever give Donald a concubine." She sobbed uncontrollably. "Even if the woman were just like Brook ma-ma . . ."

"Don't cry! I understand how you feel. I would probably never do a thing like that either — not after a Christian education that taught me to dread 'the concupiscence of the flesh!'" She chuckled at the irony. "Yung is a dutiful husband, but I can't control his eyes when so many women are willing to serve him and live a better life."

"I'm so confused! Don't I have a right to demand loyalty from my husband?"

"Of course. If only life were so simple! Even in the West many men have mistresses, and often the only way for a woman to get ahead is to marry a powerful man. Yung and I used to huddle together and check the company books. Now I do it alone because he is busy taking care of other things with Donald."

Silver Bell could hear her sister tapping a pen on her desk.

"It isn't fair!" Silver Bell stamped her foot.

"Nothing is fair in this world. The Huang family survives with dignity because you and I have married successful men. But Yung was born into his wealth and success. Where is the fairness in that?"

"I can't believe you condone such behavior. Where is your self-respect?" Silver Bell shouted, almost choking on her words.

"Oh, I'm sorry. I guess I sound callous. You're a newlywed, and I've only been married over one year," Golden Bell said, softening. "Only you can give yourself a sense of self-worth. That's why I work harder than my husband in the office. Besides enjoying literary works, you must have practical skills for earning a living."

"I can't believe it! Don't you love your husband? Wouldn't you feel hurt if Yung had an affair?"

Golden Bell kept her calm. "I suppose I'd feel hurt if Yung fell in love with some slut and wanted to bring her home. However, as long as I don't know what goes on outside, he remains my respectable husband. I'll have to live with his occasional indiscretion.

Maybe he and Donald are fellow philanderers. We're in China. Here, our role is to produce an heir. By the way," she slipped in, "I'm pregnant, and I'm glad he isn't making any physical demands on me now."

"Congratulations!" Silver Bell shouted, sounding sarcastic. She didn't mean to. She was glad that if her sister should produce an heir, her position would forever be secure in the Yung family.

Silver Bell's tears soon turned to hysteria because she could not accept the logic of Golden Bell's cynical calculations. She knew full well that if Donald and Yung really became involved with other women, they would pretend nothing had happened. The sisters would have to accept the infidelity in order to save face and preserve the family's integrity. This was what generations of Chinese women had done and perhaps some Western women too.

"Do you know that the name for my children's generation's, Der — Virtue — is the same word as Father's name, Righteous Virtue? If I have a son, I plan to call him Yung Der An. Peace is what China needs, so he will be An, or Peace. If it is a girl, she will be called Der Li. Li for beauty. Beauty is always auspicious for a girl."

Silver Bell nodded even though she was talking on the phone. Her thoughts lingered on her own problems. She was almost certain that something had happened between the cook and her husband. Brook ma-ma had been wise to maneuver the cook out of her house. Silver Bell wouldn't know how to confront Donald. She knew what her sister would have done — nothing.

"Yung agrees these are excellent names. He isn't talking about just having a son." Golden Bell hummed. He said, "Yung Der An, Yung Der Li, they will build a new China."

Silver Bell nodded again and thought that even though Yung had become progressive in America, his parents would surely insist on an heir now. "I wish your Der An arrives peacefully," she pronounced firmly into the phone.

After Silver Bell hung up, she lit a cigarette. She still felt almost like a newlywed and was terrified to acknowledge the chasm in her marriage. She and Donald filled the void between them with clouds of smoke. They strained their eyes to obscure the emptiness and communicated in syncopated puffs.

Three months later, when Donald started coming home for his meals again, she knew he had tired of his affair with the cook. Her anger dissolved into pity, and she often wondered what had become of the poor woman. Then she got busy, and the incident turned into another questionable memory.

Hostages To Fortune

Shanghai, 1948

ELATED ABOUT her pregnancy a year after her marriage, Silver Bell was convinced that her family would say, "Good fortune has come to roost." She ordered fresh roses to scent the living room. She placed Donald's slippers in front of his favorite chair. In the evening, Silver Bell applied cream and transparent makeup to her smooth face. She carefully swept her hair from the sides into two large rolls above her head, showcasing her jaw line. "I wish I had Coral Bell's large dark eyes," she mused.

She meticulously lined her thin long eyes, adding white and brown eye shadow to make them look wider. She chose a long, Western-style gown with an empire waist. The flowing green garment draped her still shapely body. She stood in front of the mirror, sure that her waist had grown thicker and her breasts fuller, but she still couldn't detect her new womanly figure under the liquid green silk.

When Donald returned home, Silver Bell danced up to the front door to greet him. Giggling, she sang out, "I have a surprise for you!"

She led him to his chair and knelt to remove his shoes. "How was your day at the office?" she asked.

"Oh, the same bad inflation news," he replied in the insipid baritone that he usually employed at home. Silver Bell ached inside whenever she remembered his ringing voice that had so energized her at her sister's wedding party. Now, his bushy brows knitted together into a dark straight line across his handsome face. "The labor unions are talking about a strike. Prices of all essential goods are galloping into the stratosphere!"

"Oh, yes. Ah Woo told me that life is impossible outside. Everyone is hoarding goods and spending their worthless cash." Silver Bell prattled on lightheartedly, untying her husband's shoelaces. "Our Hangzhou relatives supply us with all our provisions, so don't you worry!"

"I'm not worried about us." Donald reached to help his wife up, putting on his slippers. "Sit down. I want you to write a letter to your old teacher, Miss Tyler. Ask her to transfer all our money into several small accounts in non-international banks in New York."

"Why should we do that? Our U.S. dollars in Chase National Bank have served us well in this hyperinflation here."

"The news is that the government will soon inaugurate a gold Yuan. People with overseas accounts will be required to report their reserves and exchange foreign money for the new Yuan. It is safer to hide our assets in small regional banks."

"You don't trust the new currency?" Silver Bell gasped. "It hasn't even been printed yet!"

"These are desperate measures." He accepted tea from Ah Woo. "There is no gold backing the paper money they'll print, in spite of what they say. The Nationalists are spending heavily on military action against the Communists. If they can't control the economy, the government will fall."

"You suppose this could happen? The Americans are fully supporting our government." Silver Bell sipped her tea, smiling at her husband. "But I'll write Miss Tyler, just in case."

"Yes, it's best to be cautious." Donald sat back, relaxed. He lit two cigarettes and offered one to his wife. He finally noticed the roses. "So what's this big surprise you mentioned?"

Eyes twinkling, Silver Bell sang: "I'm pregnant!"

Donald snuffed out his cigarette in a hard grinding motion, and his body turned rigid. Frowning, he asked, "Didn't you learn anything in America? Why didn't you take precautions?"

Silver Bell let her cigarette ash drop; she was stunned. "No, no, no . . ." she stuttered, trembling, as she ran out of the room. "I've never considered anything like that!"

"You must get an abortion!" he bellowed after her. "The Communists are coming." He took a deep breath. "Come back!" he thundered. "I want to talk to you!"

Silver Bell returned, sobbing. She couldn't understand why Donald would reject their child. She turned her back on her husband and stood in front of the window. Cold air from the buffeting winds seeped inside. She shivered.

"You must talk to your sister," Donald stated calmly. "Yung is totally unrealistic. He thinks the Communists will be like a change of dynasties. He wants us all to stay and safeguard his factories! It would be suicide. Many of our Phi Lambda friends are already planning to leave China. The Chus are going to Brazil; the Changs are applying to enter the United States; and the Wangs want to go to England. Many more are moving to Hong Kong or Taiwan." Silver Bell didn't answer; her small world was shattering.

From her eighth-floor window, she had an unobstructed view of the street below. A bitter cold had settled on this gray day. Rows of modest brick and concrete buildings loomed dark and gloomy in the dim reflected glow of lighted windows. The trees were bare, their branches extending like hungry arms clawing the empty pavement. A beggar woman in rags huddled by the trunk of the sycamore tree across from her apartment. When a passerby approached, the woman shakily held out a broken bowl. Silver Bell's heart fluttered wildly. The sight of desperate poverty was all too common these days, but she could never get used to it. The morning's newspaper reported that government trucks picked up dozens of frozen corpses every morning. She moaned softly.

"You must persuade your sister to move to Hong Kong or Taiwan. That's the only way to safeguard our, I mean their, family fortune," Donald insisted.

Silver Bell ignored the gaffe. "Golden Bell told me many in the Western press depict the Communists as different from the corrupt Nationalists. They have brought ascetic discipline to the country. Their soldiers never looted in the territories they conquered. Our local papers carry only Nationalist propaganda — calling the Communists thieves and rebels. Just look at that beggar woman down there! Our country needs to change. We could use a new government!"

"Phooey!" Donald waved his hand in exasperation. "Your American sojourn has given you nothing but a broken basket of useless ideals! It's too late. Don't you see? There are too many poor and dispossessed people. They consider us the enemy because we have prospered under the Nationalists!"

Silver Bell turned to face her husband. "No, they will see we're different! In fact, I plan to give this woman my dinner tonight!" She pointed to the beggar outside her window.

"Fine. A lovely gesture," Donald shouted. "I'm sure that noble act will solve our country's financial problem."

Silver Bell turned to face the window again, one arm cradling her womb. She could not find a rejoinder, and her emotions roiled inside her.

Donald sipped his tea, his voice taking on a wheedling tone. "With your good English, you'll feel right at home in British Hong Kong." He rose from his seat and put his arm around his wife, guiding her toward the warm stove, away from the window. "We can encourage the Yungs to play it safe, invest, and start some textile factories there." He nibbled her neck.

Donald's embrace felt warm and reassuring, but Silver Bell stood her ground. "The British won Hong Kong from us after the Opium War. Many of my relatives became opium addicts. China's problems began with foreign invasion . . ." She stopped and shook herself, realizing that her rambling sounded just like her mother's diatribes. Her mother's distracted mind only attested to the futility of resistance to Western dominance.

"Talk to your sister," Donald implored her, hugging her close and rocking her in his arms. "You'll enjoy the warmer weather in Hong Kong. You can have a baby when we're settled there, but not now, not now . . ."

Silver Bell stood still, savoring her husband's proximity. "Maybe this is not a good time to have a child," she whispered, holding back a sob.

Silver Bell asked her sister to lunch at the Palace Hotel Restaurant the next day. As Donald had instructed, Silver Bell cautioned her about the Communists' coming and urged the family to move. Golden Bell vehemently resisted. "Who will take care of our textile mills if we leave?" she asked.

"Donald said our fluency in English will make us feel right at home in British Hong Kong," Silver Bell repeated quietly, still looking glum.

Golden Bell kept silent for a long while. Finally, she said: "Yes. I'll talk to Yung; maybe you and Donald can move to Hong Kong and manage a branch of our business there for us. That may be a wise safeguard." Both were sipping tea, but neither had an appetite.

"No one here understands communism. It is really more foreign than Christianity," Silver Bell reflected. "I don't think the

Communists will rape and kill like the Japanese, though, do you? After all, they are Chinese like us!"

"Yes, our Confucian learning, but the Japanese also adopted Confucian concepts. They are more disciplined and more brutal, though . . ." Her sentence came out sounding like a question. She paused, shaking her head. "Still, we are different. We're more civilized. After all these years of war and poverty, maybe we can profit from new ideas." Her wobbly voice didn't sound at all confident.

"There could be a brief period of disorder," Silver Bell suggested. "You and Yung should really come with us."

"Yung can't possibly leave all our factories unattended. And I want to stay by him, especially since Der An is born. We must respect the proper authorities, cooperate with them, and work under their supervision. We will help build up the industrial base of China." Golden Bell smiled at the thought. Like their mother, she sounded totally unselfconscious about her pride in Confucian orthodoxy, unaware that she had also become hostage to the family fortune.

Silver Bell remained quiet for a long time, nibbling on a few morsels of dim sum. Finally she whispered, "I'm pregnant."

"Congratulations! How exciting!"

Silver Bell lowered her head. After a long silence, she added, "But Donald wants me to have an abortion." Silent tears streamed down her cheeks.

Golden Bell put down her chopsticks and stared at her sister. "My God, how far along are you? When did you find out?"

"I've been suspecting this for more than a month. Dr. Graham confirmed it two days ago."

"You look miserable. Were you happy about it at first?"

"I was . . . but Donald and I agreed that the times are too unsettled to have a baby." Silver Bell wept on.

Golden Bell sucked in a big gulp of air and looked away, giving both of them time to collect themselves. "What, what bad, bad luck!" she finally stuttered. "I think maybe you still want the child, but it'll be very unpleasant if Donald doesn't want it." She hesitated. "Try to think on the positive side. You're still very young; you'll have many more children."

"Donald said the Communists are . . . are coming."

"Yes. These are unsettling times. We don't know what this change of dynasty will bring." She tried to smile.

"What should I do?" Silver Bell sobbed uncontrollably.

"Now, now, take a deep breath and think things through. It is risky to have a child when you're still so young. You must consider your health." She reached for her sister's hand and her eyes reddened. "You'd better talk to Dr. Graham again. Besides, partisan war is coming. You must help me hold up the sky over our family." Instinctively, she pulled out her gray silk scarf and began twisting it.

Back in the examination room, Dr. Graham thought Silver Bell's husband was most enlightened. "China is terribly overpopulated," he said in his placid voice. "Now, take two of these pills every day for three days. You may become nauseated, but they will prepare you for a scraping of your uterus. I'll schedule you for a D and C on the fourth day."

The heat churned in her stomach, tugging, pulling, and twisting her insides into convulsive retching, hiccups, and stabbing pain. Silver Bell dashed into the bathroom and collapsed over the toilet. A burning sensation rose up in her throat. The vomit was gray and yellow, laced with blood. The mess in the bowl made her retch again and again.

"I can't go on . . . taking medicine . . . for this abortion," she wailed. She pulled herself up and tried to rinse her mouth. Her eyes were bulging; tears sparkled like blazing windows in her swollen face. "This is going to kill me first."

God did not give me strength, she thought. *Clearly God has revealed Himself to be vengeful against the Chinese. The desperate people all around me are proof of that. Am I being punished for all my years of privilege? Is it now my turn to suffer?* She saw long barren years stretching ahead of her because she had consented to an abortion. She even imagined throwing up parts of the baby's arms, nose, fingers, and . . . *Oh, God, please obliterate such crazy thoughts!*

She was determined to avoid the D and C, sure that she would die from the procedure. Instead, she swallowed the drinks that Ah Woo brought her. The herbal tea spiced with ginger helped to settle her stomach. She knew Ah Woo had been consulting Brook ma-ma, who had learned all her medicinal lore from her mother. Perhaps the drinks were antidotes to the doctor's prescription? Silver Bell didn't care. She was feeling better.

When Donald came home and learned of Silver Bell's decision not to proceed with the abortion, he ranted and raved about her ignorance and pampered childhood. After much pacing and sighing, he warned: "Just make sure you have a boy!"

Silver Bell still felt too nauseated and weak to argue. Finally the savage images abated, clearing the way for the life within her.

She was relieved that her husband had at least considered having an heir, and she vowed to start praying and concentrating on producing one — Donald Junior. She would speak to Pastor Cummins and ask for special blessings from the Methodist church. Then she would ask Brook ma-ma to take her to the temple and make offerings to all the Buddhas — in case they should have influence in the heavenly court.

Corel Bell's Conversion

Shanghai, 1948

BEFORE THE COMMUNISTS entered Shanghai, the streets were clogged with cars, trucks, bicycles, beggars, miles of vibrating trolley lines, and crowds of hawkers scurrying past, carrying yoked panniers of nuts and fruits, live chickens squawking in baskets, and buckets of steaming-hot bean-curd custard. Rickshaw pullers cursed and grunted; impatient bicycle and Pedi cab riders rattled their tiny bells; motorists leaned into their horns; buses ground and grated through the jumble of pedestrians and rumbling streetcars. In the International Zone, Purple Jade, Brook ma-ma, and Coral Bell's two-bedroom apartment was an oasis of peace and refinement. Two maids took care of every domestic need. They cleaned the goldfish tank, wiped the collection of jade figurines, and kept everything spotless and bright. Every morning Brook ma-ma supervised the thorough cleaning of one room so that everything was polished and placed in its rightful spot. She added potted plants, softening the effect of the angular hardwood furniture; a soothing stream gurgled from a tiny fountain; and flowers scented the air. The house had a lively, fresh feel. Coral Bell had her own room with a canopied bed. Aside from going to the famous McTyeire School and doing homework, Coral Bell easily found activities to occupy her mind. She read in Chinese and English, learned embroidery from her mother, and played games and sang popular songs when White Lily came to visit.

Except for an occasional visit to the Yung mansion, Purple Jade seldom left her house. For exercise, Brook ma-ma would place Purple Jade's hand in hers and stroll around the kitchen, dining room, living room, Coral Bell's room, and front hall every morning and evening. After several rounds, she would settle her mistress on the sofa in her room. Most afternoons, Coral Bell saw her M-ma sitting elflike and prim on the overstuffed couch, embroidering. Sometimes she would call to Coral Bell, "My heart-and liver, come and see the flower I made." On some evenings, in a voice that seemed to have emerged from the fog of the past — all the way from Hangzhou — she would recite poems by Tu Fu, her favorite poet. "The New Moon," "The Willow," and "Sunset" would transport Coral Bell from the dust and noise of bustling Shanghai to the pathos of soldiers going to war and the longings of noble-men in exile. On these peaceful occasions the recitations sounded melodic. But sometimes Coral Bell felt chilled by the winter in her M-ma's soul:

> New phantoms appear as battle cry rings.
> A litany of woes the old man sings.
> Scudding clouds color a ragged twilight;
> Tumbling winds whirl silent snow into flight.
> A wine ladle lingers in the empty jar of green,
> Wishing the stove's red flames can be seen.
> News from many provinces vaporize,
> Writing and brooding alone, my sorrow multiplies.

When it was late, the recitations felt like a radio show, and Coral Bell would curl up and fall asleep.

Every morning, Coral Bell was told to make "a tea-head." She poured boiling water into a tiny teapot made of clay, for its healthful minerals, and added loose tea-leaves. The leaves steeped in the pot, releasing its fragrance. Then she poured almost a full cup of hot water and, adding strong "tea-head" from the tiny pot, brought it to her M-ma to wish her morning peace. Everyone drank progressively weaker tea as the day wore on.

Their diet was mostly fresh vegetables. Coral Bell often accompanied Brook ma-ma to the outdoor markets. In the bustle of haggling and bargaining, Brook ma-ma introduced her daughter to endless varieties of tofu products and many interesting vegetables.

The bitter melons tasted really bitter, but Brook ma-ma said they reduced internal inflammation and helped fight infections. After a while Coral Bell learned to expect a sweet aftertaste, and she was hooked. Her favorite was eggplant cooked with garlic hot sauce. The tender-skinned Chinese eggplants were long and thin, and Brook ma-ma would cook them whole. The pea-greens tasted so delicate in early summer that she wished they would never grow into peas. She was introduced to many varieties of cabbages and fruits, but she didn't mind being almost a vegetarian, with some help from chicken broth or other meat seasonings. She was told that by eating like that, she would enjoy longevity.

Brook ma-ma thought that Golden Bell and Silver Bell's privileged upbringing had deprived them of the simple joys of preparing food, and their Western education had robbed them of their mother's expertise in Chinese herbs. Having acquired her mistress's medical knowledge through long years of intimate service, Brook ma-ma was quick to prescribe herbal tea at any sign of a cold, cough, or stomach ailment. Brook ma-ma was an excellent cook, and even though Coral Bell was only eight, she helped her mother.

Golden Bell was too busy to visit, but Silver Bell came often. She was only eleven years older than Coral Bell. After supper, Silver Bell would often say: "Let me stay with Coral tonight. I can't face an empty house!" Coral Bell couldn't understand her sister's predicament. She loved to visit her sister's apartment building, which had an elevator. She punched the buttons for every floor and rode the lift up and down until the superintendent sent her away. She particularly enjoyed Silver Bell's company because she felt she was in a different world when speaking English with her.

One day, Silver Bell, with her carefully made-up face, was sprawled on the sofa — her dark permed hair spread out like a poodle's on the white antimacassars covering the sofa's flowery arms. She massaged her stomach and said: "Donald wants to move to Hong Kong. He has no sense of national pride! After all the humiliation we suffered under the British, he still doesn't want to be liberated!"

Brook ma-ma did not contradict her. "No one knows what the Communists are like. You'll soon be back with all of us when the turmoil of changing dynasties is over. Donald is right to keep you safe when you're pregnant."

Silver Bell nodded. "Then, before I leave, I must bring Coral Bell to be baptized. She is already eight years old."

"Would Tai-tai approve?" Brook ma-ma looked at her mistress, who was still mumbling her poetry.

"She wouldn't know the difference, would she?" Silver Bell rolled her eyes. She turned to her sister. "The Christians trust other Christians. It'll bring you more opportunities in the future."

Coral Bell looked at her mother and nodded. Brook ma-ma took care of everyone, but Coral always knew she was her birth mother and special to her. Every morning, she brushed Coral's long hair with extra care while murmuring her loving concerns.

On this summer morning in 1948, Silver Bell brought Coral a new European dress. It was a pale blue cotton knit that hung sleek and straight above her knees. Brook ma-ma said that the straight seams, hidden pockets, and soft rounded collars spoke of quality. The ankle socks had small-embroidered flowers on the cuffs, and the shiny new patent leather shoes — Silver Bell called them Mary Janes — fit perfectly. Brook ma-ma refreshed Coral's braids and put in new silk ribbons, making her feel like a princess.

Brook ma-ma then asked them to bring home a golden skinned melon, which was in season. Silver Bell's chauffeur drove them first to Chaphai, the crowded, noisy Chinese section. As usual, people were haggling with the vendors and having their haircut right on the street. Chinese music wafted out of many stores while chickens cackled in their cages and hawkers cried out their special wares of fried tofu, fish, vegetables, and roasted nuts. They parked next to a stall where a huge slaughtered pig lay on a slab. The butcher was busy hacking it into pieces in front of his customers. Coral Bell had to turn away. While Silver Bell stopped to purchase the melon, a beggar boy sneaked up on the other side and stole a sweet potato. Coral Bell didn't say anything. She looked at the chauffeur, but he turned away. He was used to the sight. The ride was like a picture show. The Chinese section of town looked old and untidy, but was always glistening with bright golden jewelry stores, fabric shops, and bustling people. When they drove into the French section, the tree-lined streets seemed like another country.

The neat red brick building of the Methodist church was not as dramatic as the Chinese temples, but it made Coral Bell feel calm and safe. The white front doors opened into a vestibule. Pictures of solemn foreign men looked down from the walls. Banners drifted from the ceiling. One of them had a design of white felt pigeons flying between these words: *I am with thee, and will keep thee in all places whither thou goest. Gen. 28:15.* The words resonated with Coral Bell instantly. Brook ma-ma had often told her that the spirits of her ancestors were always with her, so she should never do anything to dishonor them. The pigeons and the quote flew straight

145

into her heart. Until then she had never been able to articulate the presence of her ancestors. The power and confidence of those words would remain with her for the rest of her life.

In the main sanctuary, the vaulted pillars soared into a dome. The immense space, lined with rows of wooden pews, felt like a tidy theater. Elegant marble stairways on each side of a stage led to a plain altar with golden candle holders. Over the altar, sunlight streamed through a window of colored glass. On the stage, Pastor John Cummins stood by the burnished bronze railing. He greeted Silver Bell and held Coral Bell's hand for a long while after she was introduced. Pastor Cummins asked, "Do you know why you want to be baptized?"

Coral Bell was awed by the immense space and the abundance of wooden pews and columns. For one moment, she let her guard down and stuck her thumb in her mouth. It was the one thing she had always done — flex her cheeks into a comfortable rhythm, block out the intrusive world, and wallow in self-communion. Now, encouraged by the spaciousness and light of the hall, she quickly pulled out her thumb. Twining her hands behind her back, she answered: "*I am with thee, and will keep thee in all places whither thou goest.*"

The pastor smiled and nodded. "I will let the congregation know your inspired response. You speak excellent English!" He proceeded to set a date for her baptism. The soaring light from the window filled Coral with joy. She was sure she would be lifted higher, returning to her book-fragrant home of many courts and gardens in Hangzhou, with perhaps her father — who must be in heaven — with her wherever she went.

Trouble on the Horizon

Shanghai, 1950

IT WAS STRANGE to feel momentous changes on the horizon and to be unprepared for them. Despite the approaching political storm, an eerie stillness allowed the Huang women to attend to the daily routines of their lives. But inside, they all sensed something vulnerable floating around, as though the string of a paper kite was about to snap.

The Communists entered Shanghai in May 1949 and imposed a sanitized version of reality. Street committees were established to clean up the neighborhoods. Beggars disappeared. Many people were sent into the countryside. Opium addicts were forced into withdrawal by going cold turkey, and drug traffickers were executed.

What was left of the Huang family's diminished properties in Hangzhou was parceled out to tenant farmers. The family had collected little rent throughout the war years, and the farmers remained friendly. From time to time, they sent the family choice provisions from their labors, just as they had done during the years of hyperinflation after World War II. They knew they would always be paid generously, sometimes in precious American dollars.

The new government wanted to encourage industrialization. The Yung factories went into full production.

Donald established new factories in Hong Kong and looked for export markets. He sometimes returned alone to report on his progress.

Each time Donald came back to Shanghai, he stayed with the Yungs. When he trudged down the winding driveway leading to their mansion, their mongrel dog barked furiously.

"Lucky, have you turned senile like my mother-in-law?" Donald snapped at the dog. "Don't you know who I am?"

Lucky paused to stare and sniff. In a second he was humming short whimpers of apology, jumping alongside Donald, yapping and wagging his tail to welcome an old visitor. Thus, the household would be alerted to Donald's approach, and Golden Bell would immediately phone Brook ma-ma. "Donald is here! We'll have news of Silver Bell."

The family gathered around the dinner table, and the first thing they asked was: "Why didn't Silver Bell come with you?" They had been informed by mail that Silver Bell had miscarried the child, and had taken a trip to Syracuse to lift her spirits. "How is she doing now?"

"She is fine," Donald answered. "In fact, she is starting a business in real estate. With her fluency in English, she can concentrate on high-end properties for the English, the Americans, and their Chinese friends. She is too busy and too tired to travel. I trust you hear from her regularly." The truth was he had told his wife that he needed to take a two-day business trip to Singapore. When he returned, he would just say his short trip to Shanghai was only an afterthought. He could not let his wife return to visit. Her family would not understand how she had changed.

He casually lit a cigarette and began with news of friends who had joined the Diaspora. Dr. Chang and his family had moved to California, where his wife, Suzie, who was a great mahjong player, now waited tables in a Chinese restaurant. Dr. Chang was working as a hospital orderly and studying for his medical board exams. The Chu family could not adjust to Brazilian life and were applying to move to New York. Mr. Chu hoped his experiences as the owner of a Shanghai bank might land him a job in the banking industry.

Y. K. Tung had moved from Hong Kong to Taiwan because he could not practice Chinese law in the British colony. C. S. Wu, being bilingual in Chinese and English, gave up law altogether and began to write for the *Hong Kong Standard*; he was now an editor. The Hong Kong textile industry was dominated by Shanghai expatriates.

Amid his stories, Donald made a point of conveying warm regards from friends of the Yung family. He never failed to emphasize how easy it would be for Golden Bell to resume her social position if the family moved to Hong Kong. Still, Golden Bell sighed and mentioned the hardships they would endure as refugee entrepreneurs in Hong Kong.

Donald steered the conversation back toward business in Shanghai. "How are the factories running? Any trouble with the unions?"

"I've been collaborating with the Communists," Yung said. "They're really not a bad lot. They want to root out the criminal elements in the labor unions."

"You'd better be careful." Donald frowned. "The Triad and Tong members are ruthless. They infiltrated the unions long ago, so they won't be easy to get rid of."

"The Communists can be just as ruthless with the criminals. In many ways, they have done great things for the country," Golden Bell chimed in. "Women are now given equal rights in everything! A Chinese woman is encouraged to use her own family name and is called a comrade like everyone else. In Hangzhou, widowed, divorced, and single women were all given land. Even though our properties in Hangzhou have been distributed to the peasants, I think it is only Christian justice to see the poor owning something for a change."

Golden Bell had reason to be elated. Her son, little Der An, had started crawling, and she was pregnant again. Yung, now without Donald's assistance and with the puritanical Communists watching his every move, was so engrossed with running his factories that he no longer had the time or energy for philandering.

"I hear that families with large homes are obliged to share their space with other families." Donald probed, scanning the dining room and noting that the opulent display of antique silver and china of the old days had vanished.

"This mansion and Mother's apartment are considered part of the Yung factory holdings, so life has remained much the same for all of us," Golden Bell answered. "In fact, we're hoping to join the Communist Party. The Party leaders we work with say they may be able to sponsor us as members when we reach a certain production level."

"Joining the Communist party maybe a risky step. We really don't understand the ideology," Donald replied.

"You know, Chinese Communists are carrying a false label. Don't you know Chinese history?" Golden Bell raised her voice.

"I guess not," Donald shook his head. "I was too young when I left the country."

"Well, when the Western Democracies refused to help us right after the Nationalist Republic was born in 1911, the Soviets were the only ones who helped us. The Chinese all took on Communism. Chiang Kai-shek even sent his son, Chiang Ching-kuo, to study in Moscow. He only became a protégé of the Americans after he married Soong Mei-ling and supposedly adopted Christianity and Democracy. Our Hangzhou connections told us that Peony's husband is a high Communist official. He was in Yan'an when an

American, John Service who spoke fluent Chinese, visited Mao Zedong during World War II. Mao emphasized his fervent desire to befriend America. He even offered the Chinese coastal areas as a potential base for the American air force to bomb Japan. The American government didn't want to deal with Mao because he was a Communist. It was only when America rebuffed Mao that he turned to the Soviets. Now that the Chinese people have chosen the Communists by their speedy defeat of Chiang Kai-shek's American- equipped army, perhaps America will realize that their investments in Chiang are useless, because Chiang has lost the hearts of the Chinese people. Maybe America will help us rebuild again.

But enough about us; tell us about Silver Bell. How is she recovering from her miscarriage?"

"Silver Bell misses all of you. She hopes she will be successful next time." Donald lowered his head, not knowing how to address the political misunderstanding.

Purple Jade asked, "What? Who had a miscarriage?"

Donald ignored his mother-in-law. Scowling and knitting his brow, he pronounced the bitter truth. "The move and the turmoil are not conducive to having children."

Everyone became quiet. Silver Bell had never mentioned unfavorable conditions in her letters, only her disappointment at not having produced a son because she had a late-term miscarriage.

Donald said no more. He remembered the scene in the hospital. When Silver Bell was first shown the baby with the cleft lip, she burst out shrieking: "No, no, no!" Donald had to scream at her to shut up. The doctor and nurses all grimaced in embarrassment. They reassured her that she was young and would soon conceive another perfect child.

Still, it was difficult to watch the wet nurse feed baby Jenny. The large gap on her lips leaked milk, and everything was a mess after

each feeding. Donald persuaded Silver Bell to place the child with
Miss Tyler and her missionary ladies. Life would be peaceful in
Syracuse. Jenny would be able to have the best medical care when
she was old enough for surgery to repair her lips. They had heard
that such procedures were available in New York. They wouldn't
tell the family in Shanghai because the family would then offer to
take the baby instead. It would be unthinkable for the older
generation to agree to leave a child with foreigners. They also
wouldn't understand the fierce competition for social status in
Hong Kong. There were so many people down on their luck; they
would have no sympathy for an unsightly child. People shunned
those with bad luck, as if any association would rub off on them.
Silver Bell wept bitterly, but she was happy to visit Syracuse and
Miss Tyler again. There, after seeing how the baby was loved and
welcomed by the spinster missionary ladies, she accepted the
situation and swore Miss Tyler to secrecy — until such time as they
would be in a better position to handle things. Silver Bell started
her real estate business in Hong Kong and her life of social promi-
nence. People flocked to her glamorous parties.

Donald did not tell his in-laws that since the birth of the child,
Silver Bell had turned into an ill-tempered scold. Any little annoy-
ance would set her off. "You made me go for an abortion!" She
would hurl perfume bottles or whatever object she had on hand.
"Why did I listen to you and take those pills?"

Donald would hang his head and light another cigarette. He
thought Silver Bell's family might also blame him for turning her into
a shrew. If angry words tumbled out of Golden Bell, how would he
maintain his standing in Yung's eyes? Without his wife's connection
to the Yungs, could he continue to work in Hong Kong?

"Silver Bell has thrown her heart and soul into her real estate
business. She is making a lot of money," he said. He had repeatedly
advised his wife to write only about the positive aspects of their life,

so as not to burden the family in Shanghai. Brook ma-ma noticed that Donald never expressed any regret. She took a deep breath. "Both you and Silver Bell are young. You will have many more children," she said.

An uneasy quiet descended around the dinner table. Purple Jade looked from face to face. She snapped at Coral Bell: "Silver Bell, stop sucking your thumb!" Yung sighed and left the table. Golden Bell ordered tea to be served in the living room. No one mentioned Silver Bell's misfortune again.

On the train ride back to Hong Kong, Donald had a sense of foreboding. Somehow the Spartan life in Shanghai felt unseemly, but what would happen next? Silver Bell missed her family, but he knew he must not allow her to visit Shanghai. He was afraid she might blurt out everything if she were in the bosom of her family. He had finally become his own boss in Hong Kong and couldn't let his wife undermine his new status. He would have to tell her that he had visited Shanghai and that he was protecting her from the emotional demands of this trip.

A year elapsed under Communist rule. The family in Shanghai concentrated on operating the factories and ignored signs of coming upheavals. On June 25, 1950, the Shanghai press declared that South Korea had invaded North Korea. When the U.S. Seventh Fleet began patrolling the Taiwan Straits, the papers became saturated with angry denunciations of Western imperialism and all the humiliations China had suffered earlier in the century. People were urged to volunteer for the army and help North Korea maintain its territorial integrity. There were endless reminders that China needed North Korea as a buffer zone against foreign invasion.

Donald went to Shanghai again to coax the Yungs to leave. "All Western businessmen and religious people have been ordered to leave China. Your education and mode of life will surely come under attack. They are hunting spies and foreign agents!"

"Everyone here knows the best park in Shanghai once posted a sign: NO DOGS OR CHINESE ALLOWED," Golden Bell retorted. "In spite of my education, I can still recognize American arrogance. What business is it of MacArthur to threaten us with an invasion? Uniting with Taiwan is an internal Chinese issue!"

"Don't you see?" Donald banged the table in frustration. "China now considers America the most barbarous imperialist! Your education . . ."

Golden Bell did not let him finish. "Both Yung and I have joined mass rallies to condemn the United States. Americans are rebuilding Japan! They want to invade us like in the old days!"

"But . . . but you are acting against your own interests! America considers China a Soviet satellite," Donald sputtered, hoarse from bellowing. "You have hardly become used to calling the streets by their new Chinese names! You still refer to them as Avenue Joffre, Bubbling Well Road, Seymour Road —"

"Yes, we haven't been progressive, and we must change. But don't you remember why the streets in Shanghai were given foreign names in the first place?" Golden Bell rejoined heatedly. "Don't you know your Chinese history?"

Purple Jade entered the fray; her voice shrill, she blurted out, "Yes, yes, yes . . . England and France invaded China in 1860 and burned down the emperor's Round Bright Garden. Then eight foreign nations came into Beijing in 1900, raping and looting even the Forbidden City." Purple Jade was trembling. In her mind's eye, her home was burning.

Brook ma-ma wiped the sweat off her mistress's forehead, massaging her shoulders to calm her down. The family had become so accustomed to Purple Jade's interjections that they hadn't even noticed her agitation.

"We had to sign one unfair treaty after another!" Golden Bell jabbed one hand in the air to emphasize her point. "Avenue Joffre and the Bund are streets of shame — Chinese territories held as concessions. So much hard work and Chinese profits had gone to pay huge indemnities! The foreigners collected our import and export taxes. No wonder China was so poor!" She sat down exhausted, ignoring Donald's slumping figure. He had put his hands over his ears.

"You are quoting Communist propaganda." Donald sighed. "You've been misled."

"My parents taught me Chinese history. The Westerners are ignorant ingrates!" Golden Bell raised her voice. She was almost shouting. "Don't you remember that China and the West were allies throughout the two world wars? Even after the Bataan Death March and losing so many young lives to the Japanese, America is rebuilding these fanatics and joining forces with them to create a new colonialism!"

"All right, all right." Donald pushed out his palms to prevent further outbursts. "That history was a traumatic blow to our deep-seated cultural pride and dignity, but the new Korean situation is completely different! Have you read anything in the Western press lately?"

Yung's body stiffened. "No, we don't get Western magazines anymore. The factory also stopped doing business with South Carolina."

"Josie, Katie, and I all became engrossed in our families. We have only exchanged Christmas cards," Golden Bell said. "It is so hard to describe our totally different life here."

"Give me your contact information in South Carolina. I'll follow through for the Yung factory in Hong Kong," Donald said. "I can also send along any communications you need to your American friends, but be careful. Use only the most trusted courier for the letters."

"Yes, that'll be a good strategy," Yung said. "You know the Americans are imposing an embargo. Donald, what is it that you've heard in Hong Kong that makes you think China is wrong?"

"The Communists are paranoid! MacArthur took his troops to the edge of the Yalu River, but they did not breach Chinese territories as you have been told. There is much talk in the free press that President Truman may dismiss MacArthur for threatening to invade China."

"So, you do agree that China is under threat?" Yung asked.

"Yes, the Americans are stupid to go into war in a place where they don't understand its history, culture, or politics. But China's response is hysterical, and the government has whipped up the population — including you — into frenzy. You are not safe living in this steaming cauldron."

Golden Bell was about to speak when Yung went over to hug her. "Hush, hush, you've been too agitated by the propaganda. Try to remember this bright spot in our history: After the Boxers killed missionaries and eight nations invaded us, we had to pay huge indemnities. All the Western nations emptied our treasury, but America alone, urged by women's groups at home, lobbied Congress to return the money. Americans established the Boxer Rebellion Indemnity Scholarship Program on the gardens of the Qing Dynasty in Beijing. This became our famous Tsinghua University. America is not like the other European nations. The Chinese cannot tell one foreigner from the other, just like our experience in America when our friends couldn't tell the Japanese and Chinese apart. Donald is right. There is too much anti-American sentiment out here."

Golden Bell listened with tears in her eyes. She lowered her head, shaking in confusion and mumbled: "Sorry, have I been so misled? Have I lost my common sense?"

Yung rubbed her back and kissed her forehead. "There, there . . . we're in such difficult times. It's best if we never use any English outside the house. Stop attending church; be prudent. Warn Coral Bell so she doesn't show off her English and get into trouble at school."

"You should really come to Hong Kong." Donald renewed his smoking and pacing. "With the American embargo in force, you won't be able to export anything anyway. Plus, your business in Hong Kong will be a liability for you here with the Communists."

"We cannot possibly leave Shanghai now and abandon our factories. The authorities tell us our country needs us." Yung nodded toward his wife. "Golden Bell and I are committed to our homeland. Besides, we're expecting another child."

Donald leaned forward to snuff out his cigarette, but his eyes were wide with disbelief. "Congratulations on the child. But your patriotism is both alarming and naive. If you must stay, at least strip your house down to the bare necessities, and never have contact with any foreigners! We should also stop open communications. Use only the most trusted couriers for our letters."

"I've been trying to figure out some means of safeguarding our capital for little An-an and the coming baby." Yung stood behind his wife, laying both hands on her shoulders. "I think it's best if you and Silver Bell claim ownership of our factories in Hong Kong and deposit our profits into a foreign account for our children."

"Thank you for your generous offer. Yes, it is prudent to stage an open break and pretend that Silver Bell and I stole your company. But you can be sure that most of the profits will be saved for your children in America. Silver Bell is in constant contact with Miss Tyler." Donald returned to Hong Kong with a sense of vindication. Not only had he tried to avert the worst disaster for the family, he was now poised to fulfill his lifelong dream of owning his own company.

Golden Bell's Journal

June 30, 1950

CAN WE TRUST Donald — a man without a Chinese name? Though Silver Bell married him and loves him, my heart flutters and whispers my suspicions and sometimes my disgust. He never mentions his family. When we ask, he always changes the topic. After all the years of war, the innumerable stories of death and loss made us weary and so we didn't press him. We can now assume his family has been decimated. But why won't he talk about it, even to Silver Bell? He knows how the Huang household has been reduced to dependence on Yung for its survival. Surely we would understand his pain. Why won't he share it?

Yung trusts Donald. They are natural friends. After all, they both speak American English without much of an accent; they both went to school there for many years. There is an invisible bond between those of us who have lived in the States. When I was training An-an to use a spoon, Brook ma-ma was shocked. Here, a servant feeds privileged children even if the child is five or six years old and already running around. I said, "It's important for An-an to be independent." Brook ma-ma looked at me and pinched her lips. "You are thinking like a foreigner! With us, children are the center of a family. They are always served!"

This mix of "Chinese/foreign" mind-set is the cement that now binds Yung and I in our work and family life. But Yung and Donald seem to share a deeper friendship. Before the Communists came, they were drinking buddies and fellow philanderers. Whenever I questioned Yung, he reminded me that little An-an and I were at the top of his Gratitude and Wish Lists. He said our happiness was his first priority. He was also solicitous of my mother's comfort, so I'd decided not to notice what he did with Donald outside of work. Nothing must be allowed to disturb the harmony in our home. With the Communists in town and Yung's total immersion in his work, my whole self is caught up in the sweet warmth of our marriage. Under the changing political climate, it is a comfort to have Yung's bare foot or arm or shoulder within reach at night. I have been aware of the altered state of our romance. After the pains of childbirth, sex is no longer intoxicating. Yet I'm sure our attachment has deepened. It is pure happiness to just listen to him snore softly or breathe quietly beside me.

Yung's assurance that Donald is highly intelligent and responsible dispels my unease about surrendering part of our company to him and my sister. My fears about their marriage have diminished now that the Communists are in power. For the sake of our children, Donald and Silver Bell must build a second base for us in Hong Kong. I will write my sister about that tomorrow.

History and our ancient culture have shaped Yung's personality and mine. Most Chinese can accept Mao as their new emperor, but what is this "communism" all about? It was rumored that Mao and other Chinese leaders had been working toward a better relations with America until MacArthur came to South Korea. Was this information reliable? Are the Americans driving us into Soviet arms? Are we becoming totally dependent on Soviet technical know-how as well as their military, political, and economic support? Donald's visits are most disturbing. He wants us to move to Hong Kong. But I am not sure. The British are snobbish and rigid in their class system, unlike the Americans. Silver Bell said that the British residents in Hong Kong lead separate lives, and just about the only Chinese they interact with are business contacts and servants. That's not so different from the expatriate communities in Shanghai in the old days, but the Shanghai groups were more international. They included prominent families like ours.

Donald said America fears China and imagines it a Communist threat — an extension of Soviet Russia, an enemy. Communism is a Western philosophy, just like democracy and fascism. What I wonder is, why are the Americans so ignorant of Chinese history? When Dr. Sun Yat-San started China's first republic, Western democracies refused to help. Only the Soviets offered assistance. The Communists became our revolutionary heroes. Even Chiang Kai-shek sent his son to Russia to be trained as a Communist. Mrs. Sun (Soong Chin-Ling) is now a vice president of the People's Republic of China. Chiang Kai-Shek bought off the warlords and never united the country. He also depended on the triads and underworld gangs for power. We see his campaigns against the Communists as pure power struggles. He went against the Confucian teaching of building harmony in society.

I turn to Chinese history to help me understand our present situation. It is well recorded that when the government becomes corrupt and life turns oppressive, the peasants rise up in revolt and hand the Mandate of Heaven to a vigorous new emperor. Most Chinese see communism as just another "ism" from the West. After all the years of depredation from the West, we want a strong China. We see communism as a way to escape the corrupt Nationalist government. It is like a change of dynasties. But the West is isolating us. What choice do we have when the Soviets are the only ones willing to help us modernize? Are we to be drawn into a proxy fight between democracy and communism — two Western ideologies?

Am I equivocating or deluding myself?

History, like images of Father's ghost, reminds me of who I am and why it is so important for us to rebuild China. Yung and I loved America, and would have returned there if we could. But our family obligations, our duties to all the people who depend upon us for a living, make us hostages to our cultural pride and responsibilities.

My experience with the Americans shows me they are open and warmhearted. Have they also been fooled by propaganda? How can a country of immigrants obstruct China's membership in the United Nations? How can they exclude almost a billion people from the family of nations? They want to isolate us. They threaten us by building up Japan, once our common enemy. How can they think China is a Soviet satellite? We've had long territorial conflicts with Soviet Russia. When I was a child, the map of China looked like a leaf. After the Soviets forced us to recognize Outer Mongolia's independence, the leaf looked as if a silkworm had taken a big bite out of its upper edges. Most Chinese know that Vladivostok was once called Haishenwei! Anyway, it seems the Americans do not feel the Chinese-Soviet alliance can be temporary.

I wish more Americans were like Josie and Katie. They took the time to study Chinese history and came to understand me. They thought I imagined Father's ghostly visit because I missed home and had a mental breakdown. History is China's hovering phantom. Will the Americans try to understand China only after we suffer more devastation clinging to our lingering ghosts?

When I find myself questioning my Chinese sentiments, I need to remind myself that China suffered a century of foreign depredation. At first, everyone wanted to trade with us because they wanted our silk, bronze, pottery, tea, and other fineries. The antediluvian Chin emperor was arrogant and would trade Chinese goods only for silver, until the British East India Company cultivated opium and shipped it to China despite imperial objections. China went to war over this and lost. Hong Kong became a British colony, and other Western countries acquired concessions in our port cities, where they obliterated Chinese sovereignty. The gunboats in the harbor and foreign soldiers on the streets protected the denizens of these foreign concessions. In 1937, some wealthy Chinese and we, the Huang family, moved to the French Concession to escape the advancing Japanese invasion.

America shared in the British trade advantages. Such blue-blooded American families as the Delanos became fabulously rich through their opium trade. Still, I have warm feelings for America, especially its carefree, generous people. I keep reminding myself that America never asked for territorial concessions. The humiliation of our country was complete once the League of Nations gave the German Concession in our Shandong Province to Japan after World War I. Then the Japanese annexed yet more of our northern territories. They cultivated poppies on almost all the arable land, and inundated China with so much cheap opium that even the poorest coolies could afford a smoke. Before World War II, Shanghai was known as the "whore of the Orient." My parents and most book-fragrant Chinese felt outraged when they realized the implications. But as a teenager, I was intrigued. I felt modern and even proud that celebrities like Mary Pickford, Noel Coward, George Bernard Shaw, Wallis Simpson, and so many others came here for the opium, free-flowing liquor, and nightclubs that offered song, dance, and prostitution until noon the next day. After World War II, opium was no longer so plentiful, but those with means could still have it in the best hotels. I often wonder if Japan would have dared invade America if the world had not awarded northeast

163

China to them. Being a small country, it would not have had sufficient resources and slave labor to wage war. When the Japanese bombed Shanghai in 1932, they were careful to aim their firepower at the densely populated Chinese areas. The French Concession and the International Settlement (British) were never under threat. The foreigners came out of their clubs in their fancy gowns to watch the "fireworks" as if these grim spectacles were fashionable entertainments. Although I saw poverty and desperate people around me, my mind was divorced from their suffering. Maybe there were just too many of them. Like privileged people everywhere, I had adopted a common tactic — blocking emotional reactions to extreme poverty. Our daily encounters with the poor had steeled our hearts.

These historical humiliations form the foul breath that infuses our Chinese psyche. Most of us saw China as an overripe fruit that was rotting while the world came to uproot the whole tree. Perhaps a deeper part of me still views the foreign dominance in Shanghai as a humiliation. Yet at the time, we had different priorities. Anyone with means sought to live in the international areas to escape arbitrary taxation from local warlords, the old rigid social structure, and random violence. After I returned to Shanghai and married Yung, we had a separate existence from the larger Chinese society due to our wealth. We lived more like the foreign expatriates, served by a platoon of servants. We employed a nanny, two chauffeurs, a cook, a gardener, and two housemaids. Of course, we did not need all this help, but we needed to save "face." We went to foreign clubs, danced in modern hotels, and wore tuxedos and Chinese and Western gowns to parties. None of us could contemplate being excluded from our "beau monde" — our fancy parties and charity balls. What an idea —being left out of the most glamorous social scenes in China!

Yung often chides me for my naiveté. As well he should. I usually believe what I read, and I know I've bought into my parents' cultural hubris. I wonder if, like the calligraphic flourishes of their ancient art, I am holding an overly romantic view of Confucian peace and gentility. Growing up in bucolic Hangzhou, I was well protected. Syracuse was also a sheltered experience. In spite of my family's plight — abandoning our home in Hangzhou, moving to Shanghai, Hong Kong, and now back to Shanghai — I have been shielded from the unpleasant reality of struggle. The Communists have changed all that. Today, Shanghai is a bleak Chinese city. Instead of exhibiting conspicuous consumption, we dress in somber colors; we have dismissed all our servants, except for Lo-ma, little An-an's nanny, and a cook. And I myself feel torn. A part of me celebrates the vindication of this new Chinese identity.

After we were married, Yung and I conversed mostly in English, to rekindle our intimacy. Ever since little An-an was born, we spoke English to him at home, to acclimate him to that different tongue. Yet Mother's presence, and an ancient portion of my soul, would not let me fully forsake my cultural pride. The gentle Confucian scholar with his concentration on calligraphy, quiet learning, and cultivation of virtue remains my ideal. Now and always, my foremost attachments are to my family. Yung and my adopted Western values do not sit easily alongside our native pride. We had expected China and the United States would be natural allies. America had always been good to us. When the other nations collected their huge indemnity payments from the Boxer War, America used its share to found our Tsinghua University. After the second World War, the U.S. had taken pains to assure us that no foreign country would invade us again, going as far as to draw explicit eleven dotted lines in the South China Sea. The Americans even warned the Philippines against encroaching there because the charter from Spain did not include this right when U.S. acquired the territories. Furthermore, both countries embraced capitalism. The pride of owning a family business had been a Chinese tradition since ancient times. Most Chinese are not ideological. We can't tell one "ism" from another. Certainly, Mother and Brook ma-ma cannot. They thought we were going into a new "communist Dynasty." So far, the Communists have not denounced us for being Capitalists. We own so many productive factories that clothe our people. Surely the government will not destroy what is essential to our national survival? Perhaps we do have too many investments in Shanghai, but how can we just walk away from them? Are we tied down here by our comforts? Am I dismissing Donald's fear that the Korean conflict will endanger our family because I am so taken by slogans? Yung was prudent to sign over the ownership of our factories in Hong Kong to Donald and Silver Bell. Now my sister and her husband are no longer totally dispossessed, but I still worry. China has clutched the Yungs to its Communist bosom.

I am trying to become a chameleon! We've tried to blend into the new Communist landscape. Would that people could accept our efforts, and overlook our Western inclinations? Will they ever grant us Party membership? I feel we have been wedged between these two insurmountable Eastern and Western boulders!

I started this journal while attending the French Convent School in Hong Kong, where English was preeminent and Chinese and French were taught as second languages. My journal was first written in a mix of Chinese and English. In America, I wrote in English. Upon my return, I reverted to Chinese. The languages reflected my life's journey. People used to ask me whether I think in English or Chinese. Much of my formal education has been in English, and I certainly don't have the Chinese vocabulary for ideas and objects that are unfamiliar in China. I can describe a train that goes underground, but there is no Chinese term for a subway — Now, I have switched to writing in English again. Most people cannot read or understand it here. Given the present political situation, it is the safer choice.

I have tried to fill my journal with swatches of observations, worries, memories, and sometimes records of actual scenes. Yesterday, I saw myself setting the table with Yung in the Methodists' Mission house in New York City. I want to hold those dishes and chopsticks to my breast forever.

My pregnancy is going well. Dr. Chen, who delivered An-an, will again be attending. At least this important event will be normal.

I can't face Mother's blank mind, Brook ma-ma continues to speak of her in an awed whisper. She and Mother have a true marriage of mutual respect and devotion.

Like a good Confucian, Mother doesn't speculate about an afterlife. She accepts the dictates of fate. I find it easier to be a Christian. I pray to the Christian God, who directs human affairs, and I ask for guidance. I plunge head-on into life's challenges. Still, my doubts and worries multiply. Silver Bell told me how impressed Pastor Cummins was when Coral Bell recited that passage from Genesis before she was baptized. Coral Bell is blessed by an unwavering belief. I pray constantly — out of habit? Need? Desperation? It is a great comfort to believe in a God who loves and cares.

In America, my Jewish friend Marcia once said that life should be enjoyed and that one's purpose on earth is to bring love and happiness to one's community and family. That is very close to the Confucian ideal of imparting harmony and peace to civil society through respect, consideration, and generosity to people in their separate stations. Mother has brought love and happiness to others through her virtuous living, but she lacks the detachment and practicality of, say, a simple typist. She is helplessly adrift in the cruel torrents of Chinese history. Am I also going down the same path?

I was named Golden Bell, the first-born golden child. My parents spared no expense in teaching me Chinese classics and later brought in Miss Tyler to prepare me for the modern world. Encircled by the soft purl of our language, and charmed by my parents' quiet gentility, I was inculcated with enormous cultural pride. The Chinese have turned the dirt of the earth into fine porcelain, the cocoon of a destructive worm into rich silk; they were the first to use gunpowder to paint the night sky in breathtaking colors. To me, my parents personified China in all its creativity. Mother, in particular, is a living symbol of China. Mother's China, the Middle Kingdom, the center of the civilized world, has now unsettled us with her chaos. Burdened by pride of culture, by history, and by resources yet undeveloped, she drives her dispossessed children away but clutches the rest of us more tightly to her offended breast to restore her pride and rightful place in the family of man.

Mother suffered the most devastating effects of the harsh Japanese occupation. I don't know the Chinese terms for "psyche" or "psychology," but I find it difficult to live with Mother's senile dementia. I want to scream and plead for her old self to return. But I must hold my confrontational self under control at all times when I'm boiling inside with fury and sometimes experience inconsolable despair.

Maybe fatalism is the only sane strategy. Indeed, Brook ma-ma has accepted her fate. She has been Mother's hands and feet, and now she is truly Mother's alter ego. They live as if they are one person. How could anyone have foreseen that by giving her husband a concubine, my mother would guarantee her longevity and even acquire a new dignity?

Mother gives me an ache that never subsides. I feel queasy whenever I see her blank face. I have a sinking feeling whenever my mother greets me as though I were a stranger. Have I adopted Mother's cultural pride as a way of trying to win back her recognition? Still, Mother's wandering mind always ignites my aching memories. Silver Bell and I need only glance at our gray silk scarves to feel the pain and sweetness in remembering.

The only time I feel comforted is when I place An-an on to her lap, she almost always embraces him and starts to rock and recite her poems. An-an prefers to take naps in her bosom rather than in his bed, and I can feel peace and contentment settle into my every pore.

Since the arrival of Western values, Mother's world has been turned upside down. Consider the Soong family: The patriarch was a stowaway and therefore an illegal immigrant in the United States. The missionaries educated him. He returned to Shanghai as a Bible salesman — not a respected profession in the old culture. Yet his children attended missionary schools and became proficient in English. His son was the treasurer and defense minister of the Nationalist government. His daughters became Mrs. Sun Yet-sen, Mrs. Chiang Kai-shek, and the eldest married a direct descendant of Confucius. No one seemed to have noticed the irony in rewarding the Christian, Westernized scion with honor and wealth while claiming heritage from the founder of our Chinese culture. I believe my parents sent me to study in America because of the Soong family's example.

Did the Nationalist leaders work for China, or were they simply corrupt manipulators who used Western values to enhance their family's prestige and wealth? Will the new "Communist Emperor" turn corrupt and be equally destructive? I hope not.

Dear God, how much more suffering must the Chinese people endure before they receive your mercy?

America has a free press, but the truth eludes them. They don't see how the Korean menace is stoking China's deepest fears. America has invaded North Korea — practically our backyard — and is threatening to enter China. They are building up Japan. Will the Europeans again ask for territorial concessions and open ports, so that corporations like the East India Company and Japanese interests can flood us with opium? The democratic West and China were allies through two world wars, yet today, we have become "the Yellow Peril, the Communist hegemony, the Enemy." All the while, China's greatest fear is further humiliation and more invasions from Japan and the West.

The outlines of this new Communist dynasty are still blurry. We must align with its cause. This is our only recourse.

Try as one might, it is impossible not to be afraid.

Peace, Under Memory's Shade

Shanghai, 1951

ON A DAY that seemed more or less like any other, a committee from the workers' union came to inspect the apartment where Purple Jade lived with Brook ma-ma and Coral Bell. "The workers need more living space," they explained at the door.

Brook ma-ma, quaking in fear, ushered the group of one man and two women into the living room. "Please introduce yourselves to my tai-tai," she said.

"People call me Ba Hu." The man raked his hand through his hair, uncertain how he should behave. Would his co-workers report him if he was too gruff or too polite? "This is Ah Yee and Shao Lee." He pointed to the two women. Shao Lee looked like a teenager, but Ah Yee seemed older.

"Welcome, welcome." Purple Jade smiled. "Orchid, please serve tea and see if the kitchen would send us some dim sum."

The workers looked surprised. They had expected resistance. Brook ma-ma whispered that there were no servants and that Purple Jade's mind dwelled in the Hangzhou of many years past.

171

"You called her your mistress," Shao Lee said. "But you are not a servant?" Brook ma-ma placed her finger over her mouth and excused herself to prepare tea. She thought it best to explain their relationship later.

"Please be seated." Purple Jade smiled most graciously. "Loh Woo, did you bring the books for me to examine?" She mistook Ba Hu for her old accountant.

The workers looked at each other and shrugged. They sat as directed, confused by the quiet dignity of the congenial old woman. It was dusk, and now, after a day's work, they waited for the tea.

"Loh Woo, how are your wife and daughter Pearl?" Purple Jade, dressed in a blue brocade gown and sitting tall on a dais-like rosewood chair, commanded attention. She rested her bound feet on a settee.

Ba Hu nodded and smiled, but Shao Lee giggled. Ah Yee frowned and tugged on her companion to stop. "That's how the ladies used to behave," she said, gawking at Purple Jade.

"Oh, you must be Pearl!" Purple Jade strained to look at the giggling girl in the fading light. "Forgive me. My mind is often cloudy these days. It is an honor to have young people visit. Come, I must give you a gift." She rummaged through her inner pockets and produced a perfectly pressed and folded silk handkerchief.

Both women rose to look.

"Here, I embroidered this some years ago when my eyes were sharp. You see the bumpy, rice-like stitches? These are the insects swarming over the little rose!"

The workers had seldom seen fine embroidered silk. Shao Lee quickly grabbed the handkerchief. "Thank you!" she said and walked toward the window for a closer look.

Purple Jade followed the young woman to the window. She looked out at the rising fog and began mumbling a few lines about some mists in the garden. Halfway through, her mind drifted back to her past.

172

Her body swayed with the lulling motion of the rowboat; her eyes glistened as she saw the glimmering river and the layers of interconnected roof lines of her house drawing ever closer, like the flight of winged birds in formation. The gently rising courts of her house, its walls, gardens, and roofs seemed to have grown like appendages in a landscape of towering bamboo groves, protruding rock boulders, hovering willows, and the quiet flowing river.

Brook ma-ma returned with the tea service. She nudged Purple Jade, trying to wake her from her reverie.

After a sip of tea, Purple Jade resumed her gracious behavior. "Come, let me show you our gardens," she said. She forgot to allow the guests sufficient time to drink tea. The group decided to follow her. After all, they were there to examine the apartment.

Purple Jade wandered from room to room. "The suites of the house are interconnected and surround a series of landscaped courtyards."

She could feel the golden sunlight casting crisp shadows on the roof and trees, visible from every room.

"See the budding cherry tree?" she asked. "It will be a pink cloud in another month."

Ba Hu took out a notebook and began to take an inventory of the rooms and furniture as he followed Purple Jade. Brook ma-ma tagged behind, explaining in a murmur that the house in Hangzhou had been burned during the Japanese invasion and their farm properties had since been divided up. They now lived as the dependents of the Yung family.

"Be careful," said Purple Jade as she spread out her arms, holding back the visitors. "Here is a tall step leading up to the bridge." She held on to the back of a chair and gingerly mounted an imaginary step, refusing Brook ma-ma's arm. "No, I don't need any help! Orchid, you know how I love to ramble through these marble walks leading to the open pavilions." She turned to the visitors. "I often come here to read, paint, and view the terraces of bamboo groves, flowering fruit trees, and swaying willows. Look" — she pointed to the dining room table — "the lotus flowers are in bloom!" She waved Brook ma-ma away. "Orchid, tell the gardener to dig up some lotus roots near the south end of the pond. We must stuff them with sweet rice and simmer them with rock candies and dried jasmine flowers. Oh, such fragrance!" She swept her arm in an imperial arch.

Brook ma-ma didn't answer. She bowed and trailed behind the group again. Ah Yee turned to her, asking, "Are you a servant?"

"I was Mrs. Huang's personal maid." Brook ma-ma blushed.

"You mean you were a slave girl?"

"Well . . . not exactly."

"Did your parents sell you to her?"

"I was so young, I truly cannot remember. My mistress has been my teacher, my mentor, my protector, and my kind patron."

"So you never married and had a family of your own?"

"This is my family!" She explained how she had become a concubine because she was presented to Mr. Huang as a fiftieth-birthday present. "The Huangs had no sons, and my mistress is dear to me, like a mother." She stifled a sob.

"I can't understand this!" Ah Yee shook her head, placing one hand on her face while the other gently stroked her stomach. "You mean you enjoy being a concubine?"

"No, but I am able to stay near the person dearest to me — my mistress, my teacher, and now my sister-wife."

Suddenly Purple Jade began reciting the Tu Fu poem "Alone":

A hawk lingers in empty air.
White gulls drift along the river in a pair.

The hawk hovers in the wind with ease,
The gulls glide with the current in peace.

Morning dew warms the grass,
Revealing a spider web of brass.
Nature mirrors the affairs of man,
In which ten thousand sorrows span.

Brook ma-ma wiped a tear and murmured, "Yes, my tai-tai has often thought of us as the two white gulls." Everyone stopped to gawk at the old lady who was senile yet seemed to be commenting on her predicament. New edicts were arriving from the authorities every day, and turmoil roiled every segment of society, but they could not articulate the unease they shared.

Purple Jade saw Ah Yee's contorted expression. She hurried over. "What is your name? Are you pregnant? Are you having a headache?"

She held Ah Yee's hand and took her pulse. Her touch was firm and gentle. Somehow her actions conveyed authority and experience.

"Yes, I'm pregnant and I'm getting a headache," Ah Yee confessed, staring at Purple Jade in surprise. "How did you know?" She allowed Purple Jade to lead her to the sofa and promptly obeyed when asked to stick out her tongue.

The other workers tittered and rolled their eyes, muttering that Ah Yee had never told them her good news and now she had a headache. Purple Jade proceeded to massage Ah Yee's neck and head muscles, explaining the theory of chi and how it traveled through the meridians of the body. She directed Ah Yee to press firmly on the soft fleshy part between the thumb and the forefinger, saying, "This is called the *hegu*, the joining of the valleys."

Brook ma-ma explained that due to the master's anti-Japanese activities, the family had to move to Hong Kong. There, Purple

Jade served the poor boat-dwellers. "She was truly a people's doctor," she told them.

"You mean she didn't charge them money?" Ba Hu asked.

"Not a single fen." Brook smiled. "She was a Communist way before your time."

"So did you provide the family with a son?" Shao Lee asked with wide-eyed curiosity.

"No, no," Brook ma-ma stuttered. "My daughter, Coral Bell, is attending an anti-imperialist rally in school right now. She should be home soon."

"So you are still a slave girl to her?" Ba Hu pointed to Purple Jade.

"I have always been treated better than any personal maid could ever hope for," Brook ma-ma pronounced. "Look at my mistress's bound feet! She has been more oppressed than any of us." Her eyes reddened.

"Slavery is the worst form of oppression," Ba Hu said.

"She has been a mother to me," Brook ma-ma responded.

"Don't you see?" Ba Hu persisted. "She has used you. She is still using you!"

"She has given me dignity. I was a starving orphan. I owe her my life." Brook ma-ma deflected the workers' accusations in a blur of tears.

While Purple Jade massaged Ah Yee's hand, she launched into one of the ancient stories with which she used to regale Golden Bell and Silver Bell. "When the first emperor, Qin Shi-huang, was in the process of unifying China in the third century B.C., many talented scholar officials came from the neighboring states to serve the new powerful king. Some native-born Qin nobles became jealous and did not like the competition from the 'foreigners.' They convinced the emperor that these scholar-officials were spies and would foment revolt inside Qin. The emperor signed an edict to expel all the foreign officials.

"The list of expulsions included the prime minister, Li Si, who was originally from Southern Chu. Li Si wrote the emperor an eloquent memorandum, arguing that banishment due to a person's place of birth had nothing to do with his competence, honesty, or evidence of disloyalty. Instead, this blind ordinance would drive the talented officials to serve rulers of other states and thus harm Qin. That would be like *guo zu bu qian* [binding your feet in order to impede progress]." Purple Jade looked at her listeners meaningfully. "You see," she continued, "the Chinese originated everything. We became self-absorbed. We turned inward. The Japanese were not so proud. They adopted foreign technologies and grew strong."

The workers gasped. Chairman Mao had repeatedly demonized foreigners and exhorted the Chinese to rely on themselves. Mass propaganda about Chinese humiliations under foreign invasions was disseminated throughout the country to stir up patriotic fervor and incite protests. What Purple Jade was expounding could be considered treason.

Brook ma-ma threw up her arms in shock. Standing behind Purple Jade, she affected a helpless pose. Pointing to her mistress's bound feet, she said, "She has suffered so much under the Japanese and the old system . . ."

"Yes, yes, the Japanese are brutes," Purple Jade rejoined, massaging Ah Yee ever more vigorously. She seemed to have forgotten the point of her story.

The workers snickered.

"The old system oppressed women." Brook ma-ma pointed to Purple Jade's feet again. "We've been such long-suffering victims until Chairman Mao said, 'Women hold up half the world.'"

"My headache is gone!" Ah Yee exclaimed suddenly from the sofa, frowning and feeling out of place under Purple Jade's ministrations. She could see her comrades becoming disoriented in the

177

presence of this strange woman and her devoted, but politically shrewd, personal maid.

Ah Yee signaled her coworkers to end the visit. The government did not provide the medical services she would need, and she felt the old woman could be useful. She thanked Purple Jade with a slight curtsy, the way she thought the fine ladies of old might behave. The workers seemed to recognize Ah Yee as their leader, and they took their leave.

The next day, the Huang women learned that three other families from the Yung factory would move into their apartment, but they would be allowed to remain and retain the use of two rooms. Coral Bell would sleep on the sofa in the living room, where Purple Jade would practice her medicine in the daytime.

Ah Yee visited from time to time. She listened to Purple Jade's poetry recitations and ancient stories, and enjoyed her massages. Brook ma-ma assisted with her herbal lore. Purple Jade often complained that she had no acupuncture needles, but she massaged the proper acupressure points and sometimes was able to relieve Ah Yee's discomfort.

Ah Yee finally brought her some needles, and Purple Jade ministered to her throughout her pregnancy and confinement. Later, Ah Yee would come with a steady stream of workers from the factory. They all benefited from Purple Jade's services. However, they would never admit that they also liked her old stories and her poetry. The party line no longer sanctioned anything from the old culture.

Thus it was that the Communists helped Purple Jade prolong her usefulness in the fifth decade of her life. Brook ma-ma's knowledge of Chinese medicine also grew, even though she was nearing forty. She often performed massage and acupuncture under her tai-tai's supervision. She was particularly gratified that her tai-tai seemed completely lucid sometimes when she diagnosed ailments.

Purple Jade had a particular moment of lucidity when she was told she had a new granddaughter, Yung Li-li. She happily prescribed herbs to restore Golden Bell's health.

Still, their greatest fears materialized when the Korean War came. The government started hunting for spies.

Sticks and Stones

Shanghai, 1951

MR. ZHU, a Communist Party member and an education minister, had to fill his quota of catching a certain number of spies to maintain his standing. He spoke to the sixth-grade class.

His tone was strident. "Since the beginning of this century, the foreigners took land from us, forced us to buy opium, and encouraged us to become degenerates. Now they have overrun our good neighbor, North Korea. They are threatening our country's sovereignty again."

His voice softened, now warm and reassuring. "You are the future hope of this country. You can help build a strong and independent China. But you must pass the 'true tests' to become loyal Chinese. You must denounce the people who lead lives of selfish pleasure! Those who neglect their families, who indulge in wine, women, and song, who feed upon the misery of poor workers." He wiped his mouth. "You may know these people as your uncles, your neighbors, or even as your fathers and mothers. But if they are corrupt, you must realize that they are bringing misery upon you and our country. Be brave: Name them now! Turn them in and you will be honored as true revolutionary heroes, true children of Chairman Mao." He raised his hands in a wide sweep to embrace the whole room, smiling at the children.

Silence reigned.

"You will save your parents and your relatives by naming them. They will be dealt with very harshly if we uncover the truth about them later!"

More silence.

"Let us repeat Chairman Mao's teaching: It is our duty to help our comrades!" he shouted, waving his arms as if conducting a chorus.

The children repeated the slogan, muttering it under their breath.

"Louder!"

The children raised their voices.

"Even louder!"

The children started to shout, their faces turning red with excitement.

"Watch your parents and neighbors closely and report any suspicious activities. There are many capitalist spies among us. You are the hope of our future! I know you will all pass the true test!" He smiled triumphantly. His hands chopped the air to emphasize his point. "The security of the country rests on your shoulders!"

One boy in the back began to sniffle. Mr. Zhu ran to him immediately, exclaiming, "Have you some information? Do you want to denounce an imperialist relative?"

The boy hung his head and cried in earnest.

"Ugh! He wet his pants!" The girl next to him pointed to the puddle on the floor. Others giggled.

Mr. Zhu sent the boy to the principal's office, warning him, "I'll talk to you later."

He returned to the class, fanning his hand in front of his nose. "He's such a baby!" He laughed. Some children laughed with him, others snickered. "That boy is a coward. But you have nothing to worry about. You are all young heroes — Chairman Mao's special revolutionary force." He gestured again with his arms to embrace the whole class.

He turned to open a cardboard box and pulled out red scarves. "These scarves represent the red blood of our heroes who died to defend us from the foreigners. Here, pass them out and tie them around your necks." He helped one child after the other. "Yes, yes, you must all help each other."

The children chattered and giggled as they straightened their shirts and donned the red scarves. Mr. Zhu rubbed his hands together. "Now, don't you look smart? Think of it! You are all glorious members of the Young Communist League." He led the children in applause.

Everyone smiled.

"Some of you will soon become leaders of the League. Could it be you, or you, or you?" He pointed to the children at random. "The leader is always the bravest. He or she must turn in his or her corrupt relatives. The smartest boy or girl will be honored and may be invited to Beijing and given a seat at a banquet with our new Sun, Chairman Mao."

The children shifted in their seats at the lofty suggestion.

"As I said, you have witnessed cruel and corrupt capitalist behavior. Sooner or later, people will find out. You will be doing yourselves and your families a big favor by denouncing them. Remember, you'll be given great honor."

Several hands shot up.

"I'll denounce my father!" Coral Bell was surprised to hear White Lily's voice.

"Wonderful, wonderful!" Mr. Zhu nodded, directing White Lily to stand up. "Is he a spy for the Americans?"

"I don't know," White Lily mumbled, twisting a corner of her shirt, uncomfortable now with the attention. "He has another woman and kept us — my mother and me — in Chungking for a long time after the war."

"How old are you?"

"Eleven."

"What is your father's name?"

"Lee Tar-see."

"Have you seen him speak with foreigners?"

"No."

"All you children must act as the eyes and ears of the Party. If any of you see or hear your parents speaking English or contacting foreigners, you must report them! You will then become model young Red Guards with high honor. Remember, you may even be awarded a trip to Beijing to see Chairman Mao!"

Mr. Zhu turned to a boy sitting behind Coral Bell. "Yes? Do you also want to denounce your father?"

"No," the boy answered. He pointed to Coral Bell accusingly. "She speaks English!"

Coral Bell turned crimson. She lowered her head in a tremor of confusion and fear. Brook ma-ma had constantly reminded her not to be a show-off. Before the Korean War her English teacher had openly admired Coral Bell's diction and had used every opportunity to practice English conversation with her. Everyone knew she was the teacher's pride and joy.

"Oh, yes?" Mr. Zhu looked at Coral Bell in surprise. "Is one of your parents a foreigner?" He took note of Coral Bell's big round eyes and unusually fair skin.

"No," Coral Bell answered, biting her lips. "My father is dead." She twirled a tuft of hair on her forehead.

"So who taught you English?"

"My sister."

"How did she learn English?"

"She went to school in America."

"Are you going to denounce her?"

"No. She has moved to Hong Kong." She popped her thumb into her mouth.

"Ah, a pity!" Mr. Zhu looked crestfallen. "Your family must have been class enemies of the people!"

"I . . . sh-sh . . . don't know." Coral Bell made hissing sounds around her thumb; tears rolled down her cheeks.

"I'll get your name and address later." He didn't want to pressure a nervous child who could be useful to him later. He faced the class anew, urging them to be vigilant.

At recess, White Lily and Coral Bell huddled with the other children near the wire fence. They watched the high school boys in their schoolyard marching to military music.

"The boys are volunteering for the Korean War!" White Lily said.

"Are they going to get killed?" Coral Bell chewed furiously on her pigtail.

"I don't know. But I heard each of them has been given a gun and five bullets!"

"I guess they'll be able to defend themselves then. Why do the Americans hate the Chinese so much?" She turned to look at White Lily.

"I don't know. People say the Americans want Taiwan to rule China. They think Chairman Mao will make us too strong."

"I wonder why my sister taught me English?" Coral Bell asked.

"Maybe she wanted to show off?"

Coral Bell thought Silver Bell had introduced her to the most interesting experiences in her life. Aside from practicing English with her, she had paid a private tutor for special conversation lessons.

"Are you really going to denounce your father?" Coral Bell eyed her friend sideways.

"Why not?" White Lily answered nonchalantly. "Both my mother and I hate him. I never see him. He works for some foreign company. You heard Mr. Zhu say they'd find him out anyway. Maybe even my father will feel proud of me. I'm going to be honored and sent to Beijing to meet Chairman Mao!"

That evening, Coral Bell told Brook ma-ma all that had transpired in school. She wept and worried because now everyone knew she spoke English.

Brook ma-ma hugged and rocked her for a long time. She didn't remind her she was already eleven and shouldn't be sucking her thumb anymore.

"Now listen carefully," she whispered. "We have made a mistake in giving you English lessons. Go to Mr. Zhu and confess to being forced to learn English and to become a Christian. Tell him you are a concubine's daughter, and your M-ma is a cripple and has lost her mind because of the Japanese. She also was oppressed by the old system, which bound women's feet. Tell them she is now a Chinese doctor caring for workers in the Yung factories. Say you're glad Silver Bell is gone, and that you'll never have to learn anything from her again."

"But . . . but I love Silver Bell," Coral Bell protested in a blur of anguish and shame.

"We'll keep those feelings within the family."

"But you said there is no honor in lying!"

"Yes, but the greatest honor is to safeguard the family, so it is not a true lie. Now you must denounce Silver Bell to keep us safe."

"But is Silver Bell safe in Hong Kong?"

"Hong Kong is British. She will be safe."

"Because she speaks English?"

"Yes, maybe." Brook ma-ma clasped her daughter tighter. "Hear and listen: A nail that sticks out will surely be banged down. You must not stand out in anything again. Make sure you place all the blame on Silver Bell, but never mention Golden Bell. The Yungs are in a lot of trouble already."

The school hall buzzed with the whispers and whoosh of several hundred people fanning themselves. Tension rippled through the crowd. New banners and posters covered the walls, exhorting everyone to join the volunteer army and fight in Korea.

At Mr. Zhu's request, Coral Bell had come with Brook ma-ma. They found seats near a side aisle, by a wall plastered with anti-foreign slogans praising socialism and denouncing the imperialists. Coral Bell recognized many schoolmates and their parents. She did not greet them, afraid to draw attention to herself.

White Lily sat on a low platform in the front of the hall. She looked strangely disheveled and wore a rumpled cotton outfit. Coral Bell knew that her friend had spent many hours meeting with Mr. Zhu and other officials in preparation for her role in the "struggle session" against her father. Her face was flushed. Tear-filled, her eyes darted nervously about the room. When she noticed Coral Bell, her gaze did not linger; she acted as though they were strangers.

A group of men in Mao suits entered through a side door, Mr. Zhu among them. A man introduced as Mr. Wang stood up to speak. Looking pale and tense, he droned on about the incursion of foreign armies into China and how Chinese territorial integrity had been violated at the turn of the century. "You have all known a friend or relative who was addicted to opium. You have seen the shame this dirty habit brought and the destruction it wreaked upon our families and our country! Well, do you know how we became a nation of depraved, useless citizens?" Mr. Wang scowled. "England, the most loyal ally of the United States, cultivated opium in India and forced us to buy it in exchange for our silver, tea, silk, porcelain, and fine art. Why, today more Chinese treasures decorate foreign museums than are left in this country! Then the Japanese took Manchuria. They grew opium and again flooded our country with this cheap poison."

Coral Bell twirled a tuft of hair on her forehead, sucked her thumb, and leaned on her mother. By now she had heard the same speech delivered in so many different ways that she couldn't concentrate. Despite the charged atmosphere, she dozed off.

Mr. Wang's rants filled the air. "Even such noble American families as the Delanos grew rich from the opium trade!" Mr. Wang huffed. "We helped the U.S. and England during World Wars I and II. But they are ungrateful. The Americans are building up Japan. They want to flood our country with opium again!" He swallowed.

"Americans are thieves!" someone shouted.

The crowd echoed: "Scum of the earth!" "Predators!" "Down with the bullies!"

Mr. Wang raised his palms to still the audience. He surveyed the room and took a sip of water. He signaled to a man in the back of the hall to start the slideshow.

"Although we are the most populous nation in the world, we are not allowed to join the United Nations." Mr. Wang continued his harangue. "What reason do they have other than their desire to build up Japan so they can harm us again? Who among us hasn't suffered under the Japanese? Japan imitated everything good in our culture, but they bought Western guns and grew strong. Remember the Nanking Massacre! Japan has devastated our country and enslaved us for too long. The United States is reshaping South Korea in Japan's image. They are debauching North Korea and threatening to invade China again!" Grainy black-and-white pictures of World War II appeared on the screen behind him.

Voices emerged in the dark: "Not another war on our homeland!" "Kill the imperialists!" "We will never be enslaved!" "Never again." Coral Bell could feel her mother's heart pounding against her own.

Mr. Wang was pleased with the response. Spittle flew from his mouth as he announced China's imminent danger from the American invasion. "North Korea is like the lips that protect our mouth. If we don't help the North Koreans defend themselves, we will be America and Japan's next victim! We will see the Nanking Massacre all over again! You remember Nanking — how our families were slaughtered?" His gaze swept over the room like a hawk surveying field mice. The screen overhead replayed gruesome scenes. Coral Bell buried her head deep into her mother's knees.

As people shook their fists, shouting their outrage and weeping, Mr. Wang fed their frenzy with more details of atrocities: Japanese soldiers raping, looting, and sending young men and women into slavery, forcing thousands of people to push each other off cliffs; men, women, and children being shot, speared, beheaded, or disemboweled.

Not a dry eye remained in the hall. Even Brook ma-ma sobbed and gasped, "No wonder so many of us lost our minds."

Mr. Wang ended his harangue by instructing everyone to be vigilant and to help root out foreign spies.

Then he introduced White Lily as a patriotic youngster who would denounce her father. She was touted as an honor guard in the Young Communist League and one of the first to pass the "true test of loyalty to the Chairman." She was escorted to the front of the stage and made to face a prisoner who was being prodded onto the platform.

Coral Bell, now roused from her half sleep, jerked herself erect, craning her neck.

Lee Tar-see's hands were tied behind his back. His head hung low, and his overgrown hair fell in front of him. Coral Bell could not see his face. His white shirt was gray with sweat and grime, but his Western-style wool trousers still carried a crease of distinction amid the sea of men in baggy pants and gray or blue Mao jackets.

Fists clutching the cloth on her chest and tears streaming from her eyes, White Lily mumbled in a trembling voice how her father had kept her mother and herself in Chungking for a long time after the war while he caroused with foreigners in Shanghai. Then she hesitated. Pulling out a piece paper, she read as best she could how her father had been corrupted by his work in a foreign trading company and had once called her mother and herself a scandalous name: "country bumpkins!"

"Have you seen him talk to foreigners?" Mr. Wang asked.

"No." White Lily's voice was shaking. "But I heard him speak English on the telephone."

The crowd jeered, "A spy! A spy!"

Coral Bell moaned. She remembered how White Lily had complained that she hated her father because he never came home. Had she really heard him speak English on the telephone?

"Are you a spy?" Another man on the platform poked Mr. Lee.

"No, no, no!" White Lily's father knelt down in front of his daughter, crying: "I have been a bad father. I'm sorry . . . But please, please tell them I was never a spy!"

With tears rolling down her face, White Lily stretched her hand out toward her father. She turned to steal a look at Mr. Zhu, but Zhu's face remained impassive. She retracted her hand. Mr. Lee slumped in defeat. His head touched the ground.

"Have you seen your father bring home secret foreign documents?" Zhu asked White Lily.

"He . . . he took away our phonograph and foreign records," White Lily stammered, looking stunned.

"He hid them! He hid them!" the mob thundered.

"Kill him! Kill the cowardly spy!" A man in the middle of the hall shot up to point an accusing finger.

Coral Bell remembered hearing White Lily complain about her father gathering up all her mother's favorite records and taking them to the other woman. But did that make him a spy?

A roar went up in one corner of the hall. "Shoot him! Shoot the traitor!" "Drag him out! Hang him!"

Hysterical voices demanded revenge against the foreigners. Brook ma-ma, ashen-faced, drew Coral Bell to her, burying her face in her chest.

Mr. Lee lifted himself for a moment and then cowered in front of the crowd. He trembled violently and large drops of tears and sweat coursed down his face. He shouted, "No, no, no," but his protests were drowned out by wild denunciations. Several strongmen came on the platform and dragged Mr. Lee out. A frenzied crowd followed them. White Lily sank into her chair. Her mouth was twitching uncontrollably.

Coral Bell burrowed into her mother's lap and covered her ears as a shot rang out.

An Offering to the State

Shanghai, 1952

THE SEARCH for spies continued throughout Shanghai. And the Yungs had become a target. Hundreds of workers and their families packed the factory auditorium, where patriotic music blared from the corner speakers. An oddly festive bustle permeated the air, although people remained solemn. When the music stopped and an official walked to center stage, all eyes focused on him. Five Party officials, including a Mr. Hsia, sat on the platform. Yung and Golden Bell stood off to the side, their eyes blank and their hands clenched. From time to time, they shifted their weight and tried to appear unconcerned.

Mr. Chen, the official in charge of the meeting, delivered a long speech similar to the one given at Coral Bell's school, about the Opium War, China's contributions during the two world wars, Japanese depredations, and the West's ingratitude. He repeated the popular line that the Korean conflict threatened Chinese sovereignty and how Chairman Mao had made the ultimate sacrifice: His only son had been killed and buried in Korea.

Finally the speaker turned to the business at hand: "Mr. Yung Hien-Kung and his wife, Golden Bell, both attended universities in America. With their wealth and education, are they not assisting the foreign capitalists to enslave China once again?"

"Yes, yes, yes!" the crowd shouted. "They are the running dogs of the imperialists!"

Mr. Chen raised his hands to silence the audience. "Earlier, the Yungs refused to admit their guilt!"

The workers roared back with "Arrogant bastards!" "Oppressors! Capitalists!" "Freeloaders!" "They sit in the office and never lift anything heavy." "They're spies! Kill them!"

Mouthing "No, no, no," Yung and Golden Bell held hands. They stared at the people defiantly. Their icy glare scanned the crowd and locked on those they knew. They had attended enough "struggle sessions" against "spies" to know that if they appeared guilty, everyone would believe the false accusations and feel emboldened. The melodramas that sometimes ended with the execution of innocent people depended on their ability to control their feelings.

Again Mr. Chen waved his arms to subdue the crowd. "However, after weeks of reeducation and help from the workers, they have agreed to make their self-criticisms." He motioned the couple to step forward.

Still holding hands, their eyes sparkling and their faces blank, the Yungs nodded to the audience. They hoped that their model citizenship and hard work would save them. Yung fished out a few sheets of paper from his pocket. To overcome the tremor in his voice, he fixed his gaze on the opposite wall, which was festooned with the usual slogans against foreigners. In a flat monotone, he read his prepared statement. "Dear comrades, I apologize for leading a life of depravity. All my mistakes and backward reasoning grew from my feudal-bourgeois origin. My parents spoiled me and did not properly teach me to learn from you, the proletariat . . ."

"Louder!" someone cried.

"Forgive me." Yung choked back his tears. Golden Bell squeezed his hand, and he coughed to clear his throat. "I'm ashamed that I was blinded by capitalist propaganda."

A worker in the front row rose up to shout. "Yes! Shame on you!"

"Yes, yes." Yung nodded and continued to read. "I am not worthy of managing this company. I am therefore offering all these factories to you." He wiped his face.

Waves of shouts and questions filled the room.

"All your factories?"

"Yes." Tears fell from his lowered face.

"Are you a spy?" A young man pointed a finger at him.

Yung shook his head. But Golden Bell shouted: "No!"

A young woman in the center of the hall stood up. "How about the criminal elements in the union?" Her arm stabbed the air. "Did you do anything to stop them?"

"What?" Yung didn't know how to react to the unexpected question.

"The triad used to control the unions!"

"Yes, I tried to . . . I tried . . ." Yung's voice trembled. He didn't know how to tell the crowd that he had to placate them, but by collaborating with the new government, he had eradicated the criminals.

"The gang members used to bully us!" The woman swiveled her body around, swinging her pigtails from side to side to address all corners of the hall as she spoke. "They took a percentage of our pay and did no work!"

"I think I know this woman," Golden Bell whispered to her husband. "The way she moves her head and swings her pigtails reminds me of — yes, she's Peony! She used to be Silver Bell's personal maid in Hangzhou. Oh, tell her what you did." She swiped her sweat.

"I helped Mr. Hsia, our plant manager." Yung turned to indicate Mr. Hsia on the platform. "The workers helped us identify the underworld figures!"

Mr. Hsia walked to the front. "All you workers know this is true. We now have real foremen who know what they're doing!" Murmured assents swept through the room.

Peony's finger pointed to Yung and Golden Bell. "Did your families deal in opium?"

"All capitalists are opium dealers!" someone shouted.

In an instant, Golden Bell realized that Peony had tossed them a lifeline. She shouted back, "Absolutely not! Both our families traded only in silk and cotton." She poked her husband. "Peony is helping. Talk about the Opium War!"

Yung threw back his shoulders, putting away his papers. "As you've heard from Mr. Chen's enlightened speech, you must know how China was almost partitioned by the foreigners because we could not defend ourselves from their gunboats. By the turn of the century, first the British and then the Japanese flooded our country with opium. China's economy and society were debilitated. Plus, we were forced to pay huge indemnities, and the foreigners collected all our import and export taxes and we became a poor country!"

"Yes, kill the opium traffickers!" the man next to Peony shouted.

"The Opium War devastated our country!" someone yelled.

Golden Bell called out as loudly as she could, "Both my parents and Yung's parents participated in the 1911 anti-imperialist revolution!"

Yung clenched his fists. "Our parents were among the first to look for national salvation. They realized the necessity of building up Chinese industrial might, so they sent us overseas to learn new technologies." He drew a deep breath, aware that he was taking a risk. "As you know, both my wife and I attended universities in

America. We experienced firsthand the white man's arrogance and ignorance. The Americans cannot tell the difference between a Japanese and a Chinese. We were their allies through two world wars. The Japanese bombed Pearl Harbor and killed thousands of Americans. Now the Americans are rebuilding Japan and punishing us!"

Sympathetic snickers spread across the room.

"Can you imagine calling us Japanese when we suffered so much under the East Ocean devils?" Yung sensed his audience's curiosity about life outside China. However, he and his wife had agreed to recount only the most unpleasant experiences, knowing that the truth must be tempered.

"America is a racist society," he informed his audience. "The colored people, and the yellow race, which is what they consider us, do all the hard work. White men hold all the positions of power and do nothing."

Looking over the whispering and frowning workers, Yung continued: "They call us Chinks. Although they want our finest silk and porcelain, they think we are best suited to doing laundry and cooking chop suey — a dish you'll never see in China." He asked his wife to tell them about the disgraceful dish.

The audience settled back to be entertained. Golden Bell obliged. "The restaurants used to mix up all their meats and vegetables in a gooey sauce to get rid of all their leftovers."

People giggled.

"You know how we respect our teachers. My parents sent me to America because my tutor recommended it." Golden Bell continued. "I brought fine jade carvings and ancient scrolls as gifts to the school authorities to make sure they would take good care of me. Later on, when the Japanese burned down our home during the war and we lost all our possessions, my family could no longer send me money. I had to work in the school kitchen — mopping floors, scrubbing pots and pans, and washing dishes.

"The Americans gave my sister and me used clothing. Once when I sat down to eat in the dining room, some girls rose up to leave. They said: 'We're not going to sit beside a Chink!' I wanted to punch them, but I didn't dare. I was a coward, because I was alone and outnumbered. You can't imagine how lonely we were and how we suffered!" Golden Bell sobbed bitterly, unable to continue. Looking fragile and pale, her shoulders hunched over, she was no longer the boss lady with her commanding demeanor. Many eyes in the audience moistened.

Golden Bell continued through her sniffles, embellishing her anguish at being treated like a Japanese — an enemy to both the Americans and the Chinese. "They said the Japanese were sneaky and cruel because they bombed Pearl Harbor. They painted us with the same brush and would not acknowledge the holocaust suffered by us, the Chinese, in our own homeland!" Her tears flowed freely. "Forgive me." She added, pausing, "We were so humiliated in America! In all those years of war, the Chinese suffered even more than the Americans, fighting our common enemy, the Japanese. Now the Westerners are building up Japan again. They want to keep China weak, so their white faces can appear superior among us! Remember how they used to ride high in Chinese cities — protected by their own armed forces on Chinese soil and their own warships in China's harbors and rivers."

The audience was outraged. "How can the foreigners forget our suffering?" "The Japanese are not human!" "They're beasts!" "The Americans want to ally with the predators!" They cried out.

Golden Bell and Yung nodded.

"The Westerners think they can control Japan because it is a small country, but they are afraid of us. The Chinese have always helped the West, but Westerners transferred all their hatred of Japan to us." Golden Bell continued to play on the feeling of injustice. "My husband and I are patriots. We returned to build up

China, make use of our vast untapped resources, and take our place in the family of nations, as is our right. We have the finest culture. We should build up our industries and become the envy of the world!"

Golden Bell was shedding tears of regret and shame. Although the stories she told were true, they were chosen carefully.

"We both decided to remain in China after the liberation." Yung's voice rang out. "We know the foreigners will respect the Chinese only if we are strong. We've worked hard to build our industry." It was obvious that Yung spoke from the heart. "China has known nothing but war and humiliation since the foreigners arrived. Now we must prove to the world that we are an innovative and hardworking people who can contribute to civilization." His fist rose to punctuate his points.

"He is a spy!" A loud voice came from the back. "He even speaks English to his wife!"

"But he's giving up his factories!"

Yung ignored the shouts. "For thousands of years we have had the most civilized culture! Now we need to build up our industrial might!"

"So what have you done?" Peony called out.

"I have invested heavily in new machines."

"That must be a waste of money!" Peony rolled her eyes.

"Lao Chao." Yung recognized a foreman in the fourth row. "Tell them our accident record."

Lao Chao turned to face the hall. "We used to have dozens of accidents — workers having their fingers, hands, or arms nipped or chopped off by the old machines. Now we have none!"

The room buzzed.

"Who is going to run the factories when you give them up?" another foreman asked.

"I don't know." Yung shrugged, looking at Mr. Hsia.

"We need someone experienced," Peony and others yelled.

"The country is at war. We must keep up our production!"

"We can't allow the gangsters to control the union again!"

"We'll vote to pick a manager!"

Mr. Chen waved his arms to bring order. "The Party Central Committee has accepted the Yungs' self-criticism. Our glorious socialist-democratic government has accepted the six factories owned by the Yung family. You workers are now the owners of your own production. The Party will pick a new manager!"

The workers cheered and left the hall talking about the usual subjects: increased pay and better working conditions.

Due to the war, work intensified, but working conditions did not improve. It had never been the Party's intention to give the workers total control.

"How did we get it so wrong?" Yung and Golden Bell asked themselves every night amid regrets, self-reproach, and numbing apprehensions. "The Communists seem to defy all our old cultural pride in decency and respect for social order," Golden Bell said. "I've read someplace that it is the hurt people who want to hurt others. There have been too many hurt people in China."

"I don't understand the workings of psychology. Maybe we romanticized our Chinese idealism."

"No revolution in history was ever peaceful." Golden Bell huddled close.

They made quiet inquiries about leaving Shanghai. There were no legitimate channels, and it would be impossible to flee with two young children. On a dark night a few days later, the dog barked. In the light reflected off the house, Yung and Golden Bell saw Peony crunching down the gravel of their driveway with her familiar bouncing gait, her pigtails swinging from side to side.

"How did she get in? I wonder why she's coming?" Yung asked.

"Before the criticism session, the authorities made copies of our house keys. Remember?" Golden Bell sighed. "When we were children, our personal maids were our greatest friends. Silver Bell probably felt closer to Peony than to me."

"Does Peony hold a grudge against you?"

"She helped us during the struggle session, so I don't think so. I'm glad she's come. There are so many questions I'd like to ask her. When the Japanese set fire to our Hangzhou house, she was raped and brutalized by the soldiers. It was Mother who nursed her back to health. In fact, it was through nursing her that Mother became actively involved in Chinese medicine.

"After she recovered, Peony left to join the Communists — she wanted revenge against the Japanese. That was over a dozen years ago." Golden Bell strode over to open the door.

Peony marched into the house, smiling. "Do you remember me, Golden Bell?"

"Of course I do!" Golden Bell's voice shook. Peony had never addressed her by her name before. She had always called her "elder young mistress."

Golden Bell grabbed Peony's arm and thanked her again and again for helping them during the public confession. She led Peony to the living room.

Peony refused to sit. "I'm not used to sitting on fine rosewood furniture," she explained matter-of-factly. The Yungs stood before the fidgeting Peony, glad that they had put away their fine porcelain and ancient jade carvings.

"You still wear pigtails!" Golden Bell exclaimed, louder than she had intended. Sweating and bowing, she was overcome by the irony of honoring a former maid who now had the power to destroy them.

After Peony was introduced to Yung, he asked, "How did you know Golden Bell is my wife and they were holding this struggle session against us?"

"My uncle Lao Wang told me you were in real trouble."

Golden Bell had forgotten that Lao Wang, their former gardener, was Peony's uncle. She turned to her husband. "The Wang family took care of our gardens in Hangzhou for generations. Lao Wang is also responsible for sending us the produce that kept us fed during the time of hyperinflation."

"Aiyaa!" Peony exclaimed. "And that is now giving him lots of problems." She laughed, but her face furrowed. "By selling you the produce for American dollars, he became a rich man. He bought himself a farm and took a concubine. Now he has to account for all that."

"Fancy a farmer with capitalist inclinations!" Yung was unable to hide his bitterness.

Golden Bell glared at her husband. "Forgive us." She bowed to Peony. "Mr. Yung does not know our family in Hangzhou. Lao Wang is such a decent man! We paid him extra because we knew he was sharing his good fortune with all his relatives and friends in need."

"Yes, his concubine was an orphan girl. If your family were still in Hangzhou, he probably would have brought her in as another servant in your house — the way he brought me."

"I hope he won't be imprisoned!"

"No, my husband is a member of the Provincial Party Central Committee." Peony's voice was wary. She leaned against a wall. "He taught my uncle to confess to having learned bad habits from the enemy class. Then my uncle offered up his small farm to the Party. Lao Wang is now back in service. This time, he's gardening for the Party chief."

"Good, he is safe." Golden Bell lowered her head. "Property can be a real burden these days. But tell us about yourself. How did you meet your husband?"

"We met during our long struggle for liberation — facing many battles together." Peony chuckled bitterly. "You must have heard of all the hardships we suffered. The Americans supplied Chiang Kai-shek with modern weapons. We depended on the corruption in his military to win over his soldiers and the general population . . . So many of us died." She paused and swallowed. "But looking back, we were full of energy and idealism! We also made many friends. Now Comrade Deng Xiaoping is our sponsor!"

"Are you also a member of the Party Central Committee?"

"Yes, and I'm in charge of all the propaganda campaigns in this province."

"M-ma and Brook ma-ma would be pleased to know your success," Golden Bell said.

"My husband's family perished during the war. We have no children, so you've become part of our extended family," Peony reassured them.

"Thank you, thank you!" Golden Bell murmured.

"I have ways of knowing what is going on with you. It is best if people don't know that I'm helping you," Peony confided. "My husband is aware of your generosity because your mother sewed many jade pieces and gold coins into my padded jacket before I left to join the Communists. During the war, those jewels saved our lives!"

Peony seemed to know that Silver Bell was living in Hong Kong, and Golden Bell described her general well being without mentioning her unhappy marriage. Now convinced of Peony's friendship, Golden Bell openly admitted that the Yungs should have moved to Hong Kong like her sister. They simply had the wrong background. "Please advise us on what to do," she implored. "We no longer feel safe here."

"Don't bother applying for exit permits," Peony replied curtly. "The country is at war, and we need your knowledge and experience to meet our production quotas. You'll only look like a deserter if you try to leave now. They need you and will not persecute you further. But be extra careful. As the old saying goes, you must first line up your teeth before opening your lips."

"Yes — under such extreme circumstances." The corners of Yung's mouth turned down.

"My husband and I suffer from horrible nightmares!" Golden Bell confided.

Pale and tense, Peony continued almost in a whisper: "So many comrades have been traumatized through all these years of non-stop warfare that many have turned their anger toward each other. Looking for foreign spies is only an excuse. They won't hesitate to kill and destroy anyone. But the more levelheaded people want to build up China, and they know they'll need your help. Mr. Hsia is one of them."

"Yes, I think he helped us during the meeting." Yung nodded.

"You had better invite his family to share your house so that you no longer stand out as privileged people," Peony advised.

"Yes, we'll invite the Hsia family." Golden Bell agreed. "It is better to live with someone we already know than to wait for them to assign us total strangers."

"Never repeat news, gossip, or sound sarcastic. You'll be seen as too smart for your own good," added Peony.

The Yungs nodded.

"A power struggle is going on in the Party. I think it would be unwise to criticize or befriend anyone. As you've heard, Chairman Mao's son was just killed in Korea," Peony said through pinched lips. "There is now added pressure to find American spies and exorcise the demons among us. Don't even think about leaving! Never ask for economic rehabilitation. And you must join in denouncing America!"

Golden Bell grabbed Peony's hand and knelt down, thanking her profusely. Yung turned his wet face away from the women, trying his best to pull back his shoulders and retain some shred of dignity.

Peony retreated to the door. "You will never see me again. If we should ever meet by chance, do not address me! Some of my old relatives from Hangzhou will be in touch with you, when I have useful information." She turned her back and ran down the driveway.

Two weeks later, Yung learned that he had been retained as manager-in-chief, provided that he and his wife joined in self-criticism and reform group discussions. They would also study the works of Mao Zedong. Furthermore, his family could remain in their mansion, but Mr. Hsia's family would share it with them.

The Hsias were a childless couple who went to work every day. Mr. Hsia's widowed mother was so fond of the Yung children that she became a great help. Peace prevailed in the house, even though there was less privacy.

The workers now owned the factories, but they were not given any profits or pay raises. As the Korean War intensified, everyone had to work longer hours, with no improvement in lifestyle.

THE QUEEN'S ENGLISH

Hong Kong, 1960

THANKS TO PEONY'S maneuvers, Golden Bell was allowed to visit her sister in Hong Kong for two weeks. After almost ten years of separation, the sisters embraced so fiercely that it was a long time before they disentangled themselves. Moaning how they had missed each other, they wiped each other's faces and wept intermittently as Golden Bell their decision to stay in Shanghai.

Finally, Silver Bell lit a cigarette and tried to regain her composure. "We were surprised they allowed you to come at all."

"I was the only one given a permit. The authorities are keeping Yung and the children as hostages. They know I will return for the children, if not for my husband." Golden Bell stood staring in front of the huge plate-glass windows facing the ocean. "I wish they could see this."

Silver Bell drew her sister away. "Come, try on some of my new clothes." She poured herself a cocktail and tossed it down in one gulp.

Golden Bell put on a silk cheongsam and stood before a mirror. A rush of memories flooded her, and tears coursed down her cheeks. "I haven't worn silk for so many years!"

"Everything here is yours." Silver Bell puffed her cigarette furiously, creating a smoke screen. She was wearing a Western-style light wool suit. She rose to fix herself another Manhattan and took a big gulp. "Would you like a cocktail?"

"No, thank you. I haven't had one for so long, I might get sick." Golden Bell walked over to her sister and stroked her hand. "Take it easy, sister. This is your second drink, and you're smoking too much. Where is Donald?"

Silver Bell ordered tea and was promptly served.

"He's in the United States getting a contract for knit fabrics. That seems to be the upcoming fashion."

"Did I keep you from going with him?"

"No, Donald always travels alone."

Golden Bell hugged her sister close, acting like the big sister of old, but not knowing what to say.

Silver Bell could no longer hide her despair. "After all you've been through, you remain strong with your dignity intact." She shook her head. "Although I live in luxury, I'm always depressed and lonely and feel utterly wretched. My husband is never home, and since Baby Jenny was born with a cleft lip, I don't want another child."

"You have a daughter named Jenny?" Golden Bell's eyeballs almost popped out of their sockets. "You did not miscarry?"

Silver Bell cried with abandon. Dark streaks of eye makeup ran down her cheeks.

"No, she was born with a cleft lip, and I couldn't take it. When the wet nurse fed her, her milk leaked and it was a mess every time. Neither Donald nor I had the presence of mind to handle her condition. We decided to take her to Miss Tyler so she could have a normal life! We didn't tell you because we knew Mother wouldn't approve. Brook ma-ma especially would want to take care of her."

"So Jenny is in Syracuse?"

"She is well taken care of by the spinster missionary ladies. She calls Miss Tyler Na-na. Her friend Martha is Ma-ma, and her friend Darlene is Da-da."

"And we thought you miscarried!" Golden Bell sat down to calm herself, breathing heavily as she fanned herself.

"I was too ashamed." Silver Bell hid her face in her hands, muttering, "I was consumed with work and making money. We've set up an endowment for Jenny. How could any child thrive in this unhappy home? Jenny just had an operation. Now the gap is sewn together, but there is a big bump on her lips. She will need more surgeries, but she is happy with her Da-da, Ma-ma, and Na-na. Isn't it lucky that the names of the ladies fit the customary family appellations so easily?"

Silver Bell lit another cigarette. She stared into the haze.

"Yes, I almost forgot that Miss Tyler's given name is Nancy." Golden Bell remembered the dumpling-making scene in New York City when Miss Tyler told them her name. This was another world from her life in Shanghai. Indeed, all Chinese lives were in such disarray, it was good that Jenny was safe. She was probably enjoying more peace and even love from all her missionary "mothers."

"I'm sure she is well taken care of. Is Donald visiting her now?"

"I don't know." Silver Bell sobbed anew. "We were both uncomfortable visiting her, because we confuse her."

"So did you visit her when you went to the States?"

"Yes, of course. She seems very bright, verbal, and calls me Auntie Sarah."

"Why? I'm sure Miss Tyler and others would want her to know her own mother!"

"I was so confused when I saw her that I suggested she call me Auntie because she was already calling Martha, ma-ma. Miss Tyler suggested that she start calling me Mammy Sarah."

"When will you be seeing her next?"

"I've told Miss Tyler that either Donald or I will be there for

Jenny's next surgery."

"Why can't you both go together?" Golden Bell could not help asking.

"Maybe, may . . . be." Silver Bell sobbed on and on. "I cannot forgive him for what he has done! If I were in a Western society, I would have asked for a divorce long ago!"

Golden Bell hugged her sister and soothed her. "Shhh . . . shhh . . . You'll go to Jenny's next operation and perhaps bring her back with you. You've given Jenny a good and peaceful life. My children await an uncertain future." Her eyes automatically reddened. "Yung and I consider Donald our best friend. He has always been honest and shared his profits."

"Being an orphan, Donald was not born into a web of family ties and relationships the way we were. He lacks the nurturing instincts of a family man." Silver Bell calmed herself. "I think he is staying with me only because of my connection to you."

"We're sure he still feels loyalty toward the Yungs. But you have prospered way beyond our initial investments! We are lucky he is a relative. How do you track his profits?"

"I don't, and I can't." Silver Bell crushed her cigarette in the ashtray. "He supports our family. He has also written a big check to take care of your visit."

"You must thank him for me," Golden Bell mumbled.

Silver Bell gulped down the last of her drink and slammed the glass on the table. "I won't bother! Sometimes he complains of expenses for M-ma and 'her concubine,' as he calls Brook ma-ma. Maybe he has mistresses and concubines of his own. I no longer care!" She started sniffling anew.

Golden Bell spoke as if to herself, "From your letters we guessed that you have not been happy. In spite of being secure, you're living in a worse prison than we are."

"I envy you in so many ways." There were many questions Silver

Bell had refrained from asking in her letters because she'd feared their communications might be intercepted by the authorities in Shanghai. "Do you still get tea and fresh produce from our Hangzhou relatives?"

"Yes. We pay them in the Hong Kong dollars you send us."

"Have they tried to make your children denounce you?"

"I don't know. The children are mature beyond their years. They do well in school, and they never flaunt their talents or feel ashamed of their background. But they've been robbed of their innocence."

Silver Bell grimaced. "And Yung? Is he a good father?"

"Yung works so hard that he hardly has time for the children, but whenever I see him in his fraying shirt and his haggard look, I feel only love. I know he feels the same."

As if something had shattered her reverie, Golden Bell quickly lost her composure. She trembled uncontrollably and moaned, "My children will never be allowed to attend university! What will become of us?"

When the fresh supply of tears had drained, Silver Bell whispered, "I no longer need anyone to support me. I've started a new life for myself."

"That is wonderful." Golden Bell sipped her tea. "You're doing well in your real estate business?"

"I do very well in real estate but I also dabble in buying and selling antiques."

"Do you enjoy the work?"

"Yes! I scour the back alleys and find recent immigrants from China who have family treasures to sell."

Golden Bell squirmed.

Silver Bell went on sheepishly, "I know M-ma would consider my work crass, coming as we do from a book-fragrant family. But I'm independent, and I don't ask Donald for money anymore." She pointed to a bronze horse, some jade bowls, and pieces of blue and white porcelain. "I bought all these pieces."

"There is nothing dishonorable about your trade." Golden Bell did not look at the collection. She took another sip of tea. The teacup obscured her weary eyes.

"You remember M-ma always taught us humility. Modern trade depends on self-promotion. She would be horrified to hear me brag about my fluency in English — how I can fetch a better price for people's treasures because my English helps me speak to foreign collectors."

Staring at her cup, Golden Bell said, "You drink a Manhattan and dress like a foreigner. I sip tea in your silk gown. I'm afraid my pride in our old culture has bound me to a China that is still trying to find a way out of her isolation. You have progressed far into the new world."

Relieved that Golden Bell was not condemning her for taking advantage of the unfortunate refugees, Silver Bell perked up. "I know you refuse to see any of our old friends, but many of them lead really interesting lives overseas. You remember Suzie Chang, who immigrated to the United States? She worked as a waitress while her husband studied for his medical boards. Now he is fully accredited, and she owns the fanciest Chinese restaurant in Los Angeles. They live in luxury. Suzie visited Hong Kong last month and almost bragged that their children can no longer read Chinese and that the younger ones don't even speak it anymore."

"Why?"

"They sent their children to Chinese Sunday school. But the Taiwan faction and the mainland faction fought for control. To please both sides, the children were required to learn every Chinese character four ways: the old script, the new simplified script, the Romanized pin-yin system, and Taiwan's "bo-po-mo-fo" system. The kids were so confused that they wanted only English and to become totally American!"

"So Chinese partisan wars are again driving us into foreign

arms." Golden Bell's lips curled in contempt, and her eyes glistened. "Still, they are the lucky ones. The parents struggled as immigrants, but the whole family will prosper. What can I say to our old friends? How can I face their sympathy? How can I tell them that I envy their children's future while I snuffed out mine?" She pounded her chest while tears flew anew.

Silver Bell tried another diversion. "Hong Kong has changed. You must see some Hollywood movies. There is a new star getting all the attention these days: her name is Marilyn Monroe. She is quite different from Jeanette MacDonald."

"Ah, you're still in love with movies. Are you required to stand when they play 'God Save the King' before each and every show?"

"Oh, not by any means! Now we have to stand when they play 'God Save the Queen' before each and every show." Silver Bell laughed, remembering how they used to detest the requisite display of loyalty to the British sovereign. "Anyway, no one seems to mind."

"Of course, everyone knows what people like us on the mainland are going through. How can anyone imagine we need to be saved from our own people?"

"Would you like to visit the French Convent School? I'll call Sister Rose Mary. She is retired now and lives in the convent next to the school. She'll be so pleased to see you. Afterward, we can go to dinner at that new Harbor View Restaurant in the Regis Hotel. Their serving dishes are all jade! For the rest of this day, let's go down for a drive; you must see the new constructions."

"In 1938, Hong Kong had a cricket field right in the middle of town. Is it still there?"

"No, pile drivers and tall buildings dominate the skyline now."

The chauffeur took them to the center of town. Occasionally Golden Bell recognized an old building: "Look, the King's Theatre is still here!" While China engaged in one campaign of political correctness after another, Hong Kong poured its entrepreneurial energy into free trade. With access to Western information, transportation, and choices in education, the Chinese prospered.

The next day, Golden Bell wore a silk shirt with a light worsted pantsuit she had picked out from her sister's closet. She looked trim and elegant.

"You look better than many fashionable Hong Kong ladies here because you're so slim!" Silver Bell chuckled at the irony.

"I suppose that is the reward for my poverty, semi-starvation, and constant worry!"

The two sisters set off for the school they had attended before leaving for America. They brought trays of the finest European cheeses to their teachers. Sister Rose Mary looked wizened, but she still remembered the Huang girls as Vicky and Sarah. She told them there were more students now, and most of the teaching nuns came from Ireland and the Philippines. She gave them permission to tour the school grounds.

Large orange balls of Clivia bloomed in the gardens, and the soothing drone of the nuns reciting the rosary made them blink back tears. The limestone chapel, capped by a soaring steeple and lofty Gothic arches, still inspired reverence. Silver Bell hummed the hymns they used to sing in the choir. They began to pray but left quickly to avoid the flood of memories.

In the music room, students were singing:

> *Some talk of Alexander and some of Hercules,*
> *With a tra-la-la-la-la, to the British Grenadiers!*

"Remember how I used to march around our Flame of the Forest tree singing this song?" whispered Silver Bell, tugging on her sister's sleeve.

"Yes, and Father said it was strange for a Chinese girl to be imitating British soldiers."

"But this is most appropriate now!" Silver Bell exclaimed. "After all, the might of the British Empire is protecting us."

The students burst into another song:

> *Rose of England thou shalt fade not here,*
> *Though the storm of battles thunder near.*

With British patriotic airs ringing in her ears, Golden Bell led her sister away. They were tempted to sing along and indulge in nostalgia, but felt the sting of colonialism mocking their Chinese pride. They didn't realize that these were British patriotic airs when they were young.

"Even though the British didn't establish a democracy in Hong Kong, they're giving us the freedom to work, trade, and prosper," Silver Bell mumbled.

"Most Chinese now consider you lucky to live under colonialism. I wish my family were here with you." Golden Bell's eyes brimmed.

In the auditorium, a Cantonese girl was trying to recite a Shakespeare sonnet:

> *Sood I compeer dee to a summar's day?*
> *Dow art moor luv-a-ley and moor tempoor-ret.*

Sister Patrick frowned. "Arrah, what's your hurry?" she corrected in a thick brogue. "You're going entirely too farst!" She waved her hand. "Now, do you suppose them lads in love would hurry through such beautiful speech?"

The girl onstage shuffled her feet, glancing sideways with a bleak grin. "How sood we know for soor?" she asked.

"Love sonnets are the best poems altogether." Sister Patrick began reciting the lines in her heavy Irish lilt.

The girl shuffled her feet some more and tried again.

"Slow down now." Sister Patrick waved her hand again. "Don't be daft!"

Silver Bell winked at her sister as they hid their faces in their handkerchiefs, stifling their giggles.

"Remember how Miss Crosby used to make us recite Longfellow in the most proper King's English?" Golden Bell nudged her sister. "Is it possible that we were actually taught to pronounce everything in brogue?"

"I think Miss Crosby did teach us the proper English pronunciation. You remember how the Americans in Syracuse were impressed by our British accents?"

"But Longfellow was American!" Golden Bell laughed.

"We would have been luckier if we had stayed in America and not returned to our god-forsaken country," Silver Bell answered sourly, stamping her foot.

Once they left the school grounds, they could no longer laugh. The contradictions in this "normal" life were overwhelming. On the mainland, Golden Bell, her family, and most of their friends were living in fear of persecution and death. They dreaded the Communist purges the way a child feared the bogeyman. But here in Hong Kong they were safe, as long as British colonial manners ruled supreme. And voicing outrage at the imposition of colonial education seemed too petty and irrelevant. After all, though it was almost comical for a Chinese child to sing British patriotic airs and learn English in brogue from Irish nuns, the sisters knew the child must be thankful for those providing safety and a glimmer of hope.

During dinner, the forest of tall skyscrapers twinkling around the harbor distracted Golden Bell. "It looks as if someone has sprinkled fish scales all over the water. Look how it glistens!"

They fell silent for a long time. Silver Bell chain-smoked and downed one cocktail after another. She piled piece after piece of her sister's favorite seafood on her plate.

"Anyone born here is a British subject, not a citizen — the British would never allow that in their colony. I feel ambivalent about what we're about to do," Silver Bell said between puffs.

"What is that?"

"Both Donald and I are applying to become British subjects. It's supposed to be a privileged status." She ordered another drink. "We must overlook the historic humiliation because it is so much easier to travel abroad on a British passport."

Golden Bell swallowed. She had already learned to detach herself emotionally from ancient Chinese pride. She straightened herself stiffly in her seat. "M-ma's China no longer exists. Do you know what happened in early 1957?"

"No, I never follow the news closely. The news is so depressing."

"Let me tell you then. Everyone was exhorted to practice free expression. 'Let a hundred flowers bloom.'"

"Yes?" Silver Bell whispered.

Golden Bell widened her eyes, unable to control her outrage. "For five weeks, from May 1 to June 7 of that year, the so-called democracy walls appeared in Beijing and Shanghai — walls covered with essays by patriotic writers who criticized the government and advocated freedom of speech, free enterprise, and democracy. Even our favorite writer, Mr. Ba Gin, and other intellectuals fell for the ruse and answered the open invitation to express their true opinions."

"Oh, I remember loving Ba Gin's novels, especially his trilogy: *Family, Spring*, and *Autumn*. He gave such a vivid picture of the old, oppressive social structure. You'd think the Communists would honor his views." Silver Bell frowned.

"Far from it. As swiftly as the buds flowered, the Party started their arrests, imprisonment, and torture." Golden Bell could no longer swallow another bite. "So many careers were ruined and families destroyed. Peony had the shrewdness to advise us to criticize only our own bourgeois ways and no one in the government."

Silver Bell tried to compose herself. "Why is it that no one has explained to the world that communism is not Chinese? It is a foreign doctrine. Most Chinese Communists took on that name because it was the only ideology that claimed to help us. Yet we have not been helped. We are poorer than ever!"

"So why should you feel guilty that you have chosen to become British subjects?" Golden Bell slammed down her cup.

For two weeks the sisters toured Hong Kong. They took the funicular to Victoria Peak and strolled leisurely along the path that wound around the summit. Passing mountain laurels and walking under a canopy of deep emerald philodendrons cascading down the mountain with their exposed roots clinging to the rock face, they rounded a bend. A vast amphitheater of sparkling ocean edged by skyscrapers opened before them. From this vantage point, the evening sun painted the blue ocean in a golden sheen. Triangular dots of Chinese sailboats bobbed red and brown while supertankers and cargo ships lay amid the dancing lights of the harbor like toy pieces. White seagulls flew across the greenery and buildings below.

Silver Bell touched her sister's hand. "Doesn't the view remind you of the time M-ma first recited her favorite quatrain by Tu Fu?"

"Yes. I wonder if M-ma relives her time here when she recites it now."

"I am having the same thought." Silver Bell took on her mother's soft intonation and began:

> *Birds flash whiter against the blue water;*
> *Flowers flame brighter against the green mountain.*
> *Spring speeds past before my eyes.*

What year will I return?

"Beautiful." Golden Bell nodded. "Remember how Father suggested that we play at riddles? Each of us had to describe something in verse, and the rest of us had to guess what it was?"

"Yes, you rose to the challenge right away, but I couldn't come up with anything." Silver Bell gave her sister a playful punch on her arm.

"You were much younger, so naturally you couldn't participate. I still remember my riddle:

> *A mist of silken veil crowning her head,*
> *A sprinkling of gemstones around her skirt.*
> *She is a Queen,*
> *In regal repose."*

"Oh yes, I thought it was easy!" Silver Bell exclaimed. "It is the Victoria Peak!"

"M-ma's riddle was not so easy," Golden Bell reminded her. "Only Father could solve it:

> *It does not knock,*
> *It comes uninvited,*
> *When we meet,*
> *We caress, and I'm refreshed!"*

Walking on in silence, both became misty-eyed. Silver Bell finally said, "Father knew it was the wind. Our parents had a marriage of compatible minds."

Golden Bell squeezed her sister's hand to soothe her. "You and Donald are both talented in trade. You must build on that."

Silver Bell shook her head but didn't respond.

In the following days, they took the ferry to Lan Tao Island to visit the Buddhist temple, and another boat to Macao's casinos. They shopped and feasted every day, sampling the best of French, Italian, German, Japanese, Thai, Malay, Indian, and five Chinese regional cuisines.

Hong Kong was booming. Since English has become the language of commerce, the Hong Kong Chinese were learning it en masse, through whatever means available. In spite of the confusion and occasional rancor in this Westernization process, things were coming together in a way that revealed an orderly pattern of progress: higher living standards, more literacy, as well as better nutrition and medical care. And, not to be dismissed, people seemed to be gaining a broader perspective on the world.

At the end of her visit, Golden Bell wept bitterly before bidding her sister farewell. "Why must I choose between my freedom and my husband and children?"

Silver Bell could only echo her sister's sobs. All the while she was thinking, *I am free and independent, to be sure, but my true home is with you in Shanghai. Your life under political oppression is so distant that my desolate heart must strain to hear you.*

⸸arming 5⸗⸗l

Wei Village, 1962

AFTER the Korean War, everyone fumbled through two five-year plans of economic reconstruction that were doomed to failure. People sank deeper into poverty. In spite of American fears of Communist hegemony that threatened to spread from Soviet Russia to China to Korea, friction developed between the Communist allies. The Soviets withdrew all technical and financial aid. They even removed all the blueprints for the factories and industrial infrastructure they had proposed. China plunged into further disarray.

White Lily heard her father's execution in a state of catatonic shock. Later, she began tearing her hair out in chunks and walked around in a trance. She bumped her head into walls, fell down the stairs, cut her fingers, and burned herself near fires. She became so quiet people thought she was mute. Morose and silent, she never regained her former exuberance.

Coral Bell often brought her home so M-ma and Brook ma-ma could brew healing herb teas, dress her cuts and burns, give her massages, and provide the sympathy and care that no one else, not even White Lily's mother, seemed able to offer. Over time, White Lily's condition stabilized, but she followed Coral Bell everywhere

221

like a puppy. Outside of her immediate family, Coral Bell trusted only White Lily. To signal danger, all they needed to do was to give each other a certain look.

Coral Bell knew her M-ma's moments of lucidity were connected with her medical knowledge. After watching her two mothers practice medicine, she learned the value of acupuncture and massage in relieving pain — both physical and psychic. After high school, she persuaded Brook ma-ma to arrange a meeting with Peony. She told Peony of her desire to go into medicine. Peony informed them that young people in the city were being sent into the countryside to do menial labor and learn from farmers. The Communist Party did not like Western influence in the urban medical system and wanted to focus on the well-being of the rural population. Since the 1930s, the Reconstruction Movement had pioneered the use of rural health workers to provide care. The system had persisted in some villages, and Peony promised to look into it. Coral Bell was eager to minister to the people in the vast countryside. White Lily was happy to follow.

After two years of mostly first-aid training, the medical authority assigned both girls to a village outside Pingyao, a historic small town bordering the northwest region. Through Peony's influence, they were given a plum assignment: working under a "real doctor." Not only would they be taking care of actual patients, but they would also train other villagers to become health workers.

Will we have running water? Will we live in shacks? Coral Bell wanted to ask. Brook ma-ma reminded her how lucky she was to avoid arduous farm work. She took out the gray silk scarf with the orchid she had embroidered and stitched the scarf under an inner vest. This would keep her daughter warm as well as remind her of her family. Coral Bell felt like a baby bird taking its first flight. The anticipation of spreading her wings and venturing into the unknown took away her appetite and her habit of tucking her head into her mother's neck and losing herself in M-ma's poetry.

A sandstorm seemed to have covered Shanghai since the Communist liberation. The neon signs advertising Coca-Cola, Camel cigarettes, perfumes, and various fashionable products disappeared. Coral Bell had always wondered if the fancy balls the foreigners had hosted were anything like the Family Day party she had attended in the Shanghai Sporting Club so many years ago. She had seen Westerners being chauffeured about town in showy cars, patronizing the grand hotels and coffee houses. Now they were all gone. There was no new construction, and a pall had descended upon the city.

Coral Bell and White Lily left Shanghai in early May when the gray city was still shrouded in spring mist. As the train threaded its way through damp fog, the sun suddenly appeared. Its rays stung their eyes but seemed to promise a world of peace and stability.

"Look, there's a small field of camellias!" White Lily exclaimed. Although twenty-one years old, neither young woman had been out of the city since the new government had arrived. Now, the crimson blossoms amid the thick dark green foliage blazed past so quickly that they pressed their faces to the window. Their eyes lingered on the fields where a few women and children were tending vegetables and spreading fertilizer. The excitement of travel and the glistening green land added to their delight. Fresh breezes brought happy spirits. And their card-playing and tea-drinking comrades' laughter and shouts dispelled their sadness at leaving home. The train was packed with people assigned to other destinations. The girls didn't know who their co-workers might be.

As evening approached, the distant hills undulated like a mythical dragon racing alongside the train. Some students began to sing the new patriotic songs: "Destroy the Old and Set Up the New," "Oh Youth," and "Though Happy, We Must Not Forget the

Communist Party." After several such rousing tunes, their voices
grew faint. One young man shouted, "Hey, Fat Lips! Don't you
know some reactionary old songs?"

"No, I don't know anything reactionary. But I know this love
song from a Chinese minority tribe." Fat Lips began to sing in a
sweet voice:

> *In that faraway place,*
> *There is a beautiful girl.*
> *People who walk past her window,*
> *All want to turn their heads*
> *And cast lingering glances.*

A tingling arose inside Coral Bell. During long years of trying to
be "politically correct," she had ignored the emotions that were
now filling all the secret places inside her. She snuggled close to
White Lily, recalling the English romantic stories of Snow White
and Sleeping Beauty she had learned from Silver Bell.

She had neither read nor spoken a word of English for over ten
years now. The train's steady, soothing rattle sent her dreaming of
the piney woods she used to read about in English fairy tales. Now
the scent of freshly turned earth, green vegetation, sweet budding
flowers, and pungent night soil permeated the fresh air.

The next morning, they reached their destination. Wei Village,
on the bank of a small river, looked hazy in the rising sun. Boats
floated under a stone bridge, their motion barely distinguishable
from the rustling leaves of the lone sycamore tree on the shore.
The tree looked decapitated, with its top branches lopped off, but
this was not dusty Shanghai. Coral Bell rubbed her eyes and
whispered: "Paradise!" White Lily nodded her agreement, smiling.

An old villager, Loh Wei, was waiting for them at the station.
His eyes were bloodshot, and his bare feet caked with mud. When

he smiled he revealed a wide-open mouth with no front teeth. They learned that everyone in the village had the same family name and belonged to one clan. Dr. Tsai, the head physician of their team, introduced everyone: Tar Chuang, a young man of twenty-three; Bai Yue, a young woman in her twenties. Coral Bell and White Lily completed the medical group.

The team immediately went to the clinic.

The windows of the clinic were stained, and the plaster on the walls was cracked. Spots of mold, withered moss, and dust covered everything. The three women were assigned to a shed behind the main clinic, which at one time must have housed animals. The earthen grounds and walls emitted rustic odors. Wooden beams crisscrossed under the thatched roof. A few planks of wood constituted their beds. No table or chair graced the living space. Dr. Tsai had his own room in the clinic, and Tar Chuang slept on the floor of the examination room.

Everyone was now addressed as Doctor, but only Dr. Tsai looked old enough to have had proper training. He was short, chain-smoked, and had a full head of white hair. Before they could unpack, Dr. Tsai ordered a scrub-down of the clinic and the examination room. Coral Bell was delighted that a pipe from the river delivered water to a pump in the compound.

Loh Wei apologized that the honored guests had no time to rest and deplored the backwardness of the health facilities in the area. He excused himself and soon returned with two young men to help scrub the walls and floors. White Lily and Coral Bell boiled hot water to disinfect all the instruments, linens, and drapes.

"Where is your Party leader?" Dr. Tsai asked Loh Wei.

"Mr. Chen is supervising the backyard furnaces." Loh Wei smiled his toothless smile. "Our commune will produce loads of steel this year! I'm seventy-eight years old and the only one here unable to do the hard work to modernize our country."

"Yes, I know we have embarked upon the Great Leap Forward program." Dr. Tsai nodded, looking glum.

Since the Soviet Union had withdrawn all its machinery and technical help, Chairman Mao now extolled the power of the masses, insisting that common sense, and not technical know-how, would promote economic progress and help pay back the Soviet loans.

"We've been organized into a collective farm," Loh Wei said uncertainly. "We share our work now with two other villages."

"Do you have a school here?" Dr. Tsai asked.

"We used to have a primary school. But the teachers and children must all help with the backyard furnaces now. Most of us cannot read or write."

"And are the people generally healthy?"

"The furnaces belch out smoke and soot. I suppose we're all right, though many are coughing and sneezing." Loh Wei lowered his head to cover a fit of dry, hacking cough. "People will be coming to see you in the morning. We are proud to host such honored doctors from the big city!" He wiped his mouth with his sleeves. "Ah Tung here," he said, gesturing toward one of the young men scrubbing floors, "will escort you to our communal meal tonight."

"All the family pots and pans have been collected for the backyard furnaces," Ah Tung informed them eagerly. "We eat together now."

By lunchtime everyone was ravenous. As Loh Wei had not mentioned anything about food, Coral Bell took out the box of Dragon Well tea her Hangzhou relatives had given her. Dr. Tsai produced the half dozen hard-boiled eggs he had purchased at one of the train stops. Tar Chuang contributed some old steamed buns, and White Lily her dried fruit. Bai Yue did not contribute anything.

"Let's brew some tea and take a break by the river," suggested Dr. Tsai. He invited Loh Wei and the two local youths and led everyone toward the waterside. Ah Tung and his friend smiled and nodded to each other, speeding ahead.

Coral Bell and White Lily wandered down to the riverbank. When she was sure no one was near them, Coral whispered: "Isn't this a peaceful spot? If this were Hong Kong, where Silver Bell lives, I'm sure the banks would be lined with daffodils!"

"What are daffodils?"

"I've never seen them, but I know they're yellow." She remembered the Wordsworth poem. "This is the only poem in English I can still recite:

> *I wandered lonely as a cloud*
> *That floats on high o'er vales and hills,*
> *When all at once I saw a crowd,*
> *A host, of golden daffodils;*
> *Beside the lake, beneath the trees,*
> *Fluttering and dancing in the breeze."*

Ah Tung and his friend called everyone to gather under the sycamore tree. They had dug up a bowl of worms and brought a dozen little hooks made of rusty wires. Sitting by the riverbank, they invited everyone to join them in catching small crabs. Some of the crabs were using their pincers to push the worms into their mouths.

"Look, look, they're getting themselves hooked!" Coral Bell exclaimed.

"Only designated personnel are permitted to use nets, so we improvise with these fish hooks. Normally, we're not allowed to eat any of the crabs ourselves," Loh Wei mumbled. "The Party leaders sell them in the cities to raise funds for our national debt. But we're honored to be your hosts, and we've been given permission to treat our visitors just this once."

Soon, they had caught a bowl of tiny crabs. The villagers stunned them with hot water. Everyone ate them almost raw, dipping them in a sauce from the communal kitchen — soy sauce, grated garlic, wild onions, ginger, and vinegar. Coral Bell paused when a crab jerked or wiggled, but food was disappearing so fast around the table that she dug in and found herself relishing the tender, almost liquid meat. Laughing and eating, the villagers, and even Loh Wei, who hardly had any teeth left, were crunching down the shells. In fact, they were wolfing down more than their share of the catch.

As the meal ended, Loh Wei dumped all the sauce into the bowl of hot water and started to drink it. Ah Tung and his friend clamored for their share and scooped up the doctors' crab shells on the table to chew on. They took turns taking a swig of the hot water. The doctors looked away, embarrassed.

"The furnaces take all our time. We're all so hungry!" Loh Wei apologized.

"Only a few women and children are tending the fields now," Ah Tung told them. "We'll soon be running out of grains and vegetables because everyone is required to help make steel at our backyard furnaces."

The other youth corrected him. "Chairman Mao said our fields can lie fallow, because the power of the people will produce so much grain that we'll have a huge surplus."

"We're lucky to be near a river, so we manage somehow." Loh Wei sighed. "I hear that people up north are starving!"

No one seemed to know how to respond. Everyone grappled with the irony that even though the people were supposed to be the guardians of political power, they had to adhere to the Party line.

After lunch, the older men dozed along the bank. Coral Bell enlisted the young men to look for ropes and a plank of wood; she wanted to make a swing for the sycamore tree. She'd remembered pictures of swings in her English books, and this rural scene kindled her nostalgia for her foreign education.

"You'll never find any wood pieces here," Loh Wei said. "This is just about the only tree still standing. We took its top branches, but found them too damp. We've chopped down almost everything else and used the wood to feed the furnace."

Finally, one of the young men found some burlap and a long sturdy rope. Coral Bell improvised a seat after folding and tying it to the rope.

"It's your idea, so you'll have to be the first to try it," Tar Chuang said to Coral Bell. He gently pushed her several times and ran in front to look at her. Coral Bell blushed. She asked White Lily to go on the swing instead.

"Let me have a turn," Bai Yue chirped, and the village youths volunteered to push. Laughing, everyone took turns pushing, and sitting on the cloth swing. The sounds of laughter woke Dr. Tsai. He smiled.

When Coral Bell and White Lily returned to organize the medical supplies in the small storage room, they felt lighthearted and energized. In a mischievous mood, and soothed by the security of the cell-like room, Coral Bell asked her friend, "White Lily, do you want me to teach you an English song?"

"Sure, we're quite alone here."

"Silver Bell taught me this song she learned in her Hong Kong school." She started singing very softly:

Picnic time for teddy bears,
The little teddy bears are having a lovely time today.
Watch them gaily gad about:

They love to sing and shout.
They never have any care.
At six o'clock their daddies and mummies
Will bring them home to bed.
Because they're tired little teddy bears!

Almost in a whisper, Coral Bell sang each line over and over again while White Lily giggled and tried to repeat the strange words. Somehow, the melody helped the time fly by.

At dusk, Ah Tung rounded up everyone. "Follow the cooking smell. The fragrance is driving me crazy!"

"I'm so hungry, my stomach is growling!" Tar Chuang laughed and ran ahead.

The doctors had trouble following. The road was so badly rutted that their feet sank ankle-deep into the grooves. Loh Wei walked along the edge of the road, explaining, "We've been working the furnaces around the clock every day, rain or shine. The heavy carts bringing in scrap metals ruined our roads."

When they reached the open-air courtyard, rows of benches and tables had already filled with people. More were coming, their faces and clothes streaked with soot. No one bothered to wash; they jostled to line up at the serving table. The doctors were introduced to Mr. Chen, the Party head, and everyone took turns to shake his hand.

Dr. Tsai asked Mr. Chen whether he could meet the farmers he was supposed to train to become health care workers.

"I'm sorry," Mr. Chen replied, averting his eyes. "We need all the help we can get for the furnaces. We cannot spare anyone for you to train. You'll have to take care of our health here and in the surrounding villages." He did not elaborate and left to get his food.

Dr. Tsai shook his head. Higher officials had to approve every decision, and he knew there was nothing he could do. He followed Mr. Chen.

"Where do you eat when it rains?" White Lily asked Loh Wei.

"We serve from one of the rooms," he said, pointing to the sitting room of the Party chief's house. "People find a sheltered spot under the eaves."

Everyone was handed a bowl of thin, watery rice gruel with a few pieces of mushy brown vegetables floating in it. One steamed wheat bun accompanied the gruel. By the time the doctors sat down to eat with Mr. Chen, Tar Chuang and the village youths had already wolfed down their food and were standing in line for seconds.

The servers grudgingly refilled Tar Chuang's bowl. "He's a guest. You weren't even working the furnaces!" they shouted to the youths, who slumped away.

Soon, several disheveled urchins came to stand by Coral Bell and White Lily's bench, watching them eat.

Coral Bell, still holding a half-eaten bun in her hand, turned to the nearest little boy, who, except for a runny nose, seemed a model of stillness. "What is your name?"

The boy stared, pointed to the bun, and pleaded with his eyes. Coral Bell handed him her bread without a word, bending over her bowl to hide her moistening eyes.

Dr. Tsai observed the scene without comment. He was already planning ahead. "Mr. Chen, Chairman Mao said we must learn from the peasants. All these young doctors are city folks who should learn some farming ways. Please grant us permission to plant vegetables in the stretch of land in front of our clinic by the riverbank. In fact, they should learn husbandry as well. With your approval, we'd like to keep some pigs and chickens in the backyard."

Mr. Chen could not refute the quotation from Chairman Mao, but he reminded Dr. Tsai, "The Party wants us to concentrate on making steel. We're not allowed to fall short of our quota." A perpetual frown had etched his face. "However, since you are city doctors, I'll ask for permission from the Central Committee." He lit his bronze water pipe and became thoughtful. "Yes, city folks need to learn from us. You have the right —"

A loud explosion interrupted his speech. A dreadful pause followed. Everyone gasped and stared at the crimson sky. Some dashed underneath their tables and benches. Most screamed and scattered, calling for their children, husbands, and wives.

"Go check the furnaces!" Mr. Chen rose as he shouted, motioning people to follow him.

As they drew near the field, another furnace erupted. Plumes of fiery stars shot out like a giant fireworks display, shaking the earth beneath them. Coral Bell felt her eardrums pop and go silent. All the air seemed to have been pulled from her lungs. She coughed and swallowed to regain her balance. Automatically, she pulled White Lily to the ground, covering their heads with her bare arms. People cowered and cried. Children whimpered. The explosion had occurred near a row of straw and mud cottages. Tongues of fire began licking the thatched roofs, and people were shouting: "Help! Water!" "Run to the river and get water!" "We have no buckets! We've melted them in the furnace!"

The smoke was so thick, they couldn't see. Only the stench of charred flesh seemed to pierce the haze. Gurgling groans, panic-tinged shouts, and screams whirled like the fires around them.

As the wind stirred up the flames and blew away the smoke, Coral Bell saw Loh Wei kneeling by the door of a hut, stunned by the blaze that was consuming his home. His face, which was ruddy and tan from working outdoors, had turned white. His eyes were pale and round like two Ping-Pong balls. Coral Bell crawled toward him, shouting for him to move. He did not budge. Coral Bell had to call for help to drag him away.

People ran inside their burning houses to grab whatever possessions they could salvage. Others had to be restrained because the evening breeze had whipped the fire into an inferno. Weeping and wailing, the people wrung their hands, watching helplessly as their meager belongings disappeared before their eyes.

Dr. Tsai directed several men to carry the wounded to the clinic while Coral Bell and White Lily waded into the debris to look for survivors and warned each other to watch out for pieces of red-hot metal, scattered all over the ground. They tripped over bundles of charred bodies.

"Don't bother with the ones that are already dead!" Dr. Tsai hollered.

Suddenly, Coral Bell screamed and stopped short in her tracks. A severed head, like a matted red ball, lay before her. The hair was singed like caked charcoal, and the eyes were still staring in horror. Arms and legs were strewn about, like the mannequins she had seen in Shanghai department store windows. Coral Bell retched and ran from the scene. She hung her reeling head between her legs and waited for the waves of nausea to pass.

White Lily was soon sitting besides her, rubbing her back and asking, "Are you all right?" Coral Bell nodded and spat out the last of her supper.

"Let's go back to the clinic. We'll be needed there." She gasped.

As they walked in the eerie dusk, their shadows stretched out behind them like ghosts. They ran toward the swing, which, strangely, reminded them of a hung man. The enchanting scene from noontime now glistened orange like the backdrop of a horror movie. The sky had turned lavender. Flecks of gold floated down the sycamore. This surreal beauty slowed their steps.

A screaming boy lay in front of them. "Help, please help!"

Coral Bell knelt beside the boy. "Where does it hurt?"

"Something hot and hard hit me here." He pointed to his thigh.

"Thank you for helping, thank you!" his scrawny mother, sprawled on her hands and feet, cried out beside them. "I had to stop. He's too big for me to carry."

Coral Bell and White Lily wrapped the boy's arms between the two of them and hobbled toward the clinic.

"I watched the furnaces while people ate." The boy wept. "Nothing happened. Then this blast . . ."

"He was the best buffalo boy!" his mother shouted, weeping. "He never lost a single animal. He's not responsible for the fire!"

"Of course not," Coral Bell assured her.

White Lily couldn't help asking the boy where he had learned to forge steel.

"Nowhere," the boy answered flatly.

"What were you instructed to do?"

"I was told to stoke the fire and watch the furnaces."

"How many furnaces were you watching?"

"There are just two here. No one knows how to do anything."

"Be quiet!" his mother shrieked. "The lady doctors will think you're politically backward. Chairman Mao said that we, the people, could do anything." She ran in front of the three and turned to walk backward. She gesticulated wildly. "My boy did his best! Chairman Mao said we, the peasants, could move mountains. We don't need foreign technology. The whole country will become industrialized!"

White Lily asked, "Did someone come to teach you?"

"The government sent Mr. Chen to lead us."

"And does Mr. Chen know how to make steel?" she pressed on.

"He must know," the mother intoned quietly now. "He is the only one here who finished high school!"

The Poker Face

Wei Village, 1962

IT WAS FORTUNATE that the two exploding furnaces had been far from the other three. When the few surrounding homes had burned to the ground, the flames subsided. It was also a blessing that this had occurred during dinner, when most people were at a safe distance. As it was, half a dozen villagers had died, and twenty were injured. Almost a hundred people came to the clinic limping because they were barefoot or their cloth shoes were singed and their soles burned. Ah Tung kept three large pots of water boiling for cleaning and drinking. The smelly white gaslights illuminated the streaks of soot and blood everywhere.

The buffalo boy, whom everyone called Number Three, turned out to be a morale booster. While people screamed and cried demanding care, Number Three just whimpered occasionally. As soon as Coral administered anesthesia, using acupuncture needles as M-ma had taught her, he said he felt no more pain, none whatsoever. When Dr. Tsai extracted three pieces of metal from his leg, he just laughed and said, "No wonder people call me Number Three — I'll have three holes in my leg!" That was their only bit of levity the entire evening.

Tar Chuang also showed a childlike ebullience. He ran ahead and plunged into his tasks with such energy that Coral Bell wanted

235

to stop whatever she was doing and watch. Everyone came alive in his presence. The doctors stayed up all night, cutting, suturing, draining blisters, dressing wounds, cleaning, and disinfecting until the last patient had been put to bed or sent home.

"I don't know if I can get accustomed to using the outhouse," Coral Bell remarked to White Lily when they finally retired to their shed at dawn.

"So you must have lived in those modern Shanghai apartments!" Bai Yue exclaimed. She had a crass manner and spoke loudly. "I am a daughter of workers. Our family lived in the old Chinese section, and we've always used night-soil buckets." She exuded self-confidence, and her voice took on a disdainful tone. Coral Bell recognized her comment as a class statement, because she had placed herself in the exalted "Five Red Elements." White Lily shuddered, giving Coral Bell a knowing look. They both understood that they could never claim to be children of "workers, the poor and lower-middle class, peasants, revolutionary cadres, liberation army men, or martyrs." They would never again speak openly in Bai Yue's presence. Soon they became expert at affecting a poker face, which they had learned when they first met in the Shanghai Sporting Club so many years ago.

They woke up at noon that day. When Coral Bell entered the back room of the clinic to boil water for tea, she saw that Tar Chuang had already brewed a full thermos.

"Comrade, I hope you don't mind our using your tea leaves again," he said, smiling broadly. Looking around to make sure no one was in sight, he presented an egg. "Loh Wei came early this morning and brought some chickens. I was setting up a fence and rigging a coop when one of them laid an egg. I scooped it up before Loh Wei noticed. Here, you eat it."

Coral Bell shook her head, afraid to become involved with a clandestine activity.

"You hardly ate anything last night," Tar Chuang said, offering the egg again.

Coral Bell's stomach growled, but she stammered, "I . . . I'd better not."

"I boiled the egg in the tea water and buried the egg shell, so no one will ever know!" he whispered.

"Is Loh Wei bringing us some food?"

"There'll be no meals until dark," Tar Chuang said with a sigh. "Loh Wei brought the chickens here because Mr. Chen was afraid that people would steal them. Here, we'll share this." He broke the egg into equal halves as best he could. In one swift motion, he popped his half into his mouth and stuffed the other into Coral's. Coral Bell turned to pour them each a cup of tea and took her time chewing and savoring her egg.

Staring at the steam curling around her cup, Coral Bell offered Tar Chuang his tea with both hands. He grabbed her hands and bent down to catch her eyes, whispering, "You're so thin. Your eyes seem to cover half of your face!"

Blushing and trembling with confusion, Coral Bell could think of nothing clever to say. Tar Chuang took the cup from her and placed it on the table. To cheer her up, he squatted and hopped around like a monkey, making funny faces until Coral Bell couldn't help but laugh. He crouched before her, stared at her like a child, and said, "I can see myself in your eyes!"

Coral Bell's heart was thumping wildly. She wanted to hold his angular, long face, tug on his strangely flared elephant ears, and kiss his mischievous long eyes, but she had become accustomed to caution, hiding in a safe place inside herself. She lived a secret life in that church of her childhood, where memories of kindness and peace lingered in the vaulted ceiling, soaring up into a dome with sunlight streaming through a stained-glass window. She kept her poker face.

She jerked her arms back, intertwining her hands behind her to get a firm grip on herself. Then she turned abruptly and ran from the room, not even thanking him for the egg or for making her laugh.

Except for two old women, Number Three, and two children, patients were sent home throughout the afternoon. When Mr. Chen arrived to inspect the wounded, Coral Bell showed him Number Three's injuries. Dr. Tsai came over and suggested that Number Three remain in the clinic to help guide his buffalo and plow the fields by the river. Inexplicably, Mr. Chen nodded yes and sent the buffalo half an hour later.

Number Three greeted the animal like an old friend. Tar Chuang helped the boy onto the buffalo and hitched a plow behind them. With Number Three riding and talking to the animal, and Tar Chuang leading the plow, they set to work right away. Soon Coral Bell could hear them singing "The People's Army Loves the People" and "East Is Red, the Sun Is Rising."

They stopped abruptly in the middle of a stanza. Coral heard Tar Chuang say, "We should have sung 'The East Is Red, the Fires Are Rising.'" Coral Bell shuddered. Everyone knew that the "Sun" referred to Chairman Mao. If anyone reported that Tar Chuang blamed Chairman Mao for the furnace fires, he would be in great danger. Luckily, no one seemed to have noticed, and Coral Bell soon heard Tar Chuang teaching Number Three an old folk song:

> *There is a little monk,*
> *His eyes shiny with tears,*
> *As he walks up the hill to burn incense.*
>
> *Remembering my mother,*
> *Who packed me a bundle and*
> *Sent me to become a monk.*

Oh-me-to-fo, in the middle
Eighteen Loh Han on two sides,
Protect me; find me a good wife,
Give me a big strong son.

Calls me Dad, calls her Mom,
There is a little monk,
His eyes shiny with tears,
As he walks up the hill to burn incense.

Number Three repeated each line after Tar Chuang, singing louder and louder as he learned the tune.

"Why does the mother want to send her son to become a monk if he prefers to be a father?" Coral heard Number Three shouting to Tar Chuang.

"I don't know. It's only a song!" Tar Chuang shouted back. He was now knee-deep in the dirt, wading through the plowed earth. "Maybe that was the only way the mother could afford to give her son an education. Or maybe he had connections, and the Party granted him permission to lead a soft life."

"What's the use of getting an education if you don't have a son to pass it on to?"

"I can see you'll never become a monk!" Tar Chuang laughed. "Hey, get the buffalo moving. We want to start planting so we'll get a good crop before the weather turns cold."

Coral Bell made frequent trips to the window and the door to monitor Number Three and Tar Chuang's work. Their singing and bantering cheered her. The rest of the day passed in a blur of ceaseless activity: tending to the wounded, cleaning, and organizing.

When Coral Bell took her afternoon break, she found Dr. Tsai alone in the back room. By way of a greeting, she said, "I think we will be running short of disinfectant and penicillin soon."

Silver Bell normally was careful not to reveal her Western education, but her earlier encounter with Tar Chuang in the same room had lowered her guard. She inadvertently said the word "penicillin" in English.

Dr. Tsai gulped. "Do you know English?" he whispered, looking around to make sure they were alone.

"Yes, at one time I did." Coral bit her tongue, fearing she might get into trouble again.

Dr. Tsai remained quiet for a long time, staring at her. "I thought you were different — suggesting we build a swing."

A torrent of emotions and lessons learned surged through Coral; her fears, her reticence, her lies and deceits to safeguard her family, and the discipline required to spout the correct Party line all jostled for a scrap. But Dr. Tsai looked like a Confucian gentleman. She decided to tell him briefly of her background. "My sister taught me English when I was young. After 1953 I was encouraged to study Russian, but for some reason my childhood English has never left me."

"I'm a graduate of Cornell Medical School in New York." Dr. Tsai sighed. Choking back his shaky breath, he stuttered, "I . . . I was accused of being a spy during the Korean War, and everything was taken from my family. Now I've been labeled a counterrevolutionary. I had grown used to speaking frankly in the United States. My wife warned me that I would get into trouble, and so I have."

"When did you return to China?"

"I came back in 1950. I thought the Communists were true nationalists, and I returned thinking I could help heal the country." He stared at his gnarled hands.

"My sister Golden Bell and her family refused to move to Hong Kong for the same reason."

"Yes, here's where my youth has gone." His voice trembled. "They sent me here to get 'reeducated.' Only my medical skills saved my life."

He rummaged in his inner pockets and pulled out a rumpled picture of himself in a Western overcoat, standing in front of the Cornell Medical Building in New York. He was squinting under sunny skies. A blooming cherry tree drew patterns on his face. His fingers shook as he gently smoothed the cracks in the photo and carefully returned the picture to his inner pocket. Clutching his hand to his chest, he found a place to sit. All the while, he blinked and turned his head away so as not to betray any emotion.

White Lily and Coral Bell had often discussed the important lesson they had learned from Eddie, the boy who had called Madam Chiang Kai-shek Auntie. Now they lived in a true poker game. Keeping a straight face helped them defy and disengage from the daily humiliations and drudgery around them. A dull ache lingered in Coral Bell's stomach like an ulcer, which helped only when she wanted to forget her hunger.

Coral knew all too well the slippery nature of memories. So Dr. Tsai also had a secret place where dreamlike experiences resided. Though burdened by the anxieties of his present life, the images of sunlight and cherry blossoms in the photo must have swelled his heart and soothed his pain, but also intensified his longing and unease. Cora Bell felt his conflicting emotions, as if a liquid fire flowed between them. At least she had Brook ma-ma and White Lily to share her secrets with, and she prayed that he wouldn't have to bear his burden alone. She turned away to make him tea and give him time to regain his composure.

"My sisters studied in Syracuse. I never asked them whether they liked living there," she said, handing Dr. Tsai his cup of tea.

"I was lonely in America. By 1950, my parents had arranged to find a wife for me," he said. "The Communist government had also mounted a quiet propaganda campaign to facilitate Chinese intellectuals' return to China and help with its reconstruction. I was sick of the corruption in the old Nationalist government, and I thought the new regime represented progress and would bring positive changes." He sipped his tea, and his voice stopped trembling. "I thought our country would go through a period of slow reconciliation, as happened after the American Civil War. I was young and romantic. I thought I would be in the forefront of the New Order!"

"My sister Golden Bell felt the same," Coral Bell said. "Living in America must be like living in paradise!" She could not help voicing her longings.

"Yes." Dr. Tsai nodded woodenly. "The irony of being Chinese these days is that in order to live in paradise, you have to feel like an alienated foreigner. But here, being a patriot means creating a new order of hell. Where have we gone wrong?"

"My M-ma always blamed China's troubles on foreigners. Now we have no more foreign contacts. Do you think China can ever emerge from its ashes?"

"I once heard a philosopher say that the extreme of virtue is vice. For too long, we've been taught to be obedient, to honor our parents and leaders." Dr. Tsai seemed to be musing to himself. "We've been so well trained that we've become docile and humble, forever placing our family's and nation's interests before our own. On that pretext, too many of us have lost our individuality, or worse, stifled our innovative spirit."

"I was baptized in a Christian church when I was young," Coral Bell said, sipping her tea to slow her racing heart. "I remember one of the banners on the wall carrying a motif of white felt pigeons flying between these words from Genesis: 'I am with thee, and will keep thee in all places whither thou goest.'"

She watched Dr. Tsai's face, trying to detect his reaction. His face was blank, but he muttered, "I think He is with us here now."

Coral Bell gulped for air. "Are you also a Christian?" She felt a familiar rush of long-suppressed warmth and comfort. She had behaved like a criminal, murmuring and huddling in the store-room like a corrupt conspirator. Suddenly, she seemed to see a golden ray of enlightenment: they were sailing in the same boat wherein they learned life's greatest lessons — transcendence, universal service, and love.

Dr. Tsai nodded. "While I am sobered by the story of Job, I still dare to hope and pray for relief."

"Do you think the Great Leap Forward will work?"

"I doubt it." He shook his head. "Our culture may have civilized the ancient world, but how can we produce steel simply by rousing the collective will of the peasants?"

"Pride comes before a fall," Coral responded, leaning into a wall, twirling a tuft of hair by her ear the way she used to when she was a child. "My Sunday school teacher used to say that. But I was always told to be proud of being Chinese."

"Cultural pride comes naturally to everyone. Perhaps at one time we did have much to be proud of. The museum in New York displays many relics of our old accomplishments, but the world has passed us by." His eyes turned red.

Wraithlike, Bai Yue appeared. Coral Bell was startled, but acted quickly. "I learned my acupuncture from my mother," she almost shouted.

"Mrs. Wong in the north corner bed is vomiting!" Bai Yue burst out breathlessly.

"You go," Dr. Tsai said, nodding to Coral Bell. "I'll come after I finish my tea." His arm stayed crossed over his chest with his hand safeguarding his pocket. His face turned blank. Coral Bell knew their secrets would be safe with each other. Perhaps he had also learned to be a poker player.

Coral Bell ran out to take care of Mrs. Wong. White Lily was already there.

"Where were you?" White Lily asked.

"I . . . I was taking a break with Dr. Tsai," Coral stammered.

Tar Chuang was cleaning up by the door, and Bai Yue went over to help him. They were whispering and eyeing Coral Bell. She began to tremble, wondering how much of her conversation with Dr. Tsai had been overheard.

In this poisoned atmosphere, where everyone was urged to report spies that did not exist, they were afraid of being investigated, locked up, randomly smacked, humiliated, or even killed for espousing the wrong values. Coral Bell's fear also included rage — compactly bottled up and stored in a secret place within. In spite of everyone's poker face, fury threatened to erupt at any given moment — like those explosive backyard furnaces.

Ties That Bind

Wei Village, 1962

WITH THE BUFFALO firmly under Tar Chuang and Number Three's guidance, the clinic plowed more tracts of land and planted an abundance of yams, potatoes, carrots, mustard greens, spinach, turnips, peas, beans, and several varieties of cabbage. Ah Tung and his friend came to help whenever they could. They showed the doctors the commune's small orchard, and everyone began tending the fruit trees as well. No one complained about the extra work because the steady harvest was encouraging.

Loh Wei had been appointed guardian of the clinic's garden and chicken coop. He also brought a basket for crabbing and taught the doctors how to tie earthworms into a bundle as bait. He spent his time digging for worms, fishing, crabbing, weeding the garden, and feeding the chickens. The city doctors were impressed by the meticulous way he collected the chicken droppings and night soil from the outhouse. He used them to fertilize the garden.

Loh Wei took all the fish and large crabs to the communal kitchen but allowed the doctors to have the snails. He snipped off the pointy tip of each mollusk, creating a hole on the bottom of the shell. The snails were stir-fried with ginger, scallion, and soy sauce.

Coral Bell had loved eating snails since childhood. It was delightful to put a finger on the hole and wrap her lips around the open side of the shell. Taking a breath and releasing the finger at the same time, she sucked the savory, chewy morsel. In the summer, the doctors shared a large bowl of snails once a week. There was much raucous merriment during all that sucking and licking. After each meal, Loh Wei pounded the shells into a powder to supplement his fertilizer. With greens from the garden and the occasional egg, they seldom went hungry.

More and more patients arrived every day. No one knew if they came for a better meal or for legitimate treatment, but Dr. Tsai never turned them away. "Better nutrition promotes better health," he proclaimed. So many people came to the clinic that Mr. Chen had to intervene. From then on, villagers had to get his permission.

White Lily and Coral Bell were sometimes sent on "healing missions" into the surrounding villages. They walked or rode on oxcarts. They often came back discouraged because they weren't skilled enough to heal anyone. After seeing the hunger and poverty there, they brought yams to their patients rather than medicine. Life had become a game of bluff poker: The secret of staying alive was knowing what not to say while telling partial truths cloaked in the correct Party line. It was always safe to quote Chairman Mao.

"Look, look, look!" An old woman ran to Dr. Tsai screaming and crying one day. "She's trying to kill me! I'm all black-and-blue!" She extended her arm to show her bruises, pointing and cursing at Bai Yue.

Dr. Tsai took one look and shouted at Bai Yue, "Useless doctor! Don't you know how to draw blood?"

Beads of sweat appeared on Bai Yue's forehead. "I . . . I've only done it once before!" she stammered.

"Why are you drawing her blood?" White Lily asked.

"She came in yesterday complaining of a cough that had lasted two months. We gave her an extra serving of vegetables," Bai Yue said, pouting. "I felt her forehead, and she was burning up. I thought drawing blood might help."

"You don't need to draw blood to treat coughs!" Dr. Tsai sounded gruffer than ever. Coral Bell could hear him mumbling under his breath, "Dumb egg, Dumb egg!" She remembered hearing the doctor blame his forthrightness on his foreign training. She could see how this habit might have landed him in trouble.

"Our great leader Chairman Mao said we must learn to swim by swimming!" Coral Bell interjected, silencing everyone. "We're all learning through our work." She led the old woman aside, disinfected her bruises, and rolled down her sleeves.

Dr. Tsai caught on right away. "Yes, we must all learn by doing. Good try, Bai Yue." He ordered an extra meal and more fluids for the old woman.

Later, Coral Bell drew Bai Yue aside and whispered: "Dr. Tsai praised you for learning by doing. He shouted at you because he does not want you to become infected by the old woman's blood. There is lots of bronchitis and tuberculosis around."

Bai Yue had no idea whether handling a patient's blood spread bronchitis or TB. But since Coral Bell had quoted Chairman Mao correctly, she was duly impressed.

After dinner, Coral Bell and White Lily headed for the sycamore tree by the river. They often went there to be alone and talk. White Lily sat leaning against the tree trunk, but Coral Bell felt restless. She walked around a little, then came back and sat close to her friend, telling her all her conflicting feelings regarding Tar Chuang's attention.

"I'm so short — not quite five feet tall. I wonder what he sees in me."

"It's your eyes," White Lily answered. "Big round eyes are unusual for the Chinese."

"That's my mother's gift," Coral Bell murmured, the crease between her eyebrows deepening. "But what should I do?"

"You have obviously charmed him. Unlike those of our background, he comes from the noble working class. I heard his father was a janitor at a Shanghai hospital, and his mother a seamstress, so you'd do well to accept his attentions."

"How did you find out so much about him?"

White Lily turned to gaze at the river. Her composure concealed her inner turmoil. Finally she blurted out, "Bai Yue seems to know everything about him. And I had noticed his lively playfulness even on the train coming up here. We're all getting on in age and ready to marry."

"Yes?"

"We should both be looking for mates!"

"Right. But I hadn't thought of it, and you've never told me!" Coral Bell knelt beside her friend. "You're always so quiet, I just assumed you had no interest in men. Is Bai Yue interested in him too?"

With trembling hands, White Lily grabbed Coral Bell's arms, crying, "Bai Yue always tries to sit beside him at meals and find excuses to consult him in the clinic. But help me, help me, I have such intense yearnings sometimes."

"Yes, yes." Coral Bell hugged her. "I too have strange dreams and longings. Often at night, lying on my miserable wooden plank, I think I can smell the freshly cut-grass of the Shanghai Sporting Club. When I wake up, I smell the hot stench from the outhouse and imagine bizarre creatures growing and multiplying. I, I . . ." her tongue cleaved to her mouth.

"You're right." White Lily sobbed. "The last thing we should do is to dream and indulge ourselves. But my heart is so starved for something carefree. Sometimes I imagine someone will see me as beautiful. Oh, Coral, am I so corrupt and depraved to want these things?"

"No, no, your feelings are natural. In the old days, women were married in their teens. I am just as guilty as you, longing for things our country cannot afford." Coral Bell rocked her friend back and forth. "You and Tar Chuang would be good for each other, if only times were different." Anger surged through her. "Our lives are a sham. We're not qualified to be doctors. Our present drudgery is totally senseless. We all quote Chairman Mao and put on elaborate guises to appear professionally competent! What does that have to do with medicine?"

"Shhh." White Lily put a finger to her lips. "Not so loud! As a child, I was always told that China is a large country with rich resources and hardworking, clever people. How did we become such a poor and crazy country?"

"M-ma blames the foreigners, but I really don't understand. Our country is doing worse since we cut off contact with the outside world." Coral Bell looked somber and confused.

"Oh, what's the use? It wouldn't make any difference anyway. No one would look at me!" White Lily lowered her head.

"That's not true! You have beautiful shiny hair, and your skin is so creamy — like vanilla ice cream! Remember when we had that in Shanghai before the liberation?"

White Lily grinned sheepishly. "Thanks for trying to cheer me up."

"Yes, next time Tar Chuang does something funny, copy him. He'll laugh and notice you. Don't just imagine your flirting scenes. Act them out!"

"The last time I was impulsive . . . oh, I can't trust myself. Remember what I did to my father?" White Lily began to tremble. "I live with that guilt every moment of my life."

"You were very young, and the spy hunters tricked you. This time, you must try to make yourself feel lively. It will help you heal."

"Many years ago, you told me time would help me heal. But it still haunts me. It even invades my dreams."

"Yes, I've heard you mumble and scream sometimes."

"Then I sit, wide awake all night, feeling the pain over and over again." She bent forward, clutching her stomach with both hands.

"What are you doing?" Bai Yue had sneaked up beside them. Her demure look made it hard to determine whether she was curious or malicious.

"White Lily has a . . . a stomach ache." Coral Bell improvised quickly. "Here, give me a hand. Let's help her get to bed."

Tar Chuang came tramping forward, and Coral Bell said: "White Lily, you're getting heavy on my arm!" She looked at Bai Yue. "White Lily must be heavy for you to support also. Aren't you all tired from a hard day's work?"

"Oh, yes," Bai Yue replied. She often complained about having to scrub floors, clean bedpans, and do other chores that she considered beneath her dignity as a "doctor."

Coral Bell pulled White Lily's hands toward Tar Chuang for support. "White Lily has a stomach ache, and we're taking her to bed."

"No, no!" White Lily protested. "I can walk by myself. I'm feeling better now."

Tar Chuang had already wrapped his arm around her, pulling her along. White Lily stole her friend a look of gratitude and showed no inclination to push him away.

"I heard Dr. Tsai whispering to you in private the other day," Bai Yue said to Coral Bell as they trudged along. "What was he telling you?"

Starbursts of panic flashed in Coral Bell's head. Her hand flew up to her mouth, and she pretended to be picking her teeth. She couldn't answer for a moment.

Tar Chuang answered for her: "I told you: Coral Bell is fond of asking questions. She's learning from Dr. Tsai. Do as Chairman

Mao said: 'Rice must be eaten one mouthful at a time; a journey must be undertaken one step at a time.' You should ask Dr. Tsai for instructions before you do any procedure, just as Coral Bell does."

Apparently, Tar Chuang had also learned to quote Chairman Mao for safety.

Coral Bell finally found her voice. "I think we were discussing acupuncture."

White Lily chimed in to help her friend: "I understand Dr. Tsai comes from the corrupt professional class. He would have been sent to do hard labor in the country, but instead he has been given this noble assignment to work as a doctor. He must be related to someone senior in the Party. He may be spying for the higher-ups; we would be wise to learn from him."

Tar Chuang smiled at White Lily, giving her a meaningful look.

Bai Yue eyed the three uncertainly. She had suspected that Dr. Tsai belonged to Coral Bell's equally incorrect class status and had hoped for confirmation. Instead, she heard Chairman Mao quoted at her from all directions. Now she would have to be wary, because a Party connection was a very serious matter.

All her young life, Bai Yue had judged others by the firm Maoist teaching that since her father had been a store clerk and her mother was a scrubwoman, she had the right to bring down those who were more privileged. After all, the glory of communism was to level the playing field. She would never have attended primary school under the old system. Now she was a doctor, just like White Lily and Coral Bell, who belonged to the privileged class.

She resolved to write home and ask her cousin, a minor Party functionary, to check into everyone's background. Party membership and connections to the political elite were real advantages.

⸸AMINε

Wei Village, 1962

B Y EARLY NOVEMBER, all the corn and greens had been harvested, and the ground was pregnant with potatoes, carrots, turnips, and radishes. Loh Wei raked every fallen leaf and mixed it with lime and human and animal waste to prepare compost. Smiling and puttering around in the waning sun, he predicted abundance for the following year.

The nights grew frosty. A crust of ice began forming on the river. One morning, Loh Wei arrived to find the rooster missing and a patch of sweet potatoes dug up near the north end of the field. He got permission from Dr. Tsai to camp out inside the clinic's front door. "I'm a light sleeper," he explained. "I will hear the poachers."

In the evening, several young people with gaunt faces entered the fenced-in garden. Loh Wei screamed at them: "Get off the fields! Get off! The vegetables belong to the clinic!"

No one listened. More groups of ragged men descended on the small farmstead, their bare, mud-encrusted feet trampling down the rows of vegetables. They ignored Loh Wei's orders and rushed around to find rocks and sticks to dig up the field. The doctors ran out to watch as Loh Wei came to them hollering: "Look, look! There must be a dozen people coming toward us!"

A rustling, scratching sound pierced the eerie cold air as the doctors stared and the hungry people stuffed the produce into their mouths, smearing their faces with dirt.

"They're coming from the north," White Lily whispered.

"Come help me gather the chickens inside!" Tar Chuang ran off, and without a word, everyone followed him to the coop. A famished young man tried to grab the chicken Coral Bell was holding, but she gave him a vigorous shove and the man fell down. Loh Wei came by and gave him a kick. The interloper cowered, looking plaintive and fearful rather than threatening. He muttered something inaudible and slunk away. The sullen, emaciated people barely looked up to stare. They were busy digging and chewing. The doctors took all the chickens into the clinic's storerooms and locked the doors.

"Come, help me dig! We must dig up everything whether the plants are ready or not." Loh Wei passed out a few farm implements and sent everyone into the field to harvest what they could. "Don't be afraid to beat away the poachers!"

The hungry marauders were too weak or too busy eating to fight back. Soon the doctors brought bushel after bushel of their harvest into the clinic.

The few patients in the clinic were asked to leave. Two elderly female patients refused, but others clamored to go home. They grabbed some vegetables as they stumbled out the door. Coral Bell found a few ragbags and helped them conceal the food. "People will rob you if you carry the vegetables in your hands," she warned.

By nightfall, Coral Bell, White Lily, and Bai Yue decided to stay in the clinic, barricaded behind closed doors and taped windows.

"This house has solid earthen walls. We're safe inside," Loh Wei assured everyone.

Dr. Tsai shook his head. "This bitter cold wind does not bode well. More people will be able to cross over the frozen river tomorrow."

"The older and weaker stragglers will be swamping the whole town!" Tar Chuang added.

"Some of the hungry mobs will be more desperate and dangerous," Bai Yue whispered.

"They'll want more than food, and they'll steal and destroy everything." Even White Lily joined in sounding the alarm.

"We are no longer safe here," Tar Chuang pronounced.

The rustling sounds outside continued, and a low moaning wail was heard. Scratching and banging noises reverberated through the walls.

"We'd better eat our supper raw," Dr. Tsai said. "The smells of cooking might incite a riot."

Coral Bell and White Lily huddled together, trembling. Bai Yue joined them. "I should never have come here," she grumbled, crunching on a raw potato.

Tar Chuang stood up to speak. "We'd better leave as soon as possible."

Dr. Tsai nodded. "Yes. Medicine can't help anyone under these circumstances. We have to vacate." They asked Loh Wei about train schedules and the best way to escape.

"There is a train tomorrow morning at first dawn — around 5 A.M." Loh Wei sighed in resignation. "It's best to leave when the mob outside is still half frozen." Tears streamed down his face, and he said shakily: "The clinic is the best thing that has ever happened to this village. It has certainly saved my life. But you're right. All of you must leave immediately."

Dr. Tsai ordered everyone to pack the medical equipment and anything else they could carry.

"But all my things are still in the shed!" Bai Yue groaned.

"People must have broken into it by now," White Lily said, looking miserable.

"I must get into town to report this to the Party leaders," Loh Wei whispered. "The militia has been safeguarding the storehouse, and the leaders will be angry if you leave and the mob carries away all the food and remaining livestock."

"Are we allowed to leave? We've only been here less than a year." Bai Yue reverted to her strident Party-member voice.

"Do you want to wait for permission and starve to death here?" Coral Bell spat out.

Tar Chuang and White Lily stared at her, surprised at her uncharacteristic bluntness. Throughout her childhood, both her mothers had taught her to be polite and gracious, that all foolishness must be dealt with by allowing the other person to "save face." But this was a different China. Any trace of Confucian gentility was long gone.

Tar Chuang turned to Loh Wei. "I'll go to the Party leader's house after midnight. You'll need your rest. I'm sure I can fight off the hungry people."

"I need to get home," Loh Wei answered. "If I can sneak out, I'll crawl and moan like the rest of the people outside. They will leave me alone." He wept openly. "Ah, this is so much worse than the time when the locusts came! Heaven sent us the locusts, and we fought them as best we could. Everyone, including the villagers from miles around, released their ducks and chickens into the fields to feed on the insects."

The elderly woman with heart problems piped up from her bed. "We also used smoke torches to chase the critters into nets. We caught so many — enough to feed our domestic fowl for weeks! We worked like demons until the winds turned and blew the insects away. We managed to save some crops. The birds had a huge feast, and we even ate roasted locusts!" She was smiling at the memory.

"Our backyard furnaces caused this famine," Loh Wei cried. "Only old men like me are allowed to work on our land . . ." He could not continue.

The rest of the night was hectic, with everyone fumbling in the dark, packing medical equipment. After midnight, Loh Wei bade a tearful farewell. He crept out a window because sleeping bodies blocked the doors. In stunned silence, the doctors peered out toward Loh Wei's receding shadow. A suffocating darkness settled over the starless sky. Bodies lay huddled everywhere, many slumped deep inside the dirt they had dug.

Someone whispered, "They're already in their own graves."

Bai Yue debated aloud whether she should follow Loh Wei and retrieve her personal belongings from the shed. Coral Bell wanted to shout her outrage, but she kept quiet and instead gave Bai Yue disgusted looks in the dark. Bai Yue continued to worry, until White Lily finally said: "No doubt the starving people are already using our quilts in the shed to keep warm!"

Coral Bell wanted to bawl in the clinic's bed, kick her bedding, shout obscenities, and pummel her pillow. Instead, she suppressed the shouts, scratched her bedding, and buried her head under her pillow. Throughout the night, everyone dozed as best they could in the numbing cold. Suddenly, loud groans and shouts were heard in the darkness. There was heavy banging on the door. Coral Bell bolted upright in the sickbed she slept on.

"It's all right." Tar Chuang touched her arm. "It must be the soldiers coming to bring us to the station." Coral Bell was surprised to hear his voice so near her bed.

The soldiers wore Liberation Army uniforms and carried rifles. They loaded all the produce and livestock on to several handcarts and helped the two remaining patients out the door. The doctors followed, carrying whatever medical equipment they could.

A path had already been cleared among the slumbering bodies. A new moon cast ghostly shadows on their pale faces; Coral Bell saw their gaping mouths, deep sunken eyes, and limp hands. She tried to ignore them. She stared straight ahead and followed the soldiers. Suddenly a hand grabbed her pant leg, and she almost stumbled. Tar Chuang was right behind her. He kicked the hand away and helped her keep her balance.

Half of the soldiers left to bring the produce into town and the rest escorted them to the station.

The train was late because bodies had to be cleared from the tracks. Hordes of people swarmed the station clamoring for tickets, but the ticket office was closed. When the train came, everyone stormed the doors. In the end, it was the soldiers' rifles that allowed the medical group to elbow their way in.

By the time they were seated, the sun was rising. The horizon blazed in glorious reds, oranges, yellows, and crimsons; not a single cloud marred the sky. Unbidden, tears streamed down Coral Bell's face. White Lily hugged her friend and wept with her.

Patting both of them, Tar Chuang spoke to them as if they were frightened children: "The sun is up. It will be warm. The people will survive today." He had stayed close to Coral Bell the whole time.

Strangers on a Train

1962

A T THE NEXT station, a few people, wrapped in swaddling clothes, lined the platform. One was writhing and moaning; others looked dead, their faces frozen in fright. Their eyes stared skyward, but no one bothered to close them.

People on the train began pointing and whispering. They speculated that the families might be taking their dead or ailing relatives home. If these families wanted to give their loved ones a proper burial, they would have to go elsewhere. There was simply no wood left for coffins here.

"I hope they don't let these . . . these bodies on board," Bai Yue mumbled, turning her head away from the window. "With so many people dying in the fields, why do they bother?"

"We're farther south now. In spite of the famine, maybe there are still people who have the means to travel." Tar Chuang sounded almost hopeful.

Coral Bell also turned away. She would have preferred to leave the window seat Tar Chuang had grabbed for her, but the aisles were also packed with people. She was tightly wedged between the window and White Lily, whose shoulder pressed into hers. Her knees almost touched Bai Yue's, who was sitting across from her.

White Lily began to cry. "A dead father or mother is still family."
Coral Bell grabbed her friend's hand.

Tar Chuang peered out the window. "The train is full. I don't think they can take on any more passengers."

"So why don't they just go on?" Bai Yue opened the window and leaned out, straining to glimpse the engine. A rush of cold air, loud wails, and pleading voices entered the compartment.

Dr. Tsai, who had been snoring next to Bai Yue, woke up with a jerk. "What, what's going on?"

"Close the window!" people shouted.

Bai Yue banged down the window and slumped back into her seat. "They're loading water and coal. That means we'll be leaving soon."

When they were on their way again, Tar Chuang produced a carrot for everyone. Coral Bell, feeling dizzy and nauseated, refused the offer. Tar Chuang stuffed the carrot into her palm anyway, urging her to save it for later.

Once the train pulled out, fallow fields came into view; dirt roads crisscrossed mounds of earth — backyard furnaces that were no longer puffing smoke. The fanatical zeal to feed these furnaces had stripped bare the surrounding hills. Grave markers dotted the brown, desolate spot that had once contained verdant farmland. Coral Bell closed her eyes. Although queasy and nervous, she dozed off. She woke with a jolt, banging her head on the side of the train. She cried out in shock. Bai Yue was pulling the carrot from her hand; the long-ago scene of the ragged boy robbing her of chocolate replayed in her mind.

"No sense wasting good food," Bai Yue said.

"Coral Bell will need it later!" White Lily snatched back the carrot, wrapping Coral Bell's fingers around it.

"Better eat it now," Dr. Tsai said to Coral Bell. Everyone avoided looking at Bai Yue, who was staring out the window in sullen embarrassment.

Tar Chuang scowled. "Maybe I can buy us some hot water at our next stop."

Coral Bell rubbed the thin carrot on her sleeves. Patches of golden skin shone; it looked appetizing. She turned toward the window and hid the root under her hands while munching as quietly as she could.

As the train rattled on, an unnatural hush descended on the compartment. Those cramped in the aisle sat on their meager luggage and leaned against the benches. A train going in the opposite direction led to murmurs about the soldiers on board.

"A troop train!" a raspy voice announced.

"They're probably going to seal off the areas where people are starving," another gruff voice followed.

"Is this the last train going south?"

"Maybe."

Sighs and quiet whimpers swept through the compartment.

Bai Yue wriggled in her seat. "Chairman Mao had a good idea anyway." She looked at her coworkers. "Don't you think China would be a world-class country if the furnaces had worked?"

Dr. Tsai closed his eyes, pretending not to have heard.

Tar Chuang glowered at her. He wanted to curse the backyard furnaces that had caused this disaster. The steel they produced was of such inferior quality, it was unfit for constructing anything. Instead he took a deep breath. "Isn't it too bad that people worry about their growling stomachs when they should be thinking about the glory of the motherland?" he said.

The sarcasm did not escape Bai Yue. She rolled her eyes and stared out the window.

At the next stop they reached the fertile Zhejiang Province. A few peddlers at the station were selling hot tea and buns. The medical party decided to take turns to stretch and exercise on the platform. Two people were to remain in their seats to hold their places and guard their meager belongings.

Just before Coral Bell and Bai Yue's turn to be on guard duty, Bai Yue leaned forward as if to share an intimacy. "I'm sorry I tried to take your carrot," she began. "But you have rich relatives, and I come from poverty. My father died, and my mother was a poor scrubwoman," she said, smiling. "I . . . urh . . . have more respect for food."

Despite the apology, Bai Yue eyed Coral with contempt. Coral Bell lowered her head, shrinking from the reproach. She wanted to say her father had also died and that her mother once was a slave girl, but she kept quiet. She was taught to be honorable. Her mother had never felt oppressed, and Bai Yue would not have shown sympathy anyway.

"You know, your friend White Lily is really very unattractive — such tiny eyes and thin little lips! She doesn't even have a chin," Bai Yue said.

Coral Bell took in a quick breath. She fumbled with her jacket, not knowing how to reply.

"Of course I am no beauty myself," Bai Yue sneered, as if her humble self-estimation gave her the authority to judge others. "Your large eyes always catch men's attention. Dr. Tsai and Tar Chuang both seem to favor you," she continued. "But you are really too short. Just barely pleasant to look at, and nowhere near a great beauty."

"I . . . I . . ." Coral Bell stammered. She sensed not only a personal attack but also danger in Bai Yue's animosity. She wanted to say something to appease her. But her heart raced and her tongue felt leaden. She held out her carrot stub toward Bai Yue.

"Oh, the high-class lady is sharing her cold food now that she knows her hot tea and warm bun are coming!" came the sardonic reply.

"No, no, no," Coral Bell replied in alarm. "You can have my hot bun too!" She had managed to say an entire sentence.

"I suppose all the men will admire your generosity." Bai Yue waved away the thought in disgust. "You rich people just want to show off. You have no idea what poverty can do to you!"

"I . . . I'm not rich. We, we are comrades in our work." *Oh, what should I say?* She wondered.

"Humph!" Bai Yue huffed.

Tar Chuang came in with the bun and hot water and indicated that it was Coral and Bai Yue's turn to exercise. White Lily was also ambling down the aisle toward them. Coral Bell chose to stay behind.

Pale and trembling, she blurted out her exchange with Bai Yue as soon as the latter had left.

"Heavens! Bai Yue could make trouble for us when we return." White Lily held on to her friend's hands.

"My father wrote from Shanghai that people are again being encouraged to denounce the 'slackers' and the 'counterrevolution-aries,'" Tar Chuang whispered. "Does Bai Yue have any influence with people in the Central Committee?"

"She boasted of having a relative in the Communist Party."

"I think something is brewing," Tar Chuang speculated. "I heard that Chairman Mao wants young people to live a pure life and to foment continuous revolution. There is talk that they will form a radical corps called the Red Guards in order to clean out the corrupt leaders in the Party."

"We had better join the Red Guards when we get back to Shanghai," White Lily whispered.

"I wish it were that easy." Coral Bell sighed. "I belong to the wrong class and I'm too old." At twenty-one she already felt past her prime to foment revolution.

"Maybe if you renounce the East Pacific Textile Factories you still can . . ." White Lily's voice trailed off.

Coral Bell wrung her hands and shifted uneasily in her seat. It was shocking to hear her friend talk about betrayal. She remembered

White Lily's disastrous denunciation of her father and looked out the window to hide her anguish.

With no warning, Tar Chuang grabbed Coral Bell's hand. "Marry me! I belong to the working class. With our record of hard work in the country, we can both become Red Guard leaders!"

Both women looked stunned. Coral Bell recoiled from his grasp and turned to hold White Lily's hands in hers. She wanted to tell her friend that she did not love Tar Chuang and had hoped the young man would favor White Lily. But she couldn't utter a single word. Only her watery eyes pleaded for understanding.

White Lily embraced her friend. In a trembling voice, she said, "Yes, yes, you must marry Tar Chuang. You'll be safe with a janitor's son!"

The die was cast for Coral Bell.

When the train resumed its journey, Tar Chung announced his plans of marrying Coral Bell. Dr. Tsai congratulated them, but Bai Yue knitted her brows and gave them a sour look. She mumbled something about Coral Bell's luck in joining the working class and looked out the window.

Back in Shanghai, Dr. Tsai was invited to Tar Chuang and Coral Bell's wedding. Everyone debated whether they should include Bai Yue.

"She might become more spiteful if she is left out." Brook mama frowned.

"Don't include her," White Lily urged. "You should at least have some peace of mind during your wedding."

"Weddings are private matters." Golden Bell nodded. "Surely you must invite the people you like!"

"Privacy is a capitalist luxury," Yung reminded them, cracking his knuckles and pacing.

"I cannot see her attending my wedding!" Tar Chuang said firmly. "I don't care what mischief she might bring on us. My struggle for survival has been just as hard as hers. Besides, her jealousy could be more deadly." Tar Chuang would not be dissuaded.

The marriage was performed in the city registry with the bride and groom wearing the same Mao jackets and drab dark pants that had become the nation's uniform. The only touch of gaiety was the red bows that the couple wore on their chests.

A simple wedding reception was held in the Yung mansion. Many kinsmen came from Hangzhou and brought foodstuffs as gifts. Though meager by the standards of the Yung family's earlier opulence, the simple food and wine were enough for everyone. The Yungs felt blessed that they could now claim to be related to someone in the working class. To preserve her position in the Party, Peony was not invited, but she promised to use her influence to get the young couple into the newly minted all-powerful Red Guards.

A Marriage of Survival

Shanghai, 1962

TAR CHUANG and his parents shared a single room in the old Chinese section Shanghai, and so the newlyweds moved into the Yungs' factory-owned apartment.

On the first night after the wedding, Tar Chuang held Coral Bell's hand and led her to the couch where she had made her bed. He leaned down to kiss her, but she backed off a step. She looked sad, and her hand turned cold and clammy in his. "I hardly know you!" she whispered.

"Yes, but you're the most beautiful girl I've ever met." He pulled her hands to his chest, his face glazed with perspiration.

The musty smell of his sweaty body was more than Coral Bell could bear. She turned her head away, trying to keep her face blank and hard. "Have you seen the modern facilities in our apartment?"

"Yes, of course. Such luxury! I've never used a bathtub before."

"Then I must draw you a bath." Coral Bell extricated herself from his grasp. Before Tar Chuang could protest, she went to check if the bathroom was vacant. It was occupied. Instead of returning to her husband, she ran to the kitchen and boiled two large pots of water. Then she fetched her cleaning supplies and waited outside the bathroom, informing the other tenants that Tar

267

Chuang would be taking a bath. Everyone nodded and smiled, giving each other meaningful glances.

When the bathroom was free, Coral Bell scrubbed the tub clean, and Tar Chuang helped carry and pour the two pots of hot water into the tub.

"Want to join me?" he whispered. Coral Bell shook her head, blushing. She left.

When Tar Chuang returned to their room, Coral Bell faced the back of the sofa, pretending to be asleep. She had fashioned a bedroll for Tar Chuang on the other side of the room.

Tar Chuang moved the bedroll to the floor beside the sofa and started to make conversation. "I hope you're still awake and can hear me. When I was a child, my mother used to bathe me in a small wooden tub we had. Ever since, I've only used our basin to wash myself. I know you come from a different background and that you used to have this apartment all to yourself."

Coral Bell did not answer.

"I was almost ten when I saw my first flush toilet. My father had taken me to the hospital to help him clean." Tar Chuang lifted her braids like a chef checking to see if his noodles were done; he dangled them over his face.

"So how did your family manage?" Coral Bell couldn't help asking.

"Oh, haven't you ever seen the red wooden bowls with lids that look like pregnant cylinders?"

"Yes, but I thought those were chests that people used as end tables! Usually, people covered them with a thick tablecloth." They began laughing together.

In a flash, Tar Chuang had climbed onto the sofa and slipped under Coral Bell's quilt. Somehow he had already managed to take off his clothes, and his body loomed pale and warm above her in the dark. He struggled to extricate her from her nightclothes, whispering, "When I first saw you, I thought you were a movie star fallen upon hard times . . . Oh, Coral Bell, help me, help me . . ."

Coral Bell lay stiff and still in the dark. Then the fragrance of his clean, scrubbed body stirred her. She lifted herself slightly to allow Tar Chuang to disrobe her. As they coiled together, winding and unwinding they consummated their marriage.

"This is also my first time," Tar Chuang confided. He rose, wrapped his bedroll around him, and went to the window to smoke a cigarette by the luminous moonlight. "Your M-ma seems to think that I'm just another tenant in the apartment, not your husband. Obviously she has trouble understanding."

Coral Bell sat up to put on her nightclothes. Even in such an intimate setting, she felt it necessary to abbreviate her family's story, placing all the blame for Purple Jade's sense of dislocation on the Japanese invasion. Tar Chuang seemed satisfied. He returned to the couch and began his ardor anew. This time, he was less urgent. Slowly, he undressed her again, kissing and fondling her breasts, her neck, and her limbs, at last reaching into regions of secret pleasure that sent Coral Bell moaning in spite of herself.

"You don't know how it's been! I've been burning with fire inside for such a long time — especially after seeing you." Tar Chuang lay supine with his legs pressed against the back of the sofa and his feet in the air. Hot and sweaty from their coupling, he panted, "Oh, Coral, I can't wait to have a son with your eyes . ."

The new bride stiffened immediately. Before her wedding, she had secretly gone to see Dr. Tsai, asking for contraception. Uncertain about Tar Chuang's political beliefs, she had not consulted him. Although Chairman Mao had encouraged people to be prolific and build up China's greatest asset — its population — Coral Bell could not imagine bringing a child into her world of struggle meetings, famine, and hard labor. But to consider anything that contradicted the Great Chairman's edicts would be a disaster.

She knew she could share her views with Dr. Tsai, but the doctor had asked her to wait. She must discuss things with Tar Chuang and then decide what to do. Now that Tar Chuang had voiced his desire for a son, she was sure he would not agree to contraception. Her skin itched as if a stranger had touched her. She held her tongue while reaching for her nightclothes.

Tar Chuang sensed his wife's change of mood. He dropped his head on her lap. Biting softly on her inner thighs, he took her hand and guided it to wrap around his hard penis. Coral Bell recoiled as soon as the moist organ made contact. She shook herself free and wiped her hand on her nightclothes repeatedly. Taking a quick breath, Tar Chuang again hauled himself onto her, kissing and nibbling her all over. He coaxed: "All young girls are afraid of motherhood. I won't seem so . . . so lowly to you when we have a child."

Coral Bell could feel her husband weeping with ecstatic joy when they climaxed together, because her own body responded despite her unease. Still, her mind rebelled against the intrusion of this man, and she groaned.

Tar Chuang sat up suddenly to face his wife. "Did I hurt you? I'm such a fool. I was so impulsive."

His warmth and excitement were hard to resist. "I . . . I don't know. I guess I'm politically backward. I don't want a child to see hunger." She wished she could tell her husband about her excursion to the Shanghai Sporting Club and how she had always dreamed of having children that might belong there. She bit her tongue. "Don't you think it's too soon to have children?"

"Maybe, but things will change."

"Until they change, we should use some contraception."

"No! I used to envy the children that drove by in their chauffeured limousines." Tar Chuang finally dressed himself and returned to sit on his bedroll. "I also envied children attending school, because my parents were too poor to send me. Even

270

though my father worked for a cleaning service, he was never an employee of the hospital. The cleaning company paid him barely enough for our food and rent. When my mother got sick, we had to go to the moneylender. Since then, we were never free of debt — not until the Communists liberated us."

"Didn't you see the starvation and unrest in Wei Village?"

"Even though we are going through some tough times now, the Great Helmsman will lead us to victory," he assured her. "The Communists wiped out all the underworld moneylenders and gave my father a proper job in the hospital. They raised my family's standing. We have so much to be thankful for. Now I can read and write! I can add and subtract even better than you." He gave her a contrite look. "I noticed how long it took you to calculate the accounts when we were working in the clinic. The peasants even called me doctor."

Coral Bell didn't know how to respond. She had hoped to introduce him to a different world. She would dearly love to teach him English and read the Bible with him. Now she realized that while he quoted Chairman Mao in the clinic to protect her from Bai Yue, he probably believed what he quoted. He was a true Mao loyalist. There was nothing to bridge the vast chasm that separated them. She had already hidden all her English-language records and books. Tar Chuang still had not seen the shiny Mary-Janes she had saved from her baptism, now stored on the top bookshelf. She had better take them down. She must be extra careful to hide all traces of her privileged background. In the present political climate, people were known to catalog each other's transgressions — even those of the closest family members — especially if they were "drunk on the corrupt ways of old."

She remembered how the boy at the Shanghai Sporting Club had warned her and White Lily that they would share three shoes between the two of them when the Communists came. Now, his prediction had come true. Yet Tar Chuang came from the dispossessed that had worn no shoes. Should she feel grateful because she was married to him? Why was she resisting him? Tar Chuang was so proud of being a Communist. The rift between them was widening. *I must not breathe another word about wanting to use contraception,* she thought. *Tar Chuang will never accept it, and I might bring Dr. Tsai trouble. I must lie to everyone.*

To prevent any further advances from her husband, Coral whispered, "You must help me become a true Maoist. Let us read the Little Red Book together."

Tar Chuang looked stunned for a moment, but he complied for a few minutes. Then he snuggled into his bedroll, spent and exhausted from their night of passion. He started snoring almost immediately.

The very next day, Coral Bell secretly visited Dr. Tsai again, telling him that she and her husband had decided to put off having a child. They agreed no one would ever mention this politically suspect act again.

Claiming fatigue, Coral Bell did not allow Tar Chuang to touch her for many days. She often suggested reading Chairman Mao's writings together. When that failed to quench Tar Chuang's passion, and he insisted on his conjugal rights, Coral Bell complied with such frigidity and resistance that Tar Chuang began to blame himself and their cramped circumstances.

One day he came home with wooden planks and fashioned a double bed in a corner of the room. Brook ma-ma installed a curtain of bed sheets around it. In the process of rearranging the room, Coral managed to eradicate all traces of her foreign learning and bourgeois privileges, hiding her old treasures in her mother's room.

Coral Bell's ardor did not rekindle in their new bed. Tar Chuang was often petulant, and he grumbled to Brook ma-ma that his wife could not conceive after almost a year of marriage.

"Try to understand: She needs more good food and rest," Brook ma-ma replied simply.

"I admit it is unfair." Coral Bell wept while visiting White Lily. "Tar Chuang is a decent enough fellow. But despite our efforts at good cheer, we have nothing in common. I cannot begin to tell him about my aspirations to travel around the world and live in a society like the one we knew in old Shanghai."

"But we were never really part of that world either," White Lily pointed out.

"I know, I know. I should be ashamed of myself." Coral Bell couldn't help feeling discouraged by the irony of her situation. "But I always thought that if I worked hard, someday." She remembered the dancing lights filtering through the stained-glass window of her old church. She swallowed hard to get rid of the sour taste in her mouth as old memories came rushing in.

"M-ma thinks Tar Chuang is just another person sent here to live with us." Coral Bell continued. "But Brook ma-ma almost admitted that she wished he were more book-fragrant."

"How about Tar Chuang's parents? Are they difficult to please?"

"No. Since we are not living with them, they don't bother us." Coral Bell smiled in spite of herself. "I suppose I should feel grateful. Tar Chuang's parents are old-fashioned, humble people. They are also amazed that their son has married into a book-fragrant family. But of course, they're hoping for grandchildren."

"You should really count yourself lucky that Tar Chuang chose to marry you. Did you consult Dr. Tsai as to why you're still not pregnant?"

Coral Bell had always confided in her best friend. "I went to Dr. Tsai before I was married and asked him about contraception," she now said. She stopped. She saw White Lily sucking in her breath, her eyes widening and her mouth working convulsively.

Coral Bell stared again. Where had she seen this expression before?

"Dr. Tsai told me to wait until I had discussed the whole issue with Tar Chuang."

"So did you?"

"Um, I did . . ."

"So what did Tar Chuang say?"

"He wants children."

"You know Chairman Mao said our strength is the Chinese people! We must produce more children for a stronger China!" White Lily almost shouted.

"But what about all the famine?" She wondered how White Lily could go along with such warped thinking. Chairman Mao wanted more fodder against the American cannons in the Korean War. Hadn't White Lily figured out his motives yet?

White Lily's mouth continued twitching in a strange way. She said nothing for a long time. Finally she sighed. "You don't know how lucky you are! Oh, what's the use? At least you're married and safe — you're a member of the working class."

Suddenly, Coral Bell remembered. After years of sharing secrets with her friend, she had somehow dissociated White Lily from the struggle session that had led her to denounce her own father. Not so long ago, White Lily had hoped to win Tar Chuang's affection for herself. Now her mouth was twitching uncontrollably just like the time she was onstage and saw her father kneeling before her. Coral Bell shuddered, disturbed by the strangling clarity of her memory.

"Um, erh . . . Dr. Tsai never gave me any contraception. I just don't let Tar Chuang touch me very often." She lied. White Lily didn't respond, but the contortions of her mouth was just as if she was on that stage again.

Coral Bell turned her head away and muttered that she had an errand. "I have to run," she said.

That night, Coral confided in Brook ma-ma, recounting her conversation with White Lily. "I have no solid proof, only a panicky fear that both White Lily and Tar Chuang may cause harm to Dr. Tsai and people like us. Sometimes they don't seem to want to think for themselves. Tar Chuang hangs on the 'Great Helmsman's' every word. White Lily may not be able to control her jealousy. Would they do anything to endanger us?

"I understand." Brook ma-ma wiped her forehead, which was suddenly moist with sweat. "I know you would never harm a friend just to survive. I hope they won't either. It isn't noble to be suspicious of your own husband and your best friend, but it's prudent not to mention forbidden topics like contraception anymore."

Coral Bell felt relieved her mother no longer mentioned honesty. She was also grateful that Tar Chung's desire had lost its urgency. Now a generalized anxiety pervaded their work in the Red Guard Movement. She grew angry and depressed when the Guards scheduled a purge of each politically incorrect person or family. The moments of marital rapture never returned.

Wu Wei—Positive Non-action
Golden Bell's Journal

August 1968

I NO LONGER know what day it is. With so many units of Red
Guards running wild outside, fear has become my constant
companion and I've lost track of time. Miss Tyler once explained
that the Christian definition of hell is a state of total separation
from God. Is God absent from China in these terrible days?

No philosophy or religion has been able to explain to me why
suffering exists. I remember that the old tiger balm garden in
Hong Kong displayed a diorama of hell. The lurid scenes were
carved in bas-relief on serpentine walls. Devils with bulging eyes,
pointy ears, and rat-like tails were performing heinous deeds, each
more horrible than the last. They carried daggers, forks, and
spears to cut out tongues, gouge out eyes, and disembowel terror-
stricken sinners. At the time I wondered whether anyone had ever
been wicked enough to deserve such punishments. Now the stories
of torture and cruelty make me think hell has taken over Shanghai.

I remember my parents started to teach me the *Three Character
Classic* after I turned three. I had to commit the whole book to
memory. As I grew older, they used to recite key passages to me

and asked me to explain their meaning. Then, I had to memorize the passages all over again. They told me that it was this learning that made the Chinese superior. The center of our culture can be distilled into these two lines:

Yuē rén yì lǐ zhì xìn

曰 仁 義 禮 智 信

cǐ wǔ cháng bù róng wèn

此 五 常 不 容 紊

(To be humane to all living things is "ren."

To cooperate and do the proper thing is "yi."

To practice proper respect to all according to their station is "li."

To deploy your talents based on the best of your understanding is "zhi."

Honesty in all your actions breeds trust. That is "xin."

These five constants must be observed and never confused.)

How can such violence erupt in a land that has valued the Confucian rites, propriety, gentility, and harmony for so long? How can such mayhem consume the young, who had been taught obedience and discipline? No, these youngsters have never been taught the Chinese spirit. They have known nothing but war.

They indulge their most beastly instincts of survival, self-interest, hatred, and revenge. What will be our country's future? After the Great Leap Forward Movement led to widespread famine, our supreme leader now wants to regain Party control. For months he has unleashed the Red Guards, who are mostly high school and college students, to destroy the old culture and traditions. Shouting their slogans, they rain violent "retribution" on book-fragrant families, the capitalists, the landowners, and the ruling officials. Chairman Mao has become a god, and his edicts commandments. Since time immemorial, the dynasties had repeatedly relied on our Confucian ethos of reverence for learning, profound dedication, and sacrifices for the family to fortify this larger community we call China. When the young have wiped out the old, will we be Chinese anymore?

What is this madness gripping our country? Young people burst into song one minute, then roll their eyes, raise their fists, and shout invectives to kill and destroy. These histrionic outbursts seem to titillate them, but they send chills down my spine and paralyze the world around us. This dissonance, the total desertion of reason, makes M-ma seem sane. The Japanese invasion and World War II embedded shrapnel in Mother's psyche. How am I to confront my fate?

My journal is a lifeline to sanity. I must write but must be careful. Though I make my entries in English, I am afraid someday people will translate my journal and harm those who helped us.

Yung and I figured that if we tried to escape as a family, the state's secret service would hunt us down. So we stayed. God only knows how long the "thumb sucker" can keep us away from the savageries of the marauding Red Guards. The thumb sucker and her husband may be in danger themselves. The Red Guards are young and disorganized. Staying out of sight is our only chance. We hope the Red Guards will forget we exist and leave us alone.

I feel I cannot breathe sometimes. Maybe my inner self realizes that during all these years of war, I never shared the trauma of my parents' generation. How did they cope with the loss of dignity and status, and how did they retain or fail to retain their identities? I was taught to be modest and clear-eyed in my expectations. None of that prepared me for this madness. Are we to be tortured? It is better not to think about it. Was our criticism session during the Korean War a harbinger of what is to come? How can there be any rehearsal for such horrors? Will we be paraded through the streets as revisionists, like Deng Xiaoping? He lived, but his son was pushed out of a window and was crippled. The Flower Maid told us his fate and thought it best to send An-an and Li-li into hiding. Yes, we will endure anything, but we must protect our children.

Will we be jailed? Will anyone be able to visit us? Will we be forced to tell them where our children are hiding? In truth, we don't know the exact location, because we don't want to reveal anything under torture.

Because the Flower Maid had enjoyed Deng Xiaoping's sponsorship, she is now imprisoned. No one dares speak up and remind people of all the years we have contributed to our country. Any hint of our service is glossed over. Our factories are labeled "engines of oppression," in spite of our excellent record of production.

Yung and I have been biding our time. We hope to survive but fear that we may never see our children again. Lucky also misses the children. He goes into their rooms, sniffs all about, and whines. I used to share our meager meals with him. Now he disappears outside the house for a few hours every day and never begs for food when he is home — he knows so much. His presence warms our empty days. Still, an ominous cloud hangs over us and creeps into our conversations.

Yung said one day, "I keep seeing the face of Lee Der-chin."

Lee was in our Phi Lambda fraternity. He was a brilliant electrical engineer who graduated at the top of his class from Jiao Tong University — China's equivalent of MIT. He received his advanced degrees on full scholarships at Cambridge University. He spoke English, German, and several Chinese dialects fluently. He returned to Shanghai after World War II and became the department head of engineering at Jiao Tong.

When he was brought before the mob for "self-criticism," he had already been imprisoned in a small closet for months. His hair had turned white. It hung, matted, down to his shoulders. He reeked of excrement and other noxious odors. As soon as they dragged him onstage, he fell to his knees and begged to be executed. With his shoulders hunched over, he sobbed and tucked his head into his body. No one could see his face; he slobbered uncontrollably.

The howling youths accused him of mismanaging his department, giving bad grades, and training cadres of slaves for the capitalists. Lee admitted every charge leveled against him. He apologized as he wailed and asked to die. Torrents of gibberish came with his replies. They kicked him some more, and then triumphantly put him back in his closet.

Recounting the incident, Yung grabbed the clothes on his chest and thumped on it. He could not seem to catch his breath. My own heart was racing so fast that I thought I was about to have a heart attack. From that day on, we never dared guess or mention what might happen to us.

Grief, regret, and fear rear their ugly heads at random moments. Sometimes the stabbing pain, pounding heart, and torrent of tears are unbearable. At other times they appear like bits and pieces of someone else's story from which we seem emotionally removed. Sometimes anger grabs hold of me, and I fly into a fit of destruction, throwing dishes and glasses against a wall, cursing.

"Easy, easy, my dear." Yung, ever the gentleman, tries to calm me down. "You don't want to become like our oppressors."

"I'm sorry," I cry, or moan or curse some more. Neither of us can utter the word "sorry" without acknowledging the bitter taste of futility.

We see no escape. I understand why some of our friends have committed suicide. We have talked about killing ourselves too. But we cannot take this easy route without endangering our children. Even amid our despair, something precious is brewing between

Yung and me. I have never felt so close to another human being. It is such a comfort to feel his shoulder or his leg beside me in bed. Even his snoring, which used to annoy me, reassures me. Acceptance has entered our union; we sense something sacred there, a renewed beauty of spirit that binds us to one another.

Yung often appears to be reading, but mostly he just stares into the void. As the only son of a leading Shanghai industrialist, Yung never had to lift a finger to care for himself. Now I make him sweep the floor, wash our dishes, and trek out to the garden to tend our roses. One day he brought me a rose and was as happy and pleased as I can remember. Suddenly, color drained from his face and he grabbed the doorframe so tightly that his knuckles turned white. I helped him sit on a kitchen chair and ran to get him some water. After his drink, his face became flushed and I took him to bed. Neither of us had to explain what was going through our minds.

For thousands of years, servants pampered their rich masters. Now I realize that those who served us had something we did not: pride of self-sufficiency, an outlet for their frustrations, and the joy of knowing their essential worth. The Communists have grasped part of this truth: We could have learned more from our helpers. I never understood Mother's eagerness to take care of the sick, but now I realize her service to the workers keeps her spirit free.

I did try to emulate Mother when I managed the Yung factories. I treated the workers with respect, and always asked about their families. I even imitated Mother's firm but soft voice of concern. Now I'm emulating Brook ma-ma, who told me her gentle labors soothed her mind. I've scrubbed our house from top to bottom. I mop everything with only water and no soap. The work steadies my nerves. My greatest joy is cooking for Yung because I treasure the moments when we can behave like normal people. I have not written in my Gratitude and Wish lists for ages.

Today I recorded my gratitude for another peaceful day and wished for the reunion of my family.

It is past 1 a.m. Images of leering, screaming, violent crowds play in my head. My heartbeats run amok, and I am immersed in the fuzzy images of the old newsreel. Finally, I splash myself with cold water and decide to start practicing my calligraphy to control my mind. I remember Miss Tyler reminding me that many Chinese characters are not only works of art, but imbued with meaning. For example, the central concept in educating children in China is the word *ting* (聽) — "to hear or listen." A Chinese mother never calls her child a "bad boy or girl," but she may twist the child's ear and scream: "You don't listen!" The word *ting* is written in the most descriptive way: the left side carries the "ear" (耳) symbol sheltering the "king" (王) symbol. The right side carries symbols for ten (十) eyes (目— turned sideways) over one (一) heart (心). In one pictogram, it tells how one must listen: The ear is king and one must listen with ten eyes and one heart.

The heart of Confucian philosophy is *Der* (德) — virtue. Again, it is written in a telling manner. The left side is a symbol for "man" (人 — in a standing position.) To this, a stroke has been added on top to indicate a step higher. Again, the right side carries the symbols for ten eyes and one heart. This pictogram tells a man to step higher and attain virtue through the use of ten eyes and one heart. This word was my father's personal name and the generational name of my children. Indeed, our family is steeped in Confucian humanism, which seeks to make everyone a moral being through virtuous practices. Ah, how our country has drifted from these ideals.

Wu (無) means "no." *Wei* (為) means "action." The word *Wei* is again imbued with symbolic meaning. The strokes are developed from a claw like hand sitting on top of an animal. *Wu Wei* literally means "do not claw around like a wild animal." This is a pictorial exposition of being non-egotistical and non-combative. I see this as the essential beauty of Chinese philosophy and the adaptive steel of the Chinese character. Its strength is its moderation and deliberate acceptance of the tasks of the day. As Mother used to say, "The Chinese may moan and bend like the bamboo in a storm, but never break" — except now the Cultural Revolution is encouraging the young to tear down every vestige of ancient wisdom. The government is talking about using a simplified script. It is supposed to be more practical, but it will be robbed of its instructive meaning. We, the older generation, will have to learn our characters all over again! Will we be able to read and understand Chinese? Am I really Chinese anymore?

When I first learned how White Lily was led to denounce her father and the Yungs had to forfeit their property, my mind became chaotic. My thoughts tumbled over each other. I was in a panic and tried to distract myself. I was so jittery that I grabbed on to anything. I signed up to do a night shift in the factory. With my emotions raw from worries and fear for my family, and not having any experience in factory work, my labor could have been a disaster for the company and me. Luckily, Yung caught my "make work" order and scheduled me to serve tea during the night shift. I was distracting myself with "wei," acting like an animal trying to claw its way out of a dark hole.

Perhaps the Taoist philosophy of Wu Wei is the only rational way to prepare for our coming ordeal. If we were to die, we would want to keep our integrity and dignity intact. Hopefully this is also the way for us to prepare for the process of aging. I find pride in my Chinese cultural heritage, but I see the solutions to China's problems through my American education. Mother probably can recite a Tang poem to express these dilemmas, but I can only remember the popular phrase "Let what will be, be." Oh, yes, I think Robert Frost wrote that about the darkness of night in "Acceptance" and coined the phrase.

Although I learned it when I was only three, I still remember the opening stanza of the *Three Character Classic*:

> *Origin of man*
> *Is always kind.*
> *Nature brings close*
> *Habit channels away.*
> *If not taught*
> *Nature will change.*

The youngsters roaming the street to find things to destroy have never been taught the fundamental tenets of our cultural heritage — that it is our duty to maintain a harmonious society. Most Chinese do not believe in an impartial God who rewards good and punishes evil. When they obliterate our heritage, they have neither a God nor the nobility of a Chinese soul! Oh God, how can chaos rebuild our nation? You have punished us for our pride. Please send us your mercy.

Hiding in the house feels claustrophobic, but the dread of what lurks outside keeps us indoors. I fear venturing into the market to buy necessary foodstuffs. Once, I did that and ran into a worker from our factory. She stared at me, dropped her jaw, and exclaimed, "You're still around?" I was so shaken that I ran home. I thought she might report us for existing.

No one dares to visit us now. Once, people loved to call us their friends; now they're afraid to associate with us. For our safety, we no longer communicate with Silver Bell. The thumb sucker is wise not to come near our house. Brook ma-ma visits only occasionally. She brings us whatever she can.

I try to be creative with our limited supplies. My biology classes and erstwhile independence in America are helpful. I add jasmine flowers to our rice, and stew our store of dried peas and beans with rosehips from our garden. One day, I even dug up some earthworms, slit them open to clean them, and stir-fried them with onion grasses from the garden. Yung thought I had found some dried bean curds. I didn't tell him the truth, but I couldn't eat any of them myself. Indeed, if I come back in my next life, I hope I'll be a bird who can enjoy the sun, the rain, the trees, and the flowers. I see myself as a mother bird that finds the tastiest morsels for her family.

Reality intrudes. We are hungry most of the time. My legs are weak. My frame is hollowed out and I must lean against a wall to stand. I gasp for breath and fear gnaws at me constantly. The gloom in this empty house drifts through the air and penetrates my every pore. We are past indulging in regrets and blame. We're running out of food. I cooked the last handfuls of rice tonight. Dare I go out and buy more? No. Maybe I'll go into the Hsia portion of the house and see if they have some provisions left. Will I be reduced to stealing? The Hsias are already in jail. Like the Flower Maid, they were also Deng Xiaoping's followers. I fear they will never return.

We are not without sin. When I was young, I remember telling Mother that I should get a bigger share of her jewelry than Silver Bell because I am the older sister. Mother replied that she wished none of us would ever need the jewelry to buy respect or our survival. After Yung's father died, Yung took over the management of his father's factories, and I helped him. His sister and her husband were never consulted. The family wanted things to be that way because Yung is the son. When Yung's mother was dying, she gave most of her jewelry to his sister but saved the most important pieces for me. I did not protest because it felt good to be favored, and it is in the Chinese tradition for the son to keep everything in the family. Before the Communists entered Shanghai, Yung and I gave his sister a large cash settlement and she and her family moved to Taiwan.

In peaceful times, many families squabbled shamelessly out of greed and jealousy. Now we are chastened and left with the sting of our privilege. Yung's family endowments have weighed us down, keeping us anchored to Shanghai in the midst of this whirlwind.

Thumb sucker tells me she and her husband are consumed with guilt and recriminations. They couldn't deal with the brutal struggle for control within the Party. We appreciate whatever they have done to protect us. If she has participated in any evildoing, she will surely ask for forgiveness from whatever beneficent spirits still remain in our godless country. We know she never meant to do any harm or take pleasure in others' misery. May the healing waters of time wash over her.

Yung and I are at peace. Truly, we often feel blessed and thankful. We have enjoyed an abundance of wealth, not only in material possessions (none of which we can carry to the grave anyway), but also in the devotion of so many people: our family, our precious children, the Flower Maid, so many of our workers in the factories, and the farmers in Hangzhou.

I ask for forgiveness from all of them for our preoccupation with accumulating worldly goods and for failing to take the time to know them better. They brought food, light, good sense, and laughter into our lives, and we have not thanked them sufficiently. They have displayed nobility when we hardly noticed. We seem to have lived like walking blind people! We should have enjoyed our garden, our children, and the sunshine in our lives; instead we worried about "keeping face." We fought for status and recognition, dwelled on imagined slights and hurts, and refused to let go of the glittering things that would surely slip from our grip. And all the while we were surrounded by love, and gave so little in return. I hope they forgive us.

To reach our peaceful harbor, Yung and I have agreed to also forgive ourselves for all the anger, hunger, and endless want that we witnessed but refused to acknowledge. It seems fate has dealt us a heavy hand of sorrows. But Yung and I accept our responsibility. I hope we've made a small difference in the world around us. In the end, we agree that the Taoist philosophy of Wu Wei is most suitable in our present predicament. We practice yielding to resistance. We've tried to reach the state of "knowing in not-knowing," to master the power of "being positive in not thinking." We have already taught the children there is a God of goodness in spite of the horrors they're experiencing. We also taught them to honor our heritage as well as the workers who enriched our lives. These are the lights that make our lives worthwhile. I pray that they have learned from our mistakes.

I hear a lumbering truck approaching; horns are blaring and people are shouting slogans. The cacophony is made more ominous by the steady drumbeats that grow louder and louder. We have no heart to participate. We don't know what is happening outside, nor do we wish to know.

Is that a gong I hear clanging in the distance? I fear I have written too much and must hide this journal.

Tides of The Red Moon Rising

August 1968

THE DISTANT GONG sent a tremor through the night. As the truck neared, the predictable Party slogans could be heard, high-pitched and shrill, chilling the humid air.

"Down with the capitalists!" "Running dogs of imperialism!" "Class enemies!" "Kill them — kill the capitalist vermin now!"

Golden Bell and Yung were in bed. She closed her journal while he kept reading. She was still wearing her rumpled Mao suit. He had changed into a white T-shirt and pajama pants. The noise sent chills down her extremities. She ran to hide her journal on the bookshelf and lunged back to bed. She grabbed her husband, grateful for his warm body.

"Oh my God," Yung groaned. "My bowels are loosened." He jumped out of bed and ran to the bathroom.

The racket ceased at the garden gate.

For a moment, Golden Bell exhaled. Maybe the bitter cup from the Red Guards would spare them again this night. Perhaps they would be able to work in their rose garden tomorrow.

"Open the gate! Open the gate!" Fists rattled the heavy iron grill.

"It's not locked!" A young man's voice exclaimed.

The gates clanged open. The Yungs could hear the sounds of a truck, bikes, and running feet crunching gravel down the winding driveway.

Lucky whined and barked, racing around the room in circles. Shaking with fear, he relieved himself and finally jumped into bed, whimpering in Golden Bell's arms.

"Lucky, Lucky, let your name protect us tonight." Golden Bell nestled into his yellow fur. She shivered so hard that Lucky clawed at her shoulders and whined even louder.

A band of thirty or forty shouting youths crashed through the front door. Wielding sticks and iron pipes, they smashed windows, tables, chairs, vases, and bowls — anything within reach. They pulled books and ancient scrolls out of bookcases. Like a herd of stampeding animals, they screamed, amplifying the mayhem.

Coral Bell, wearing the Red Guards' red kerchief around her shoulders, jostled with the crowd. She shouted slogans like a broken record, all the while praying she wouldn't be recognized as Golden Bell's half sister. She picked up some books and took them outside to the patio, where she started a bonfire. White Lily and several other youths joined her in stoking the blaze. Rising smoke masked the scent of jasmine in the garden. An unnatural stillness settled around the fire, while shouts, howls, and bursts of crashing glass and tumbling furniture broadcast the chaos inside.

A young man and two women charged into the room and dragged the unresisting Golden Bell and Yung downstairs. Lucky darted out of the house and cowered in a corner of the garden.

"Take them to prison, take them to prison!" Coral Bell shouted, but no one listened.

"Take what you want! We won't run away!" Golden Bell pushed away the grasping arms. Anger galvanized her.

"You bloodsuckers of the proletarians, stop your chatter! Your dog is better fed than we are!" The young man gave Golden Bell a vigorous push, and she fell. Yung reached down to help her, but a young woman with fiery eyes had already yanked her up by the hair. Pipes and sticks were flying toward them.

Yung crouched and ran forward, trying to cover his face and head with his bare arms.

"I've given you my permission to loot all you want!" Golden Bell shouted in defiance, her hands shielding her bruised face.

"You dare to speak of looting?" The young man swung his pipe. It came down hard on Golden Bell's chest. She lurched backward. "You live in luxury while we work and starve!"

"No, no, no," Yung pleaded, kneeling beside his wife. "We worked hard to create jobs for thousands. Please, please, spare her!" A fist came down on him like a sledgehammer.

Again, Coral Bell shouted, "Bring them to prison, bring them to prison!"

No one took note because everyone was milling and rummaging around the house. More Red Guards rushed down the stairs, carrying a carved cedar chest of furs. "Get out of the way! Out of the way!" In the chaos, unknown hands dragged Golden Bell and Yung outside. Amid the shouts and confusion, they were dumped on the patio like two bags of garbage.

Coral Bell averted her eyes from the melee. "Burn everything! Burn all the poisonous books and old decadent calligraphy!" she cried as loudly as she could.

Golden Bell recognized her sister and shuddered. Yung gasped, "Help, help."

Coral Bell faced the fire. She stoked it with all her might and tried to still the tremor in her limbs. After a few minutes, she rallied those gathered around the fire to enter the house and collect more books.

"Degenerate!" she shouted as she passed her sister. She raised her arms and whispered furtively, "Run to hide behind the rose-bushes by the garden wall." She clapped her hands next to her sister's face. An observer would have thought she had reached down to slap Golden Bell.

Yung helped his wife to her feet. They half ran and half crawled into the rosebushes in their walled-in garden. "I can't go any farther. I think they shattered my ribs!" Golden Bell whimpered as they huddled in the dark.

Yung looked all around. "We can't get out of this garden. The Red Guards are everywhere, loading things onto the truck." Stabbing pain cut his words short.

"Where can we go? Where?"

"Oh, I . . . I should have sent you away with your sister!" Yung sobbed. He rested and gasped for breath.

"But how, how could we have known?" They fell into each other's arms.

"Oh, the savagery!" Golden Bell wailed. Tears streamed down her cheeks, but her chest was too inflamed to sob.

"It is so easy to appeal to people's individual frustrations, ha-tred, and material ambitions! Just mayhem!" Yung cried out.

"Shhh! Not so loud." Too weak to speak with passion, Golden Bell watched the bonfire. She whispered: "In the old days, Mother would not have allowed any of us to throw away a single piece of paper that had words on it." Tears caught in the back of her throat; she desperately tried to stifle a cough despite the dizzying pain.

"Thousands of years . . . pure and gentle . . ." Yung watched in astonishment as his collection of ancient watercolors and manu-scripts were hurled into the fire. Book after book burned, curling into black cinders and disappearing in the eerie moonlit night.

Small rhythmic contractions convulsed his body. His abdominal muscles sent him into rounds of spastic retching. In one massive expulsion, the contents of his stomach emptied as if someone had just uncorked a champagne bottle and started pouring. Some of the vomit hit the rosebushes, but much of it landed on his pants and Golden Bell's sleeve. "Oh God," he moaned.

Golden Bell tried to wipe her sleeve on the ground, but her injuries prevented her. She sniffled and hung her head.

Yung shifted away a few paces. Ignoring the mess all over him, he focused on the fire. "I don't feel so nauseated now," he said numbly, rubbing his stomach.

Coral Bell and her friends were hoarse from chanting. They stoked the fire and watched their comrades carry load after load of family treasures into the truck.

"I hope An-an and Li-li are safe," Golden Bell mumbled.

"Yes," her husband replied, still mesmerized by the bonfire in the distance. "We can trust Lao Ma to take care of the children. Oh, dear God!" he cried, rending the soot-laden air with his bruised arms.

"Shhh! You're too loud!"

"I know, I know." He wept. "But how is our country or anyone to be helped by such destruction?" They huddled again, mourning as quietly as they could.

"Oh Yung, do you recall our youthful passion when we first made love?"

"Yes, yes . . . How can I forget?" Yung huddled close and held his wife's hand. They were quiet for a long time. Sweet memories flooded them and eased their agony. But their stabs of pain returned. Yung groaned. "Thanks to our passion, we explored our bodies and our world," he whispered, "but these youngsters are exploring all their base instincts. How can people become so insane?"

"Where are the prisoners?" Shrill voices came from the house. The Red Guards scanned the faces around the smoky fire. Coral

Bell and the other students stopped working to disclaim any knowledge of the prisoners' whereabouts.

"There is so little jewelry in the house!"

"We must find them."

"Question them, the dirty capitalists!"

"They're all thieves!"

"Where are their servants and children?"

The Red Guards fanned out into the garden. It took them only a few minutes to find the injured couple. Golden Bell and Yung were again dragged onto the open lawn in front of the bonfire. The Guards circled around them. Brandishing their sticks and pipes, they screamed, "Tried to run away?"

"Confess, or we'll kill you!"

"Where's your jewelry?"

"In the bank, in the bank," Golden Bell cried.

A blow fell on Golden Bell's head, and more followed. She heard voices ringing out. "Trying to cheat us?"

"Capitalist liars!"

"Where are your children, your servants?"

"They ran away!" Yung mumbled.

"More lies, more lies!"

A wave of hysterical yelling descended on them. Hard blows from the sticks and kicks rained from all sides. The squall drowned out their moans.

No one noticed that the victims had started spitting blood. The flying pipes were crunching bones and bringing up hair and messy red emulsions.

Coral Bell and her friends joined the frenzied circle. Coral Bell punched the air with her fists and let out a hoarse shriek. "Confess, confess! That's the only way out!" She had seen people confess to all kinds of crimes they had never committed just to stay alive. Maybe this was the only way out for her sister too.

The dreadful shouts continued: "Where have you stashed your gold and silverware?" "Where are the servants?"

"Confess! Confess! Do you wish to die?"

"You have bars of gold! We know you have them!"

Stamping feet took on a rhythmic cadence. Threshing sticks and pipes punctuated the incantations. Thick smoke billowed over everyone, obscuring the two bundles of blood-soaked flesh and bones and the ghastly faces streaked with sweat and soot.

"Stop! Stop!" A male voice rang out. A young man elbowed his way into the circle. "We still need to bring them to a struggle meeting." The frenzied mob froze.

Arms stopped flailing. The hard breaths and panting gasps were amplified in the sudden quiet. The occasional pop from the fire sounded like firecrackers. As though tired from an ordinary day's work, the young women, with tearing eyes, turned away to rub them. Young men pulled off their shirts to wipe their sweaty, gleaming faces.

"Someone should call the hospital," a soft voice whispered. A lanky youth bent down to turn over the bleeding bundles lying in a heap before him.

"Don't bother," he answered, recoiling from the bodies. "They're dead." He ran onto the grass, rubbing his shoes over and over the dewy lawn. "The bloody slime is sticking to my shoes!" He did a kind of macabre dance.

The mob followed his example, cleaning their shoes but ignoring their blood and soot-streaked clothes.

Sweaty faces glistened under the moonlight, and tears of panic coursed down Coral Bell's cheeks. Murmurs arose: "What happened?" "Who started this?" "I didn't!" "I used my stick because all of you were doing it." "But they're dead! I didn't kill them." "I didn't even know they were dead! Beaten to death!" "They wouldn't confess!" "We got carried away." "Who did?" "We were all shouting." "Serves them right." "Yeah, serves them right!"

In the crowd's subdued mood, the voices sounded all the more riotous to Coral Bell. A loud ringing in her ears made her feel that her head was exploding. The blood-soaked figures before her appeared to twist and spin, following each other around and around in circles. Splashes of red swirled over the moon and splattered onto the stars. She sat down and cradled her head between her legs. Others followed.

Lucky appeared out of nowhere. He sniffed and whined, circling the dead bodies, avoiding the pool of blood as best he could. Finally he ambled over to Coral Bell. He licked her, first crying and whimpering, then howling inconsolably. Other Red Guards stopped to stare at the dog.

White Lily realized the implication. "You crazy dog, go away! Leave us alone!" She hit the dog with her stick and he scurried off. She sprang up shouting, "We have orders to dig up the flower gardens!" She pulled Coral Bell to her feet, pushing a bloody stick into her hand. "Decadent symbols of capitalism!" She hustled others into the rose garden. Many followed, glad to leave the harrowing scene.

Lucky trailed behind, still whimpering, his tail hanging limp between his legs. He continued to whine and to circle while Coral Bell and her comrades dug up the roses.

The Book of Revelation — Red Moon Rising

August 1968

A SWEEP OF glossy black birds screech and dash headlong in my direction. I run, protecting my head with my arms. They spiral around me, their long beaks pecking each other, but they do not touch me. Their macabre dance leads me toward a glimmering light ahead. Black streaks of wings brush against me and crisscross the patch of light in front. I open my mouth to shriek and howl, yet no sound comes.

What is happening? Where am I?

The dirt road turns into a wooded marsh. I stumble and slosh through the undergrowth, mute from fear but sweating in the icy muck. I grasp a young sapling, firm my stance, and hear wailing voices calling for help. I bury my face in my sleeves and join in the call. Again, I make no sound. The birds continue to swirl but still do not touch me. They seem to want me to move on. I stamp my feet. I cry and shout, but it seems I am only miming...

A surge of fury energizes me as I desperately claw my way toward the light. In my oddly angled view, a pair of weird, glittery eyes swims by. They look drugged. No, they are not listless but moist and on the verge of tears. These are my sister Golden Bell's eyes — bitter and contemptuous, as I remember her looking when she was angry during her visit to Hong Kong. A swelling rises in my throat, and I scream and scream —

Donald was shaking Silver Bell. "Wake up, wake up!"

"Oh, what a horrible dream!" Silver Bell sat up. Her throat was throbbing.

"Are you having a nightmare right in the middle of the afternoon?"

Is he criticizing me again? Silver Bell pretended to yawn. "I fell asleep reading about the Cultural Revolution and the Red Guards." She pushed away the newspapers covering her legs.

"You sound like a drunk. Have you been drinking?"

"No . . . yes, well maybe I had a cocktail before I read the papers," she said, adjusting her shirt. "What a horrible nightmare!"

Donald looked away. Silver Bell thought he must be disgusted with her again. She checked her mother-of-pearl buttons. "Why are you home?"

"Tell me about your dream." He sat beside her and held her hands.

He had not held her hand for years. She cringed, her face flushing at his unusual tenderness. "Yes, yes . . . I had such a strange, frightening dream."

"Tell me about it." Donald wrapped his arm around her shoulder.

She shifted away. "I . . . I . . . ." Her breath came in pants. "Such a scary dream! Black birds swooping, voices calling for help, and Golden Bell's eyes staring at me."

He squeezed her hand, his face contorting.

His closeness aroused all her fears and old suspicions. "Why are you here?" she asked again.

Donald stared at her, obviously on edge. His shoulders twitched, and his eyes shifted around as if trying to focus. Finally he muttered, "I don't want to bring you bad news when you're already upset."

"What bad news?"

"From Shanghai."

She jolted upright. Her insides rumbled and the throb in her throat felt like a thumping hammer. "What happened? Tell me!"

"Maybe you should have some tea first . . ."

"I don't want tea. Just tell me what happened!"

Donald walked away. He gazed out the window and said in a hoarse whisper, "A few days ago, the Red Guards killed Yung and Golden Bell."

Silver Bell saw her sister's teary eyes hovering over her again. "No!" she screamed. So many reports of the Red Guards' savageries had reached them that she could easily picture the mayhem and destruction.

Donald knelt down before her and took her hand. "Are you all right?"

"All right? No, no, no!" She bawled.

Donald smoothed her hair and rubbed her shoulders. Even though it felt strange to accept his solicitude, she screamed, "Tell me what you know."

His eyes moistening, he hugged her again. "You're sure you want to hear this?"

She nodded silently and went to blow her nose.

"You know Peony has many relatives working in the Yung factories and the Communist Party. The foreman in our factory here, Lao Sing, is also her husband's cousin. Even though Peony and her husband are now imprisoned, we still communicate with the Party officials through him. He said that two days ago, the Red Guards went to raid the Yung mansion. Coral Bell had scheduled only a denunciation session, nothing more. But the young people got 'carried away,' as he put it." His voice was shaking. "Both Yung and your sister were beaten to death."

"No! This can't be!" Silver Bell buried her face in a cushion. Images of torture and cruelty overpowered her.

"What's worse, both White Lily and Coral Bell were with the Red Guards in the Yung mansion. Lucky, of course, recognized Coral Bell. The faithful dog clung close to her and wailed with her the whole night." Donald took her head into his hands and gazed into her eyes. Tears rolled down his cheeks, and he hesitated, unable to go on.

"Oh, oh, Coral Bell, the last letter said she was doing well in the Red Guards . . ." Silver Bell choked back her sobs. "But I don't understand . . . why are you ?" His kindness was too sudden. She had long ceased to think of him as a caring man.

Donald sat very still, his lean face creased with pain. "No doubt you think I married you to earn a fortune through Yung? You probably hate me."

"Um, um, well, I . . ." Silver Bell couldn't respond. For years now, she had called him a bastard and worse.

"So what does it matter anymore? I hate myself." Donald rolled his eyes and stifled a sob. "Golden Bell and Yung are both dead, and what good have I ever done to them?"

"You managed their factories here, and you sent money to everyone in Shanghai," she reminded him. Silver Bell couldn't believe she was comforting her husband, whom she had called a monster and blamed for her misery.

"That's nothing. I hate myself!" He said it again with greater vehemence.

Silver Bell was shocked to see him crying openly.

"Yung liked me and trusted me. I feel as if he died in my place." He looked away. "I sometimes thought Golden Bell was too bossy, but Yung was like a brother — the only one who appreciated my work."

Silver Bell sat gaping at him. All his infidelities, his vile scheme to get rid of Mr. Ching, how he had encouraged Ching to molest her — could this be the same husband she had come to hate?

300

"I was the lucky one who always got away." Donald lit two ciga-rettes. He handed one to her, and they both puffed as they used to when they were first married. "How many times have you been told that I went to Japan when China was occupied, and that I went to America before Japan declared war on the whole world? Now I'm in Hong Kong, the haven of successful capitalists!"

"I suppose we never understood . . ."

"You're a baptized a Christian." Donald squinted at her through the blue haze. "Talk about a life of the Cross. It seems that your God has given China a cross to bear in the last hundred years."

Silver Bell sensed his tears behind the cloud of smoke.

"Nothing makes sense to me." She sobbed, crushing her ciga-rette in the ashtray. "People in China live in terror while we wallow in luxury." She started to hiccup. "But still we manage to hurt each other — such pettiness!"

"I know your family thought of me as a scheming bastard." Donald snuffed out his cigarette on the coffee table, missing the ashtray. Suddenly he slumped forward and curled up on the floor. Wrapping his arms around himself like a cocoon, he shivered and rocked. "And they weren't wrong. After the Japanese massacred my family in Nanking, I survived — survived by any means . . . unspeakable treachery!" He choked, babbling his tale in fits and starts. "The Japs, the beasts, sent me to, to service . . . depraved, so depraved . . . the generals. An aide to the ambassador took me to A-America. Yes, yes. I survived . . . became one of them — a predator." Tears streamed down his cheeks and he began to wail. "It would've been better to be dead!"

His family decimated in the Nanking Massacre? Was he one of those young men chosen by the Japanese to service the soldiers? He is tall, handsome, with unusually wavy hair. I still feel a thrill every time I hear his booming baritone voice, yet no one has ever heard him sing. Was he a toy for the generals?

Although a thousand questions crowded her mind, Silver Bell couldn't utter a sound. Somehow the sight of him in a fetal position on the floor paralyzed her.

Still trembling and rocking, Donald held his head in his hands. "I remember — I remember," he cried. "How they used me . . . a piece of meat . . . sapped my soul . . ." He choked on his tears and wailed on and on. "I couldn't tell anyone anything because I was ashamed. Even though I was 'a kept boy,' I was grateful to be spared torture and death. I came to love my captor. It was only when I thought I was one with him that I could function without shame."

Silver Bell pinched herself and felt the pain. No, she was not dreaming. She stared silently and knelt beside him in a stupor. She was convinced he would never have admitted all this if it weren't true. She threw herself on him and they rocked as one. "Whatever happened to you when you were young is not your fault!" She smothered him with forlorn kisses. "You now support my family. That is your true self, your true decency and nobility!"

Still hugging and entwined in each other's arms, they managed to edge themselves onto the sofa. She nudged him to lie down. "Now, you must take a rest." She stayed on her knees, penitent before him.

His whole body trembled. He closed his eyes, folding his arms over his chest. He seemed to be dozing, but his breath was uneven, his face warped by a pitiful grin. His long sighs and short gasps convinced her he was trying to regain control of his emotions.

Silver Bell gently stroked his cheek. Realizing he was still wearing his suit, she helped him take off his jacket and felt his tense muscles twitching. She massaged his arms and shoulders.

He finally opened his eyes as if awakened from a trance. He let out a raw yell and stood up to pound the wall. Totally beside himself with rage, he let loose a string of invectives, cursing himself, the wars, the Japanese, and the Communists. He slapped his face and hardly stopped to breathe. "I don't deserve you!" he shouted.

Silver Bell couldn't go near him. He was kicking and punching the air all around him, as if imprisoned in a magic circle. Listening to his rants and raves, she got an inkling of his full degradation: how he had participated in orgies and performed unspeakable acts. Disregarding his wild swings, Silver Bell threw herself into his arms. They shrieked and bellowed out their outrage together.

Suddenly, they held their collective breath as they realized the servants had been peeking in. Silver Bell shouted to them to leave them alone and dragged her husband to their bedroom. They fell into each other's arms, crying and howling as if possessed. They collapsed into their bed, mourning Golden Bell and Yung's deaths, and cursing the cruel hand of fate.

Donald sat up with a jerk. Wiping his face on his sleeve, he shook her. "Listen, listen to me. We must do something! As soon as they're sure Coral Bell is related to Golden Bell, they will arrest her too!"

"What can we do?"

"We should get Coral Bell here, if at all possible. The Red Guards are still in a state of confusion."

"What about M-ma and Brook ma-ma? Where are Golden Bell's children? How can we possibly save them all?"

"Listen, listen, Silver Bell." He reached out for her hand, looking grave but animated. "We must put our heads together and plan a rescue mission."

The confidence and precision of his words startled her. "Can we do this?"

"Yes, we must try. I can sail our company tanker into Shanghai with a load of cotton, as if we're still carrying on our trade. The harbor authorities will be only too glad to accept the goods when I tell them we're under contract to deliver them."

"Thank God you're still using your head," Silver Bell said, her mind shuttling between his past and the present turmoil.

"Yes, I suppose I've developed survival mechanisms." He stared into the void once again, and his eyes lost their focus.

"Of course, you've been trained under . . ." She stopped herself, afraid that he might lose himself again in his memories. She turned to their rescue plan. "So we'll slip ashore and bring everyone to the tanker?"

"Yes, we'll try to bring out whomever we can." He lifted his chin, wide-eyed with newfound excitement. "Who are these Red Guards after all? — Just packs of frightened youngsters running wild and venting their frustrations. The chaotic conditions will make our escape possible."

"Yes, yes. We must bring the family to safety, what's left of it anyway . . ."

"We have no time to lose."

They finally calmed down enough to plot their rescue mission. Try as they might, they could not see a way for both of them to go on shore in Shanghai.

"I can easily slip ashore when the workers unload the cotton," Silver Bell proposed. "But you must stay on board the tanker to direct the operation."

"You've never had to risk your life or experienced anything like this before. How are you to manage now?"

"Please, please, let me. I must. I've always relied on Golden Bell's experience and largesse. Now I must take what I've learned from her and save her children."

"You know if you get caught, you will be killed without mercy, just like Golden Bell."

"They'll kill you too!"

"But I'm used to taking chances."

"Yes, but Golden Bell came to me in a dream!" She described her nightmare. "Her eyes silently pleaded for help."

Impatient, Donald stood up to pace. "I owe it to Yung to save his children."

"Coral Bell may not want to come with you. Remember, my family does not trust you. It's strange no one mentioned the children. Maybe Brook ma-ma won't tell you where they are," Silver Bell reminded him.

"I suppose you're right. Your family has never trusted me. And I don't know if your M-ma can negotiate an escape."

Silver Bell nodded. "If M-ma cannot leave, I know Brook ma-ma will not want to leave. But I'll make that decision when I get there. What if some official should come on board to inspect? You must stay on the ship to keep order and deal with the authorities that patrol the harbor."

"Yes, you're right."

"The rescue may take days or even a week. What will you do if someone asks why the tanker has remained in Shanghai Harbor for so long?"

"I'll claim we have engine troubles, and we're working on some mechanical problem."

"That sounds credible!"

"I'd better get some cash for bribes."

"For the harbor officials?"

"Yes, and you should be ready to bribe everyone you meet as well. You should take most of the money, and wrap it into hundred-dollar bundles. People in China love to have Hong Kong dollars."

Their voices grew firmer as they continued planning. They decided to implement their strategy right away. Donald left to get cash and buy up-to-date maps: Shanghai no longer carried the foreign street names that were familiar to Silver Bell.

It had been almost twenty years since Silver Bell had left

Shanghai. She had to learn her way around. She also needed clothes that would make her look like a Communist worker.

In the evening, Lao Sing came to coach her on the ways of the new Shanghai locals. Silver Bell spoke perfect Shanghainese, but she must now address everyone as "comrade." When Lao Sing left, he promised to get in touch immediately with his Shanghai relatives and arrange fishing boats to take Silver Bell ashore and then to wherever she needed to go. The rest would have to be arranged when she arrived on the scene. No one knew what to expect.

Silver Bell packed and tried to imagine what she might need for her mission. Recalling the darkness that pervaded her dream, she included a flashlight. She decided to change into the drab clothes and plastic shoes Lao Sing had brought, to get used to them right away. She cut her hair so no trace of her Western-style perm would be visible. Donald helped her trim the back of her head. They did such a rough job, they had to laugh when they were finished: She looked like a country bumpkin who couldn't afford a proper haircut.

Later, Silver Bell added first-aid equipment to her bag, and Donald slipped in many chocolate bars so she wouldn't need to stop to eat. She couldn't think of anything else to take.

Early next morning, they embarked.

While the company tanker plied the South China Sea northward to Shanghai, Donald and Silver Bell were constantly agitated. Donald's feverish eyes often filled with remorse and shame. Occasionally, he would burst out crying and mouth "I'm sorry," then run into his bunk to hide. Silver Bell would follow him there, kneel beside him, rub his back, and make soothing sounds as if she were petting an injured child.

Donald began drinking heavily. In his delirious state, he would stumble about like a whirling dervish and wave Silver Bell away as if she were a pesky fly. Most nights, he downed drink after drink, pausing occasionally to light a cigarette. Back in bed, he tossed from his back to his chest, turning from side to side until his liquor took hold and he fell into a stupor.

Silver Bell knew Donald needed a catharsis. She also wanted to learn more about his past. She remembered Golden Bell taking psychology classes in Syracuse and mentioning a "talking cure" for injured psyches. She instructed the steward to hide all the liquor and gave Donald cups of coffee. She let him walk and talk while he draped his arm over her shoulder. After a day of hearing him rant, writhe miserably, retch, and declare, "I don't deserve you!" she encouraged him to tell her about his family.

In a moment of lucidity, Donald poured out his tale:

"My family name is Tung, not Ting. My given name is Da Ming, not Donald. My father was an administrator at the University of Nanking. His post was a sinecure obtained by my grandfather, a senior official in the Nationalist government. Father was the only son of a powerful family. The marriage was arranged because both families had been friends for years. My mother used to rail at him for being a useless playboy because he was so spoiled. My mother always bemoaned her fate. She came from a banking family. She thought she would never want for anything.

"But the marriage was a sham. My father philandered, and my mother tried to alleviate her boredom and drown her sorrows at the mahjong table. She spent nights and days gambling. My younger sister and I were brought up by servants and witnessed constant bickering. Sometimes my parents fought and threw things at each other like a pair of unhinged children. Gossipy women fluttered around my mother. At the time, I hated her.

"Father tried to befriend me when I turned ten. He said we 'men' must stick together and not let women's pettiness control us. He said that people considered Mother a beauty because she was

307

tall and slender, but he often spoke of her in a crude way. 'What is the good of a stiff board when you don't have the soft melons to play with?' He would laugh and open his hands to form cups. On hot and humid summer nights, Father would sit bare-chested and play with his own breasts. Even as a child, I was exposed to lewdness and cruelty.

"Father always wore the façade of a flamboyant playboy — quick to offer drinks and cigarettes and cracking jokes that denigrated women. For a long time, I believed that my mother persecuted him because she was so cold and showed such disdain toward him. From my perspective, while she might wipe away a tear sometimes, she seemed more preoccupied with sitting in front of the mirror, shopping, conferring with the tailor, or giggling and gossiping with her mahjong friends. I took my father's 'manly' behavior as a template for my future. I bullied my sister and got away with it.

"When Chiang Kai-shek ordered all the government officials to evacuate Nanking, almost all our family's friends and relations left for Changsha, Hangkow, and Chungking, packing whatever they could. The smart ones went overseas. When the treasures of the National Museum were emptied and crated to Chungking, and the generalissimo left by plane on December 8, my grandparents followed. Mother pleaded with my father to leave. Father steadfastly refused. Mother accused him of wanting to stay because of his mistress.

"Father dodged her accusation but was ecstatic. He had learned a smattering of Japanese and thought his language skills would enable him to enjoy a drink with the conquerors, continue his sinecure at the university, and perhaps live openly with his mistress, given that both his parents and my mother's family had left town. When the Chinese military made a disorderly retreat, he hired bodyguards to defend our home." Donald's mouth turned down into a sneer, but he continued.

"When our bodyguards learned that the Japanese soldiers were going from door to door, looting and rounding up women, they fled. My parents sent my sister and me to Ginling College in the foreign-run safety zone. We left in the dead of night; we had hardly gone two blocks when we encountered a Japanese patrol. I was fifteen and my sister twelve. We were grabbed like two meek lambs and sent to our separate destinies. I was taken to a general's house. I never saw my parents and sister again; I shudder to think what happened to them."

He swallowed and seemed reluctant to continue. But then he grabbed his chest and groaned. "No, no . . . no. I must go on!" He jerked himself upright. "I have to . . . I have to!"

Silver Bell messaged his back, murmuring, "You'll feel better unloading your burdens."

"I lied about going to study in Japan. My degradation began and ended in Nanking — in the Japanese general's house. I was treated like a piece of meat." He paused, wiped his face, and shook himself. "I would be dragged out and forced to witness the torture of others. Nights and days fused into a blur. I wanted to die quickly and lost all memory of faces, names, and my surroundings. But on one fateful day, the sadists — reeking of whiskey, sweat, cigarettes, and danger — wanted to be entertained." Donald started sobbing and stuttering out curses.

"They brought in a family of three, a father, mother, and daughter. They stripped the girl naked and cut off the father's pants. They forced the father to rape his daughter and the mother to watch. The mother screamed, cried, and finally fainted. They poured water on her to revive her. The father begged to be killed, screaming his refusal to continue. Veins bulged like webs of twine around his neck and urine trickled down his legs. The girl cried and cursed in defiance. When a soldier taunted her, saying that she shouldn't care, because she had been violated so many times already, she spat at him. The soldiers slapped, kicked, and stabbed the three with their bayonets. The official sitting next to me also poked me with a gun to make sure I was watching. All the while, he snickered and tried not to laugh out loud.

"Suddenly, the door opened and the room turned deadly quiet. Mr. Tanaka, a Japanese embassy official, came in with John Rabe. Rabe was a German businessman, the leader of the Nazi Party in Nanking and the head of the International Committee that had set up the Nanking safety zone around Ginling College. The silent backdrop only intensified the smell of urine, liquor, and vomit. Rabe gave everyone a poisonous look and pointed to his Nazi medals. The Japanese soldiers cowered and shot the miserable family in a hurry. Brains, flesh, and blood splattered everywhere. Someone announced that they were executing spies.

Mr. Tanaka, in a loud but calm, sure tone, asked to speak to the commanding officer. The official next to me wobbled to his feet, saluted, and left. When told that the commanding general was ill and they would have to return another day, Mr. Tanaka ordered me to go with him and Rabe. We all left together. I didn't know what would happen to me, but I was glad to flee. As we drove, I saw dead bodies stacked like hillocks all over the streets. Dogs were rooting through the piles and feasting. An early red moon hung low in the darkening sky. Its dull orange-red glow highlighted the macabre scene. Under this red moon, we had to drive over masses of black and purple corpses because there was no other way to proceed.

"Once in the Japanese embassy, I was led to a place where I could clean myself. When I emerged, Mr. Rabe was gone. I later learned that he was considered the Buddha of Nanking because he had used his Nazi credentials to save thousands of lives.

"From the very beginning, Mr. Tanaka treated me with kindness. He spoke several languages and was a consummate politician and manipulator. I learned all my survival skills from him. He was a cultured man — you might even call him book fragrant. He was delighted that I was willing to study hard and learn Japanese and English quickly. Officially, I was his assistant, but I also became his lover. Through him, I first experienced candle-lit dinners and soft warm lips. Later, I learned that Japanese education was regiment-ed and that violent punishment was meted out at any sign of individualism or disobedience. The military institutionalized brutality. The soldiers were fed a steady diet of pornography through graphic pictures, books, and even films. The soldiers considered dying for the emperor their greatest glory.

"In early 1941, Mr. Tanaka was sent to Washington, D.C. I ac-companied him. By then, I was given freedom of movement because he trusted me completely. After Japan bombed Pearl Harbor, the mood in the embassy turned dark and stormy. Every-one was busy burning papers. Tanaka walked around with a pistol in his small, shaking hand. Life became disorderly and confusing. We knew we would soon be arrested, sent to jail, or sent back to Japan.

"By this time, I knew I wasn't a homosexual and greatly resent-ed Tanaka's sexual advances. I bought old clothes from a beggar, changed, and went into an Episcopal church in Maryland to seek asylum. I told them I was a stowaway Christian from Nanking. By then the church people had some inkling of the Nanking Massacre. They enrolled me in school and did everything possible to recon-nect me with the Chinese community. Despite their charity, I was consumed by guilt, shame, secret gratitude for Tanaka, and remorse — a poisoned man. I decided to change my name so I would never have to speak of my experience.

"It was easy to avoid talking to the early Chinese immigrants in Washington's Chinatown because they were mostly Cantonese or Fukienese, whose dialects were alien to me. Many newly arrived refugees were eager to share their tragic stories as part of this Chinese Diaspora. I avoided them. I had already settled on a new agenda for myself: to finish my education and strike out on my own. I remembered only too well how my grandparents had ruined my parents' lives by pampering them. No one would pry a single word of truth from me. I thought I would die if I relived my experiences. When the war ended, the church sent me back to China to find my family. I never went near Nanking. I was much taller by then and knew my appearance had changed.

"Sometimes, when I walked into a room, I was surprised to see that it was normal — that there was no blood or gore. Other times the nightmarish images were vivid, more persistent. Whenever I see the Japanese flag, I only see the red moon instead of the sun it is supposed to be." Donald wiped his eyes; sweat coursed down his face. "The sense of degradation, anxiety, fear, and guilt never left me. I had to keep quiet. I don't deserve you. I am a bastard, a degenerate, and I have ruined your life."

"No, no, no." Silver Bell listened, slack-jawed, to her husband's harrowing account. Her heart raced and her tears flowed, but his revelations buoyed her spirit and sent it soaring. She hugged and kissed him. "Now I understand. You have condemned yourself because of your humiliation. You are kind and you have saved the Yung family's fortunes and ensured the Huang family's survival." She explained her Christian understanding of grace and mentioned Coral Bell's answer to Pastor Cummings before her baptism. She assured Donald that his actions had not been egotistical but a reaction to his trauma and the natural will to live. Then she reminded him of their rescue mission. Though her stomach churned, she felt a strange elation. A radiant affection permeated her being. She didn't know what dangers lay ahead, but the old shadows faded and she was ready to face future challenges.

She vowed she would someday persuade Donald to search for his family. Assuming they had remained alive, a reunion would bring a measure of peace to Donald's tormented psyche.

"It is enough," Silver Bell soothed. "We need never mention your past again." From then on, whenever she saw him weeping or shaking in bed while covering his face, she would give him a sedative and try to focus on their rescue plan. She gave him her Bible. She brought him on deck for walks and fresh air. As they paced, she tried to discuss Christian notions of love, transcendence, forgiveness, and grace.

"Let's tell Jenny," Silver Bell whispered one day while they were walking around the deck. "Not all the gruesome details, but since she took Chinese history last year in college, she already knows about the Japanese atrocities in China. She will forgive us and understand our love for her."

Donald straightened himself to face the sea breeze. "I really need to apologize to her. All these years, my sordid secret was a story that tortured me, in dreams and waking, and gave me a sense of separateness that I must box myself in shame and despair. I was uncomfortable seeing her deformity when she was young. As she grew, she looked more and more like my mother and sister. It was torture to see her and be reminded of my past." Donald shook himself to remain erect. "She was so tall and thin and even had the same voice as my sister. I felt as if the ghosts were haunting me. I was a coward. I mostly chose to be away on business when she visited. Whenever I saw her I didn't know how to behave. She never had a father. She was probably also uncomfortable visiting us because she could sense the tension between us." He sighed, took a deep breath and hung his head.

"I have no excuse for being a bad mother. I lived with a model mother, and I was so close to Coral Bell when she was young."

"You were too young and immature when she was born and couldn't handle her deformity. I was to blame for that too." Donald squeezed her hand.

Silver Bell let her blowing hair cover her face. "I did try to be with her for each of her operations. When she was young, she was always confused to see me. She also seemed so happy living with the missionary ladies that I vowed to take time to establish a non-intrusive bond." Silver Bell's voice wobbled and she swiped her wet face as she pushed her hair away. "In the early years, after her lip reconstructions were complete, she was truly ill at ease whenever she visited us. She clung to Miss Tyler or one of the ladies who brought her. But since she turned thirteen and was able to travel alone, we made sure she comes home on all her long vacations. She's adjusted."

"Do you think I should write her a long letter about my past? It'll be easier than telling her in person." A gust of wind pushed them forward and he had to shout very loud to be heard.

Silver Bell nodded. "I'm sure she'll appreciate hearing from you. She remembers the times you took us out to dinner and drove us around the island to show her the sights — things you're used to doing with your clients." She reminded him. "Oh yes, you also introduced your friends who had children her age." Silver turned to pat his back and smile into his eyes. "Now she even corresponds with several of our friends' daughters."

"Oh yeah? I didn't know that!" Donald said.

"The girls here all envy her because she lives in America. She did ask me once why our little family is separated and why you always seemed so preoccupied." Silver Bell grimaced and hooked a hand into her husband's arm and they resumed walking.

"What did you tell her?"

"I told her we wanted to give her the best treatment in America. She did remember me being with her whenever she had surgery. I was a coward too and didn't tell the whole truth. I also tried to excuse our alienation by blaming how hard we both worked. But she has been my Sunshine and the Love that has kept me going all these years."

"I'll make sure I'm home the next time she comes. We'll have a heart to heart talk. She may come to feel truly at home with us." Donald grasped Silver Bell's hands.

"Perhaps we should all go visit her. She is very involved with the church and her work and studies in the University. If our rescue mission is successful, we'll bring Coral Bell, Der An and Der Li there as well. We can all go and stay a while." They nestled close with their heads tugged together as they moved onward against the blustering wind.

One evening, the captain of the ship joined them, telling them he was a Buddhist. Every evening thereafter, he talked about letting go of one's ego and emptying oneself of hatred, jealousy, anger, and bitterness. He spoke about the manifold desires for worldly things blinding us to the sublime truth that we are mortal and cannot take anything with us. He explained how building up good karma for the next life is central to the Buddhist faith. "Buddhism is simple," he said. "Avoid evil, do good, and master your mind. The last part is real work."

Despite some resistance, Donald turned his attention to the immediate challenges. He was playing an essential part in preparing Silver Bell for her rescue mission. The captain said that when it came time for Silver Bell to go ashore in Shanghai, he would keep close watch on Donald.

Tides of the Red Moon Waning

August 1968

"THROW OUT the old, bring in the new!" Coral Bell cried out. She raised her arms like a robot, shouting slogans. Her hair tangled around her face like dead seaweed, as if she were still rampaging through the streets. Her dark round eyes blazed in her unnaturally ruddy face. She couldn't stop her harangue.

"What's the matter?" Brook ma-ma asked nervously.

"Throw out the capitalists!" Tears streamed down her face.

"Are you all right?"

"Yes." She thrust her fist into the air like a mechanical arm. "I . . . I am such a progressive woman! I help burn old books, dig . . . dig up flower beds!" She hiccupped.

"What happened? You're hysterical."

"Tra . . . trappings of capitalism!" She gasped, her arms flailing. She twirled and stumbled around in her room, as if riding a cyclone.

Brook ma-ma came over to restrain her. "Stop this instantly! The neighbors can hear you."

"Trains are coming in, in late, late . . . because the ca . . . capitalists wanted them to come in on, on . . . time!" She coughed,

317

choked, hyperventilated, and sputtered out the words: "We, we want everything Chi, Chi . . . Chinese! Red is our color — the red light means 'go' — the green, green . . . light 'stop'!"

"Hush, hush." Brook ma-ma pushed her onto her platform bed. "You'll wake M-ma. She's resting next door."

Coral Bell collapsed onto her pillow. "I, I've been . . . digging up flower beds in Golden Bell's mansion all, all night," she wailed, trembling like a woman rescued from a drowning.

"Aren't you just a dispatcher for the Red Guards?" Brook ma-ma said, covering her daughter with a worn silk quilt.

"I had to go. I thought I might protect her . . . Now both she and Yung are dead!"

"What? No, no, no . . . What, what happened?" Brook ma-ma opened her mouth and stared. She looked from her daughter to the disorderly room. Her mind whirled. She took the longest breath she could remember; she coughed and swallowed, trying to control herself while rubbing her chest to slow down her heart's chaotic rhythm. Finally, she gulped down a mouthful of air and mumbled, "You've been protecting her and all of us." Brook ma-ma placed her hand on Coral Bell's forehead. "Do you have a fever?"

Coral Bell's teeth chattered in her now ashen face, but she didn't answer. She closed her eyes. Lurid scenes of death and destruction continued to feed her waking nightmare. She moaned.

"What?" Brook ma-ma stood up mumbling. "Your forehead is cool — too cool. Did you say you went into Golden Bell's house?"

"No," Coral hissed, curling up and putting her thumb in her mouth. "No one knew I was her sister."

"Are you sure?"

"Um . . . I'm so tired!" she cried, yawning and spitting out the dirt she tasted on her thumb. She knew she must not breathe another word. "Tar Chuang told me I must put the Yungs on the schedule . . . so we'd be safe. Most often, the kids were so busy looting that they just pulled the owners to prison . . ." She pretended to fall asleep, but the memories kept flooding in.

I, Huang Coral Bell, just participated in my half sister's murder . . I did not want any part of this mad destruction, but my husband, Tar Chuang, an administrator in the Communist Party, thought I should display more concrete proof of my loyalty. I joined the Red Guards to protect our family. By 1966, in the name of Chairman Mao and revolutionary democracy, the youths were unleashed to loot homes, burn books, and kill and destroy anything that represented Confucian rectitude or capitalist realism. They called for a new spiritual purity. Anyone with an education or wealth was subjected to mass meetings of denunciation, beatings, and torture. I scheduled the Red Guard raids and joined in the purge. For months and months, Tar Chuang and I pushed the Yung family to the bottom of our list. We finally had to schedule their cleansing, thinking that they would only be arrested and imprisoned. Tar Chuang convinced me that leaving them alone would invite more brutal treatment. People know we live in the Yung family's business housing. None of us knew that someone had given the students iron pipes instead of the usual stick or two.

All these years, Golden Bell and her husband supported M-ma, Brook ma-ma, and me. Is this how I repaid them?

I remember lolling around the Yung family's garden with Li-li and An-an in peaceful times. We watched the parade of ants with fascination. We tracked the movements of their segmented bodies as they hauled oversize leaves, grub, or some musty dirt into their underground home. Once, An-an squashed a few ants under his feet, leaving a tiny brown patch that showed no sign that the ants had ever existed. Now Golden Bell and Yung have been reduced to pulp; will they be forgotten like the crushed ants? Life is so cheap these days.

Scenes of the days we played catch haunt me. Sometimes I would crawl around as if I were a giant monster, threatening and growling that I

319

wanted to eat the children. They giggled and ran, but always came back to let themselves be hugged, kissed, and tickled. Now I have brought monstrous savages into their house and devoured their parents. Oh God, where were you? You promised to be with me! How can anyone endure such insanity? How are the children to survive?

Coral Bell's reverie kept her quiet. The baby wailed in the next room of their shared apartment. Sounds of cooking and bantering came from the communal kitchen. Someone was splashing water in the bathroom and mumbling aloud. Coral Bell's shivers subsided. Ordinary activities of life made images of last night's rampage seem unreal. She looked at her dirt-encrusted fingers and saw specks of blood on her hands; she trembled anew.

She needed a wash, but the bathroom and the kitchen were occupied. She smelled her own sour breath and groaned as mysterious pains pricked her all over. She tossed and turned on the lumpy bed and remembered how White Lily always reminded her that she was lucky the revolutionaries had not sent her back to be reeducated on the country farms.

The sky turned dark. She wondered when her husband might come home. Pain and despair gripped her like a disease in her chest. Obviously the dog had sniffed her out. The other Red Guards would find out she was related to Golden Bell. Would her husband protect her? Peony could no longer help. All the leaders in the Party, the same Communists whom the Yungs had collaborated with — led by Liu Shaoqi and Deng Xiaoping — were labeled revisionist; sent to "struggle meetings"; wore dunce caps; were paraded before screaming youths; were imprisoned without judicial review; and their whole families were tormented.

The naked ten-watt light bulb in the hallway flickered, obscuring the smelly, soot-filled apartment. She moaned and turned to the wall. Fate had dealt her a disastrous hand. In public, she had grown accustomed to fumbling through lies, cruelties, and hysteria. But at home she must keep her experiences under lock and key and feign innocence. Suddenly, she heard the familiar blare of a Red Guard truck down the street. The sounds of screaming slogans and clanging gongs floated up the seven stories of the apartment building, filling every nook and cranny. She burrowed deep into her bedding, covering her ears.

Brook ma-ma nudged her. "Coral Bell, Coral Bell, tell me what happened."

In the next five days, Coral Bell lapsed into hysteria and long periods of numbing sleep. Tar Chuang held her tightly whenever he was home. He apologized repeatedly and together with Brook ma-ma forced her to drink soups and herbal tea.

Brook ma-ma took a deep breath. Pronouncing each word with firm puffs of air, she said, "It's no use pretending. White Lily told me everything." After much secret weeping, Brook ma-ma had decided to show no fear or sorrow. It was essential that she appear strong to her daughter. She came into Coral Bell's room carrying a tray. "I brought you some tea and leek dumplings."

"I think I . . . I have a cold." Coral Bell blubbered, hiding her face in her pillow.

"You do sound congested." Brook ma-ma placed the tray on the table and felt her daughter's forehead. "No, you don't have a temperature. Your tears must have stuffed up your nose. Look, your eyes are puffed up like a bullfrog's!" She tried to smile. "Come and eat."

Brook ma-ma's loving gaze softened Coral Bell, and she instantly felt warm. "How can I live after what I did to Golden Bell?" she blurted out.

"Oh, Coral, you did not beat her. White Lily told me you didn't even touch her!" Brook ma-ma rocked her daughter in her arms.

She rubbed Coral's back and smoothed her disheveled hair. "Hush, hush. You've been lying here for almost a week. It's about time you returned to work."

"Resume my evil work? Yes, I was the efficient one. I organized the smashing, killing, and defacing of every old decency!"

"You did it to keep us safe." Brook ma-ma subdued a sob and choked. She took a sip of tea.

"Everyone said I had to do it. Even White Lily and Tar Chuang said Golden Bell was a capitalist. I had to schedule her for a cleansing!"

"You did what you could." Brook ma-ma turned away to wipe a tear.

Coral Bell knew Tar Chuang had instigated her actions, but that did not alleviate her guilt. Tar Chuang had not expected the savagery. She couldn't abide the bitter irony of it all. "Week in and week out, we join in these atrocities. Then we return home, huddle in our warm beds, and bemoan the hysterical, hideous deeds going on with our Red Guards."

"What other choice do we have? Now eat!" She stamped her foot to show she was in control. Her sudden movement startled her daughter.

"Brook ma-ma, I know you've taken pains to make these dumplings." Silent tears coursed down Coral's cheeks. She ate but couldn't taste anything.

There was a soft knock on the door. A woman slipped in, wearing a faded blue Mao suit that was standard attire for a Communist Party member.

Brook ma-ma shrieked with recognition. "Silver Bell!"

Coral Bell stared. It took her a minute to recognize her sister. Silver Bell's straggly, dirty hair stuck out of her Mao cap. Her rumpled suit made her look like a Party member just returned from a night of marauding. No trace of the Westernized socialite remained.

Silver Bell put her finger to her mouth, silencing the stunned women. The incongruous apparition sank down into the sofa, panting. "I first went next door. M-ma was stroking and stroking Golden Bell's gray silk scarf."

"Yes," Brook ma-ma answered. "Tai-tai doesn't know about Golden Bell's death, but she seems to feel that something is amiss. White Lily found the scarf in Golden Bell's house and brought it to Tai-tai."

"M-ma's hair has turned all white, but you've kept it in the same chignon . . . she just sits there staring. She called me Ah Yee and apologized she is not well enough to give me a massage today!"

Brook ma-ma's eyes turned to pools of crystal. "Yes, Ah Yee is a worker from the Yung factory. She and some other workers often come up here to consult Tai-tai when they feel sick. Why have you come? You've entered a tiger's den!"

Silver Bell acknowledged the danger with a nod. She pressed her hand to her chest. "I must rest. I held my breath all the way here from the harbor." She gulped down the tea on the table. "Oh, it is good to see you!"

"How did you get in?" Brook ma-ma refilled the cup.

Silver Bell ripped off her cap to fan herself, explaining that she had come to rescue Coral Bell and Golden Bell's children. She had already decided it would not be wise to take her M-ma and Brook ma-ma to Hong Kong. She could see they were in no danger here and might jeopardize the mission if she included them.

"How did you know what happened to Golden Bell and Coral Bell?"

"Yes, we know. We also know that the Red Guards will soon find out Coral is Golden Bell's sister. All her efforts in the past to help the Yungs may be held against her."

"I . . . I can't leave M-ma and Brook ma-ma, and . . ." Coral Bell stammered. It would have been proper to add Tar Chuang, but something inside stopped her. No one noticed the omission.

"Who told you Coral Bell is in danger?" Brook ma-ma gasped.

Silver Bell sipped her tea, leaned back into her chair, and felt calmer. "We have been in contact with Peony and her relatives all along. White Lily informed them that some of the Red Guards must have noticed Lucky was friendly to Coral Bell."

"My God, Coral Bell, you never said anything about that!" Brook ma-ma ran to hold her daughter's hand, tears falling down her cheeks.

"Lucky came to sit and wail with me." Coral Bell looked up in wide-eyed alarm.

Silver Bell blinked back her tears and refrained from more questioning. Donald had instructed her not to dwell on the murder scene. She turned to Brook ma-ma. "Where are Golden Bell's children?"

"Lao Ma, their nanny, has taken them to the Bamboo Hills we used to own in the Yellow Creek Village." She whispered the long-held secret.

"I remember visiting there!" Silver Bell exclaimed.

"Yes, Lao Ma's father had been the keeper of the hills for ages. I remember going there, before the liberation." Coral Bell brightened.

"What liberation?" Silver Bell spat out her outrage. "We've been liberated into chaos!"

Coral Bell dropped her head into her arms on the table.

"We've no time to talk. Donald and our company ship are sitting out in the Hwangpo. A fisherman's boat is waiting for us in the harbor. Coral Bell and I must leave immediately!" Silver Bell put down her teacup and slapped on her cap. "We'll go to the Yellow Creek Village later."

Brook ma-ma squeezed Coral's hand. "Don't worry about us. You must flee now. The Red Guards can come after you any day, anytime!"

"I . . . I can't!"

"You must!" Brook ma-ma stood very tall. "When people ask about you, I'll just say that you had orders to go to Changsha and organize struggle sessions there. Maybe in the confusion, people won't find out for months. If you're arrested, you might endanger M-ma and me."

"But how are you to survive?" Coral Bell asked, sobbing.

"You know Ah Yee and the workers from the factory rely on your M-ma's medical care. They will protect us. Tai-tai doesn't know where she is. No one will harm us here."

"And . . . and Tar Chuang?" Coral Bell finally had to ask.

Silver Bell grabbed a slip of paper and scribbled down the location of the fishing boat. "Here. Ask Tar Chuang to come to the boat when he can. Donald will be waiting on board every day and night."

"I'll tell Tar Chuang you've gone to rescue the children. As soon as I get word that you're safe, I'll give Tar Chuang this paper. He'll have to decide what to do."

Coral Bell sat dazed, immobilized by so much new information.

Brook ma-ma quickly packed a small bundle of clothes and helped her daughter change and tidy up for the journey. Looking at Silver Bell, she gasped, "I never expected Donald to be our savior." Her voice broke.

"Donald suffered more than we can ever imagine." Silver Bell bit her lower lip. "I have no time to explain now, but I'll tell you someday."

Silver Bell stood up to leave. Brook ma-ma tried to smile through her tears. She held on to her daughter's hand. Silver Bell tugged the clothes bundle under her arm. She boldly dragged Coral Bell out the door before she could protest or dawdle. In the hallway, she announced loudly that Coral Bell had orders to report to duty in Changsha.

Walking down the tree-lined street speckled with sunshine, Coral Bell hunched over as she trudged alongside Silver Bell, who strode like an energetic Party member.

Coral Bell was sweating. She wanted to cover her face. She felt as though lights were searching her out and that she was exposed in front of all the Red Guards. She dragged her feet, and her mind conjured the many scenes of savagery that she had helped orchestrate. She cringed at her own thoughts and imagined hearing shouts. She raised her hands to cover her ears. She was sure there would be ropes coming out of nowhere to bind her hands, rocks ricocheting around her, and cries of "Traitor! Capitalist! Intellectual!"

At the end of their street, Mrs. Chen stopped to stare at them. She opened her mouth as though to speak, then closed it and lowered her head.

Coral Bell paused, her whole body quivering. Sweat trickled down her face, and her palms rose automatically to wipe it away. She wanted to say good-bye.

Mrs. Chen turned, shaking her head, and went on her way.

Silver Bell tugged on Coral's sleeve. "She probably thinks I'm arresting you. You look wretched enough . . . let's go."

They tucked in their chins, afraid to encounter more familiar faces. They shuffled on, gaining strength when they saw no one approaching them. Walking by grimy gray buildings that once housed elegant retail stores, Silver Bell felt her heart lighten with the memory of dancing in the Paramount, the city's biggest nightclub. Her eyes filled as she remembered the countless hours she had spent shopping in the towering Wing On department store. It now stood solemn and glum. Since the Korean War, there had been no new construction or renovation in Shanghai. The peeling paint, broken windows, and warped and dented doors led to empty, demolished stores or government-sponsored small vendors with few goods to sell. The more elegant stores that used to line Nanking Road, carrying Western goods, now looked like bombed-out shells — gutted and vandalized by the Red Guards. Not a vestige of foreign charm remained. Coral Bell trembled, remembering the frenzied attacks on the stores. The teenage Red Guards had been full of hysterical energy. *So much savagery . . .*

The streets were eerily quiet. The Red Guards must have been at their midday meal or were still resting from their night's activities. The trucks that usually drove them were absent. Since many high-up Party members had been imprisoned, cars had disappeared. People even refrained from using their bicycles for fear that some young Red Guard might confiscate them. They hid in their shabby homes. Even in the middle of the day, Shanghai seemed to have gone into hibernation. Coral Bell felt an urge to wail her good-byes and confess that she had helped destroy the bustling streets of this once vibrant city. The people they did see on the street turned their heads to avoid meeting their eyes. Coral Bell realized her puffy eyes, her shuffling gait, and Silver Bell's energetic pace and solemn face told the usual story around town — an unfortunate woman taken to struggle sessions, interrogations, or worse.

Gazing at the pyramid-shaped roof of the Cathay Hotel, Silver Bell silently bade farewell to well-known landmarks on the Bund: the tree-lined esplanade, the Hong Kong and Shanghai Bank, and the Custom House tower. Strangely, she found herself longing for the human sweat and exhaust from the teeming traffic in Hong Kong.

They reached the waterfront, and Silver Bell felt her pulse racing. Foreign warships flying colorful flags of many nations no longer crowded the Hwangpo. Instead, sampans and small wooden boats, hung with laundry, cluttered the waterway and the area around the wharfs. They reminded her of the wobbly wooden shacks that covered the hillside in Hong Kong. Her hands tightened around Coral Bell's bundle of clothes. Her balled-up fists steadied her shaky legs. They walked past their boat. Few people were about, and no one was idling. Coolies, stripped to their waists, with sweat running down their foreheads and torsos, tended to their own affairs — loading or unloading goods, just like the old days. The sisters walked back and scurried inside the waiting boat.

Coral Bell had held her breath for so long that she panted for air. She peered out from the straw mat that formed a cave-like hood over the sitting area. Her heart was thumping fiercely in her chest. "I hope no one saw us coming in!" she murmured.

The fisherman's wife served them tea and a small repast.

"I'm surprised at how well it all went. Here, have some tea." Silver Bell sighed with relief, sitting Buddha-like in front of the low table.

Coral Bell slumped forward. Her voice shook. "What about M-ma and Brook ma-ma? What about the children? Are we ever going to see them again?"

"No use crying now." Silver Bell touched her weeping sister. She had long discussed with Donald the importance of keeping a calm demeanor during this perilous mission. "Sit up. We must talk." She let out a bitter laugh. "And yes, someday we will see our M-ma and Brook ma-ma again. The Red Guards will leave them alone, seeing M-ma has already lost her mind." She turned to the business at hand. "Tell me, do you know how to get to the Yellow Creek Village?"

The confidence and precision of her words calmed Coral Bell. "I . . . I'm not sure exactly. I know it is south of Hangzhou."

"I remember visiting, many times, some cabins in the Bamboo Hills that our family owned near that village. We always went by boat." Silver Bell couldn't help smiling wistfully at the memory.

"Yes, yes." Coral Bell's eyes brightened. "I remember Lao Ma's father meeting us."

Silver Bell took small sips of her tea, her manner formal and melancholy. "Good. Yes, I still remember our trips there — always turning right into small creeks from Hangzhou." She took out her maps and studied them.

"Here is Hangzhou." She pointed it out to her sister. "And here is the Yellow Creek Village. On its south bank are the Bamboo Hills." She left to consult the fisherman. When she returned, she said, "The fisherman's wife has gone to make arrangements. As soon as it gets dark, we'll go up the river." They remained quiet, waiting and fidgeting. They had no plan and knew they would have to follow their instincts in order to save the children.

A pregnant silence prevailed for a while. Finally, Coral Bell whispered: "You've come to save my life! Now you have enlisted me in helping to save the children. I will do my best."

In the stillness of the afternoon heat, Silver Bell felt a rush of sorrow. Like oil boiling inside a cauldron, her emotions surfaced as though all the suffering were alive within her once again. In the old days, she had unburdened herself to Golden Bell and asked her advice. Now she missed Golden Bell's wise counsel. With her only living sister before her, the struggles that she had bundled inside for so long rushed out. "Coral, I want to tell you everything about Donald's past so you can understand him.

Coral Bell nodded, though her thoughts were racing ahead anticipating their coming mission.

While her stomach felt as if it had been stitched together, Silver Bell could not help pouring out her husband's experience of degradation. She tried to immerse herself in his misery, but was beside herself knowing her pains were totally inadequate in helping him heal. How he must have suffered all these years in maintaining his lonely false façade! Still there came a measure of relief in the telling. Amidst tears of horror and ceaseless dread, she finally said, "I am sorry to unburden myself on you."

Coral Bell was shocked by the unspeakable trauma inflicted on the man her family despised. She mulled over things to say about

Donald's past, but decided not to say them. She moved to sit beside her sister and reached over to hug and clutch her sister's hand. Mumbling her words of comfort, she whispered, "I'm so glad you told me."

Still rattled and with more urgency, Silver Bell said, "Golden Bell must have told you that you have a niece, my daughter Jenny, living with the missionaries near Syracuse, New York."

"Yes, Golden Bell did tell us after she returned from visiting you in Hong Kong." Coral Bell's lips quivered just mentioning Golden Bell's name.

Silver Bell did not notice. She dove straight into the bright side of her life — her daughter. "Jenny was born with a cleft lip. I was too young and too bitter about my marriage to accept her. Childishly, all I wanted then was to become independent. As you know, I soon became quite successful dealing in real estate and antiques in Hong Kong. However, Miss Tyler made sure that I visited Jenny every time she had an operation. I had grown more confident as time went by, and while my heart banged like the cymbals when I saw this beautiful little girl, I knew I would be visiting as much as I could.

As Jenny grew older and her lip reconstruction progressed, I found myself offering Miss Tyler and the other missionary ladies several trips a year to bring Jenny to Hong Kong. When Donald first saw Jenny with her repaired lip, he scrunched up his brows as if hit by some unbearable complications. He did not apologize nor admit guilt, but lowered his head without a word, and wiped his forehead as if he needed to swipe away the sweat that was not there. In a moment, he collected himself and extended his arm, almost touching mine, but moved his open palm toward all of us and in a voice tinged with an undertone of excessive tenderness, offered to drive us around to tour Hong Kong. I was too consumed with guilt and confusion to understand his reaction. Now I know it was his past trauma that had overtaken him, robbed him of the peace and confidence that were needed to restart our family. Donald usually stayed away during their subsequent visits — for his 'business trips' — as he claimed, but he never complained about the expenses involved for Jenny's home coming.

When everyone grew older, I went every year to bring Jenny home for her summer and winter breaks. Often Miss Tyler joined us, especially in the winter. I found myself fighting for Jenny's affection in a more ferocious effort than I had ever spent on nailing down or closing a sale.

One summer, I learned to make chicken salad from Jenny. I told her I couldn't believe how the chicken breast could be so tender. Jenny was amazed that I was ignorant of preparing simple dishes, even though she knew I had a full time cook for our Chinese meal."

Silver Bell smiled and took a deep breath, wondering if she should explain to Coral Bell what chicken salad was. Coral Bell smiled back. Sensing her sister's need to connect them all, she whispered: "Tell me more about Jenny."

Silver Bell continued: "Music saved our relationship. As you know I had always loved singing. Jenny had learned to play the piano. When she played some hymns from church one day, I couldn't help singing along. She often joined me, and our voices blended and soared with our spirits. We always laughed and hugged afterwards. I had stopped attending church for many years and then only when Jenny visited, but music really brought me back.

As Jenny grew into her teens, Donald started to stick around more often. Aside from his usual habit of taking us out to dinner and driving us to see the sights, he introduced some of his business friends who had children around Jenny's age. Jenny began to feel more and more at home in Hong Kong. I was grateful for his attempts to normalize our family, but I was still ignorant about his life — his past and his everyday business. I couldn't forgive him.

The most astonishing experience I had was once I saw Donald standing next to Jenny by the window. Their two faces before me had obviously borrowed features from each other. Jenny had inherited his high forehead, large, wide piercing eyes and his straight long nose. I quickly noted to myself that she had my pointy chin line and slightly pouty mouth. She has a long waist and was already almost a head taller then me. No doubt she had inherited her father's stature.

Donald lifted his arm and for a moment. I thought he was going to put his arm around Jenny, but he snapped his head back and patted the back of his ear and looked puzzled. He screwed his eyes together, turned toward the window and stared into the distant sea. I realized in a flash that the outlines of their robust bodies formed a domestic scene that was made up of all these separate things that were strange to me. A shot of pain sped from my foot to my spine and head, while I felt as if I was standing on an Indian Holy Man's nail board. I zipped up my quaking lips, took several deep breaths and lit a cigarette.

Jenny still doesn't know about her father's unspeakable experiences and my struggles to cope. Donald is in the process of writing her but we've decided that saving you and Golden Bell's children is more urgent . . ."

Silver Bell's excitement made her sound like she was prattling on and on but she was teary-eyed and sweating. She could not stop until her account was complete. When she had finished, she shivered and wept as if a fever had broken.

Coral Bell didn't know how to respond. She was used to being the younger sister. Silver Bell had taught her so much about the modern world. She had always thought how lucky and blessed Silver Bell had been, living a life of luxury in Hong Kong. Now she understood the different burdens everyone carried. She leaned close to wiped her sister's forehead and smooth her hair as her own mother might have done, murmuring, "Thank you for coming and risking your life to save us. I've prayed and thanked God for your endless kindness since I was a child. It is important to understand what happened. And it is a huge relief to learn about Donald and Jenny. Their goodness gives me hope and a reason to live. Now I know I can trust my brother-in-law. I also feel blessed that you have told me about your angel child, Jenny. I know she will lead me back to the bosom of Grace I've always longed to belong."

She realized that she was behaving like Brook ma-ma — the comforter and the pillar that maintained the family's dignity. Yet, she felt different. Her strength came from her God. Still holding her sister's trembling hands, she recited the psalm that had given her so much solace: "Yea, though I walk through the valley of the shadow of death, I will fear no evil . . ."

Silver Bell repeated each line after her sister, and her racing heart slowed. After years of not practicing her faith and blaming God for her troubles, she was embarrassed to pray. She smiled weakly at her younger sister and whispered, "I'm going to rest now." She closed her eyes, folded her arms on the table, and dropped her head on it. Silently, she prayed again and again for guidance. She seemed to be dozing, but her breath was uneven. Coral Bell suspected she was having a hard time suppressing the anxiety and desperation that both were now feeling.

"Even if we lose our lives in this rescue mission, we will have done our best." Coral Bell spoke to her sister's slumped body and tried not to stare. She wished she could also unburden herself, but it was too soon. She was too wound up to talk about what she had witnessed. What would happen if the Red Guards caught them? She had seen the punishments they meted out and didn't want to share her fears. Still, the thought of their solidarity was a balm to her. She wanted to get up and pace, but the space was cramped. Leaning against a beam, she recited "The Lord Is My Shepherd" under her breath. She must have fallen asleep afterward. When she awoke, Silver Bell was bending over her.

"It's getting dark," she whispered. The boat slid off into the river.

The Rescue

August 1968

WHEN they had left the city far behind, they meandered through several sleepy villages. On the open glistening water they felt exposed, so they hid in the cabin. Adrenaline rushed through their veins; no one could rest or talk. Coral Bell's throat throbbed in sync with her heartbeat.

When night fell, they went up to the small deck to take in air. Fortunately, it was a moonless night. Only a few stars peeked through the patchy clouds. Finally, the boat glided toward a deserted stony beach. The fisherman, pointing to an eight-foot-long bamboo raft, maneuvered the boat to anchor beside it. This fishing raft would have to carry them farther on their journey.

Two startled black cormorants squawked and flapped their wings from their tethered perch on a bar mounted in front of the raft. The sisters jumped in fright and hugged each other to still their trembling.

Silver Bell wondered if these were the same black birds from her dream. The cormorants also looked dangerous. No. The cormorants were fishing birds. They wore rings around their necks to prevent them from swallowing the big fish they caught. In her nightmare, the black birds had looked ominous, though they had only brushed against her and led her to the light. She hoped that Golden Bell had sent the cormorants as a guide.

Silver Bell took out a wad of bills and paid the fisherman who owned the raft and the birds. She asked their boatman to wait for them. She signaled for quiet and herded Coral Bell onto the raft.

Silence reigned in the dark mud huts on shore. Coral Bell thought the huts looked like the stunted burn victims she had seen in her doctoring days in Wei Village. It seemed to her that the patients' dark eyes were tracking their movements. She sweated despite the cool night air.

Silver Bell took hold of the fisherman's thick bamboo stick and poled her way upstream. "From a distance, we probably look just like fishing folks on this raft."

Coral Bell felt much better after the raft began moving. "Let me take a turn poling. I'm used to physical labor."

Water was seeping through the cracks between the rows of bamboo that formed the bottom of the raft. The women took off their shoes and tied them to the near end of the stick, where the cormorants were perched. The black birds stirred about, again squawking in protest. Coral Bell felt animated by the poling. She had lain in bed for too long. Now a strange calm descended upon her.

Silver Bell hunched in the back of the float, used a paddle to steer. She was surprised that the scenery looked somewhat familiar. She prayed to Golden Bell's spirit to continue guiding them. With the black birds perched in front, like ship mascots pointing the way, she was sure they were being led to the children's hiding place.

They sped along hugging the shore, cruising past sheltering willows, clumps of bamboo, and nondescript brown farmhouses. They whispered when deciding on a course, relying on childhood memories, instinct, and their earlier scrutiny of updated maps.

Soon they entered a rivulet where the land on both sides was partitioned into walled-in rice fields. Volleys of wind whipped the ripening rice stalks like rolling waves. The soughing, which sounded as if it came from the wilderness, confused them. Coral Bell poled slower on the shallow black stream. "Do you know where we are?"

"I'm not sure." The shapeless darkness was playing tricks on Silver Bell's childhood memories.

"Take out your flashlight," Coral Bell whispered.

Silver Bell obeyed. She pointed the beam of quivering light toward the water's edge. She swept it across the banks to make out their whereabouts. The cormorants followed the light and attempted to dive for fish. They were tethered to the bar, however, and could only squawk in frustration.

The women slowed again and stole forward without using any light. A sense of desolation haunted them. Soon, a hill of dense bamboo loomed ahead, and they entered a stretch of swampland. Drifting past patches of starlit reflections, they reached reeds that grew thicker amid dwindling puddles.

"This is it!" Silver Bell pointed. "I remember this approach. Sometimes the boatmen had to jump into the water and pull us close to that beach. There were so many of us on board . . ." Her whisper trailed off. Memories of happy faces gave her a gnawing cramp in the pit of her stomach.

Coral Bell anchored the raft in tall weeds, and Silver Bell tied it to a sapling. They put on their shoes and prowled toward the hill, sloshing unsteadily through shallow water. They scrambled under wires and stumbled over rutted bamboo groves. The dark green tops of the bamboo swayed in the gusty wind; their cracking and sighing sounded as if the heavens were crying. Huge fallen bamboo canes and dead stumps blocked their way. They detoured around these obstacles only to be snared by brambles underfoot. A swarm of buzzing insects rose up around them. Coral Bell sneezed. "I think one got into my nose!"

Each time they stepped on a dead cane, it broke apart with a small explosion, startling them. They pushed on.

"Can't see a damn thing on this ground," Silver Bell muttered in the dark. They dared not use their flashlight again. Soon their eyes adjusted, and they picked their way uphill. Nothing disturbed their approach except a sudden flight of crows. The flock flew around a corner. Silver Bell recognized the birds of her dream. She decided it was another signal from her sister, and they followed the crows.

A cabin came into view.

"Lao Ma must be about Golden Bell's age." The women squeezed water out of their shoes.

"I hope this is where they're hiding. Let's see . . ." Coral Bell tried the cabin door, but it was locked. She tapped on it lightly. There was no answer. "No one seems to be inside."

They peered in the window. "Hmm, too dark to see anything."

"Coral Bell, you call out to them through the keyhole. The children know you better."

"Li-li, An-an! This is" — her voice caught — "your aunt Coral!" She pressed her mouth to the door and called as loudly as she dared. No answer came. "Maybe there are other cabins around?" They looked around but didn't see any.

"Try again."

"Li-li and An-an!" Coral Bell chanted in a hoarse whisper. Finally, she tried another voice. "Lao Ma, come out! You know me. I'm the fourth mistress and the thumb sucker!"

At last, the door creaked open. Three people emerged from the dark shelter. They huddled together, sniffling and sobbing into the arms of the two sisters, whose legs were soaking wet from their odyssey. Silver Bell looked at the three adults dressed in coarse peasant garb and cried out: "Where are little An-an and little Li-li?"

"I'm Der An."

"I'm Der Li. But where are Mama and Papa?"

No one answered. Silver Bell turned to the matronly woman. "You must be Lao Ma."

"Yes," Lao Ma said. "We thought you might be the Red Guards trying to trick us! But when the fourth mistress called herself the thumb sucker, I knew it had to be you. No one outside the family knows that the third mistress died a long time ago when the Japanese bombed Hong Kong, and mistress Coral used to suck her thumb."

"I'm Silver Bell. Lao Ma, don't you remember me?"

"Yes, yes, second young mistress. But it's so dark, and your clothes . . ."

The children started to say how they had heard so much about their aunt. When they asked about their parents again, their aunts remained teary and mute.

Silver Bell announced, "We're all going to Hong Kong; we must leave right now!"

As the group edged down the hill, Der An asked: "Are Mama and Papa waiting for us there?"

Coral Bell turned away to blow her nose. "A mosquito flew into my nose," she said.

Silver Bell's hands rose to slap at the mosquitoes on her face and wipe away her tears. "How long have you been here?"

"We've been hiding here for months, I think. We sleep during the day and come out for air at night," Lao Ma answered. "Did Master Yung and the mistress send you?"

Coral Bell coughed in reply. Silver Bell looked toward the beach, asking: "Do you think we can all fit on the raft?"

"Oh, no. You must go without me." Lao Ma looked at the sisters. "I'll be safe here."

"Lao Ma, don't leave us!" Der Li wailed.

"Hush, hush. Your parents are waiting for you." Lao Ma hugged them. "Besides, what will my father think when he comes in the morning to bring us food and finds no one here?" She managed to smile.

Silver Bell thanked Lao Ma profusely for taking care of the children. Then she slipped five hundred Hong Kong dollars into her hand. "Go to your father's house in the morning and tell everyone in the village that the Yungs in the city have dismissed you." Lao Ma was too astonished to say anything. "Now we must hurry." Silver Bell turned to leave.

"Mama and Papa are waiting for us!" Der An ran ahead.

The others followed.

Coral Bell held on to Der Li's hand as they rushed to the marsh-land. "I'm so happy to see you." Her voice came out in huffs.

Silver Bell stumbled, fell, and picked herself up, panting and gasping for air as she waded through the swamp. "I don't think I've run so fast since I was a child." She was the last to reach the water's edge.

The cormorants' squawking startled the youngsters.

Coral Bell whispered, "Don't worry! The villagers along the river are used to these birdcalls." She picked up another bamboo pole and two planks of wood.

Everyone embarked on the raft, and Der An volunteered to pole.

Softly counting the beats, they coordinated their poling and paddling. With two poles and Silver Bell and Der Li paddling, they reached the mouth of the stream in record time. Still, when they slipped into the river they could already hear the chattering of sparrows — the heralds of morning. A gentle fog had descended. The huts along the riverbanks were barely visible, but the fisher-men's lanterns dotted the water. They could no longer whisper their rhythmic counts to coordinate their poling and paddling.

Coral Bell frantically poled from the back and urged Der An to pole harder. He tried, but looked exhausted. Coral Bell worked as if possessed.

"Auntie Coral, you're so strong!" Der Li cried.

"Shhh! Quiet . . . if you want to see Mama and Papa." Der An poked her.

Silver Bell shook herself to attention. The children looked pale and emaciated. "What did you eat while you were hiding out in the cabin?"

"Lao Ma's father foraged for mushrooms and bamboo shoots in the woods. Sometimes he brought us rice and fish," Der Li said.

"Here, have some chocolate." Silver Bell passed everyone a bar.

"Oh, I remember eating these!" Coral Bell exclaimed.

Der An wolfed down his bar, and Silver Bell gave everyone more. "Yum!" the children cried.

"Mama packed more books than clothes for us to bring to the bamboo mountain," Der An mumbled with a full mouth, poling harder now. "We hid the books under the floorboards. We read and slept every day but came out to walk in the woods at night." His voice sounded stronger now.

They soon saw the waiting boat. The fishermen were squatting on deck, smoking their pipes.

"Can we trust these fishermen?" Der An asked.

"Yes, we can," Silver Bell answered. "Peony's relatives arranged for this boat. I slipped them some money and promised them more at the end. One of them grumbled about the Red Guards, so they are unlikely to harm us."

Many Red Guard rampages occurred in the evening. The marauders then slept late into the day.

"Let's go!" Silver Bell nodded to the head fisherman as soon as everyone had clambered onto the larger boat.

When the rescue party reached Shanghai Harbor, a foggy morning was dawning. The air was laden with foul odors. There were so many suicides, rotting debris, and the usual river flotsam, they didn't dare look into the water.

They met no patrol. Streaks of darkness shrouded their approach to the East Pacific Textile's cargo ship, whose silhouette was barely discernible in the haze.

Return of a Native Daughter

August 1968

WHEN EVERYONE HAD boarded the tanker in Shanghai Harbor, they found Donald waiting with Brook ma-ma, but not Tar Chuang.

Brook ma-ma pulled a small package from her old satchel and handed Coral Bell her Hong Kong birth certificate and Golden Bell's charred journal, wrapped in Coral's own gray silk scarf. The journal was a true ghost-book, with exposed shreds of the stringy spine that now held the remaining pieces of paper and parts of the half-torn hard cover. It was stained with smoke. Brook ma-ma leaned forward and was on the verge of collapsing when her daughter grabbed her and hugged her close. Brook ma-ma whispered that Tar Chuang wished her well but didn't think he could ever adapt to a Western society. He had decided to stay and take care of his parents as well as M-ma and Brook ma-ma. He apologized for scheduling the Yungs for the cleansing and said he understood why Coral Bell had to flee. He didn't even send a token for Coral as a keepsake. Still numb from exhaustion, guilt, and confusion, Coral Bell couldn't utter a single word but hugged her mother ever tighter.

Der An and Der Li ran ahead into the ship to look for their parents, and Silver Bell rushed in after them. Soon, the two teenagers' howling grief shattered the misty air.

Brook ma-ma broke loose and assumed her mask of dignity. She told her daughter that the scarf had been woven from the silk bred in their original home in Hangzhou and that M-ma had personally embroidered the orchid for Coral Bell shortly after she was born. She urged Coral to lead an exemplary life representing their book-fragrant family. She quickly turned to Donald and charged him with the care of Coral Bell. Then she trudged toward the exit ramp and the boat that would take her back to shore. She didn't look back.

Coral Bell stood there, clutching the silk scarf, the birth certificate that would turn her into a returning native — a British subject — and the pages of Golden Bell's journal, which might help her understand her sister and maybe ease her conscience about the maelstrom in the Yung mansion. The crewmen pulled anchor and sailed toward Hong Kong almost immediately.

Instead of feeling relieved, Coral Bell had one nightmare after another. Each one had the quality of a newsreel — like the newscasts of World War II during White Lily's ordeal denouncing her father. In her dreams, the Red Guards were on the prowl again. *Ingrate! Dirty Revisionist! Traitor! Devil Incarnate!* She saw herself raising her fists and leading the chants as usual.

A cracked head, with blood streaming down one cheek, floated over her. It was Golden Bell, weeping and wailing. She would not die. Instead of shouting, she whispered in a voice etched with fury, mouthing the words of the other Red Guards and the Bible stories about the passion of Christ. *Traitor! Devil! Judas!*

Silver Bell, Der An, and Der Li tried to wake her. They told her she was moaning and babbling. Still, the ghost hovered while she tried to rest, droning on and on about the atrocities she had witnessed in the awful frenzy of those days. The voice bounced from wall to wall and filled the cracks and crevices of her cabin. Sometimes the words became a screech, like a persistent door buzzer. The sound rang in her ear and jangled every nerve in her head. Then the ghost's fierce, steady gaze returned. It was omnipresent. Coral Bell pounded her head against the wall and begged for deliverance.

Silver Bell gave her painkillers, pinned her down on her bunk to calm her, and offered words of comfort. "You're safe now, you're safe now," she crooned. Other times she and one of the children would hold hands and weep together.

As a diversion, Silver Bell told them about her daughter, Jenny, in America, and how they would all visit her soon. "She is almost 20 now, so you'll have a relative who is almost all American."

"Mom did tell us we have a cousin in America," Der-li said. "Why isn't she here?"

"She is in college and spends all her vacations here if we're not visiting her." Silver Bell did not want to go into details of Jenny's early separation. "I'm sure she would love to see you and feel glad that she now has close cousins."

"When Mom packed books for us to bring to our hideaway, she mentioned how she loved reading *The Great Gatsby,* and to her, the green light on Daisy's dock, across the water was America," Der-an added with misty eyes.

Since the Communist bureaucracy was in disarray, and most of the Red Guards were students, they didn't encounter any trouble on the way. Once they landed in Hong Kong, they drove to Silver Bell's home in Repulse Bay. The sight of towering buildings, double-decker trams, neon signs, and jumbles of retail shops was overwhelming to the rescued party. Instead of human voices screaming slogans, they heard Chinese music wafting from the market, pounding pile drivers, creaking construction cranes, and endless traffic. Soon they grew aware of the heavy humid air, and the once familiar smell of frying fat, ginger, garlic, and five-spice seasoning permeating the streets.

In Shanghai, they had been reminded over and over again that the foreigners had plundered China and enslaved its people through opium. They were told that the humiliation persisted. If this were true, there would be starving slaves in Hong Kong. Streets would be lined with brothels, and tipsy foreign soldiers and sailors would ogle Chinese women on street corners. What the newcomers saw instead was the energetic Chinese, laughing and chatting everywhere as if they owned the land. An abundance of goods spilled out of every storefront — clothes, fruits, radios, TVs, luggage, shoes — and made their eyes bulge with wonder. Sorrow filled Coral Bell as images of drab storefronts, empty shelves, and the desolation of Shanghai flitted through her mind.

When the car left the city center and glided up the winding road hugging the mountainside with its spectacular ocean views, she thought she had finally reached paradise. The warm, gentle sea breezes relaxed her. The setting sun painted the glittering sea in rosy hues, and her heart swelled with gratitude.

Donald invited the captain of the company tanker to dinner one night. He told everyone how the captain had helped him accept the trauma in his life. After dinner, he gathered everyone around him when tea and fruits were served in the living room. He asked the captain to tell everyone this Buddhist story:

"Two monks were crossing a swift-running stream. They caught sight of an attractive young woman also attempting to wade through. She slipped and fell. Now in those days, monks were not allowed to smile at or even speak to any woman, let alone touch her. Nevertheless, one monk ran over, lifted the woman onto his back, and carried her over the river. After the young woman alighted from the first monk's back and thanked him, the second monk hung his head in shame and scurried away.

"The two monks continued on their journey, but the second monk kept wondering how his brother monk could have violated such a fundamental precept and whether a grave sin had been committed in his presence."

The captain paused, reflected for a minute, and resumed in a hushed voice:

"When darkness fell, they took shelter in an abandoned temple. The first monk immediately fell asleep, but the second one's thoughts churned. He tossed and fretted. He brooded on and on, alternating between frustration for his brother monk's carelessness and pity for his sinful behavior. He became so agitated and angry that he had to wake up the snoring monk.

"Don't you know what you have done?' he screamed. 'How could you violate the sacred precepts we have both observed for so many years?'

"The first monk shook himself awake. 'What? What happened?'

"You know you held a woman on your back? I could not sleep because I was praying and trying my best to minimize your sin.'"

"Oh, you mean the young woman I carried over the slippery stream?' The first monk rubbed his eyes. 'I dropped her off way back at the shore. Oh my brother, why are you still carrying her on your back?'"

The rosy rays of the setting sun had turned people into lengthening shadows on the walls and ceilings. Everyone remained still, ruminating on the story. In the darkening room, Coral Bell, who had tucked her chin into her chest, finally asked: "How about M-ma and Brook ma-ma?"

"We have not forgotten them!" Silver Bell almost shouted, putting down her teacup. "Donald and I have been in constant contact with the Yung factories, and we suggested that the factory cannot afford to support two old ladies and that we would pay handsomely for anyone who would escort them to Hong Kong."

"Several managers were interested in taking over the two rooms in their apartment," Donald said. "By Shanghai standards now, they're considered luxurious. I'm sure they'll allow the ladies to leave as soon as they think it is safe."

"Actually, I heard from Tar Chuang this morning." Coral Bell swallowed, choking down her emotions. "He said it might be necessary for him to divorce me to show solidarity with his proletarian background. He said he would do everything necessary to resettle M-ma and Brook ma-ma."

"I'll write to him right away. Maybe he can talk to the factory managers and bring the old ladies here," Donald said.

"Will Tar Chuang still want his divorce?" Silver Bell asked her sister.

"I think Tar Chuang prefers to take care of his parents. He doesn't want to live in Hong Kong." Despite the imminent dissolution of her marriage, Coral Bell smiled and sighed with resignation. "I believe Tar Chuang is decent enough to bring M-ma and Brook ma-ma to the border. The common ground of our marriage had always been survival, but he also wanted children, which I do not." She looked visibly relieved.

Everyone turned quiet. In these times of continuous turmoil, marriages of convenience were only too common, and having children was too private a topic to probe in a family gathering.

"What's more, White Lily is with him almost all the time." Coral Bell announced: "I had always thought White Lily and Tar Chuang made a better couple. White Lily is grateful that M-ma and Brook ma-ma took such good care of her when her father died. She's helping him take care of our mothers."

Der An, hunched over his seat, broke the silence by suddenly whispering: "I . . . I think Papa visited me last night."

Der Li also burst into tears and muttered: "Mama also came to me in a dream."

Everybody turned to the children with glistening golf-ball eyes.

Silver Bell sucked in her breath and choking on her words, reminded everyone: "F . . . father v . . . visited Golden Bell in Syracuse after he died. Everyone thought she was too homesick."

"But it was so real!" Der An exclaimed. "I was looking out my window last night, enjoying an ocean breeze. It was a very clear, dark night. There was no moon, but a sprinkling of stars and the bright lights of the tall buildings around the harbor seemed to scatter shimmering crystals all over the water. I was reluctant to go to bed, and all of a sudden a ball of amber light brought Papa to me. Without a word, he waved his arms and directed me to join him and Uncle Donald for a ride. He insisted that I sit in front of the car with Uncle Donald, and off we went cruising down the mountain roads, with him in the back seat giving Uncle Donald directions. As we drove, the earth and sky seemed to have fused together with no visible edges. I loved the wind rushing at my face and I laughed and laughed, overjoyed to feel the roving stars tumbling and embracing me in harmony with the night. I don't remember when I went to bed." Der An, his eyes shining like two silver coins, stared at everyone.

No one knew how to respond.

"Mama came to me in a dream too," Der Li said with tears coursing down her cheeks. "I was somehow only about six years old and wearing my favorite pink nightgown, the one with the teddy bear on my chest. Mama also came in a shaft of amber light. She picked me up. She h . . . hugged and ki . . . kissed me." Der Li began sobbing so hard, she had to stop. Silver Bell edged close and held Der Li's hand, kissing and rubbing it against her face, muttering: "Li-li, Li-li . . ." Her wet face glistened with despair.

Der Li sucked in a deep breath and continued: "Ma-ma put me on Po-po's lap, as she used to do when we were young. Po-po started to rock me, reciting some poems about ink sticks and ink stone going round and round. I can't remember most of it." She burrowed her head into Silver Bell's chest.

"Oh, I know that poem!" Bright-eyed with recognition, a tear slipped down Coral Bell's cheek. "M-ma used to recite the poem in her singsong way and told me to memorize it because that's what our family must hold as its essential truth. She sang in a soft lilting voice:

> *An ink stick glides on ink stone round and round;*
> *Serenity descends without a sound.*
> *Fingers caress the brush,*
> *Dip, lift and press the slush,*
> *Swivel, pause, and swirl the wording,*
> *The spirit is emerging.*
> *Listen true!*
> *Rise to Virtue!*
> *Reach for ancient vitality:*
> *The harmony at home—a reality.*

"Oh, I can't wait to have M-ma here to recite this to us in person!" Silver Bell exclaimed, patting and rubbing Li-li's back.

The captain rose to bid farewell. He thanked his hosts for sharing their touching family journey. Donald thanked him in return for his enlightening faith. Someone turned on the light, flooding the room and illuminating their awkward, somber faces. Silver Bell's make-up had left dark streaks down her shirt and everyone's tears had formed Rorschach blots on their chests.

Der An led his sister to the veranda. The day's heat had dissolved into a dense fog, obscuring the sparkling harbor view. Some drifting clouds walked across a crescent moon. Patches of darkness enveloped the gray evening. The adults followed the youngsters onto the veranda, wiping their eyes. They jostled to tuck the children into their bosoms, murmuring words of comfort. Donald said to Der An, "I'll be listening to your father's instructions very carefully." Just then, a distant foghorn sounded a lonesome call. Der An stiffened, feeling as if a damp hand had pulled him under water. He shook his head and gasped for air.

Der Li mumbled: "That sounds like a mourning call from Father."

Donald quivered inside, but his strong hand grasped Der An's shoulder. "You both must have never heard a foghorn before," he said. "The horn warns the sailors in the dark, dense fog that they're approaching danger."

Silver Bell and Coral Bell instinctively approached them and gave them a group hug. The foghorn sounded again. Der An's eyes shimmered in his flushed face. Peering into the dark, he muttered with resolution: "I will be listening carefully as well. . ."

Sensing the reigning gloom that shrouded them like the mists obscuring the harbor lights, Silver Bell ran inside to turn on some music. Reaching for her Sunshine, she announced brightly: "I've asked Jenny to look for a house to rent for our coming visit." She looked from face to face, giving Donald a meaningful glance. "She'll be so happy to have our family together. Everyone, watch and see if you can do this dance Jenny taught me last time she was home." The music's throbbing rhythm infused her whole being and she found herself praying, thanking God for the blessings of these children and beseeching for guidance and continued protection. She began to sway and move with the vibration, then started to do the Twist that was all the rage in Hong Kong. Donald took up the tempo and gyration, while waving his arms to urge everyone to join in. The new arrivals felt the new sounds touching them in their innermost chambers where joy had lain dormant for a long, long time. They raised their arms, swishing their hands in the warm, moist air — rocking in tempo, feeling the weight of their recent ordeal slowly drain away from them. The young ones caught on with the twisting motions. From time to time they leapt into the air and let loose shouts that seemed to come from a total surrender to a force beyond their reckoning. Coral Bell felt the swelling of her heart and while her feet moved in time with the others, her deep breathing released the years of heavy burden. She clapped, smiling with her usual graceful, dignified movements. Soon, An-an, Li-li and Coral Bell started giggling and laughing, feeling a great sense of lightness, lifting their heads high to acknowledge each other. "From now on, only goodness, and happy challenges will assail us." Silver Bell shouted. "We'll be leaving as soon as M-ma and Brook ma-ma gets here!"

Light from the sliding glass door lit up their damp, radiant cheeks. The warmth of their dance dispelled the roving mists.

Author's Note

LANGUAGE

Language can be a window into the mind and heart of a culture. Translations of Chinese terms and words do not carry the same effect and tend to obscure the landscape of that culture. This book is written in English to give the readers a more vivid and direct experience.

The Chinese often speak in metaphors. For instance, a stupid person is called a "dumb egg," and when Purple Jade—the grandmother—refers to "our book-fragrant family," it is clear how proud she is of her cultured family and the widespread respect for book learning.

The Pinyin system for pronouncing Chinese characters in Romanized alphabets was not adopted as the international standard until 1982. I have rendered the Chinese names in the Wade-Giles system familiar at the time of the novel. The Pinyin system is used only for some recent translations of old poems and place-names, such as Hangzhou and Beijing, which have become modern tourist attractions.

CULTURE AND STATUS

For centuries, neighboring countries in Asia recognized the Middle Kingdom as the center of the civilized world. Its wealth and culture were also renowned in the West. The Chinese had a self-perception of cultural supremacy, and their language reflects this pride. A person deprived of the old culture, whether Occidental or Oriental, was considered a "barbarian." When the barbarians became terrifying, they were called "foreign devils." The "East Ocean devils" were the Japanese; Westerners were the "West Ocean devils."

In Chinese society, a person's standing is often dependent upon his or her family's status. The word for "individual" has connotations of selfishness and secrecy. The word for "independence" translates as "standing alone." To many Chinese, "one" is an unlucky number.

The Chinese do not call each other by name except when addressing children, servants, and others of lesser station. Instead they employ relational terms that delineate their positions in the family clan. For example, Soo-soo means "father's younger brother." Jeo-jeo is a "mother's younger brother." These appellations are still used today. For generations, the emphasis on a child's place in the family and society provided stability.

ABOUT THE NOVEL

I was born a blue baby. Ill equipped for active play, I embraced the gifts of reading and listening. This novel is a fictional account very loosely based on my family's history. The places, the characters, and their experiences are composites, drawn from stories I have heard. They are not intended to represent real people, exact locations, or events. The main characters in *Under the Red Moon* are introduced in an earlier book, *A Concubine for the Family*, which begins in Hangzhou, China, in 1937 and ends with the family's dispersal in 1941.

Hi5Torical Background

Like many other civilizations, China developed along river valleys. The fertile plains of the Yellow and Yangtze Rivers nurtured a sophisticated culture thousands of years before the West learned of its existence — a culture that flourished, remote and undisturbed, thanks largely to its geographic features.

To the north and northwest, the sere Mongolian deserts shielded China, while the Himalayan Mountains loomed to the south and southwest. Along the eastern shore, a rugged coastline ran from Siberia to the jungles of Southeast Asia. The vast Pacific Ocean was an effective obstacle to intrusions from the east.

For thousands of years, China's neighbors have borrowed from Chinese culture. One can see the finest examples of these in Kyoto, the cultural capital of Japan: Chinese architecture, bonsai trees, bronze and porcelain ware, paintings on silk, calligraphy, and origami. The national costume of today's Korean women is in the style of fourteenth-century China. Whenever a meal is served in a Southeast Asian country, one can taste soy sauce, eat with chopsticks, and sample Chinese culinary touches. Cognizant of their tremendous influence, the Chinese feel an ancient pride that is far more enduring than twentieth-century concepts of nationalism and patriotism. Not until the thirteenth century and the famous travels of Marco Polo were the Europeans alerted to the existence of the fabulous wealth of an empire in the inaccessible Orient. The advent of the Renaissance led every major European sovereign to launch his galleons — including those of Christopher Columbus — to find a shorter trade route to the fantastic riches of the East. Most Chinese know that before the ascent of Westerners, they would never have been described as "primitive" or "underdeveloped."

By the nineteenth century, when the industrial revolution poised the Western powers on the brink of mercantile imperialism, the Chinese were experiencing the twin ravages of deforestation and overpopulation. The Chin (Pure) Dynasty (1644–1911), a Manchu government, had ruled the majority Han race for almost three hundred years, but its vitality would soon dissipate under the reign of Empress Cixi (1835–1908.) Jung Chang's book *Empress Dowager Cixi*, published in September 2014, portrayed her as a progressive thwarted by conservative factions. Previous scholars and historians had depicted her as the corrupt, capricious consort of Emperor Hsien-feng. She had maneuvered herself into a position of absolute power by allying with conservative officials and powerful court eunuchs, who helped her suppress badly needed reforms.

At a time when the West had acquired a taste for tea, silk, porcelain, and other fineries, the Chinese were weak, divided, and incapable of safeguarding their treasures. A Western flotilla arrived in the nineteenth century to end China's "splendid isolation," and China was introduced to the world community under the muzzle of a gun.

Supported by Britain's supreme naval forces and its sovereignty in India, the East India Company cultivated poppy plants in India and shipped opium to China in defiance of Chinese imperial prohibition. China went to war in October 1839, and lost. Hong Kong became a British colony. One unequal treaty after another followed, until the major powers — Russia, Germany, Japan,

France, Portugal, and Britain — held Chinese territories as concessions in which Chinese sovereignty was curtailed and
extraterritorial rights and privileges were granted to the interlop-
ers. Although the United States did not acquire territorial rights in
China, U.S. traders participated in the opium trade alongside the
British and benefited consistently from advantages gained by the
British through the unequal treaties.

These early Chinese encounters with unruly European sailors
confirmed their opinion of the foreigners as barbarians. The
traditional regard for the liberal arts and disdain for military
matters further blinded the Chinese to the power of Western
technology. They stubbornly refused to open the country to
foreign trade. In 1860 England and France sent another expedition
to Beijing to force the government to open North China and the
Yangtze Valley to trade. The Chinese handled the delegates with
brutality. The response was the invasion of the capital by the
united forces of Russia, Germany, Japan, France, Portugal, Britain,
and Holland. The emperor's favorite residence, the Summer
Palace (Yuan Ming Yuan, or Round Bright Garden), was burned to
the ground. England and France not only achieved their objectives,
but also received eight million dollars each from China as added
indemnities. Russia pretended to mediate the conflict and for its
noninterference, it received the confirmation of treaty advantages
it had gained in Manchuria, including the Ussuri River territories.
The Chinese town of Haishenwei became Vladivostok.

Japan defeated China in the war of 1894–1895. The treaty of
Shimonoseki forced China to cede Taiwan and the Penghu Islands,
pay a huge indemnity, recognize Japan's hegemony over Korea,
and allow Japanese industries in four treaty ports.

The ignorance and corruption of the dowager empress's court
weakened the country's defense against foreign intrusions, but
engendered a hatred for foreigners that simmered, finally boiling

over into the court's fatal support for the Boxers. The Boxers claimed to hold sufficient magic in their bodies to withstand bullets and guns. In late 1891 the court sanctioned the massacre of missionaries. By June 1900, the Boxers' siege of the legations led to the punitive invasion of Beijing by twenty thousand troops representing eight foreign nations. (US, UK, Russia, Germany, Italy, Japan, Austria-Hungary, France) In September 1900, the Forbidden City — the emperor's residence — was sacked. Chinese and Manchus alike, regardless of social rank, suffered looting, rape, and other atrocities. Priceless national treasures were carted off to Europe, vandalized, or destroyed. The foreigners also collected China's import and export taxes from their treaty ports. China descended into abject poverty.

At the turn of the century, the Japanese and European scramble for territorial concessions had reached its zenith. China was saved from dismemberment only because of competition and jealousy over the spoils among the invading powers.

Altogether, Chinese history in the early twentieth century was a study in national humiliation and defeat. Out of the chaos, spurred by internal strife and foreign aggression, rose Nationalism. Nationalists saw the need to liberate China not only from Manchu rule but also from foreign imperialism. In 1911, under the leadership of Dr. Sun Yat-sen (1866–1925), the first republican government was born.

Western democracies refused to aid the young revolutionary party. In the summer of 1918, the Soviet government announced that it was relinquishing the privileges it had obtained under the czarist regime. It retained the territories in the Maritime Provinces, but assisted the Chinese Nationalist Party (Kuomintang) with money, training, and military organization. Chiang Kai-shek (1887–1975) sent his son Chiang Ching-Kuo (1910–1988), who later became the president of the Republic of China in Taiwan

(1978–1988), to Soviet Russia for training, where he married a Russian woman. The divisive interests of the workers and peasants on one side and the landowning gentry, businessmen, and warlords on the other soon shattered the unity of the Nationalists. By 1930 the Kuomingtang, under the leadership of Chiang Kai-shek, had begun large-scale campaigns to extirpate the Communists.

China sent coolie labor to help dig ditches for the Allied causes during World War I. The Japanese drove out the German interests in China's Shangdong Province. The Paris Peace Conference of 1919 ratified Japan's claims to Shandong. Massive student demonstrations broke out in Beijing and Shanghai against Japan, the Allies, and the inept Chinese government. This was the unifying Nationalist May 4 movement. Japan later annexed Jehol and other northern provinces near Shandong. On this land, Japan established the puppet regime of Manchukuo in 1932. The irony for the West is that as a small island nation, Japan would never have the resources to challenge the West. Now it could take advantage of China's riches and slave labor to create an industrial base for launching its war machine in World War II.

Soon, Japan cultivated opium in almost all the arable land in the Chinese provinces they controlled. Opium became so plentiful that the poorest coolie could buy a day's supply for a few Chinese pennies. Opium poisoned vital segments of Chinese society. Its government, industry, and economy all deteriorated due to the addiction. Ambitious foreign elements wasted no opportunity to exploit the complicated situation. They played off one power faction against another, supplying one warlord with arms, another with opium trade privileges, a third with ideologies. Communism, fascism, Nazism, Christianity, and democracy all claimed rival adherents.

The Communists and the Nationalists were nominally united after the Xi'an incident in December 1936. Faced with Japanese aggression and Communist unrest, Chiang had stated to Theodore White in an interview: "Japanese are a disease of the skin, and Communism a disease of the heart."

Japan's surrender on August 15, 1945 ended its dominance of East Asia. Japan returned all Chinese territories and the U. S. sought to reassure Chiang Kai-shek by drawing 11 dotted lines in the South China Sea and proclaimed it Chinese territories. The sea had always been the route the West took to invade China. They further reminded the Philippines (a US territory) not to encroach upon the South China Sea, because it was not included in the original charter when US acquired the territory from Spain.

However, the autocratic Chiang Kai-shek failed to implement much needed political, economic, and social reforms. Galloping inflation and the greed of the politically connected further sapped the resources of a traumatized nation. The Communists, by contrast, were disciplined and offered well-organized political and military leadership dedicated to liberating the long-suffering peasants. In the ensuing civil war, the Communists rapidly triumphed over the Nationalists. On October 1, 1949, Mao Zedong formally proclaimed the birth of the People's Republic of China, or PRC.

The United States continued to view Chiang Kai-shek's government on Taiwan (Republic of China) as the legitimate government and blocked the PRC's representation in the UN until October 25, 1971. The US held that China's Communist regime was little more than a Soviet satellite. China considered North Korea a buffer against Western and Japanese imperialism, calling North Korea China's lips. The Chinese could not understand why the West was rebuilding Japan. The dread of foreign encroachment into Chinese land persists to this day. The Korean War drove China further into the Soviet sphere for moral, political, and economic support.

When the Sino-Soviet relationship soured, Mao reverted to isolationism and promoted the belief that human will alone could fuel industrial productivity. In January 1958 he initiated the Great Leap Forward program. Many projects, such as the building of backyard furnaces, were pursued wholeheartedly, with disastrous results. The failure of the Great Leap Forward led to a decline in Mao's personal authority. To diminish the power of the bureaucratic and institutionalized government, Mao started the Great Proletarian Cultural Revolution in 1965. He used youngsters, namely the Red Guards, as the vanguard to restore his godlike image. The Guards destroyed books, art, and anything deemed "old," "foreign," or "reactionary." They ransacked homes, temples, took many landowners, scholars, and other government leaders captive. They beat and tortured them. The excesses deteriorated into chaos, and the army had to step in to restore order. After 1969, the Red Guards themselves were sent to forced labor in the countryside.

The Chinese-Soviet alliance had never been easy. In the summer of 1960, when the Soviets distanced themselves from China, they withdrew their technicians and even took back all the blueprints for the plants and machinery they had helped build. The split gradually led to a rapprochement between the United States and China during the 1970s.

Glossary

- Bataan Death March —After the Battle of Bataan, the Japanese army, on April 9, 1942, forced 60,000–80,000 Filipino and American prisoners of war to march eighty miles to Camp O'Donnell. The march was marked by widespread physical abuse, brutality, and murder. Later, it was judged by the Allied Military Commission to be a war crime.

- Bonsai — The Japanese term for the ancient Chinese art of *penjing,* or the cultivation of trees in shallow pots. These miniature trees are considered living sculptures.

- Book-fragrant — Scholarly.

- Bund — The waterfront in downtown Shanghai, located in the British concession.

- Chiang Ching-kuo (1910 – 1988) son of Chiang Kai-shek by his first wife. Ching-kuo was sent to study in Moscow in 1925, when his father was the head of the soviet-trained Kuomingtang army. He twice denounced his father's anti- Communist activities while in Soviet Russia. He returned to China in 1937 with a Russian wife, shortly after the Xian Incident, to help negotiate the integration of the Chinese Communists in the Nationalists' anti-Japanese effort. In later years he claimed that he had been detained in Russia, and forced to denounce his father. He was the president of the Republic of China in Taiwan from 1975 until his death in January of 1988.

- Chiang Kai-shek (1887–1975) — Ruler of China from 1928 to 1949. He remained president of the Chinese government in exile on Taiwan until his death. He was popularly referred to as the generalissimo.

- Chungking — The capital of the Republic of China during World War II.

- Concubine — In the old days, it was customary for Chinese men to have several wives. The first wife held a position of power, and the other wives, or concubines, owed her services and deference. This is no longer legal in China.

- Cut off his pigtail — This act symbolized republican aspiration and rebellion against the Manchu emperor of the Chin Dynasty (1644–1911). The Manchu are a Chinese minority that came from Manchuria. Throughout the Chin Dynasty, the majority Han people was required to follow Manchu custom and wear a pigtail to indicate their subjugation to the Manchus.

- Dim sum — Literally, "to dot" (dim) "the heart" (sum). An expression referring to a meal of dumplings and small delicacies, eaten in the morning or late evening, before bedtime. This is the Cantonese pronunciation. In Mandarin, it would be pronounced "dian shin."

- Dumb egg — Stupid person.

- Dragon-dee — younger brother Dragon.

- Eleven dotted Lines — after WWII, US tried to reassure the Chinese Nationalists (Chiang Kai-Shek) that no more foreign invasions will come from the South China Sea. They drew an eleven dotted line deep into the Sea to indicate Chinese dominion over the area. They further warned the Philippines that they were not to encroach upon the area because it was not included in the Spanish charter from which America acquired the territories. Later the People's Republic of China (the Communists regime) abbreviated the eleven to nine dotted lines.

- Foreign concessions — Chinese territories held by foreign powers. In the nineteenth and early twentieth centuries, the West acquired a taste for tea, silk, porcelain, lacquer ware, and other Chinese fineries. Smug and unable to appreciate the advantages of Western technology, China did not want to buy anything from the Western powers. Britain shipped opium to China, in defiance of Chinese imperial prohibition. In October 1839 China went to war and lost. Hong Kong became a British colony. There followed one unequal treaty after another, until the major powers — Russia, Germany, Japan, France, Portugal, and Britain — all held Chinese territories as "concessions." Colonialism gave the Western nations economic advantages in trade, political and military power to protect their interests, collecting Chinese import and export taxes and religious opportunities to proselytize. Until Japan bombed Pearl Harbor, Japan did not consider itself at war with the Europeans, so the inhabitants of the foreign concessions enjoyed the rights of non-belligerents.

- Hong Kong — An island south of Kwangtung Province, in southern China. It became a British crown colony in 1841, after the Chinese lost the Opium War. Before the Second World War, many Chinese thought Hong Kong was a safe haven from the Japanese.

- Hwangpo — A channel of the Yangtze River, where Shanghai is situated.

- I Ching—The Book of Changes. It is one of the oldest texts for divination.

- Jeo-jeo — mother's younger brother.

- John Service — A Chinese speaking "China Hand" sent by FDR in 1944 to Yan'an to talk to Mao Zedong and Zhou Enlai to see if the Communists could be allied against the Japanese. Mao told Service that Chiang was not democratically elected and he only held the "bayonets and secret police" over the people; that China needed to industrialize and the Soviets were too debilitated by the war and that the American and Chinese had the same interests in strategic and commercial developments. Service later wrote that if America had a less biased understanding of China in 1945, the Korean and Vietnam wars would not have happened and that China would be a "different place."

- Kang bai — Dry cup. A toast and a gesture of good fellowship to shout "kang bai" as one tosses down a drink, and then holds the cup upside down.

- Manchuria — Land on the northeastern part of China, abutting Korea and Russia. The pine forests and rich mineral deposits of the area provided an industrial basin coveted by all its neighbors. In *China: A Short Cultural History*, C. P. Fitzgerald writes: "The name, Manchuria, is a foreign term coined by Europeans. The Chinese called it Tung Pei (the North East,) and it had been divided into nine provinces."

- Madame Chiang Kai-shek (Soong Mei-ling, 1897–2003) — One of the famous Soong sisters. The first sister, Soong Ai-ling, married H. H. Kung, a direct descendant of Confucius. Kung later became the finance minister of the Nationalist government. The second sister, Soong Chin-ling, married the father of the Chinese revolution, Dr. Sun Yat-sen. She later became the v-president of PRC, because Dr. Sun was a firm proponent of a United China and did not support Chiang's campaigns to wipe out the communists.

- The third sister, Mei-ling, introduced Chiang Kai-shek to Western culture and Christianity. She was educated at Wellesley College and was a spokeswoman for China during World War II. She moved to New York after her husband's death in 1975 and died in 2003 at the age of 105.

- Manchus —A Chinese minority from Manchuria. They conquered China and were the ruling class of the last Chinese dynasty (Ch'ing 1644–1911). They adopted the Chinese form of government and were totally assimilated into Chinese culture. Today, they're indistinguishable from other Chinese.

- Mao Zedong (1893–1976) — The leading Chinese Communist revolutionary who established the People's Republic of China.

- The McTyeire School for Girls was founded in 1890 by the Southern Methodist mission, and named after Bishop Holland McTyeire who founded Vanderbilt University. It was a private school for girls from Shanghai's wealthy families. The school's most famous graduates were the three Soong sisters.

- Melon-seed face — A face that is broad on top, with a pointed chin.

- M-ma — Mother.

- Moongate — A circular opening in a wall. It is often lined with tiles or lacquered wood, usually without a door.

- My heart and liver — My precious darling.

- Nanking — The capital (1928–1937) of a united China during the Republican Era. At the end of World War II, from 1946 to 1949, Nanking resumed its status as the capital of Chiang Kai-shek's Nationalist government.

- Personal maid — Poor families often sold their daughters to rich homes to serve as housemaids or personal maids to the mistresses of the house. These maids did not receive a salary but were given money, clothes, and personal items during the holidays. The maids were never resold. They were married off with dowries when they reached marriageable age. Since the maids' fortunes closely followed those of their mistresses, they often became the mistresses' confidantes and closest allies in the large, multi-generational homes. The system persisted well into the twentieth century.

- Po-po — A child calls his/her mother's mother po-po.

- Skywell — A small courtyard attached to the front or back of a house. It is surrounded by high walls on all sides and looks like a well from the sky.

- Soo-soo — Father's younger brother.

- Sun Yat-sen, Dr. (1866–1925) — Leader of the Chinese Revolution who established a republican government in 1911. The Chinese honor him as the George Washington of China.

- Taihu rocks — Rocks that are most prized for garden designs. They are limestone boulders found on the bottom of Lake Tai, west of Suzhou. The rocks were eroded by the water and sand of the lake, giving them the look of miniature mountains, or natural sculptures of birds, animals, or gods.

- Tai-tai — Mistress.

- Taoism— The best-known classic of Taoism is *Tao Te Chin*. The authorship is popularly attributed to Lao Tzu (circa 490 B.C.). Taoism preached a rejection of decadence in society and a return to primitive simplicity.

- *Three Character Classic* — A beginner reader in the Chinese classics. All verses are composed of rhyming couplets of three characters.

- To lose face — To lose the respect of society.

- T'ung Ming Hui— An alliance, mostly of young people, which was formed under the leadership of Dr. Sun Yat-sen. It was dedicated to the republican cause and the overthrowing of the Manchu Dynasty. Later, the T'ung Ming Hui was amalgamated into the Kuomintang, which is still a dominant political party in Taiwan.

- Wu Wei — One of the precepts of Taoism; it advocates peaceful non-action — that is, a mode of being without any egotistical, combative effort or clever tampering. A person must first find the "Tao" (Way) and through this passive example lead people.

THE AUTHOR

Amy S. Kwei — A graduate of St. John's University (BA) and Vassar College (MA). She is retired from teaching in Bennett College and Dutchess Community College. She has twice won the Talespinner Competition sponsored by the *Poughkeepsie Journal*. One of the judges, Michael Korda, wrote: "[*The Visit*] has a very strong cultural appeal, and gives the reader a quick, instant understanding of Chinese values, and how they differ from our own. As well, it is simply written, perhaps the best written of all the stories here."

Her short stories and essays have appeared in *Prima Materia, Short Story International, CAAC Inflight magazine, Westchester Family, Dutchess Magazine, The Country*, and *Dutchess Mature Life*. Andover Green published one of her children's stories in *Six Inches to England, An Anthology of International Children's Stories*.

Her YA book, Intrigue in the House of Wong, was published in 2008. An action-packed adventure, it delivers a taste of the modern Chinese-American teenage experience.

Kirkus Review called her adult novel, A Concubine for the Family, (2012) "An engaging family saga by a talented storyteller . . . It artfully reveals the practices and attitudes of old China."

KR also notes: Under the Red Moon — A Chinese Family in Diaspora, (2016) chronicles the family through exile, homecoming and Maoism. It is an absorbing exploration of mid-20th century through the story of a fractured family. . . A powerful saga of love and survival."

More information can be found here: www.amykwei.com

CPSIA information can be obtained
at www.ICGtesting.com
Printed in the USA
BVHW031811051119
562988BV00001B/16/P

9 780981 549965